One woman's bloody crimes. One man's chilling legacy.
A novel of seduction, madness, and murder...

"DISTURBING...READS LIKE THE BROTHERS GRIMM AS
REVISED BY THE MARQUIS DE SADE."
–The Boston Sunday Globe

P9-DMT-947

"SUSPENSEFUL."
–Bellingham Herald[2]

HIGH PRAISE FOR
ANDREI CODRESCU AND
THE BLOOD COUNTESS

"AS COMPELLINGLY READABLE AS IT IS
THOUGHTFULLY INTELLIGENT . . . *The Blood
Countess* is that rarest of things, a new American novel
of serious literary merit that is actually about
something."—*San Jose Mercury News* (Ca.)

"A BRILLIANT WORK that reveals much about
power and politics and obsession."
—*St. Petersburg Times* (Fla.)

"CODRESCU'S WRITING IS RICH . . .
suspenseful and chilling . . . a fascinating book."
—*The Bellingham Herald*

"*The Blood Countess* is a wonderful and accurate
re-creation of history by a very knowledgeable author.
A page-turner!"—William S. Burroughs

"Codrescu has woven together Hungarian history,
politics, psychology, and religion (with witty asides on
the vampirism of Christianity) in a book of high gothic
drama."—*Entertainment Weekly*

"A historically rooted nightmare that is hard to resist."
—*Publishers Weekly*

Please turn the page for more extraordinary acclaim. . . .

"A JUICY AND GUSHING STORY that overflows with horror and, surprisingly, humor . . . Codrescu brilliantly parallels Elizabeth's saga with the modern-day court testimony of her direct descendant, Drake Bathory-Kereshtur."
—*Williamette Week* (Portland, Ore.)

"The Blood Countess will frost your plasma, curdle your goulash, and stir your nightmares with a golden shiv."—Tom Robbins

"Codrescu's hallucinatory reconstruction of Elizabeth's bloody deeds reads like the Brothers Grimm as revised by the Marquis de Sade. . . . [The novel] serves disturbingly as a personal vision of the persistence of evil."—*The Boston Sunday Globe*

"The Blood Countess is beautiful and horrible in its depiction of raw violence beneath the formal measure of court life."—*The Miami Herald*

"CODRESCU HAS WRITTEN A VIVID NARRATIVE OF THE 16TH CENTURY and has made the history of Hungary and its shifting contemporary situation entertaining and compelling."
—*Rocky Mountain News*

BOOKS BY ANDREI CODRESCU

Zombification: Essays from NPR (1994)
Road Scholar: Coast to Coast
Late in the Century (1993)
The Muse Is Always Half-dressed
in New Orleans (1993)
The Hole in the Flag: An Exile's Story
of Return and Revolution (1992)
The Disappearance of the Outside (1991)
Belligerence (1991)
Raised by Puppets Only to Be Killed
by Research (1989)
The Stiffest of the Corpse: An Exquisite
Corpse Reader (1988)
At the Court of Yearning: The Poems
of Lucian Blaga
Monsieur Teste in America (1987)
A Craving for Swan (1987)
Comrade Past and Mister Present (1987)
In America's Shoes (1983)
The Life and Times of an Involuntary Genius (1975)
The History of the Growth of Heaven (1973)
License to Carry a Gun (1970)

Andrei
Codrescu

The BLOOD COUNTESS

A Novel

A Dell Book

Published by
Dell Publishing
a division of
Bantam Doubleday Dell Publishing Group, Inc.
1540 Broadway
New York, New York 10036

If you purchased this book without a cover you should be aware
that this book is stolen property. It was reported as "unsold and
destroyed" to the publisher and neither the author nor the
publisher has received any payment for this "stripped book."

This book is a work of fiction. Real historical names, characters,
places, and incidents have been used fictitiously. Any resemblance
to actual events or locales or persons, living or dead, is entirely
coincidental.

Copyright © 1995 Andrei Codrescu

All rights reserved. No part of this book may be reproduced or
transmitted in any form or by any means, electronic or mechanical,
including photocopying, recording, or by any information storage
and retrieval system, without the written permission of the
Publisher, except where permitted by law. For information address:
Simon & Schuster, New York, New York.

The trademark Dell® is registered in the U.S. Patent and
Trademark Office.

ISBN: 0-440-22191-9

Reprinted by arrangement with Simon & Schuster

Printed in the United States of America

Published simultaneously in Canada

August 1996

10 9 8 7 6 5 4 3 2 1

OPM

PREFATORY NOTE

ELIZABETH BATHORY (1560-1613), known as the Blood Countess, was real. She lived most of her life in the second half of the sixteenth century. She is said to have tortured and murdered 650 virgin girls in order to bathe in their blood. Investigated for her alleged crimes at the beginning of the seventeenth century, she was never convicted. Nonetheless, she was sentenced to live her life walled inside a room of her castle at Cahtice (now in the Slovak Republic).

She lived five years within that walled chamber, refuting the charges of priests and preachers on the other side of her permanently barred door. While they attempted to make her confess her crimes, she reasoned instead against the failure of their faiths. At this time, the Protestant religion of Martinus Luther coexisted uneasily with the Catholic church. Every soul was a battleground. Elizabeth, who had been raised by a Catholic monk and taught by Protestant teachers, had an especially complex and difficult soul, one that warranted the clergy's full attention.

The details of Elizabeth Bathory's life as they appear in this book were taken from historical documents in the Hungarian State Archive.

The contemporary character Drake Bathory-Kereshtur is a descendant of the Blood Countess. He is a Hungarian American who returned to Budapest after the collapse of Communism. While there to write stories for a newspaper and to search the archives for documents relating to his notorious ancestress, he became involved in the murder of a young girl. He successfully escaped prosecution in Hungary, but when he returned to the United States, he turned himself in to the D.A.'s office in New York. His original testimony, unsupported by witnesses, is the basis for the story told here.

To be sure, the light itself is also varied by the surface of the body whence it comes, as it shows now this and that color, but the degree of the heating power is obtained from the interior disposition of its body.

> JOHANNES KEPLER,
> *Concerning the More Certain Fundamentals of Astrology*

.

It is difficult for us to evaluate the distance that then separated the man (magnified by birth and fortune) who did the crushing from the insect crushed between two stones.

> GEORGES BATAILLE,
> *The Trial of Giles de Rais*

.

The witch-burning stakes covered Europe; the Reformation would have preferred that the only book surviving on earth be the Bible, but in any case it was not inclined to tolerate either Eros or magic or the contiguous "sciences" of the Renaissance. A magic invocation of an alchemical experiment could cost a man his head. Fear justified everything.

> JOAN P. COULIANOU,
> *Eros and Magic in the Renaissance*

.

Immortality is a clock that never runs down, a mandala that revolves eternally like the heavens. Thus the cosmic aspect returns with interest and compound interest.

> C. G. JUNG,
> *Psychology and Alchemy*

O N T H E L A S T D A Y O F T H E S I X-teenth century, Countess Elizabeth Bathory of Hungary, despondent over the irremediable passage of time, angered at the betrayal of her flesh, and sorrowed beyond measure at the passing of her youth, ordered her maids to break all the mirrors in her hilltop mansion at Budapest.

The frightened girls lowered the heavy frames from the walls and carried them out into the cold. Some of them cried without knowing why, suspecting that their mistress's whims had taken an even darker turn. When they reached the center of the courtyard, they laid the mirrors tenderly on the snow. The leaden sky reflected gloomily in them, but then it seemed that even the sky fled, leaving the polished surfaces dark.

From her perch at the window, Elizabeth signaled to them to begin. Watching her swarm of black-clad women smashing glass with shovels under the still-falling snow, Elizabeth felt a cold flame rise within her. They looked like crows, her women, laboring to bury the vanity of her flesh. When all the shards succumbed to a fresh blanket of snow, she vowed to erect a monument over the site, something powerful and cold that would commemorate the end of her temporal beauty.

She had supervised the shattering of her expensive collection of looking glasses hoping that what they had seen was being shattered as well. They had seen her transformation from a young girl to a woman, the blossoming of her flesh. They had seen the care she had taken with the vessel of her body, her intimate attention to its contours, her studious delight in the expanse of her skin, which she had studied as an explorer studies a map. They had seen also her abandon and the frenzy of her love sports, of which she was as proud as any artist. They had seen her try on faces and strike poses for official functions and clandestine assignations. Her mirrors held the discarded forms of her whims, her rejected poses, her failed selves. They had seen also her despondency, her defeated womanly being, her tear-drenched weakness. They had seen her humiliation at the hands of demons when she was alone with horned and winged creatures and no one could help her. She had allowed no human creature to see her defeated, but the mirrors had seen it all. And now they too, though made only of glass, had to be destroyed, because they had seen.

Elizabeth was not going to allow them to watch her grow old.

She had tried to put a stop to the passage of time, but her mirrors and her skills had failed. Time itself was her enemy, its very passing the darkness that cursed all with corruption and death. She had been gripped, as her friend Andrei once told her, by the pride of Lucifer. She despised nature in her star-bound course, in her slowness, her indifference. She had made *contra naturam* her credo, had emblazoned it on her stationery. What those mirrors had seen was a struggle no less fierce than the clash of armies all about her. Her victories had been brief and fraught with danger, and the hostility unending. But while her husband and his troops knew what they were fighting, her enemy had always been as elusive as it was ubiquitous.

But Elizabeth Bathory was not without hope. Andrei de Kereshtur, the friend of her childhood, had become a great magician. He had promised her shyly but firmly that he would use his magical arts to defeat time on her behalf. He had not yet completely mastered the formula, but he was nearing success. Should she die before he completed his work, he had promised her resurrection, in a beautiful body, at a future time. It might be a time far in the future, a different century even, but his promise would come to pass. Elizabeth believed him. Her time had been nothing but sorrow. She looked forward to being beautiful in a different century.

The heavy snow that fell throughout the afternoon and evening did little to lighten her spirits. She saw the whiteness as a shroud laid over her youth. From the ogival window of her bedroom she watched the fat flakes dancing over the cupolas and spires of the royal capital. One by one they buried her century, the century when she had been young and alive. The weightless crystals that she had welcomed with shouts of joy in her childhood were like nails now. She stared fixedly at the snow and thought she discerned a grinning shape in it, a skeletal woman holding a broken hand mirror. Elizabeth did not shrink from the apparition. When the gaunt form came close enough, she saw that it was none other than herself, mocked in the playful dance of the snow.

She would have turned for reassurance to her floor-to-ceiling Venetian glass, but it was no more. She continued to stare instead at the figure of her death, which she knew to be true. Looking glasses had outlived their capacity for flattery.

That evening, she chose her black garments for midnight Mass with the greatest care.

In the Church of Holy Mary in Budapest, Ilona Harszy, who had just turned fifteen years old, sang so beautifully that the Augustinian monks wept.

The Hungarian aristocrats attending the service showered the pale girl with praise. Some of them stripped their arms and necks of jewels and offered them to the church in gratitude.

Ilona stood modestly amid this storm of affection with her head bowed, inwardly thanking the holy Virgin for the inspiration that had caused her voice to soar to angelic heights. In her white shift she looked made out of nothing, a wispy white cloud in an otherwise empty sky. Her voice had been made of the purest and barest substance; the grit of this earth had not yet adhered to it. She shut her eyes tightly even as two tears made their way down the tender skin of her cheeks.

Watching closely from the front row, Palatine Thurzo of Hungary and his niece Countess Elizabeth Bathory seemed equally entranced.

The palatine fought the urge to rise from his seat, walk to the girl, lift her face in his hands, and drink those crystalline tears. They were doubtlessly ambrosial, a sort of holy water that would heal the weariness in his bones and lift from his shoulders, ever so briefly, the heavy mantle of state and his worries about his wild niece Elizabeth. The century that was about to end had been full of strife and sorrow. He had risen to the highest position in the land through cunning and ruthlessness, but there seemed to be no end to war and religious quarrels, and he was tired.

For her part, Countess Bathory was equally compelled to touch the divine instrument of the angels who stood in virginal shame before the worshiping crowd. But, unlike her uncle the palatine, the countess had no need to suppress her urges. The girl's purity was like spring water to her thirst.

That day the countess had buried her vanity, and freedom welled within her.

Her uncle had mildly reproached her for wearing "widow's cloth," and she had laughed in his face. Her husband, the renowned warrior Franz Nadazdy, was on his deathbed in Castle Kereshtur. While not yet a widow, Elizabeth had been wearing the color of mourning for many years now. Franz had died for her more than a decade ago. The mere presence of his rotting body on a bed was no impediment to her widowhood.

"And anyway, dear Uncle," she whispered to the palatine, "today I mourn my own passing. I am my own widow."

She could see by the narrowing of his eyes under the bushy brows feared by so many that he did not understand. And this made her glad.

The ground in front of the church was strewn with the silk of noble overcoats, shed so that Ilona would not have to walk on the snow.

Her performance caused Baron Eszterhazy to write to her parents: "Her pure voice was one of the best in Europe, better than I have heard in the opera houses of Italy."

By then, of course, his words came too late, and they brought no consolation to her parents.

The Augustinian monks who lived across the street from the Church of Holy Mary sewed a robe for Ilona. Their abbot, Teronius, admonished them to "sew the robe purely, with thoughts of gratitude for the angel Ilona Harszy whose voice was sent from heaven."

And whose voice was now, doubtlessly, in heaven, though her body lay in its grave covered by the beautiful robe.

Barely two hours after Ilona's astounding performance, an elegant carriage bearing the Bathorys' coat of arms had arrived at the girl's house, and a messenger had delivered a perfumed note and a gift of a gold locket set in precious stones. The note requested Ilona Harszy's presence that same night at the house of Countess Bathory, who desired a private performance. The messenger waited for the answer.

Ilona's father and mother, Gepy and Olyra Harszy, were modest landholders and petty nobles from the area of Kereshtur, which belonged to Countess Bathory. They too belonged to the powerful Bathory estate; no matter that they had gained some roundly disregarded and fleeting liberties from the Hungarian Parliament.

They could not refuse. Fearful to the bottom of their hearts, they bade farewell to their daughter. They had heard dreadful things about the countess and they feared for the health of their frail child, whose miraculous voice was a triumph over a weak constitution prone to fevers and fatigue.

Ilona stepped into the carriage, still wearing her white shift, her shoulders covered by an ermine fur that had been a gift from a noble.

It had stopped snowing and was dreadfully cold, the kind of cold said to spawn wolf stars. The peasants believed that on such cold nights the stars came down from the heavens to mate with wolves. Their offspring terrorized the world on the dark nights of winter.

During the short ride to the Bathory palace, Ilona prayed to the Virgin. She begged her luminous protectress, who had given her voice such strength at Mass, to help her to enter the good graces of the powerful countess. She saw her plea leave on the cloud of her breath and dissipate into the icy night. She watched the black horses breathe clouds of steam. She looked back on her life but found little to give her strength. Her happiest memories were the moments when her voice had soared in praise of God. She had had but little joy in her childhood, when she had been sick most of the time and unable to play with other children. Love she had not known. She had glimpsed a young man's burning eyes upon her in church, but she had felt such shame that she had given all her heart to her singing.

Elizabeth Bathory received the singer in the rose

salon, a room paneled in rosewood and covered in rich
Oriental carpets. A fire roared in the marble fireplace,
making the room unbearably hot near the fire and cold
just a few feet away from it.

The countess lounged close to the flames on a Turkish divan, clad only in a black silk robe. In her hand she
held the gold mouthpiece of a Turkish hookah, on which
burned a ball of golden hashish.

She rose slightly from her pillows, which were
quickly readjusted for her by two maids who stood behind their mistress. The maids' faces were lit by the red
tongues of the flames, which accentuated the circles under their eyes and their air of fatigue.

The countess motioned Ilona to come close. The girl
had begun to tremble when she saw the famed Elizabeth Bathory. She could not take her eyes off the white
hand with long black fingernails grasping the gold
mouthpiece.

The curtsy she attempted was clumsy.

"Sing, my child," Elizabeth ordered. She lay back on
her pillows, allowing her robe to fall open. She stroked
the inside of her white thigh with her free hand without
taking her eyes off the girl. She then drew smoke from
her hookah.

Ilona opened her mouth but no sound came out.

"Don't be afraid," the countess encouraged her.
"Sing to me like the angel who sang before us tonight."

Once more the girl tried to sing, but fear had paralyzed her vocal cords, and she made no sound. All she
could see were the countess's black fingernails moving
slowly and hypnotically on the white flesh of her inner
thigh.

The countess rose from the divan, her face no longer
composed. Fury twisted her features. She stood before
the girl and first slapped her across the face, then
scratched her cheek with her nails. Blood streamed

through the skin. She then tore the white shift from the girl's body.

Her maids, who had quietly come to stand behind the singer, tore off the rest of the girl's meager garments. She now stood naked before Elizabeth, her head bowed, her hair streaming over her thin shoulders, tears falling from her eyes. The pale opals of her nipples rose from her small breasts, wet with tears. Her thin hips were boyish but her pubis was pronounced, covered in luxuriant soft dark curls.

The countess pulled fiercely at her own robe until she too stood naked. Her full breasts, fleshy hips, and loose abdominal skin faced defiantly the insubstantial form before her.

Thrusting her hand under the girl's chin, she brought her head up sharply.

"Behold womanhood!" she cried.

The countess bit the girl's nipples, first one, then the other, drawing blood. She caressed the length of Ilona's neck, then pressed softly, looking for the pure notes that had moved everyone to tears. Where were those notes? She squeezed harder, expecting those angelic sounds to rise unbidden from the depths of the girl's soul. But nothing came out, not even a cry of fear.

The girl had fainted. Elizabeth had been thwarted again by that nameless thing which had always taken from her what she truly wanted. She recognized it with familiar bitterness. Throwing the singer's ermine over her own nakedness, Elizabeth dragged the unconscious girl outside, followed by her maids.

The snow had given way to a brilliant, star-studded sky. A quarter moon shed its feeble light over the courtyard. The temperature had fallen greatly. It was fiercely cold. Shivering, the women helped pull the singer to the top of the slight mound where Elizabeth's mirrors lay buried.

The countess held the still-unconscious girl close, feeling the heat leave her body and seep into her own. The harsh cold pierced by the faraway stars made a music of its own, a desolate, high-pitched sound that Elizabeth remembered from her own childhood. As a young girl she had stood often at a window of her castle listening to the cold wind slice the endless night of the Hungarian *puszta*. Despite the castle's blazing fires, she had felt no warmth, though she could imagine in fine detail, as in a woodcut, the savage mating of stars in human form with she-wolves. She had heard their cries and had called on the stars to come to her. They had ignored her, perhaps because she had not been hot-blooded enough for the icy stars.

Elizabeth felt the girl's meager heat now, but it was too late to enjoy it, and there was too little of it to augment the small flame of memory that had flared within her.

Her best maid, Darvulia, brought a pail of water from the house. The maids held Ilona upright while Elizabeth poured water over the pale form. The water iced quickly and the girl froze on the spot.

The women stood gazing for a moment at the living statue. A blade of ice, sharp as a sliver of Venetian glass, curved forward from between the girl's legs. Above this blade her pubis glistened with crystals. Her navel had filled with crystals as well, a sparkling cluster of small jewels.

"Beauty," said Elizabeth coldly, "how easily you cling to the docile!"

The wind picked up just then, but if anyone heard her words they gave no sign of it.

The ice formed evenly around Ilona's girlish hips. Her waist became a smooth sheet of glass. Her breasts were encased by two bells of ice, the coppery nipples visible beneath the glass like clappers. Under her chin, the dripping water had constructed closely knit icicles that looked like a scraggly beard.

Only Ilona's blue eyes remained innocently open under their transparent sheet. They looked through Elizabeth at something she could not see, but she resisted the temptation to turn around. That's where her mirror had always been.

She shivered and headed back to the house.

Gratefully her women followed her in, out of the terrible cold.

From the window of her bedroom Elizabeth watched the ice statue standing over her broken mirrors. Her thoughts came to her in splintered shards, reflecting the hundreds of faces of people, mostly girls, whom she had known, loved, and been disappointed by. Like the moonlit ice outside, they had all begun bathed in angelic grace, only to shed it when she needed it most.

When the first light of the sun rose over the snow-bound capital of the kingdom, Elizabeth ordered her servants to wake everyone and to pack for the long trip to Kereshtur.

By nine in the morning, the Bathory house in Budapest was deserted.

Weeping before the closed gates, Gepy and Olyra Harszy, Ilona's parents, soon attracted a crowd.

The suspicions that had now gathered around the feared Countess Bathory like a black cloud of rumor and fear gave the crowd courage to break down the gates.

Inside, a gasp went up from the enraged crowd as they beheld the statue of their beloved singer eternally frozen atop the snow.

Gepy and Olyra fainted, but such a clamor arose from the people that there was little doubt that this time the niece of the palatine would finally be brought to justice.

All the rest of that week, the Augustinian monks beat their bowls on the street in front of the Parliament, where the palatine Thurzo resided, making a "dreadful noise, calling for the choir singer's vindication," as reported in the *Chronicles of Andrei de Kereshtur.* The monks, according to Abbot Teronius, "had been kept awake many nights by screams of anguish from Bathory's house, but never had God been so blasphemed before."

The outraged Augustinians did not let up their demands for justice. They accompanied Ilona's parents from royal office to courts of justice and from noble house to noble house, demanding an inquest.

But bringing to justice the most powerful noble in Hungary was no easy matter, as the palatine Thurzo, King Matthias, and Emperor Rudolf all knew. Castle Kereshtur, where Elizabeth now resided, had withstood the armies of two empires.

*S*tanding before a New York judge, in the absence of a jury, without a lawyer or witnesses, a mustachioed man in his early fifties accused himself of a heinous crime. He had already been remanded to the custody of the district attorney's office and was residing in a private cell at 100 Centre Street. This hearing was for the purpose of establishing a motive and providing the court with enough evidence to corroborate his testimony.

He said that his name was Drake Bathory-Kereshtur and that he had killed a young girl in Hungary. He begged the court to find him guilty and to sentence him to death.

He would provide details beyond what was required and implicate the person who had caused him to commit the crime.

Up to a point, the judge did not find his confession extraordinary, but then the man claimed that his accomplice and instigator had lived over four hundred years ago. The man claimed to have been driven to his action by one of his ancestors, Countess Elizabeth Bathory, who had been born in the sixteenth century.

I killed her with my hands but not with my mind, Your Honor. I am incapable of murder. Elizabeth Bathory killed her, as she has done many times in the past.

"And what might her *reasons have been?" the judge asked, aware that in certain mentally disturbed people, excessive logic tends to create a dramatic result.*

But the self-accuser was not flustered.

She felt mortal at a time when there was no need to, Your Honor, because at the time nearly everyone believed that they were immortal. She had everything. She had angels, Your Honor. In a sense she resembled us more than she resembled her contemporaries.

"However," the judge said, "this hearing is not about her."

If only this were so. But there was a conspiracy. Its nature is only partially known to me. Its scope is beyond all of us. I have been set up by an alchemist and by a woman. His name is Andrei de Kereshtur. Her name is Elizabeth Bathory.

To the judge's next brief questions, Drake Bathory-Kereshtur answered in the following manner:

Of course I am going to explain. Whether you will understand or not is another matter.

I am an American.

I am also a Hungarian.

Call me Drake. This is America. I used to be Bathory-Kereshtur. Still am.

I am going to make a lengthy statement, Your Excellency.

I will talk. Your scribe can take it down. I mean your stenographer, Your Highness.

OK, I will call you Your Honor, because this is America. You can call *me* Your Highness.

I know it's not a joke.

I will start at the beginning. Bathory-Kereshtur. B-A-T-H-O-R-Y. Like *bath.* Rhymes with *laboratory. Hortatory.* It suggests *bath* and *whoredom* in English. In Hungarian it does not. In Hungarian it is a sigh. This name is key to what follows. And the reason I stand before this court accusing myself of a murder that was not my doing.

I have spent forty years trying to escape my name, Your Honor. I have enjoyed the blessed anonymity of America since the day I came here, a refugee, in 1956. I have thanked this country every day for affording me the opportunity to be but one citizen among many. I submerged myself in the day-to-day life of America, my country right or wrong, because here it doesn't matter what your name used to be, as long as you're not wanted by the police.

I would have been content to remain anonymous, but events have decreed otherwise. Even if I hadn't turned myself in to your justice, I would have been pursued nonetheless by the faceless shadows of authorities as old as time.

I am now telling my story in the hope that I shall be nameless by the end of it, free of the curse of identity. To be perfectly honest, I want to be no one, a nameless something, gone in the light, spent by wind, a sliver of shadow passing over a rock. I don't even want a name on a tombstone. I don't want a tombstone. When I'm gone I want to be turned into fine ash and poured into a hole at a construction site. An American-style death, Your Excellency, a comical and informal death. I hope you find me guilty. I am. Guilty of murder. But also of innocence. And of forgetfulness.

It has been said that we Hungarians are passionate people. This may be true for others, but as for myself my only passion now is for my disappearance. I want it to be total.

I petition the universe for cancellation through the agency of this court, Your Honor.

The judge leaned forward and admonished the witness to refrain from overly dramatic demonstrations.

I am sorry, Your Honor. If anything, I am greatly more subdued than my compatriots. I wish I'd had a greater appetite for living, but the vitality that might have been mine has been sucked from my family tree by the woman whose name I bear. She lived more than four centuries ago, which is a long time for the dried limbs of an exhausted line to drag on all the way into the twentieth century.

Drake Bathory-Kereshtur paused to drink from the water glass in front of him. He drank down to the bottom swiftly. He did not appear to the judge to be suffering from a lack of vitality. On the contrary, his movements and speech suggested the actions of a much younger man. After putting down his glass firmly, he said:

These are the facts. I am a Hungarian-American, born during World War II in the city of Budapest. I emigrated to the United States after the Hungarian Revolution in 1956, following the street fighting that left my country bloodied and many of us homeless.

My last glimpse of Budapest was from under the tarp of a truck. There were dead bodies on the street, and buildings were burning. I left behind my mother and father, the friends of my childhood, and the sounds of my native language.

But in New York, Hungary reconstituted itself around me.

My classmate from first grade, Ficzko, owned the Golden Paprikash, an émigrés' hangout filled every evening with people far from home. We hatched plots as thick as the cigarette smoke before closing time. We spent our ingenuity and our youth dreaming of ways to overthrow the Communists. But in our heart of hearts we knew that we would never go back. Over plates of homemade nostalgia and glasses of Tokay wine that brought a lump to the throat, we bemoaned our fate and rhapsodized over our lost country, which had grown without blemish in our minds.

Sitting among my fellow exiles, I often had the feeling that we had grown more fond of the melancholy country of our longing than of the real place. Given a chance, most of us would have chosen our sorrow over the uncertainties of return.

And in the end, that is exactly what happened.

When Communism collapsed and there were no longer any impediments to return, many of us preferred to stay, citing mundane and practical reasons that in no wise matched the grandeur of our laments.

That was not my fate. I did return.

From the outset of the events that toppled the Communist regimes in Eastern Europe, I felt great apprehension. The faces of people who had been shut away from public exposure for forty years began to appear on television. I watched the nightly news with nervous anticipation. I expected at any moment to see old friends or relatives or the faces of my schoolteachers.

Western reporters combed the streets of Budapest interviewing people. New political parties appeared. Their spokesmen looked both younger and more spirited than the dour bureaucrats who had run the country in my day.

Then something strange happened, Your Honor.

The more I watched the faces of common Hungarian people and those of their new leaders, the more anxious I became. I couldn't explain the dread that seized me in seeing my liberated countrymen. It was something in their eyes.

Then one day while watching television I saw someone I actually knew. It was an old friend and classmate of mine, a once thin boy named Klaus Megyery. He had become a rather portly man. He appeared on a program about the political future of Hungary. What he said was bizarre, but it is not what he said that filled me with dread. It was his eyes. They emanated twin beams of cold blue light that pierced me. The impression that I was addressed directly grew so strong I tried to get up and turn off the television. I couldn't.

I thought I heard him call my name.

He can't be calling my name, I told myself. But that's what I heard. Klaus was my oldest friend, by which I mean *earliest.* We had lived on the same street since we could barely speak. We had stayed friends throughout our schooling. Klaus was always preaching to me on behalf of the nationalist cause, which caused me great distress, for reasons I will explain shortly. I suffered his tirades silently, and he never suspected the emotions he aroused in me. I was afraid of him, so I cultivated his friendship as a form of self-protection. I had not given him a thought since 1956. And now, here he was inside my television, affecting me so forcefully it was as if no time at all had passed.

In elementary school, we had nicknamed him Shaky Stringbean because of his long bony body that never stopped trembling. Others called him Puppet for the same reason. In our sophomore year he had appointed himself my bodyguard and followed me everywhere. He never tired of reciting forbidden patriotic poetry, particularly after a few glasses of Tokay. After I escaped from Hungary, I heard that Megyery had led a group of drunken patriots to the houses of "Communist Jews" and set them on fire. I was not surprised. But if the story had been true, Klaus would have doubtlessly been executed by the Soviets after the revolt. But here he was now, decades later, unexecuted and beaming evil rays out of my TV.

After the program, I had two water glasses full of whiskey. I was shaking.

By morning I had convinced myself that I'd been hallucinating. Only, it wasn't that easy. In the mail that day was a letter from my old friend Klaus Megyery.

Klaus wrote to me that God, after an absence of nearly half a century, was smiling on the Hungarian people again. The coming days provided a unique opportunity to the "keepers of the faith" to unite the Hungarian people under the banner of a monarch. This was the time, Klaus wrote, to create a true Hungarian kingdom under the rule of a native-born prince.

The purpose of Megyery's letter was to summon me, a descendant of the noble Bathorys, back to Hungary. Hungarian aristocrats, he said, were being summoned from all over the world by members of Megyery's monarchist organization, Saint Stephen's Knights. Saint Stephen's Knights was not solely a promonarchist organization but also a political party, duly registered to participate in the first free elections of the post-Communist era. Klaus enclosed a murky pamphlet entitled *Proposal for a New Constitution for Royal Hungary*. This document envisioned a constitutional monarchy with a House of Lords drawn from among the Hungarian diaspora.

I would have liked this to be a nightmare, Your Honor.

I tried to laugh at the solemn naïveté of the whole idea.

Bringing back monarchs was as loony to me as returning to the Middle Ages. If, after its failed utopian experiment, Europe was ready to go back to the Middle Ages, that was its business. I wanted no part of it. I was an American now.

Next morning, when I checked into my office at the *Chronicle,* where I had a humble and perfectly satisfactory job as a reporter covering the Board of Education, I was summoned by my editor. She was brief: "Events in your native country are becoming very interesting. We are sending you to Budapest immediately."

I protested. It was no use. Travel arrangements had already been made. I had the paranoid thought that Klaus Megyery, beaming from the depths of our TV sets, had influenced everyone, including my editor. Her abruptness was unusual. We often exchanged banter, and once upon a time we had been intimate. But now, behind her indifferent gaze, I thought I saw the steely glint of my old chum's eyes.

Of course, I could have quit my job. I had quit plenty of jobs before and survived just fine. This is one of the best things about America: you can walk proudly out and begin again. This is the theory, anyway. But at that moment I forgot the theory. I told myself that this was an opportunity, not a punishment. After all, how many times had I sworn, along with my exiled friends, that I would return as soon as it became possible? I accepted because it was in keeping with the conventional lie I had been telling myself for years. I did the conventional thing, Your Honor.

Drake Bathory-Kereshtur stopped abruptly.
The judge asked him what the trouble was.

I have a request, Your Honor.

The mirror. I respectfully ask that the mirror bolted to the wall in my cell be removed. I have tried covering it with the blanket. It keeps slipping. That mirror is always there.

The judge considered for a moment the man standing before her. Broad shoulders, fierce black eyes, thick black hair, rich mustache, determined jaw, high cheekbones, sensual lower lip. There would be little to be ashamed of when he looked into the metal mirror bolted to his cell wall. He projected determination and dignity, but there was something else too, something vulnerable and immense.

She granted his request.

I N 1569, WHEN ELIZABETH WAS nine years old, a band of peasant rebels came into Ecsed Castle, where she was spending the summer with her two older sisters, Anichka and Shandra. The rebels set fire to the granary and killed the soldiers guarding the outer court where the stables and the garrison were.

Elizabeth and her sisters were hastily bundled up in blankets by their nurses and carried through a secret passageway under the castle into the forest.

From their hiding place they watched Ecsed go up in flames.

The four women and three children shivered in their shelter under a big rock, wondering what to do next. As night fell, they watched the peasants drag women out of the castle and rape them on the edge of the forest. Men were hacked to death with axes or had their skulls crushed with spiked clubs.

The cries of anguish that filled the night washed over Elizabeth, a frightful music of such raw force she was unwittingly drawn to it. On her belly, propelled by terror and curiosity, she crawled to better see the flames and the shadows of men and horses in the fields around the castle. She found herself at quite a distance from her sisters and the nurses.

She felt the rough bark of a large tree under her hands, and she nestled between its roots. At that moment there was a clatter of crude weapons, and she saw men enter the woods and head directly for the rock sheltering the others.

Her heart beating wildly, Elizabeth remained where she was. She stood still as a stone, fearing to let out her breath. She heard her sister Shandra cry out. Her companions had been discovered.

Elizabeth scrambled up the trunk of the oak sheltering her. She was a good climber. Lying on her stomach on a thick branch, she watched from above as the dark shades of men, whose blood-soaked lambskin tunics she could smell, dragged her sisters and their guardians from behind the rock.

She heard the nurses plead for their lives in high-pitched, frightened voices. She heard what she thought was the hiss of snakes and then the sound of bubbling water, but did not realize until morning that it had been the sound of curved knives slitting the women's throats. The blood sounded like a gurgling brook.

She heard her sister Anichka say haughtily, "Do you know who we are? We are Bathorys! You will pay for this!"

She heard the men laugh and imitate the young girl: "We are Bathorys! We are Bathorys!"

Then a voice deeper than the other men's spoke

clearly, chilling her to the bone: "Do you know who I am? I am Dozsa, the death of nobles! I have come to avenge the blood of my father and brother!"

She heard Shandra cry softly like a hurt kitten. Then there was a sound of ripped silk, and Elizabeth saw the heavy shades of the men swarm over the bodies of her sisters.

She heard and saw nothing else until the morning.

She woke still stretched on the branch of the oak that had saved her life. When she looked down she saw her sister Anichka's blue eyes staring straight up at her. But the eyes did not see her. Hanging upside down from a lower branch beneath her, her sister's naked and bruised body swayed slightly in the breeze.

Hanging from another tree was Shandra.

On the ground below lay the grotesquely sprawled bodies of her nurses, their throats slashed. Their blood had drained into the moss at the foot of the oak, turning it rusty red.

Tatters of her sisters' clothes had caught on ferns here and there, waving like small flags.

Elizabeth remained on her branch.

Ecsed was still burning, but there was no sign of life anywhere. The rebels had gone on to attack another castle, and no one was left alive at Ecsed.

She lost and regained consciousness several times but was too frightened to climb down.

Near noon, when the sun was high, she heard the sound of someone walking softly. To her relief, it was a white horse that had somehow survived the slaughter. Its color reminded Elizabeth of a white moon.

She called to the animal with a timid whistle, but the white horse did not heed her. Then she called it by the Latin name of the moon. "Luna." At this, the mare lifted her head and looked up with warm brown eyes, the most beautiful and kindest eyes Elizabeth had ever seen.

She dropped down from her tree and approached Luna, who did not mind the girl mounting her. Horse and girl became one body as they headed for the dark depths of the forest.

Elizabeth didn't dare go into the open countryside. The forest had sheltered her so far. Only in the depths of the forest would she find safety.

The darkness enveloped her in a soothing embrace.

The forest smelled like mushrooms and rot and bitter green things. The girl and her horse leapt over a fallen tree and followed a faint path. The noises of the wood were different from the noises of the field. The sound of crickets and frogs was replaced here by a more mysterious, deeper, lower music. Elizabeth thought she heard moans and wails rising up from deep under the moss, and there was a sweet, calling sound, as of a woman crying to herself, but it was only her dying sisters' voices echoing within her own mind.

They came to a creek and followed it. It climbed to a place where she could no longer see it, but after riding for a while, she found it again. It was pouring down the side of a big boulder in a narrow but strong waterfall. At the bottom was a deep pool.

Elizabeth dismounted and told Luna to wait for her. The horse looked placidly into her eyes and she felt safe.

She stripped and dove into the clear water. It was wonderfully bracing. When she looked about her, she saw nothing but clear water moved slightly by the mighty splash of the waterfall a few feet away. She swam toward the splash and let herself be pounded by the stream until a delicious numbness spread through all her limbs.

She dove all the way down to the sandy bottom and

walked on it on her hands. She felt very much at home in the water. It was transparent and penetrable, and it embraced her completely. It was the only element she trusted. Water was utterly unlike people, those compact, dense, impenetrable, murderous creatures that belonged to the night.

Elizabeth wanted to see through everything in the world the way she saw through this water. Of all the people she knew, her sisters had been most like water. The rest were like moss drenched in blood or gnarled like the roots of a tree. Dust to dust, Preacher Hebler had once said. There was no dust, no blood, no moss, no rough wood in her clean bright green water.

Elizabeth floated for some time in the pool at the foot of the waterfall. She didn't know how long she had been there, but it was already dark. The last rays of the setting sun were sinking somewhere beyond the trees, and the last warmth of the day had begun to evaporate, causing little wisps of fog to chase one another across the mossy forest floor.

She called Luna, but Luna didn't answer.

Elizabeth clambered out of the water and looked about her. There was nothing but the unbroken silence of the forest. The first stars of the evening had appeared in the sky.

Her surprise turned to dismay when she looked for her clothes and could not find them. She remembered laying them on a stump. The stump was there, but her garments were not on it. She shivered slightly, not so much from the cold as from the thought that she might have to spend the night naked in the woods, like her sisters swaying alone from the ends of their ropes. Nights this time of the year were cold.

And then she saw her petticoat. A large lion was lying on it, staring at her with burning round eyes.

Elizabeth had never seen a lion before, except in books.

She sat down on the ground and stared back. The lion moved his head lazily from side to side and flicked his tail. Elizabeth was not frightened. Something in her caused her to become very calm. She did not want to scream, but she did when she felt a damp furry hand on her shoulder.

Standing behind her was a creature perhaps four feet tall with human eyes looking out of a matted mass of curly white hair. The creature smelled damp and sour at the same time. It was dressed in bark with leaves still sticking out of it. Its feet looked like roots. While her mind flipped furiously through the many books of exotic creatures that she had seen, trying to identify the monster, another one appeared on her left.

Elizabeth fainted, not so much from their appearance as from their smell.

She woke up in the dark feeling exceedingly warm. She judged by the foul air that she was in an enclosure of some sort, and then she heard the loud snoring of all kinds of creatures around her. She moved her hand, and it met with the hot fur of something that stirred and moaned. Now she knew where the heat came from. On all sides of her were sleeping furry beasts.

She tried to crawl out, but she was wedged tightly between them. She was still naked, as she soon ascertained by running her hand over her stomach and chest.

She spent what remained of the night with her eyes wide open, staring at the shapes about her. There must have been at least fourteen of these beasts crowded inside a round lair of some sort. She did manage to free herself bit by bit, one toe and one finger at a time, from the snoring mass. By the time she had worked herself to the top of the heap, light came streaming through the cracks.

One by one the creatures came to life. The one that had put its paw on her shoulder was the first to rise. Elizabeth stretched out her hand, and the creature clasped it. Together they crawled out a three-foot doorway into the morning dew.

"Perchance you are the fairy sent to feed us," the creature said.

"Perchance you can tell me what you did with my clothes!" Elizabeth said threateningly, and then, so as not to seem too rude, she added, "And then perchance you can tell me what you are."

Elizabeth's clothes had been washed and laid out to dry on a rock. The creature said it would be a good hour before they would be dry enough to wear but that meanwhile they could have breakfast and get acquainted. The creature said that its name was Himlat and that she—it was indeed a she—was the oldest member of her family of forest-dwelling herb doctors.

Himlat made a small fire and plucked a couple of skinned rabbits from an overhead branch. She explained that her family was only partly natural, that most of them had in fact joined voluntarily. They had come from villages and towns where they had been abused because of their ugliness. She herself had seen so many wicked things and had been employed to such foul ends that she would never return to the people's cruel world. Since childhood she had been employed in one capacity or another to help with rude peasant sports. She had had to nail cats to posts for a village game where players with their hands tied behind their backs battered the animals to death. The cats scratched and clawed, occasionally gouging out one of their eyes, an occurrence that gave her grim satisfaction. Later she had had to clean the village green, where men with clubs had beat a pig lifeless while their wives and children cheered. As a young woman she had been charged with taking corpses off the gibbet and removing heads stuck on posts by the village gate when they began to rot. At the time of her first blood, a kindly woman had taken her into her employ, paying her two copper coins for the hands and penises of corpses. She had learned many things from this woman, but in the end this life became disgusting to her, and she took herself to the woods, where she met many others with similar stories.

While Himlat laid their hot rabbit morsels on some large green leaves, the rest of the creatures began to creep outside and stretch. In the light of the sun, Elizabeth saw just how hideous they were.

At the sight of so much deformity she forgot that she was naked. The creatures stretched and blinked and ran into the woods to urinate. When they returned they gathered about the fire and about her, looking in wonder at her pale, smooth flesh.

"This one was bathed in milk," one of the biggest creatures, with a cloven hoof for an arm, said, touching her neck. Elizabeth cringed and looked helplessly at Himlat, who struck the hoof with a burning stick she withdrew from the fire.

The beast was offended. "I was just seeing what she's made of," he said crossly, spitting on his sizzling fur.

It seemed that everyone had withdrawn food from some hidden nook: they were eating salted meat, dried fish, and large loaves of black bread with coarse mustard. Some of them fried birds or rabbit together with mushrooms.

Elizabeth's presence aroused them to a great pitch of excitement. They all started talking at once, telling her woeful stories of the life they had left behind. All had run from the foul human world of corpses and disease. Many of them had been tortured, and they hastened to show her their scars and their still-open wounds. Elizabeth saw the deep-seated grooves of lead-weighted whips, the craters left by hooks, bones broken on racks, legs that had atrophied from being chained, faces that had grown paralyzed from wearing shame masks, the still-oozing seals of red-hot iron brands, the round scars where breasts had been cut off.

Many other body parts were missing; these had been smashed, amputated, or burned for trivial infractions. One of the creatures had been castrated for looking too boldly at a countess. While he told Elizabeth what had befallen him, he kept his eyes on the ground, not daring to look at her.

The world the forest people had escaped had been so merciless and brutal it had been hell on earth. Some of them had been hunted by knights in games of sport and bore the traces of arrows and spears and maces.

Elizabeth's nakedness now seemed shameful to her, because she was so smooth and unmarred, except for her birthmark, which, like a signpost on a snowy field, somehow made her seem even more naked. Eyes fastened so longingly on her untouched whiteness that she felt like an icon being adored at High Mass.

"You are a sapling," one of them said.

More and more, as their tales of woe continued, Elizabeth felt herself privileged to look on so much writing on the surface of so much skin. She noticed also that the furry, scarred, wounded, and tortured skin of the forest creatures was very much alive. Their souls had stretched to touch every patch of their dolorous surface. The creatures were as full of soul as they could be, and their souls had expanded.

Her teacher Silvestri had once told her that most people are asleep and that only great suffering can wake them. He said that pain was a kind of fire in the body that burned through the sleep of the mind. If this was true, before her now were the only awake creatures she had ever known.

"Where is the lion?" Elizabeth asked.

There was great laughter all around.

Someone dragged a lion skin from behind a tree and got inside. He then came up and lay across Elizabeth's skinny lap. The lion's skin was not even lion but some sort of straw. The forest creatures explained that they had many such tricks to scare trespassers.

When Elizabeth looked at the hovel where she had spent the night, she was startled to see that a knight's helmet and visor stuck at an angle out of the roof. The door she had crawled through was in fact an armor breastplate. She asked for an explanation.

Himlat said, "We ought not to tell you this, but since you will now live with us, I will tell you."

She said that when the forest creatures first started living together, they wandered around much more than they did at the present time. One day they came to a battlefield where Hungarian knights had fought a Turkish army. Everyone had been killed or wounded. At nightfall they had sneaked into the field of blood and stripped the fallen warriors of their armor. Their house was made of knights' suits of armor, while their other hideouts were likewise made from Hungarian and Turkish chain mail and other items.

Elizabeth suspected that this wasn't the whole truth. She guessed that the forest people hadn't just stripped the knights. They had killed them as well and used more than the armor. She now noticed that many of those around her wore bone jewelry and ate meat with intricately carved bone ware.

It worried her that Himlat had assumed that she would be living with them.

Elizabeth did not dress right away after her clothes had dried. This was partly because she did not wish to seem in a hurry after the revelations she had been made privy to, but also because she enjoyed her pristine whiteness among the savagely scarred creatures. She thought of herself as a field of fresh snow surrounded by the remains of burnt villages.

She stayed close to Himlat for the rest of the afternoon, learning from the old woman how to gather herbs and make medicines and poisons from them. As Himlat worked, carefully removing roots and cutting leaves, she told Elizabeth how to bandage wounds, let blood, cut cysts, set broken bones, and suck out snake poison.

After her work was done, Himlat gave Elizabeth a mandrake root that looked like a little man. On the neck of the mandrake man she had embedded two small datura flowers good for telling the future. Himlat told Elizabeth to keep her mandrake safe until the time her first woman's blood came. Then she should soak the root in her first blood until the root was sated with it. After that, she should let him dry under the full moon. The power of that doll would be so awesome that a few simple words of Elizabeth's would cause the doll to bring her whatever she wished.

When Elizabeth put on her petticoat the sun was already in the west. She noticed that the forest creatures had mostly disappeared, either gone to hunt or asleep like Himlat, who had been telling her about gingerroot one moment and began snoring the next.

Elizabeth thought with a shudder about her first woman's blood, which she half knew about but had never given much thought to. She had heard the women at Kereshtur speak endlessly about it and about the changes of mood and mind that it brought them every month. She knew that the bleeding was somehow connected to the moon. She had even watched her aunt Klara one morning tying a kerchief to her bottom and had seen two deep red flowers blossom on the white cotton between her legs. She had been alarmed, thinking that Aunt Klara might be dying, but she was reassured when Klara laughed heartily and told her that women bled this way in sympathy with the wounds of our Lord on the cross. This was a singular honor accorded to women by Christ for love of his mother, Mary. Men, who could not bleed monthly, were obliged instead to shed their blood in war.

Elizabeth saw that she was alone. None of the hairy creatures were watching her. Clasping her mandrake man confidently, she began walking away from the setting sun in the direction she remembered coming in.

As she walked through the forest, she heard the cries of all sorts of creatures, mostly birds, but now and then a sound low and deep, made, she imagined, by a bigger animal. She hoped to find the end of the forest before nightfall. Now and then she called softly for the horse, Luna, but there was no sound of hooves.

It was getting dark again, and the sounds of the forest became more menacing. She could feel the eyes of beasts watching her from the foliage, and she hurried on. She stopped now and then to catch her breath and to listen. She heard the murmur of the stream she had first followed into the woods, and soon found it. It was quite narrow, and Elizabeth was sure that she had seen this part of it before.

Just before nightfall the trees thinned out, and she emerged into a field made a deep burnished gold by the setting sun. She could see a village church and, far in the distance, the walls of a castle.

It was not Ecsed.

She heard a horn and the baying of hounds, and she wondered why there was a hunt at this time of day. She did not know that the woods were swarming with armed men and hounds looking for her.

* * *

Elizabeth arrived in the village just as the moon was rising. The square in front of the church was mobbed with people on their knees, praying and crying.

Tied to high stakes all around the square were naked rebels, captured near Ecsed. The highest stake had been reserved for a coarse giant, their leader, Dozsa. The prisoners awaited the arrival of Palatine Thurzo's guard with the palatine himself at the head.

Pastor Ponikenuz stood on the highest step of the church like a lean crow cawing to the crowd.

When Elizabeth neared the square she heard his high-pitched voice and was surprised to hear her own name.

"God, who makes and unmakes all things in this world, is going to bring Elizabeth Bathory back to us, unworthy sinners. We beseech God in his wisdom to bring back Countess Bathory to us. If she comes back sound and safe, we promise to give God a great feast of thanks and to thank every one of the saints in this church."

The crowd cried "Amen," and many of them made individual pledges to God should the countess return safely. One of them promised to crawl on his knees to the cross on the hill behind the church and to remain fasting there for three days and two nights. A silk merchant promised five bolts of celestial blue silk to make all the saints in the church new dresses. Another said that he would give alms to the poor every day for a whole year.

Elizabeth had the impression that no one expected her to return, Pastor Ponikenuz least of all. He was thinking already of ways to counter the blasphemous idolatry that the people, no matter what the great Martinus Luther had told them, still practiced.

She stepped slowly forward. The astonished crowd parted before her, and many people fainted, thinking that they had seen a ghost. She walked deliberately and slowly, remembering all the pledges she had overheard. She thought with a delicious inner trembling that she would hold them all to it.

The palatine Thurzo arrived that same day.

Elizabeth heard the public reading of the proclamation that listed the rebels' grievous crimes, including the murder and "buggering" of her innocent sisters.

She did not know what that word meant but was glad when the fire was lit under Dozsa's great iron "throne." Count Thurzo had ordered an iron chair made for the chief of the band.

Dozsa's lieutenants were lowered from their stakes and made to sit at a long table as if they were guests awaiting their supper at an inn.

When the iron throne became red hot, the smell of Dozsa's cooked flesh seeped into the air. Elizabeth inhaled deeply, fighting back an urge to vomit. The sweet, sickening scent permeated her clothes and infused her whole body.

She watched the heated crown melt the flesh of Dozsa's head, but she forced herself to look even as curled morsels of brain flew out of his skull.

When the body cooled, the undertaker scooped large portions of cooked flesh and threw them on the table before Dozsa's helpers. Those who refused to eat were dragged away and dismembered before the palatine, who was seated at the top of the church stairs.

Not many refused. Some ate grimly, their heads bowed, as if they were indeed hungry. When the meal was finished and nothing remained of Dozsa but grizzly charred bones, those who had consumed him were also put to death by quartering, and their entrails were given to the dogs to eat.

Elizabeth watched the entire punishment and felt so much joy at the rebels' suffering that she wet herself and the ground where she stood.

The palatine thus avenged himself for the murder of his two nieces, Elizabeth's sisters.

He expressed also his regrets to Elizabeth Bathory, now the only remaining daughter of the great family. There was no affection in his manner, and Elizabeth did not expect any from her famous and fearsome uncle.

The palatine had put all but one of the rebels to death. This one, Csarkom, a tall dark man, he kept to take back to Budapest in order to try on him one of his mechanical inventions, a torture wheel.

T hank you for removing the mirror, Your Honor.

I can now concentrate on my deposition without fear of encountering the face of that terrible woman when I return to my cell.

"She lives in a mirror?" asked the judge.

Yes, she lives in mirrors.

"Continue then."

I was born in Budapest, Your Excellency. I know I have already said that, but it needs reiterating.

I am the son of Julius Kereshtur, a mine inspector, and Eva Bathory, a printer. Both of them were descended from the aristocratic families that gave Hungary three kings and several princes over a period of six centuries.

My most notorious ancestor was Elizabeth Bathory,

who came to be known as the Blood Countess and who is the true object of this hearing. She first lived in the latter half of the sixteenth century. She was an educated woman who saw the rise of cities, the struggle between the Reformation and the Counter-Reformation, the Turkish wars for the conquest of Europe, and the settlement of the New World. She tortured and killed hundreds of girls in order to bathe in their blood, because she believed this would keep her young. She did not succeed in her lifetime.

Stung by what she conceived to be a sexist statement, the judge said: "Mr. Drake Bathory-Kereshtur, I would like to remind you that the desire to stay young and beautiful is universal and that few people kill because of it."

I understand. I am not being simplistic, Your Honor. Elizabeth Bathory wanted very badly to remain young for reasons that will become clear but which are quite complex. You or I might accept more or less gracefully the natural order of time. She did not. I will try to shed light on her refusal later in my deposition.

When I was growing up, her name was used casually whenever someone wanted to make a point that something was gruesome. For instance, people would point to a scary old house and say, "Looks like Countess Bathory lived there!" Mothers told their daughters: "If you do not obey me, you're going to Countess Bathory's house." As a child, I was sure that it was my house that they spoke of. The fact that it was my mother's name made me ashamed.

My father once told me that the name was common among Hungarian nobility, but until I went to school I knew very little about my family's history. I knew only that there was something strange about me, because kids snickered behind my back and adults often stopped talking when I was in the room. I became a shy and reclusive child.

One day I overheard two men on a park bench whispering about Jews. The Jews, they said, were people apart who needed to be shunned because they did the work of the devil. They were everywhere, often disguised to look just like everyone else. It took cunning and an extra sense to spot a Jew.

Sitting at the far end of the bench, I made myself small and inconsequential. I wanted to sink into the ground beneath my feet. I was sure that they were talking about me, because that was precisely my condition. Looking seemingly like everyone else, I passed my days under a cloud of suspicion. I conceived the thought then that I was a Jew. This was the reason why people regarded me with hatred and dismay.

I found my fears confirmed everywhere. Two boys who entertained themselves by pissing crosswise against a wall said to me as I walked by: "Every time we piss like this, a Jew dies!"

Jews cropped up in whispered conversations that ceased as soon as I approached. I had always known that I was different, but now I knew why. A mute rage rose in my soul. I began to hate everyone, even my parents, who had kept such a thing from me. I vowed to become so great and feared one day that I would show everyone just how wrong they had been. I wrote with invisible ink across my most precious possession, a much folded map of the world, I AM A JEW. One day, long after I had become rich and famous, someone would unfold the map and discover what they had all known, confirmed in my childish hand. I AM A JEW. Nothing dissuaded me from this notion, not even the facts, which I discovered after I began attending school.

The facts were that, far from being a Jew, I was a Hungarian aristocrat.

* * *

I beg the court's indulgence, Your Honor.

The judge leaned forward and granted her indulgence. Something akin to compassion was welling within her for this seemingly strong man before her who had had such sensitive and difficult beginnings.

I must now describe certain incidents of my childhood that should prove beyond the shadow of a doubt that I am not essentially a murderer, that I may indeed be organically incapable of committing the crime of which I accuse myself.

It made no sense to the judge, but she bid him continue.

The name *Bathory* was on nearly every page of our history book. We had to memorize long lists of Hungarian and Transylvanian princes, many of whom were named Bathory.

The ruins of the Bathory castles stood along a spiny ridge that marked the border between two great empires, the Ottoman and the Austrian. On a clear day, from the top of the hill behind our house, I could see the ruins of fortifications that had faced the armies of empires for a millennium.

The house we lived in was held up by a stone wall of such antiquity its origin was lost in the mists of the already shrouded history of the city. Over the sixteenth-century gate stood a statue of a horsewoman in knightly armor. Under her horse was the trampled body of a half-dressed wench in a pose of begging supplication. Affixed to the knight's shield was the Bathory coat of arms: the torso of a woman with outspread wings and wearing Athena's helmet above a dragon swallowing his own tail. In the middle of the circle formed by the dragon were three wolves' teeth.

If your scribe does not mind, I will make a little drawing of it.

Although my father took great pains to conceal everything that might have reminded people of our family's aristocratic roots, I discovered a trunk in the attic filled with medals and dinnerware stamped with the Bathory seal.

I told my good friend and classmate Klaus Megyery that my family had treasures hidden in the attic. Next evening, just as we had sat down for supper, the police came. They ordered us to remain at the table but not touch our food. While my mother's paprikash got cold, the men searched our house. They found the trunk in the attic and brought it down. They shouted at my mother to clear the table, and they took everything out of the trunk.

I remember one of them, an unshaven man in a long leather coat. He ran a thick, nicotine-stained finger over the raised seal on one of the plates.

"So this is the Jews' secret sign," he said.

"It is the sign of our family," my father said meekly.

Then they took my father away. He returned three days later. He had been beaten. My mother had saved him food, and he ate it ravenously, like a wolf. I knew that my father knew that I had been the one to tell about the trunk. But he didn't say anything to my mother. I watched him anxiously as he ate, sure that as soon as he was sated, he would rise angrily and seize me. But he didn't beat me. He didn't even reproach me.

In a way, this was worse. He had been beaten because of me. I swore to myself to be discreet and wary from that time on. I knew better than to speak about anything having to do with my family. Like my earlier discovery that I was a Jew, this aristocracy business meant only more trouble.

Our family did not have many friends. My father had a chess companion, a Doctor Thurzo, who smoked a pipe. The two of them sat immobile under the small arch in our living room until it became too dark to see. When the cuckoo clock struck eight, my mother came in and announced dinner. Doctor Thurzo always rose, made his excuses, and went off into the night. I used to sit on a chair watching them. They never spoke. Ours was a house of silence. I don't remember my father and mother speaking to each other. Instead of speaking there was always listening. We all moved furtively, listening for something. We stretched on our toes, pricked our ears, always listening. I never knew what we were listening for.

While ostensibly doing my homework, I gazed at the moss-covered seal over the gate in the stone wall. Those three wolves' teeth at the center of the Bathory shield were as familiar to me as my mother's face.

The seal was also prominently displayed below the clock on the fourteenth-century cathedral in the square. This clock could be seen from every house in our neighborhood. In addition to hours and minutes, it showed the phases of the moon and the changes of the constellations. This clock had maps of eastern and western Europe on its sides. It was made in 1566 by the astronomer and astrologer Philipp Imser from Augsburg for Sigismund Bathory, who donated it to the church.

Whenever I needed to know what time it was, I simply lifted my eyes to the sky, and there, from his tower, God and my ancestors gave it to me. It was said that this clock only stopped working twice: when the Turks sacked the town in the seventeenth century and when Soviet tanks rolled over the cobblestones in 1946. Earthquakes did not bother it. Nor did the frequent flooding of the river. God's clock was political, like everything else in a fortified trade town fiercely buffeted by the winds of history.

History, by the time I started studying it, had been rewritten to conform to the ideas of Comrade Stalin, Your Honor.

Our teacher, Comrade Hebler, was often at a loss to explain just how our history fitted into the prevailing ideology. I had been made to sit in the front row, which suited me fine. I did not want to see any of my classmates. And history interested me. Unfortunately, what we were taught hardly qualified.

Hebler recited his explanations with eyes closed and without any conviction, a yellowed flake of tobacco embedded sadly in his mustache. I was sorry for him, though I didn't know why. At the same time, Hebler physically revolted me. He was in the habit of spitting when he spoke too fast, chewing up the words of the Hungarian language into a paste of dates and names, as if the Hungarian language wasn't strange enough on its own.

The judge, who hated to hear discrimination against anything, even mild self-mocking at one's own tongue, admonished him mildly.

"What is so strange about your language, Mr. Bathory-Kereshtur? And can I ask you to confine yourself to the facts as they pertain to your confession?"

It was never clear to anyone how our language came about, Your Excellency. Yes, I will confine myself to the facts pertaining to the case, but the background is absolutely necessary. It sheds light on my innocence. It may also explain how it is possible for an alchemist, using the elements of time and matter, to use my blood and body for his purposes.

"Go ahead," said the judge, seized by sudden lassitude, as if she were lying on a divan listening to a man's thousand and one nights.

The Hungarian language, Magyar, resembles Finnish, Your Honor, though its lack of vowels could be attributed to them having been snatched by the wind when the horse-mounted nomad warriors shouted to one another. Allow me to quote Illirio Tepius, a Byzantine traveler, who wrote in 1232 that "when Hungarians speak, there is a windlike whistle that propels the words forward, as if they never dismounted."

This is important, Your Honor, because it establishes the fact that language, like blood, is a living thing that proceeds forward in time. Even much later, when Hungarians became settled people, a typical nobleman like my ancestor Count Franz Nadazdy, Elizabeth Bathory's husband, spent most of his life on horseback. He fought many campaigns against the Turks, leaving his mount only when it was absolutely necessary—to procreate, conclude treaties, or sit in the king's council.

Knights were a species of centaur, Your Highness, uneasy when separated from their horse bodies. Franz Nadazdy's horse wore armor made of the same plates as his own. The pleated gold horn thrusting from the head plate of his horse was made of the same gold as the cross on his own chest. Our history book said that "Franz Nadazdy was well aware of his family's contributions to the Christian reform, but in his heart of hearts he was loyal to the pagan Arpad, whose hot blood boiled in his veins."

The first Hungarian king, Arpad, forged the Hungarian nation from ten unruly tribes of animal-worshiping nomads who lived by conquest and plunder. They raged in a wide area, from the Caucasus to the Black Sea. Arpad's blood, in a considerably attenuated form, runs also in my veins, though I never had the slightest desire to rage and plunder.

On the contrary, as a child I preferred books to horseplay or even sports. I was completely inept at soccer, for instance, and my skinny legs caused my classmates no end of merriment.

Some of my ancestors appeared to be as degenerate as Communist propaganda made them out to be. We Bathorys were all related to one another. It has been said that the penalty for such close kinships was madness, weakness of limb, perversion, religious fanaticism, spells of prophecy, and tenderness for charlatans.

I suffer from none of these afflictions, Your Excellency. I stand ready to take any test you care to order, mental or physical. On the contrary, I suffer only from a surfeit of reason, as if I had no body at all.

On the other hand, I admit that I have changed under the occult influences of the past month, from a shamed and modest working drudge enjoying his American anonymity to an unpleasantly guilty murderer, which is, quite rationally, my birthright.

I have not changed, however, to such a degree that I cannot see the absurdity of my position. It is small consolation.

The others in my family were blessed neither with reason nor with a sense of proportion. Elizabeth Bathory murdered virgins. Elizabeth's father, George, suffered from memory loss and temporary bouts of paralysis. He spent the last ten years of his life in his favorite chair, carried to the table by servants. He slept upright in his chair and submitted to cursory washing only with great difficulty. Her brother, Stephen, was a drunkard and a lecher who liked to appear naked in the marketplaces of strange towns and get himself beaten senseless. Elizabeth's uncle Gabor, who lived reclusively on the family estate at Ecsed, often got up in the middle of the night, donned his armor, and fought invisible attackers until he collapsed from exhaustion. During these battles with unearthly foes, Gabor shouted in unknown languages. Elizabeth's aunt Klara, who was a great influence on her, was shunned by many Hungarian nobles because she liked to dress like a man and kept a large retinue of beautiful young girls whose only job was to pamper their mistress. All these extraordinary people lived in the sixteenth century, Your Honor, but in subsequent centuries there were others, afflicted in curious and perverse ways. It is true that they became fewer and fewer as time went by, but this may very well be because their power waned and they weren't much heard from by the nineteenth century.

On the other hand, the Bathory family had more princes, kings, and illustrious members than any other in the kingdom. It is on the basis of this statistical advantage that my Hungarian supporters decided to draft me to their hopeless cause.

Anyway, to return to the days when I was a schoolboy, I somehow managed to insult Comrade Hebler's political rectitude, and I was asked to write a paper criticizing my aristocratic family by applying the Marxist dialectical view of history as explained by Comrade Stalin. Unfortunately, all of Hungarian history seemed to be my family history. It was an immense job that would have taken me well into the next century if events had not intervened.

I am not sure why, but I was rather pleased that I had been asked to criticize this aristocracy. I don't know what I would have done if I had been asked to criticize the Jews instead. I hadn't seen anything written about that part of myself. Thus far, my profound conviction that in addition to being an accursed aristocrat, I was also a Jew had received little confirmation from my parents, though the world was quite blunt about it. In any case, both Jews and aristocrats were officially enemies of the state. Unofficially and officially I was a through-and-through pariah.

But at the very moment that I began pondering the immensity of my family's history for Comrade Hebler, a teary voice came over the school loudspeaker and announced the death of Comrade Stalin.

All assignments were canceled.

The world as we knew it was canceled.

Your Honor, what I am going to tell you now is the sole aberration of my otherwise eminently conventional sexuality. I am aware of the psychoanalytic bias in all modern discourse, including the law. For this reason I will tell all, so that obvious questions will have been answered. There is entirely too much complex matter to discuss to get bogged down in the obviousness that has been cast by Doctor Freud on a perfectly enigmatic world.

The judge gave her permission with some alacrity.

In my adolescence I spent long days at the Thurzo Museum, the former home of Count George Thurzo, judge of the commission that investigated the alleged murders of his niece Elizabeth Bathory—and incidentally, the great-great-grandfather of my father's chess companion.

This massive stone palace stood on one side of our square, flanked by other great buildings that had once housed Hungarian nobility but had become either museums or offices of the Communist Party. The Thurzo house contained medieval and Renaissance paintings, jewels and household objects, but mostly mechanical torture devices, which had been this count's overriding passion.

Thurzo invented the rack wheel, a unique torture instrument created as special punishment for a peasant rebel. In addition, he commissioned intricate mechanisms from the German clock makers, all of which he had first dreamt of and designed for maximum infliction of pain. Elizabeth Bathory also ordered such mechanisms later in her life, but it must be said that it was none other than her severe uncle—and later, her judge —who had instructed her in the effectiveness of these instruments and introduced her to their makers.

Speaking of the rebels, who were ostensibly the object of his preoccupation, the palatine remarked in a letter to his wife: "Death is not enough for such men. We must add mechanics."

This phrase haunted me for years. The sound of the phrase "Death is not enough" gave me a strange sensation in the pit of my stomach. I didn't quite understand it. Raised in Communist schools, with little religion at home, this phrase made me feel oddly separate from my body. How could death not be enough?

I gazed at the skeletons depicted on the case of a rusted torture wheel at the Thurzo until my eyes blurred. I became convinced then that I had a soul, separate from my body. I arrived at this conclusion all on my own, without help from anyone. This was perhaps the major revelation of my adolescence, made quite momentous by the fact that discussion of such things was forbidden. I was terribly disappointed later when I found out that the soul was a well-known phenomenon described in a large and boring body of literature.

The documented existence of this entity gave me no comfort.

If I had a soul, it was a dense and dark object that yielded nothing to my probing. Obliged by some kind of noblesse, perhaps my family's, I undertook an investigation of the theological, philosophical, and literary descriptions of the soul in the literature available sub rosa at the time. It was amazing, actually, how much of this literature was still available, even though none of it had been printed since the end of the war.

I concluded, as I knew I would, that the soul described by all those learned texts was not the soul I had discovered all by myself while daydreaming at the Thurzo. Its texture, feel, and capacity were utterly different. Mine had the weight of lead, the color of ash, the stubbornness of rock. Whatever it held was locked within by a curse. I knew that I would eventually have to crack it open and withstand its contents. I feared this event just as I feared the future. Or maybe I feared the future because I knew that it would contain such an event.

The palatine's original rack wheel was suspended from the ceiling over a narrow bed that had cuffs for the legs and the arms. The cuffs were attached to a pulley turned by a crank. The crank was used to stretch the rebel's strapped body. The wheel with its bent iron spikes was then lowered to crush his every bone. It was a rusted primitive instrument that showed its age, but it had a strange power over me, perhaps because it had been the actual instrument used to destroy the rebel. I pressed my cheek to the iron and smelled something intoxicating and troubled that sent the blood rushing to my head.

The peasant army had risen against the feudal barons of Hungary and succeeded in burning down four castles, including the Bathorys' Ecsed, and killing some nobles, among them the young nieces of the palatine, who had been hiding in the forest with their nurses. The peasants found two of the girls, raped them, and hung them naked upside down from trees in the Ulra forest.

By the time Thurzo's dragoons reached them, vultures and wolves had eaten most of the flesh from their bones. The only one to escape was Elizabeth Bathory, who was but nine years old at the time.

Many years later, after he had served as chief judge of the commission that investigated Elizabeth Bathory, Palatine Thurzo wrote about the terrible fate that had befallen his nieces—that "wolves were kinder to them than Elizabeth Bathory would have been." He wrote this in his old age, showing no compassion for his remaining niece, the only one of the three sisters to survive. The way he remembered it, Elizabeth's older sisters, Shandra and Anichka, who were only twelve and thirteen years old when they met their horrible deaths, had been sweet and eager to please. Elizabeth, on the other hand, had always exhibited, since her earliest age, a propensity for extravagance and disrespect, flaws that were made so much more vexing by her superior intelligence. This child, who could recite thousands of verses from the Latin and Italian, could, if the fancy struck her, embarrass her elders and blaspheme the holy teachings of Meister Luther. Why Elizabeth should have survived was a source of constant sorrow for the palatine in his old age. He wished that Elizabeth had been the rebels' prey instead, but he rarely admitted this to anyone until, in his old age, he wrote, "Wolves were kinder to them . . ."

This was the most shocking phrase the king's palatine ever wrote. He admitted it himself. "What I have just said is not pleasant, but it is the terrible admission of the fact that the world as we know it has come to an end. If it were not for the specifications of Martinus Luther, we could distinguish no longer between noble blood and the clever rich, between the crimes of peasants and the madness of nobles. I have spent my life upholding these distinctions."

In writing this, the palatine sensed a larger truth but did not see, perhaps, the obvious: that Elizabeth had been the victim of the rebels even if she had not perished at a tender young age. She had seen the murders of her sisters. This may have freed her to be reckless and fearless, or it may have bound her to the terror that ruled the latter part of her life. But then the palatine would not have believed such nonsense: the age of psychology had not arrived. And besides, he had never liked his niece, Your Honor, not even at the peak of her dazzling beauty, at age fifteen, when she married Franz Nadazdy.

Sharing the room with the rack wheel at the Thurzo was an iron maiden, a metal statue of a woman. This was a great example of this sort of object, a unique construction from one of Germany's greatest clock makers. She had breasts, arms, legs, and two faces, one in front and one in back. The front face was round, with oval eyes that peered down with a look that could be alternately filled with pity and enigmatically amused. The small mouth was finely etched with hair-thin wrinkles. The eyes in the back face were closed, but the mouth was slightly open, as if she was about to whisper something. Long fine blond hair covered her head and came down in two braids over her ears, past her waist. She was dressed in a ballooning dress of worn velvet folded thousands of times, spilling over her feet. Her bare breasts were round and shiny from the generations of furtive schoolchildren who had rubbed them on visits to the museum. Two strands of pearls and a gold necklace with a black stone on the end were draped about her curved swan's neck. She opened from the front, Your Honor, along a seam between her breasts that was invisible when she was closed. The trigger that caused her to open was hidden in the black stone at the end of the gold chain. When the stone was pressed, her hands moved to embrace the person who had set off the hidden mechanism. When she opened, she revealed a hollow interior with sharp iron spikes. Her arms pulled in her victim, and then she closed up, piercing her prey.

The statue's forbidding interior fascinated me. I experienced a kind of vertigo every time I saw her.

By climbing on the window ledge, crouching, and stretching out, I could press the black stone. There was a noise like the turning of a door on rusty hinges. Then her chest opened, revealing the rusty spikes inside. Her arms shot out, looking for her prey. Finding nothing in front of her, they just froze stiffly, like two polished metal branches.

She stood gaping obscenely like that until I pressed the stone at the end of the chain again. Wearily, she creaked back to close, her arms returning to her sides. I found it hard to believe that this clunky female giant had once been quick enough to snatch someone.

At sixteen, when I was having trouble choosing between my two girlfriends, Mari and Eva, I used to come to the Thurzo Museum to think.

I liked to sit on the floor in front of the statue and indulge in a timeless reverie that blotted out everything. The iron maiden soothed my anxieties and replaced them with arousal edged slightly with fear. The two-faced torture machine vibrated oddly with my adolescent sexuality.

In that dim room with dust motes dancing on the shafts of light that came through the high ogival window, I became someone else. I felt like a supplicant of some sort, intoxicated by a sweet sense of abjection and insignificance. I was not being called upon to decide things any longer. My only job was to wallow, obey, and suffer.

One time, carried away by a wave of sensuality and self-denial, I opened her and squeezed inside. The spikes were fractions of an inch from my skin. A sudden gust of wind from the open window could have closed her up. I would have been pierced then, like Saint Sebastian. I tried to imagine the pain and the blood flowing out of the many small holes in my body. Seeing myself pierced like my favorite painting caused me to swoon with pleasure.

I leaned lightly into the long rusty spikes. Their ends were too dull to penetrate my skin, but they scratched me lightly. I felt them to my core.

There were never any custodians in this room. The old museum guard liked to sleep on a little cot on the first floor, behind the large statue of King Matthias II. If the old man had surprised me, as I often thought he might, I would have said grandly, "Death is not enough. We must add mechanics," the phrase that I quoted inwardly over and over.

But mostly I had the place to myself. I liked being alone in the presence of artifacts imbued with the dense psychic substance of people in ages past who had been killed by them. It was a crowded and erotically charged solitude.

Mari kissed me passionately, but she rejected all my other, more daring advances.

I brought her to this room and tried to explain my fascination with the metal woman. I showed her how she opened; then I squeezed inside as I had done before on my own. I asked her to guide her hand through the spikes and to touch me.

Mari refused. I said some harsh words. She ran out of the room crying.

For weeks afterwards, I was filled with shame and anger for having revealed my secret.

My other girlfriend, Eva, kissed me too, but she didn't reject any advances. In fact, she made sure that we advanced quickly and as far as possible.

When I brought her to the maiden, she grasped the game immediately. She put her greedy adolescent hand quickly through the spikes and took hold of me. She did not let go until she had gathered my sticky soul in it.

When she withdrew her hand, she nicked it on one of the rusty spikes. Her blood and my semen mixed.

With a heartfelt "ouch" she put her hurt wet hand to her lips and sucked the tiny wound.

That clinched it for me as to which girl was my true object of desire, but for obscure reasons I married Mari anyway.

That was long ago. Shortly before escaping from Hungary in 1956, during my last visit to the Thurzo, I looked up the history of this iron maiden, Your Honor.

I discovered it had in fact belonged to my ancestress Countess Bathory. Girls no older than Eva and Mari, and often younger, had perished inside her. My first lover had mingled her blood with that of Elizabeth Bathory's victims across the centuries.

And that blood had been mixed with my sperm.

I want to add only that, since that time, whenever I heard the name Elizabeth Bathory, I experienced a feeling of vertigo. For a long time I deliberately avoided reading anything about her life for fear of falling too deeply, not into history, but into myself. I felt, every time, as if I was coming close to an abyss, a feeling I have now had throughout most of my life.

This concludes the story of my youth, Your Honor.

I hope that you can see that I have been swayed since my birth by forces that are poorly countered with reason.

TWO YEARS AFTER THE MURDER of her sisters, in 1571, when Elizabeth Bathory was eleven years old, her cousin Stephen became ruling prince of Transylvania. Elizabeth traveled from her home at Kereshtur Castle to the mountains of Transylvania in the company of her mother, Anna, and her aunt Klara. Their female staff came along, carrying trunks full of clothes, mirrors, beauty powders, and jewels. Dragoons guarded the carriages, which were crammed full of gifts, a temptation for the bandits who infested the wooded slopes of the Carpathian Mountains.

Squeezed between the portly figure of her nurse, Darvulia, and the sweet-smelling frills of her aunt Klara's dress, Elizabeth quivered in anticipation of the festivities. King Matthias II of Hungary, the Hapsburg emperor Maximilian, his son Rudolf, and the flower of the Hungarian nobility were going to be in attendance. She wiggled so much that Darvulia told her gruffly to be still. But Klara hugged her, and she was dizzy with happiness.

From the window of her room later that day she saw King Matthias arrive with a retinue of two hundred courtiers in a carriage train that took two hours to ride into the castle. The king wore knightly armor with the cross of Saint Stephen flashing brightly from his chest. His visor was lowered so that she did not see his face.

Before sunset, the trumpets heralded the approach of Emperor Maximilian, who rode in on a white mare at the head of 120 horsemen, followed by a whole choir of young boys dressed in white satin robes and mounted on black ponies, who were followed in turn by a motley assortment of sorcerers, alchemists, armorers, an illuminator, and carriers of an organ that was his gift to Stephen Bathory.

Even Selim the Drunk, the successor to Süleyman the Magnificent, who had conquered and burned half of Europe, including Hungary and Transylvania, had sent his vizier, Pasha Iskender Bey. The pasha, a fat man with a red beard, wore an enormous turban with a sparkling sapphire on it. He had brought fifty of his most magnificent concubines and a retinue of eunuchs to watch over them. For the new prince he brought a renowned Turkish carpet. It had been woven over a period of fifty years by three hundred children, who had gone blind creating its intricate pattern. This carpet had hung in Süleyman's own harem for many years, but at his death it had been rolled up. Selim hated it for reasons he could not explain, so he seized the opportunity of Stephen Bathory's coronation to dispose of it. It was not an entirely benign gift.

So many noble pennants fluttered from the walls that the castle looked to Elizabeth like a ship with many-colored sails flying into the dark blue Transylvanian sky. Enemies and allies, many of whom would soon exchange places, sat side by side at the lavishly illuminated banquet tables, drinking hot wine, eating venison, trout, salmon, goose, and wild pig, and watching musicians, actors, mimes, jesters, fire eaters, dwarfs, and dancers perform.

There was a tournament and a hunt every day, except on the Sunday of the coronation. Every hall of Stephen Bathory's castle was full of guests who seemed to be perpetually departing for the woods and returning bloodstained and drunk, followed by servants with big birds or animals over their shoulders. Elizabeth relished the clanking of armor, the brightness of swords and gilded lances, the rustle of satins and silks, the whispers of velvet. Daytime and nighttime she watched the nobles of various courts at their gayest. Elizabeth rode her own horse, the silver-maned Luna, to the hunt, and had falconry lessons. She was praised by the hunt master for being a good falconer.

But she had much time to herself between the organized activities. Her mother, Anna, and her many attendants were busy tending to a myriad of things. Elizabeth was pretty much left alone to explore. She darted in and out of rooms and halls, a lithe flash of quicksilver, observing everything, filled with expectation and delight.

Two great streams had been diverted to make separate bathing areas for men and for women. One had been an underground river that was made to flow around a hot mineral spring to flood a limestone quarry big enough for a thousand bathers. Steps were cut into the flesh of the mountain to allow the guests to descend into the small lake, which was illuminated at night by torches affixed to stone boulders. Additional lighting came from torches carried by servants. Musicians and acrobats performed on the sides of the pool while steam swirled about them. The cold mountain air mixed with the hot springs and made clouds of steam. The bathing women looked like fantastical figures from a mystery play. Their shadows on the mountainside were immense and otherworldly.

The baths were used mostly at night, serving both to relax the guests after the exhausting ceremonies of daytime and to clean the bodies constrained in the difficult garments of the time. Elizabeth was frightened by the immensity of the black water and by the fantastic shapes of unknown bodies moving in it. She was helped down the stairs by her faithful maid Teresa.

Elizabeth wore only a cotton nightgown over her boyish body, on which breasts had yet to make an appearance. As soon as she entered the water, she experienced a marvelous feeling. She liked the way her gown wrapped itself tightly around her. She floated on her back, looking at the stars. She was a fortunate girl. She had been born into a rich and powerful family. Her sisters' souls were in the keeping of God, and the bad dream was beginning to fade. After she had returned from the forest, Preacher Hebler had tried to frighten her with visions of hell, where demons eat the flesh of sinners and fires burn bones to fine ashes, but she had not paid much attention. She had witnessed the eating of Dozsa's flesh, and bone turning to ash, right on earth. She had no need to imagine such things, since they took place before her eyes. She was more impressed by the descriptions of the monk Silvestri, who had read Dante and was therefore inclined to endow the afterlife with variety, nuance, color. Sins were finely and vividly distinct from one another, as were their punishments. Fire and ice were used as subtly as nakedness and clothing. Best of all, in the Italian heavens, where the innocents congregated, a profusion of angels created light, harmony, and poetry for the delight of the thirsty senses. Silvestri once described to her a masked ball in Venice, where it had been impossible to distinguish clearly between hell and heaven because the masked revelers belonged simultaneously to both. That's where her sisters were, dancing the night away. It seemed to Elizabeth that Silvestri believed primarily in variety and beauty and that it was a matter of indifference to him whether these were produced in hell or in heaven. What mattered to him was their sophistication. Pain and pleasure, he once told her, are equals. Both are the result of celestial movements that ruled everything, including her body. After the punishment of Dozsa, Silvestri had consoled her by telling her how lucky she had been. She had survived the massacre. She had not yet experienced a frightful siege of the kind that had visited her elders. The Black Death, which had raged so many times in her century, had not yet provided one of its cyclical spectacles of disease and agony. An uneasy peace reigned between her family and the Turks, and with the Hapsburgs as well. Above Elizabeth's head, the stars of Transylvania sparkled in all their glory. The mountains of Transylvania protected her.

While Elizabeth floated, suffused by well-being, she bumped against a soft island of flesh and was startled. Two girls, their hair undone, their eyes closed, were swaying in each other's arms. Elizabeth felt the force of the heat between them. She felt it strongly, the way a hot flagstone in July would sometimes sear her naked foot at noon. But the two floating girls did not pay heed to the gentle bump of Elizabeth's body against them. They held on, glued together by a force whose origin and mechanics aroused Elizabeth's curiosity. She floated alongside, watching them. Their lips were sealed together in a kiss; their limbs were intertwined like the floral motifs sculpted in stone above the Kereshtur gates. When they came apart for a moment, with their eyes still closed, Elizabeth saw that they had womanly breasts with large, dark nipples. The breasts of one were much larger than the other's, but they soon came together again, and their breasts merged with a soft motion.

Elizabeth dove under the water and encircled both of them with her skinny arms. She felt the curves of their buttocks on her forearms. She wanted to make a circle, but she could not reach all the way around.

Surprised, the girls pulled violently apart. Elizabeth

found herself floundering, and she nearly drowned. She began to scream. Soon she was escorted safely to shore, where someone delivered her into Teresa's arms. The two girls had disappeared. Teresa carried her, still screaming, back to their wing of the castle. She searched for Lady Klara, Elizabeth's aunt, who doted on her niece, but she was nowhere to be found, so Teresa carried the sobbing girl to her mother's chamber.

Anna Bathory was an uncommonly beautiful woman and one of the richest nobles in Hungary. She'd had two husbands, Antal Drugeth and Gaspar Dragffy, before marrying Elizabeth's father, George Bathory. Since the deaths of her oldest daughters, she had become remote in her beauty, preoccupied with the management of her estates and detached from Elizabeth. She had Elizabeth brought to her on special occasions, mainly on birthdays. At those times, the girl sat quietly in her presence, watching the velvet folds of her mother's dress rise immeasurably high into the inaccessible peaks of her handsome face. When Anna looked at her it was from a great distance, like a falcon floating over a tiny house in a valley. Elizabeth adored her mother.

As soon as Teresa opened the great door of Anna Bathory's darkened chamber, Elizabeth began screaming louder. There was a great rustling of silks, the jingle of spurs, and sounds of breaking glass. Believing that her mother had been murdered in her bed by demons, Elizabeth set off an awesome wail. As servants came running in from the halls, someone lit a torch.

Elizabeth's mother, the baroness Anna, emerged from the darkness of her canopy bed with her long red hair undone, her gown half lowered and exposing her breasts, her wide round eyes showing emotion for the first time in Elizabeth's memory. Only, that emotion was anger.

Moving closely behind her a naked man emerged also, holding one of his boots in his hand, a gesture so pathetic it was actually funny. Elizabeth knew the man. He was Captain Moholy, of her father's guards. Elizabeth stopped screaming and started laughing instead.

Baroness Anna had taken Captain Moholy for a lover shortly after her husband, George Bathory, was taken ill by a fever that confined him to his bed. It was said that George Bathory had himself chosen her lover so that she would continue to be in good spirits and to exhibit judiciousness in the management of their estates. Elizabeth knew the whole story, but she had never seen them together like this. Now, unable to stop herself from laughing, she tried to curtsy but tripped and fell instead. Her mother saw the clumsy curtsy as a further insult. Quivering with anger, standing very still before the assembled servants, Anna Bathory shouted at her daughter. It was the first time that Elizabeth had heard her mother's cultured voice speak this way to her. It sounded to Elizabeth as if she said, "Your time has come, little monster!" Later, however, Teresa swore that Anna Bathory said, "Now is my time for rest."

Elizabeth experienced auditory hallucinations all day. She heard things people swore they didn't say. Innocent remarks by her servants, heard in passing, seemed filled with menace. After throwing her full chamber pot at a maid who may have said to her, "You trickle of bloody piss!" Elizabeth decided to go to sleep early. She hoped that by morning her mishearing—if that's what it was!—would subside.

By morning, things did return to normal. People's remarks resumed their respectful banality, like a river returning to its banks after the floodwaters subsided. Elizabeth decided that she had misheard her mother's remark. As the day wore on, Elizabeth became more and more convinced that her mother had not said what she thought her mother had said. But a nagging doubt of a philosophical nature remained. She had always been maddened by the desire to know the meanings of words she did not understand, but now she felt the strong need to question the sounds of words that were familiar. What if everything one heard was not what people said? What if everyone heard things that were not said, and everyone said things that were misheard? Suppose, Elizabeth told herself, using the principles of logic that her tutor Silvestri had taught her, that everyone lived under the wrong impression conveyed by words misheard. Hence, all that people did in the name of words would be wrong, because they were the wrong words. It was a good thing she had studied logic. She called Teresa. "Count your teeth, you silly cow!" she commanded her. Teresa looked with some astonishment at her mistress. Elizabeth's smooth face betrayed no feeling. "I will bring it to you right away," the maid answered, returning a few moments later with a pitcher of milk. It's just as I thought, Elizabeth exulted to herself. But was that truly what she thought? Elizabeth felt that this line of inquiry might lead to madness, so she postponed it.

Too much excitement swirled about anyway for her to dwell long on the night's eerie events or their implications. Next day, while watching a puppet play outdoors, she met a fifteen-year-old boy. The puppets were ten feet tall, representing animals and clergymen. The crow flapped his motley rags about, shaming a drunken monk for something he had done to a nun, who cried in a corner. The boy was laughing uproariously. Elizabeth, who didn't find the scene all that funny, asked him where the humor was. The boy blushed, curtsied, and said, "I have seen monks like that one. We have monasteries full of such monks!"

The boy's name was Johannes. He was a member of Prince Rudolf's choir. Prince Rudolf, the son of Emperor Maximilian, was already being referred to as Rudolf the Mad because he spent all his time with alchemists and astrologers instead of learning the business of the empire. Refusing to live in Vienna with his family, he had established himself in Prague, a city full of Jews and heretics, known also for the active workings of the devil. Prague was densely inhabited by demons, many of whom had been enslaved by rabbis to make gold. Rudolf had surrounded himself at Hradschin Castle in Prague with alchemists, sorcerers, astrologers, witches, palmists, and every other variety of Satan worshiper, whose combined activities emanated vile smells that caused many travelers to faint. Excrescences from putrid substances gurgled in huge vats in the castle's chambers, spilling over the rims and trickling down halls and stairs, spewing fumes and noxious clouds, frightening the foreign ambassadors and nauseating God-fearing Christians. Even his father, who loved him to distraction, had felt obliged to mutter some ineffectual reprimands. But Rudolf's addictions to magic and alchemy were not even his worst defects. In addition, he was debauched and was said to bugger the boys in his choir.

Johannes spoke German, Latin, and Greek, but no Hungarian. Elizabeth, who knew all those languages except Greek, was proud to show off her skill. Her tutor, the monk Silvestri, had taught her languages at a very early age, using a method of his own that flew in the face of convention, which held that a child is incapable of great knowledge until she is much older. Silvestri believed, on the contrary, that the best time to inculcate languages, as well as philosophical precepts, in a child was at the age immediately following the advent of speech itself.

Johannes explained that his own gift in acquiring languages had come entirely naturally, without any help from a teacher. At Hradschin Castle he had listened to the conversations of so many scholars from everywhere in the Christian world that he had found himself conversing in many tongues without any difficulty. The children conversed for a time in Latin, telling each other about their interests and their schooling. The boy said that he had been studying geometry and astrology. Elizabeth told him about her great interest in words, which went beyond even the urgings of the monk Silvestri.

"Is it true that Rudolf buggers the choir?" Elizabeth asked him, repeating what she'd overheard her maids say about the Crown Prince. By this time, the Eagle Judge puppet had appeared, demanding that the monk demonstrate exactly what he'd been doing to the nun.

The laughter and commotion around them were too great for Elizabeth to hear what Johannes said. She repeated her question on a much quieter occasion next day. They were seated on a stone bench in the great chapel during the most solemn moment of the whole affair, the coronation. Bishops in resplendent purple robes followed by retinues of monks were advancing toward the bejeweled throne on which a slightly drunk Stephen Bathory sat looking dazed. The archbishop carried a gold crown on a black velvet pillow.

The boy blushed. "Yes," he said softly.

Elizabeth, who had no idea what *buggering* meant, though she remembered that it had been one of the charges against Dozsa, nodded her head thoughtfully. At that moment the great pipes of the cathedral's organ let out their music. Voices singing hymns of praise filled the vaults. Stephen Bathory had become prince of Transylvania. Two years later, after his marriage to Anna Jagellon, he also became king of Poland. The drunk teenager seated on the princely throne was heir to large portions of Hungary, Austria, Slovenia, and Transylvania. Together with his family, he owned more land than the king of Hungary. He was heir also to the Bathory traditions of tolerance, which had allowed trade to flourish, had approved the formation of professional guilds, and had given a home to the Szekely people, a tribe of Asiatic warriors so reputed for their fierceness that, it was said, "no one lived after seeing the naked blades of their swords."

After the ceremony, Elizabeth walked with Johannes along one of the stone halls leading to an ancient donjon in the oldest part of the castle. She asked him if he would allow her to watch him being buggered. She understood very well, she told him, that she wouldn't be able to watch him being buggered by Rudolf himself, given his well-known objection to the presence of women in his vicinity, but she hoped that he could arrange some buggering for the satisfaction of her curiosity.

Johannes, who was young but not unaware of the countess's rank as well as her charm, agreed. He was himself a baronet, a petty noble, the son of an impoverished courtier, but he nursed great ambitions. Countess Bathory was from the greatest family in the land, an exalted being who had greatly honored him by her attention. In his heart, Johannes pledged himself to her service and vowed to please her in any way he could. He was amused as well by the countess's innocence, since she clearly had no idea what she was talking about. He was bothered, only slightly, by the possibility of pain, because while he had engaged many times in sexual play with boys of his own age, he had not yet experienced penetration. They discussed the possibility of asking one

of the archbishop's monks to perform the deed, but neither one of them knew how to approach a monk and,
besides, they were both scared of monks.

Just then a Gypsy puppeteer with thick black hair
and a fierce mustache walked up to them with his palm
outstretched. He fell to his knees, turned his handsome
face up to Elizabeth, and begged her for a coin. He
praised in flowery Hungarian the beauty of the countess
and commended, in addition, her discriminating taste in
choosing the "fearless knight" by her side to walk with
her. Johannes, who looked anything but a fearless
knight in his velvet tights, without even a sword,
blushed.

The Gypsy was a slave attached to one of the lesser
Hungarian nobles, who owned the puppet troupe. Elizabeth bid him rise and walk with them. With her quick
intuitive knowledge of castle interiors, she guided them
to a little-traveled passage. The three of them climbed
onto a wide stone ledge below a window. When Elizabeth explained to the Gypsy that she wanted him to
bugger Johannes, he looked confused for a moment.
Elizabeth was afraid that what she was asking was perhaps too daring. To reinforce her wish, she looked at
him severely and commanded him in Hungarian: "I am
Countess Bathory. I have the power of life and death
over you. You must do what I tell you!"

The Gypsy looked up to her quickly and gave a short
laugh. It had never occurred to him, he explained, to
doubt the legitimacy of his mistress's command. He had
only been pausing in order to ponder how much he
should be paid. He confessed also that he was most
reluctant to bugger a baronet, since the position demanded rather that the baronet bugger him. Should the
word get out that he had done such a thing to a baronet,
his head wouldn't last long on his shoulders. But knowing that it would be dreadfully foolish of him to refuse,

he stood completely at her service. Elizabeth had no doubt about that. Even at her tender age, she had already delivered disobedient servants to Kereshtur authorities and had watched them without regret as they were whipped for having offended her. She had also caused three young peasant boys to be deprived of their manhood by castration because they had attempted to rape her when she was only eight years old. But although she had begged and insisted, she had not been allowed to watch this punishment.

Today she felt generous. Her command to the Gypsy slave would have been sufficient, but she was moved to impress Johannes, her erudite new friend. Elizabeth took from around her neck a gold chain from which hung a small garnet and threw it at the puppeteer, who then nearly fell off the ledge trying to kiss the hem of her dress in gratitude.

Johannes, who had watched the proceedings with a mixture of excitement and dread, thought that the time had come to make his presence felt, since he was part of the deal. "Not here," he said in German. He too wondered about the propriety of being violated by a slave but consoled himself with the thought that the act might serve as practice for the future, when Rudolf himself might be moved to take him.

It was agreed then that, come nightfall, the three of them would meet by the fountain in the smallest courtyard, which was near Iskender Bey's harem, and the place least likely to be trafficked by anyone who might recognize them. Emperor Rudolf's retinue had been lodged in another wing of the castle, as far from the pasha's concubines as possible.

Elizabeth feigned sleep. As soon as she looked to be well ensconced in dreams, Teresa tiptoed out of the room. She had her own plans. The girl rose as soon as Teresa had closed the door behind her. She put on a dark dress over purple leggings, an outfit that made her look like a boy, and slipped out. She skirted groups of revelers by hugging the walls. Here and there she heard voices speaking Hungarian, and she gave them a wide berth. The great halls were still full of diners watching spectacles by torchlight. She went quietly past their doors. Servants and soldiers were sleeping everywhere, and she had to step over bodies that did not notice her pass.

It was entirely dark when she reached the bottom step leading to the inner courtyard with its small fountain. She felt the damp walls with her hands. There was no light or noise coming from the pasha's quarters. The sky was cloudy, but a sickle-thin Turkish moon that looked as if it had been brought by Iskender Bey from Constantinople hung over the courtyard.

"Countess?" Johannes's soft German voice came from somewhere near her. Elizabeth whispered her acknowledgment. She felt for his hand in the dark.

The Gypsy was nowhere to be seen. Elizabeth was disappointed at first, then enraged at the thought that he had taken her gold necklace and not lived up to his part of the bargain. But she did not have long to be disappointed. Slipping swiftly behind her like a knife blade into a deerskin sheath, the puppeteer said, "Your devoted slave is here, Countess."

Without speaking a word, Johannes, still holding her hand, bent over the outer rim of the fountain. He wore a short tunic that barely covered his behind, and velvet leggings just like Elizabeth's. The Gypsy pulled these down, revealing the boy's white buttocks. He then undid his cloak and guided something that looked to Elizabeth like a small roast toward Johannes's buttocks. She was still holding Johannes's hand when he tightened it over hers so hard she thought it would break. She reached for the Gypsy's round flesh with her other hand. It was

warm, covered with fine velvety skin, finer than the texture of her tights. She parted the slit at the top of it, and
a drop of thick, slippery substance met her finger. She
rubbed it between thumb and forefinger. She then felt
under Johannes's tunic and drew the tip of her wet finger around the tiny puckered flower at the center of his
buttocks. She guided the Gypsy's manhood to the place
and held on to it until it slipped between her fingers and
buried itself in the boy. The sensation of touching the
two boys made Elizabeth very warm, as if a small flame,
beginning at the center of her spine, had shot suddenly
upward, filling her brain. Her mouth was dry, and her
boyish tights clung to her legs with her own wetness. At
the center of this delicious sensation there was also a
thought: if this is what I can make happen because I am
Countess Bathory, think of all that I may experience in
the future. I am only eleven years old now, and I know
very little about pleasure.

The night before, she had experienced something
nearly this pleasurable when she had circled with her
arms the two naked girls at the bath, but her near
drowning and her mother's anger had drained all the
pleasure from it. She will soon be dead, she thought of
her mother, and I can do as I please. But this thought
filled her with remorse. The sensation of delicious head-
iness evaporated, and she watched with no interest as
both Johannes and the Gypsy shuddered and came to a
sudden stop.

So that's what *buggering* means, she thought to herself later as she lay back on her pillows. Teresa had still
not come back, and it was well past midnight. Elizabeth
stayed awake until almost dawn. She thought of everyone she knew, including all her maids, and imagined
them being buggered one by one by the Gypsy. She
paraded through her imagination all the people she
knew and bent them like dolls, subject to her whims.

But she did not think of her sisters. Nights were long in the sixteenth century. She remembered what her dear friend Andrei de Kereshtur, who was afflicted with insomnia, had once copied for her from an old chronicle: "The endless nights without light make us turn dreamlessly until time comes to mount our horses to make war at daybreak." He did not say what women did during their sleepless nights. Elizabeth's last thought before she fell asleep was to write Andrei to tell him. "Women," she thought she would write, "make dolls out of those they know."

Elizabeth did not speak to Johannes again, though she saw him walk past next day in his choir robe, following Prince Rudolf. He blushed when he saw her, and lowered his eyes. But she did see the Gypsy again, sooner than she expected.

Elizabeth was taking her afternoon nap, still exhausted from the night's activities, when Lady Klara burst into the room. "They've caught the thief who stole your necklace!" she exclaimed.

Elizabeth protested in vain, saying that the necklace had been lost, not stolen. Aunt Klara insisted that she follow her immediately and then took her to a chamber filled with shouting men. The young Gypsy, shackled in irons, was lying on the floor among them. The men made room for Elizabeth to walk through to look at him. The judge, a captain of Stephen Bathory's guard, had Elizabeth's necklace dangling from his finger. "Is this yours?" he asked.

"Yes," said Elizabeth.

"Do you know this filthy Gypsy?" he asked.

Elizabeth remembered his black eyes looking up at her on the window ledge, and she felt for a moment the heat of his flesh as it was when she was holding it. "No," she said.

That sealed the young man's fate. The case of the

Gypsy thief aroused great interest in the castle. The presence of so many foreign dignitaries and the opportunity to display Transylvanian justice made it necessary that Bathory's judges mete out an exemplary punishment. Stephen Bathory relished the opportunity to show off one of his newest possessions, a mechanical device made by the Saxon craftsmen of Hermannstadt. Called an iron maiden, it was a tall metal woman, with two faces, who opened from the middle to reveal an interior full of sharp spikes. She had blue eyes and blond hair like a real woman, and but for her size, she would have been a handsome female. Elizabeth thought that she looked fascinating and quite alive.

Before the eyes of all the assorted guests, the Gypsy was brought forward and thrust inside the maiden. His black eyes wild with fright, he scanned the hall looking for Elizabeth. He found her only moments before he was pushed all the way inside. When the iron woman slowly closed up, Elizabeth heard the spikes piercing the Gypsy's flesh. His cries filled the room, but when the statue was entirely closed there was only the sound of the long needles piercing the bones. He had died before he could hear that sound. His eyes, black and filled with fear, but also with blind anger and supplication, stayed in Elizabeth's mind. She felt no pity but, curiously, was aroused to the same sensation she had experienced in the dark courtyard. Holding the dying Gypsy's eyes before her mind's eye, Elizabeth felt the same wetness between her thighs and shuddered with pleasure. Also, she was glad to have her necklace back.

Before the Bathorys' scheduled departure, Lady Klara appeared in Elizabeth's chamber in an unusually ceremonious manner. She even curtsied. Behind her came Darvulia and Teresa, then her mother's entire retinue of young and old women. Teresa carried draped over her outstretched arms Elizabeth's formal dress, which she had worn at the coronation. The dress had been newly pressed. At Klara's urging, Elizabeth allowed herself to be stuck back into the formal folds of the jewel-encrusted costume. Shortly after, her mother, Anna, made her entrance. Elizabeth curtsied, and her mother asked if she could sit down. Bewildered, Elizabeth nodded her assent. When Anna was seated, she asked her daughter to sit by her.

"My daughter, I am pleased to announce that you are engaged to be married to the noble knight Franz Nadazdy. It has all been arranged by the councils of our families under the tutelage of Lord Palatine Thurzo. You are going to travel at the beginning of next week to the Nadazdy family castle at Sarvar, where you will live under the supervision of Franz Nadazdy's mother, Ursula Kaniszay-Nadazdy. Go with God, my daughter!"

Then Anna rose, and Elizabeth was left sitting like a prisoner within the folds of her formal dress, bewildered by the events happening to her. Only the day before, she had witnessed the execution of a boy who had obeyed her whim. The night before that, she had been privy to a mystery whose warmth still spread in her like a flower growing in her blood. And now, without any prior warning, she was to be given in marriage to a strange knight. All the power she had gained on her own by making the two boys perform to her command had been canceled by her mother, who treated her like a dumb doll. She was too drained by the insult to scream. She pulled the strand of pearls from her neck and tore the chain. The pearls rolled over the flagstones, and the maids hurried to catch them. Aunt Klara put her arms around her bare, skinny shoulders, and Elizabeth collapsed sobbing against her. "I hope she dies!" she managed to say between tears. Aunt Klara patted her head understandingly. She wasn't very fond of Baroness Anna either.

I have no doubt that my editor's motive in sending me to Hungary was generosity, Your Honor. Like many Americans at the time, she was genuinely moved by events in Eastern Europe, and she wished to give me an opportunity.

My assignment was of a general nature. I was to report back on the political, social, and economic changes sweeping the region, in a series of first-person dispatches. In other words, it was up to me to find and name my subjects.

My situation was, you must admit, of some interest. I had been summoned back by the head of a newly hatched monarchist party to participate in a royalist exercise by dint of my ancestry. There was plenty of opportunity here for a unique perspective on events. Hungary had not been a monarchy in a long time, but evidently the fascination was still there. A strong royalist movement had also sprung up in neighboring Romania and Bulgaria. Even in the former Soviet Union there was talk about the return of the tsar. Perhaps it wasn't such a crazy idea. In Spain, King Juan Carlos had provided a smooth transition from Francoism to democracy.

While I repeated this argument to myself on the eve of my departure, I was still uncertain about my own role in this affair. I felt quite anxious about the coincidences preceding my trip to Hungary. My TV-induced summons was not exactly the stuff of serious journalism. Klaus Megyery, with his sinister aura, was not exactly an altruist. I wondered what his motives were.

I called a friend of mine, a well-known anthropologist, who had just returned from a field trip to a remote Hungarian village, I asked her how people in that region viewed the momentous changes taking place. "There is a revival of pre-Christian religion," she told me. "I met a young shaman who is so powerful I can't even tell you his name. If I do, he'll be here within moments. I'm not joking. My problem is that I cannot write the truth in this case and still be taken seriously as a scientist."

It was astonishing. The lightly settled soil of democracy and atheism was rapidly turning over, releasing dormant agents. The return of the monarchy was not inconceivable. Nor was magical practice, apparently.

When I packed my small suitcase, I put in a locket with a photograph of my first love, Eva. This was the only thing I still had from Hungary. Now I was taking it back—for protection.

My first sight of Budapest was at an angle, like an old photograph, because the pilot banked the plane as he flew low over the Danube, so that we might have a full view of the glorious imperial city. The royal palace and the great buildings on the hills of Buda were shiny with early morning sun. There was snow on some of the roofs. Now and then the statue of a horseman sent up a blinding glint of light from its gilded armor. But, as a reminder of time, the monument to the Soviet soldier, which rose higher than all the rest, also shone brightest.

From the ground, Budapest looked much as I remembered it. The grime of forty drab years still clung to her nineteenth-century buildings. The wide boulevards were noisy and polluted by steady streams of dented little East German cars. Bundled pedestrians walked carefully to avoid icy patches on the narrow streets. The Danube flowed lazily between Buda and Pest, under the history-weary stone bridges.

My little taxi from the airport seemed deliberately to tour some of the important places of my youth. We passed by the Thurzo Museum, which beamed its full charge of memory at me from its high ogival windows. We went through the little square where I'd left my friends for dead. We even went past the entrance to the alley through which I'd fled from the Russian tank with the smell of Molotov-cocktail gasoline all over my hands. And just before we reached the hotel, we passed the little park by the Danube where Eva and I had sat locked in a motionless kiss from early afternoon until sunset. There was snow on the benches. No lovers had sat there in a while.

I checked in at the venerable old Gellart Hotel, another landmark of my past. This establishment had survived in dignified and aristocratic disdain both Fascism and Communism. The famous steam baths in its bowels still played host to portly men who read their morning newspapers religiously until they disintegrated in the steam. It was a locus of civilization.

After I dropped my bags in the room, I sat in a small café by the Danube. This Café Carmen, two blocks from the hotel, had not been there in my day. It was one of the new private businesses that had sprung up overnight in Hungary. A sullen-faced old woman, who may have been the proprietor's mother, brought me a plate of paprikash and a bottle of Tokay. She looked at me over her order pad with the suspicious eyes of one who trusted nobody.

She reminded me of my grandmother, a dour woman I visited during the summer in a mountain village in Transylvania. She was always dressed in black and never smiled, but she favored me nonetheless by saving little delicacies for me, like pigs' tails and chicken livers. She had once had servants, but in my childhood she trailed chicken feathers behind her and was never without a wet soup ladle in her gnarled hand, which looked like a root. When she died she was bathed in traditional oils and rubbed by professional mourners with fragrant herbs. When I passed her coffin, which had been laid in an empty stone hall of the vacant family castle, I could still smell boiled chicken under all the layers of perfumes.

Nonetheless, I savored the rich flavor of the Hungarian paprikash. Café Carmen smelled like bitter wormwood, another of my grandmother's smells.

The wine was full bodied, filled to bursting with the stubborn grape that has clung immemorially to the hillsides of Hungary. The burghers of medieval towns paid their taxes to the Turks and to their lords with this Tokay when the rich gold veins of the Transylvanian mines were exhausted.

Outside the café window, the spectacle was more contemporary. A group of skinheads was loitering in front of an ancient building across the street. The young men wore leather jackets and boots like their counterparts in Western Europe. But for their shaved heads, they looked to me like leather-jacketed KGB men of the fifties. They were smoking cigarettes and passing around a bottle. It was cold outside; the windows of the café were steamy. I soon ignored them and lost myself in reminiscence. I would have doubtlessly continued along this pleasant road of nostalgia if an empty wine bottle hadn't sailed through the air and cracked the window right by me. The plate glass filled with spidery cracks but did not shatter. When I looked out, the skinheads were laughing.

The proprietor, a red-faced man with a dirty apron tied around his potbelly, ran past me out the door and began shouting and shaking his fist at the boys across the street. It wasn't such a good idea. They made obscene gestures back, and two of them started belligerently in our direction.

The *padron* withdrew hastily inside, apologizing to us, his customers. "You can own your own business in Hungary," he said, "but who'll defend you? No one! Savages!"

He withdrew behind the counter, where he began to dial an old-fashioned phone in search of the police. His mother, meanwhile, took a defensive position in a corner, with an iron skillet in her hands. I had no doubt that in a confrontation she would be exceedingly dangerous.

The two skinheads had now reached the front of the café. One of them withdrew an aerosol can from his jacket and spray-painted first an Arrow Cross, then the word JEW on the cracked window. The Arrow Cross was the Hungarian swastika. It had been the symbol of Hungary's Fascists.

I found myself standing. I opened the door and shouted into the face of the pimply lout with the spray can: "What the fuck? Is this 1939? Goddam Nazi!"

Things could have ended badly, but at that moment a police car shrieked to a halt.

A freckled policeman with a fading red star on his blue cap came out swinging a nightstick. He brought the stick short inches away from the face of the spray-can vandal. They exchanged a few words that I could not hear. But he did not arrest him. The boys withdrew back to their spot across the street and then strolled calmly away.

The policeman watched them until they turned the corner. He then pushed open the door of the café with his nightstick. He surveyed the clientele angrily and shouted to the owner: "Get that window bricked up! You have private property now . . . It provokes people."

He then strode out unapologetically, every bit as angry and hateful as his pals with the shaved heads. Most of the customers rose, left coins on the tables, and tiptoed out. The fear was as thick as the crusted marmalade that had come with my toast.

It was an extraordinary scene. My memories of Budapest had only two modalities: a peaceful, sleepy world ruled by the invisible hand of the police and an explosive city in the midst of revolution. The scene I had just witnessed was something in between, something anxious and unsettled. The world had changed in a very short time, as plainly as the dirty winter light outside. Dingy old Europe was fretting and foaming at the mouth again. The tight lid that Communism had kept on people's hatreds had blown away. Older things now stirred from their slumber, blind creatures that lived in the deep mud of ancestral memory, things with horns and tails.

I had been given a startling welcome back.

Without the skinheads, the street was eerily silent. I wiped a circle in the steam on the window. Between the black bars of the letter E in the word JEW and the star-shaped cracks in the glass, I could see the fortresslike building in front of which the skinheads had stood. It looked as if it had been shuttered and shunned for hundreds of years. A thick blanket of snow smothered the sloping roof of the pointy tower. Between the grimy pillars flanking the entrance was the raised effigy of the dragon swallowing his tail. I was home. It was a Bathory edifice.

I beg the court's indulgence for what I am going to say.

I was then and am now perfectly aware that the young hoodlums who broke and spray painted the window of Café Carmen were in fact human beings.

Some of them doubtlessly had mothers and fathers.

And yet, just as I am sure of that fact, I became convinced at that moment that the entire mass of them had been hatched inside the dungeons of that Bathory house. They had hatched in there, Your Honor, an evil germ culture that took flight and swarmed the street when I showed up.

I became convinced that afternoon in Budapest that I was the key that fit the lock that opened the door to evil. These angry children with their Arrow Crosses and ancestral hatreds were released by my arrival in Hungary.

You have cause to declare me insane now, Your Honor.

I am not pleading insanity.

I know, beyond a shadow of a doubt, that these skinheads had sprung full grown from Elizabeth Bathory's torture chambers.

Let me put it another way.

History in our part of Europe is an unending dream of horrors. The very day I returned, Serbs had begun their campaign of ethnic cleansing in Bosnia. In Transylvania there were violent confrontations between Romanians and Hungarians. There were threats of pogroms against Jews. Gypsy villages were being burned.

I know the perpetrators of these atrocities. I know these raging peasants, Your Honor: they are my history. Their faces are etched in my mind; their fury is familiar. I have seen them depicted a thousand times at the Thurzo Museum. Century after century they stand in the middle of flames, eyes burning red with anger, bloody scythes in their hands. The only difference is that now we see them on television. They wield .20-caliber machine guns and surface-to-air missiles instead of pitchforks and scythes.

Your political scientists and psychologists may scour

the learned treatises in search of some explanation, but the roots of this evil are not planted in reason. They spring from the soil of the sixteenth century, the time of my ancestress, Countess Bathory. Forgive this pedantic aside, Your Honor, but this is the time when dramas of identity, nationality, authority, gender and religion, beauty, immortality, eternity, temporality were played out with unique intensity. Elizabeth Bathory's madness was threaded with all the gore and ideas (and gore of ideas) of what the scholars call the early modern age. That time's secret springs still pump poisoned blood into the heart of Europe.

The answer to the horror of Europe lies also in my own psyche, Your Honor. Somewhere inside me is a small core of hatred that is my legacy. It spans centuries.

I must be found guilty and destroyed.

Understand me. I am begging the court to kill me. But not before it understands me. If I am not understood, I shall return like Elizabeth and haunt the future.

Next day, properly chastened by the judge and a bit ashamed of his outburst of pedantic passion, Drake Bathory-Kereshtur resumed his story in a decidedly more sober key.

I came to America precisely in order to abandon my haunted European self. Until I saw our coat of arms again, adorning that building in Budapest across from the Carmen Café, I was sure that I'd done a pretty good job. But now, back on the slippery slope of memories and the icy streets of Budapest, I felt myself losing control.

I should have come back to America immediately. Like the hero of a fairy tale, I had but one chance.

I did not.

Looking over the dirty snow that matched the ashen

faces of the chilled pedestrians in their shabby overcoats, I knew that there was something holding me here.
It wasn't paprikash. Or nostalgia for my meager childhood. I felt no urgent need to contact the few of my old
pals still in Budapest. I didn't look forward to hearing
Klaus Megyery rave about royalism. It was something
else. It was *her.*

After I married Mari I thought often about Eva.
Somewhere in me a nearly voiceless child was asking to
know the rest of a story that had been interrupted. The
sight of that snowy bench in Budapest had brought back
her nearly forgotten warmth. I remembered the round
heaviness of her breasts under her knitted wool sweater.
I remembered her small hand resting in mine like a
scared bird. And this, Your Honor, is why I did not
immediately return to New York. For the sake of this
creature nearly effaced by time, I thought that I might
chance spending some time walking alone on the streets
and through the squares where we had once played. I
could still hear the smoky sound of her voice rising into
the twilight by the Danube. I remembered lifting a
strand of hair stuck in the collar of her schoolgirl uniform and kissing the warm skin below. She smelled
damp and bittersweet, like a wet leaf. I wanted to im-
merse myself in the smells wafting from behind the walls
of the old houses. Scents of a gone world. That was the
world of my innocent love, Eva's world.

Once, when we were leaning close on the railing
over the bank, watching the sky over the Danube, the
sunset seized us and lifted us off the ground. The sun
did not simply sink behind the palaces of Buda. It fell
over the old empire, over history, and it took us on its
journey. We were dust motes in an old dance. The river
turned deep plum and red. The shadows of the imperial
buildings sank into the darkening waters suddenly, as if

they had been driven there by an angry fist. We were roughly brought back to our railing and set back down on the hard asphalt. I had a chilling premonition. Eva drew me close to her, and I hugged her back as if making a promise. That gesture stayed with me through the years.

I wanted to walk the old streets, listen to the sounds of my native language spoken naturally and carelessly in cafés, parks, street corners, buses. And then I wanted to run into her by chance. Without looking. She would be there, just like my youth, come out of the sounds and smells of Budapest, city of our love. And she would be young, like the day I left her. And my younger self would be there, too, coincidental, casual, immortal.

We would resume our conversation where we'd left it off, in mid-sentence. I would tell her that after my divorce from Mari, I drifted. My personal life had been unsuccessful, but my adopted country had been good to me. I was a reporter at the *Chronicle,* a good newspaper. I wrote stories about people, stories that did not require a great deal of thought or introspection. I thought myself a good observer of human nature. I avoided thinking about myself or even about happiness or contentment. I convinced myself that they were not necessary. It was as if the feminine principle had been withdrawn from me. I had only my typing fingers and my keen gaze. It seemed to be enough.

I would have told Eva all this in the hope that she would be able to read the subtext—that she had been my intended all along, that I had made a great mistake to choose Mari over her.

Alas, the woman of today was doubtlessly a different creature from the slender, impatient girl I once loved. Still, she would certainly be able to read the subtext. Everyone in Hungary had been reading between the lines for forty years. And Eva had been a lot sharper than everyone.

I wanted to see her.

I'd crossed the Rubicon, Your Honor.

WHEN ELIZABETH BATHORY SET out for Castle Sarvar to live with her mother-in-law, she was certain that her life was over. She looked sadly at the castle of her childhood as her carriage and horses pulled away. She'd asked her mother that she be accompanied by her nurse Darvulia, her maids Teresa and Lena, and the young notary, Andrei de Kereshtur. The poet of Castle Kereshtur, Melotus, also came along because Ursula Nadazdy, the mistress at Sarvar and Elizabeth's future mother-in-law, had heard of his talent and wanted to hear his songs.

Darvulia, Elizabeth's nurse since her earliest days— she had only escaped the massacre by Dozsa's rebels by the grace of God and because she had been gathering herbs in another part of the woods—was sent from Kereshtur because of certain rumors about her that reflected badly on Anna Bathory. It was said that Darvulia was holding midnight masses for the devil in the village cemetery. The Lutheran preacher Hebler had started preparing a case against her, hoping to have her burnt at the stake as a witch. Anna Bathory's solution was to separate Darvulia from her friends and to send her with Elizabeth to Sarvar. Darvulia was by no means an old woman, though to Elizabeth she seemed nothing short of ancient.

During the long journey by carriage over the hardened mud roads of the Hungarian plain, Darvulia attempted to improve her mistress's disposition with tales calculated to amuse or shock, or with whatever else might help lift the gloom. She was a short, dark woman with a beauty spot in the shape of a sickle moon under her left eye. She used black powder to make her eyes bigger. The tops of her enormous breasts, with the nipples often exposed, startled her interlocutors. Darvulia knew everyone, and everyone came to her for help. Girls who'd gotten themselves in trouble with soldiers came for abortions, grown women for herbs to restore their husband's interest. Darvulia was privy to all the secrets of the castle.

But Darvulia's greatest secret was Elizabeth. She had nursed her with milk from her own breasts. She had held her, told her stories, and praised her brightly. From her tenderest years, the countess had been inquisitive and intelligent. She would not rest until she understood to her satisfaction what a particular word meant. She wanted to know everything that was said out of her earshot, and to this end she questioned everyone mercilessly until she was satisfied. She had been born with an inordinate gift for mimicry and language. Darvulia remembered her mistress, swaddled in her infancy cloth bearing her family's coat of arms, looking inquisitively up at her. Immobilized though she was, her eyes followed with lucid—some said eerie—interest the slew of women knitting and gossiping around her crib. Their voices had been a sweet cradle of sound, like the murmuring of a beehive. Little by little, Elizabeth began distinguishing their voices and matching them to faces. After her first year, she had already begun to understand many words and was particularly delighted when Darvulia told her fairy tales.

At the beginning of her second year she could repeat many tales herself. When Darvulia unwrapped her tight swaddling to bathe her, Elizabeth reenacted with gestures and uncanny accuracy some of Darvulia's tales. She also mimicked conversations she had overheard. Her performances as she splashed around in the pumpkin-shaped gold tub that also bore her family's coat of arms occasionally embarrassed those she mimicked. Fortunately, her babyish way of pronouncing words kept the women from fully understanding what she was saying. This was some relief to them, because their conversations often concerned intimate matters.

Only Darvulia knew that Elizabeth's gift ran even deeper than mimicry. The tot remembered everything. While swaddled in her ornate baby prison, Elizabeth had memorized details of the women's husbands' and boyfriends' failings, rumors about the interventions of horned devils in everyday affairs, recipes for making poisons and medicines, examples of the cupidity of priests, and the strange ways of lust, which irrupted in unfathomable ways at the oddest times. Not knowing but suspecting that the child was strangely gifted, the women started taking care to speak in whispers while Darvulia told fairy tales to cover up their gossiping voices. Darvulia told long and beautiful stories that were sad and sweet like her milk. Elizabeth was alternately dreamy and happy at her breast.

Darvulia had been carefully chosen by Baron George Bathory, Elizabeth's father, when he had still been relatively lucid. He had interviewed hundreds of peasant women before settling on Darvulia. Everything customary was taken into account—the size of their breasts, the quality of their milk—but there had also been a requirement for the women to be good tellers of stories. George Bathory had been nursed by a storyteller himself, and he thought it important. "Stories are the milk of the people," he was fond of saying. For the real milk, there were certain criteria. It had to be "white, sweet to taste, and free from unnatural savor, and it is better that it should be too much than too little, and it should be of medium consistency, not too watery and not too thick . . . A drop placed on a fingernail should roll slightly but maintain its form." There was no such precision defining "the milk of the people." He had not taken such care in selecting nurses for Elizabeth's older sisters, two pretty but dull children who were predictable in every way.

The telling of stories went along fine until Elizabeth realized that they were being told in order to distract her. She became aware that during the time she was listening to (and memorizing) the fabulous doings of magical beings in fairy tales, other conversations were taking place. She strained to hear the sounds of this outer wall of speech, and often she succeeded, because she had uncommonly acute hearing. She soon became capable of following simultaneous conversations. When she innocently revealed this ability, the women began crossing themselves. It was downright uncanny, and she was deemed to possess certain unholy powers. One of the younger girls said that perhaps Pastor Hebler ought to be informed. She was laughed at by the other women, who instructed her that all unholy powers in a girl child were good; that these powers were precisely what one kept hidden from preachers; and that, furthermore, if she uttered a word about Elizabeth's remarkable gift she would be thrashed and possibly killed. The girl, who was already attending Mass three times a day, became utterly terrified. She believed that the women, especially Darvulia, were perfectly capable of carrying out their threat. But she was more afraid of losing her eternal soul, and in the end she confessed all to Pastor Hebler. "Our mistress Elizabeth is like a mirror," she told Hebler. "She renders back whatever she sees or hears."

This was the first denunciation of Elizabeth to a church authority. Many others would follow.

Hebler was not impressed, but he looked into it anyway. He made a surprise visit to the nursery and demanded that the child tell a story. Elizabeth, dressed like a miniature of her mother, Anna, in a ruffled pink gown and purple stockings, looked more like a bald doll than a precocious demon. Coaxed by Darvulia, she began a monotonous recitation of incomprehensible words from which Hebler made out that she was rendering the well-known Hungarian tale of the girl who bathed in mare's mlk. There was nothing unnatural about it, Hebler sternly lectured the women. Memory is a function that develops sooner in some children. It was obvious that the infant did not understand much of what she repeated. Hebler concluded menacingly: "And if you women have nothing better to do than gossip, let your own shame guide you to better thoughts. This innocent child is but a mirror of your shame."

Hebler swept out of the room, followed closely by the now truly terrified girl who had carried the tale to him. She was not seen again at Kereshtur. Charitable rumors claimed that she had returned to her village under cover of the night. Uncharitable ones circulated to the effect that she had been strangled by Darvulia and thrown into the Vah River.

In the end the women, unlike Hebler, decided that the child, because of her gifts, had to be protected from men, and from preachers in particular. She was deemed by Darvulia to be one of those elect, born every hundred years, whose mission is to lead womenfolk on the paths of their secret religion, about which men knew nothing but which, nonetheless, had been practiced under their noses for thousands of years.

After a time the women about her crib decided not

to fear their charge and went on embroidering and gossiping as before.

Elizabeth did not know exactly what had happened, but she sensed that she no longer had the absolute attention of her keepers. She became a tireless (and tiresome) asker of questions. But the answers never satisfied her, though Darvulia answered each one to the best of her knowledge, which was considerable, particularly in the area of womenfolk ways.

At the age of four, when most children can be trusted to entertain themselves with dolls for long periods of time, Elizabeth still demanded the undivided attention of her wet nurse, not for her milk (the child had been weaned) but for her ability to explain and answer Elizabeth's innumerable questions.

One time, when Darvulia drew a breath, Elizabeth demanded to be heard. Present also were her aunt Klara, her two attendant maids, Teresa and Lena, both of them fourteen-year-olds, and several other women with their own babies and young children. Elizabeth told a fairy tale but then related also a conversation between Teresa and Lena, who had been sitting not far from her playpen speaking in soft voices, sure that no one else could hear them. With vivid and droll gestures, the child repeated word for word the conversation of the two maids, which concerned Teresa's husband, a squire twice her age who was in charge of provisioning the garrison. The man had gotten very drunk the previous night and had beaten and raped Teresa so meanly that under her concealing garments she was covered with bruises. Teresa told Lena that he had accused her of deliberately withholding herself, denying him an heir. He then left her weeping and went to spend the night either among the horses or with a wench he kept in the village. That morning Teresa had consulted Darvulia, who had made her disrobe and had dressed her wounds with herbal compresses. Darvulia then asked Teresa to join her and some other women at midnight in the church graveyard for a consultation with the devil concerning the potential baby. Teresa did not know what to do and was asking Lena's advice on whether she should go to the graveyard or not. Lena told Teresa that her husband of merely six months had not yet touched her. He was a very gentle man, a harness and boot maker, who spent all his time puttering about with his tools. Lena was furious with the man for his gentle ways, but any attempt to broach the subject, such as presenting herself to him naked, had been ignored. She too had gone to Darvulia with her problem two weeks previously and had been asked by Darvulia to come to the graveyard. She had gone once, and it had been beneficial. Nine women had been present: they had all been naked in a circle with a black rooster in their midst. They beat the rooster to death with sticks, and then they drank a bitter-tasting brew. After that, Lena felt very warm and had flown over the village. Unfortunately, the devil did not come that night. Lena was planning to attend that evening's session, and she strongly advised Teresa to go.

Darvulia was engaged in storytelling, so she had paid no attention to the maids. But Elizabeth had overheard them even as Darvulia was talking to her. The child's tale-telling had an extraordinary effect. The women were not in the least surprised by Teresa and Lena's conversation—well, some of them were—but they feared the worst from such things being repeated by their little mistress. When Elizabeth finished relating this conversation and laid her exhausted but triumphant little body back on the embroidered pillows of her playpen, both Lena and Teresa burst into tears. In their terror they pulled at their hair and their vestments. Finally Teresa fainted, while Lena stared straight ahead of her as if she had turned to stone. Only Darvulia kept her wits about her, staring at her charge with a mixture of wonder and adoration.

Elizabeth's aunt Lady Klara had been present during this event. She spent much of her time with Darvulia, and she adored her little niece. Lady Klara prevailed on all of them to be quiet. Lady Klara was only eighteen years old herself, but in a world where fourteen-year-old wives with two children were commonplace, she was practically an elder. She was unmarried herself for complicated reasons, some of which had to do with her stubbornly independent personality, some of which could be credited to her diplomatic skills. Her family would have liked her to conclude a beneficial alliance as soon as possible, but there was no one strong enough to persuade her.

Lady Klara said, in a firm and clear voice, that they had few choices. Allowing the word to get out about Darvulia outside their small circle would have swift consequences. Teresa and Lena would be accused of witchcraft, tortured, and put to death. Darvulia would also be tortured and made to reveal the names in her circle. These names might include women one would be very surprised to find in Darvulia's company. Lady Klara paused here and looked deeply into the eyes of each woman in turn. Most of them turned away.

"Just as I thought," said Lady Klara.

She explained that it would be much better for everyone concerned to have a little indulgence for the scrambled fantasy of a small child whose gift of mimicry was well known but whose understanding of facts was not great. Wasn't it entirely possible that the wicked fairy tales she was being constantly told were in themselves a kind of devil's brew that stirred the imagination so much it caused the production of phantoms? It was well known that some of these old tales were so vivid that people after hearing them often experienced rides on the backs of flying horses. Clearly, some such thing had been at work. Men, who had little imagination, often thought that such fantasies were real. They unjustly punished women who appeared to take such dreaming seriously. Worst of all, the church, notorious for its lack of either imagination or a sense of humor, had taken upon itself to punish and torture innocent wives and mothers. No, said Lady Klara, a thousand times no. This tale must not leave this room. And just to make sure that everyone in the room kept the vow, all present had to participate in Darvulia's moon dance that night. This was agreed to, and little Elizabeth fell asleep—not before committing to memory, of course, everything her aunt Klara had said.

Huddled in a corner of the bouncing carriage, trying to ignore the effect of the road on his spine, was Andrei de Kereshtur, the young notary of the Bathory family. His memoir about his friend Elizabeth Bathory would one day become one of Hungary's greatest historical writings. Andrei was the son of the castle's chief notary. The name of de Kereshtur had been bestowed upon his great-great-grandfather when the Bathorys first acquired the fort in 1413. The position of notary was hereditary, being passed on to the heir most likely to honor the position. By the time Andrei, the oldest son, was five years old, it had already been decided that he would follow in his father's footsteps. He would become the official scribe of the Bathory family, in charge of official documents, taking down depositions at trials, copying writs, and keeping the archives. It was a job for which the boy felt himself ideally suited. He was receiving the best education the castle could afford, the same offered to the Lady Elizabeth. In the round room called the Hall of Tapestries because of its many beautiful hangings, the Florentine monk Silvestri taught them languages, philosophy, rhetoric, grammar, arithmetic, geometry, astronomy, music, and drawing. The instruction itself was conducted in Latin, the language that Andrei and Elizabeth used whenever they spoke to each other.

Their religious instruction was conducted by the Protestant theologian Hebler, a man who in all respects was the opposite of the monk Silvestri. The children feared Hebler. They loved Silvestri. The freespirited, capricious Elizabeth did not often hold her tongue in front of the theologian, who noted all her remarks in an ominous black book that he carried with him at all times. He also carried the writings of Luther and the enormous volume of Janosz Silvay's translation of the Bible into Hungarian. His gaunt black-clad form appearing suddenly in the doorway of the study was enough to subdue the children and take all the pleasure out of the room. Theoretically Elizabeth could have had the theologian hanged if she wanted to, but he was under the protection of her mother, Baroness Anna, who strangely enough found some solace in the gloomy bird's company.

Andrei de Kereshtur was cautious by nature. He had the notary's need for strict order among his things. His quills were always sharp, and he arranged them by age, using the oldest and dullest ones first. His many pots of ink were likewise severely aligned in a row on top of the desk where he wrote, standing. He took pleasure in Elizabeth's adventurous disposition and was most interested in her escapades, but he preferred only to hear about them. He was a good student, but he plodded instead of leaping. Nonetheless he never forgot what he had once committed to memory. Andrei was like a library of sorts: one could ask for a date or a name, and if he had once heard it or read it, it would spring immediately to his lips. If asked, he was equally obliging with the dates of Emperor Maximilian's anniversaries and with the number of mares necessary to draw enough milk to bathe the maiden in "The Maiden Who Bathed in Mare's Milk," one of Elizabeth's favorite fairy tales.

Amdrei was particularly fond of the winter of 1568, when unusually cold blizzards raged through Pannonia. It was still a full year before Elizabeth's fateful journey to Ecsed Castle, where her sisters would be murdered. Life was slow but interesting, and the children greatly enjoyed castle life that winter. "You would think that we were in Transylvania," de Kereshtur noted later in his memoir. Transylvanian winters were renowned for their fury and for the hunger of the wolves that came into villages to snatch away livestock and occasionally children. "January is the coldest month in Hungary," a sixteenth-century traveler wrote, "but even then the average temperature does not fall below freezing." Be that as it may, the fierce winter of 1568 drove everyone indoors and gave notice that outside life must cease. At Kereshtur, games, entertainments, and contests had been carefully planned. The cellars and larders were stuffed with wines, viands, and fruit. Hunting parties had brought back pheasants, bear, moose, and deer, whose salted carcasses now hung from hooks in limestone rooms. Barrels full of lard and salted fish along with rows of dried meat lined the pantry walls. Travelers unable to leave before the second week in November found themselves compelled to spend the winter. They paid for their room and board with tales of strange places, songs, poems, and lies of every sort. There were always travelers at Kereshtur, many of them poets, singers, or painters looking for a place to spend the cold months, but also merchants who sold spices from the

Indies, ivory from Africa, and blue-and-gold macaw feathers from New Spain. This particular winter there was also a troupe of acrobats from Russia, in addition to Siamese-twin musicians, one of whom played the harp with his feet while the other sang mournful ballads in a language no one had heard before. Together they looked like a two-headed musical fountain. Both Andrei and Elizabeth loved music. She had a cherrywood music box that was topped by an angel. When you pulled his wings back, the box burst into song.

The thick walls of Kereshtur Castle kept out the cold wind that howled in from the desolate Hungarian plain. The two children sat before a roaring fire in one of the small halls at Kereshtur discussing the fragility of existence. Her own existence seemed particularly tenuous to the young Countess Elizabeth Bathory this afternoon because she had been caught cutting to shreds with a pair of sharp scissors the fox-fur hat of her tutor Preacher Hebler. She had been punished by being given to memorize the entire text of Dr. Martinus Luther's teaching concerning the desired behavior of women, a hefty book entitled simply—and misleadingly—*Commentaries*. Luther's stern injunctions to the members of her sex had left the young countess feeling both weak and irate. Dr. Martinus Luther had no love or even liking for members of her sex, whom he accused of being the devil's chief conduit. He was undoubtedly more fond of roasts and gravy, thought Elizabeth, who knew that Doctor Martinus was proportioned like an oak barrel full of pig lard.

Her friend sympathized with his young mistress but was shocked when she expressed the unconscionable opinion that peasants, priests, and nobles were made of the exact same materials and were therefore equally perishable. She argued that no one had been able to find exactly where nobility was located in the human body. Therefore nobility, unlike the soul—which had been seen, studied, and located in the liver—offered one no guarantee of durability.

Andrei de Kereshtur was used to the radical opinions of his friend, but this was too much. "How could you think this, my lady?" he stuttered. "Nobility is in the blood. The blood is immortal. You are making the mistake of the Greek atomists!" The children had been well drilled in Aristotle.

"Is it?" asked Elizabeth. She unfastened the lace collar from around her neck and took out the gold pin that held it together. With pursed lips and a look of glee on her face, she stuck the pin into the pillow of flesh at the top of her small fist. A drop of blood appeared. "Noble blood?" she shrieked, forcing herself not to acknowledge the pain. "Then drink it, friend, and you can be noble too!"

Andrei would not normally have taken this request seriously, but the expression on the girl's face left no doubt as to her determination. He bent his head to her hand and gently licked the drop of blood from it. Andrei de Kereshtur endowed this scene with ceremonial significance and likened it to a blood oath between brothers.

It had been an unusual day. That morning Elizabeth had seen an old kitchen maid carefully wrap the head of a chicken in a piece of cloth, take it outside, and bury it under a tree. The old woman mumbled a spell over it and cried. Elizabeth had been curious enough to wait for her to leave and to dig up the reeking head. She had learned nothing about the significance of it, however. Perhaps, she told herself, she is preparing a special dish for our Siamese-twin musicians. (The Siamese twins were known to eat only raw meat and fruit.) Later that very same morning, Elizabeth overheard two scullery maids talk about putting blood from their bodies in the food of the men they wanted to marry. When Elizabeth asked them about it, the girls bowed low, blushed, and wouldn't utter another word.

Elizabeth then disguised herself as a boy and followed the two girls around, hoping to hear something more. By the age of ten, she had already mastered many disguises. She could make herself look like a peasant girl or boy by wearing an embroidered blouse, a short skirt, and a sheepskin vest. She could even make herself look like a tiny old woman by carefully painting wrinkles around her red mouth and putting black circles under her big eyes. She had to squint so that her eyes wouldn't give her away. Andrei once told her that her eyes were like the bottomless pools in the forest. These black pools housed creatures from another time that came out only at night to bathe in starlight. No stick, no matter how long, could reach the bottom of such a pool. Elizabeth liked that. When people made her angry, she fancied that she could call those creatures from the depths of her eyes to punish them. In disguise she had been able to pass unnoticed many times, because there were always so many people of all ages running around, particularly around the kitchen area, that few of them stopped to look very carefully. This day, however, her disguise did not fool the two girls, who didn't speak at all when the "boy" was around.

In her eagerness to pursue the matter of the blood in the food, Elizabeth forgot about her lesson with Preacher Hebler. When the preacher was unable to find his noble charge, he complained to her mother, who became furious. Anna Bathory shouted at her daughter, making her cry. Elizabeth saw her mother so rarely that each encounter was an occasion, like a visit to a faraway and sweet-smelling land. She was therefore more than commonly angry when her audience with the beautiful Anna turned out to be an occasion for recrimination.

Shortly after lunch Elizabeth crept into the preacher's monastic cubicle and cut his hat with scissors. Unfortunately, Preacher Hebler, who usually took his time eating lunch, came back sooner than was his custom and caught her.

The Lutheran tutor thought of himself as one of the foremost exponents of the teachings of Dr. Martinus Luther. He had studied with the great man at Wittenberg, where he had the honor of being invited to the table on more than one occasion. He had absorbed the radical theologian's words as if they were heavenly manna. The discussions between Luther, Melanchthon, and other disciples, in which he did not dare participate, had remained forever branded in his memory. At one time Martinus Luther, a large man with a ferocious appetite, had deigned to take note of his presence and had urged him to eat. "You won't get far eating only words," the great man had admonished him, advice that resounded in his ears at all times, particularly since he never had much appetite. This matter was the only point on which he disagreed with the founder of the Protestant faith. Hebler sometimes preached against gluttony and praised frugality. Martinus Luther had doubtless been a glutton, but even this resounded in his favor, because without this flaw he would have been as perfect as Jesus Christ himself, and this was not possible. Hebler burned with the desire to make the world understand the brilliance of Luther's reform. To this end he had developed a pedagogical philosophy aimed at creating a hitherto unknown creature: Lutheran man (and woman). The end result of his applied pedagogy would have been a God-loving being who'd had lechery, gluttony, and laziness bred out of its very essence. Hebler believed in suppressing all excessive stimuli, whether beautiful paintings, adornments, immoderate music or poetry, lascivious tales, puppetry, or (especially) newfangled spices from India, pepper, cinnamon, tea, and chocolate. In his pursuit of perfection for his charges he was thwarted only by the monk Silvestri, the Italian who not only hated and mocked him but was a passionate adherent of all the ecstatic images and songs that aroused Hebler's wrath—and a gourmand besides, who could lose himself within a delicately perfumed French pastry and act more indecently than a woman buggered by a centaur. And of course he obeyed the pope in Rome, which was the greatest of his failings.

Upon sight of his shredded hat, Hebler's first instinct was to grab hold of the rotten girl by her hair, bend her in half over his knee, and whip her raw with his riding crop. But of course he could hardly do such a thing to his future employer, so he swallowed his rage and ordered her to memorize Luther's pamphlet on the wickedness of the female sex. When she had left, Hebler, his rage unspent, tore off his breeches and hit himself as hard as he could on his arse and between his legs with his riding crop. Only then, when he was stung by pain, did some of the anger drain from his body.

"We children talked of many things," wrote Andrei de Kereshtur half a century later.

Darvulia, the wet nurse of my mistress Elizabeth, was as full of stories as she was of milk. My Mistress had great Memory and the Gift of Mimicry. She also liked to go about in disguise. When she was only four years old, after being told the Hungarian fairy tale about an old woman who bathes in mare's milk and becomes young and beautiful again, Elizabeth demanded a bath in mare's milk. Her nurses told her that mare's milk was very difficult to obtain, but Elizabeth cried so much that in the end the women gave in, seeing her beautiful eyes swim with tears. They had a bath of cow's milk prepared, but told my mistress that it was mare's milk.

The monk Silvestri looked with bemused enchantment on the friendship of the two children, but since he was especially fond of the notary's son, he felt obliged to warn him against letting his affection run away with his better sense. Noting that Andrei spent all his free time with the young countess, the monk told him that he himself was fascinated by Elizabeth and quoted Aristotle on the matter of women's eyes being a kind of fire. He then assigned to Andrei, for memorization and comment, a passage from Agrippa of Nettesheim commenting on Ficino: "Fascination is a force that, emanating from the spirit of the fascinator, enters the eyes of the fascinated person and penetrates his heart."

Elizabeth often accompanied Andrei to the castle archive, where old Notary de Kereshtur, his father, instructed his son in the mysteries of the rolls of parchment dating back centuries. Elizabeth liked to study random ledgers and rolls while the notaries talked. One day she picked up a map of Kereshtur Castle, made a century before, showing all its many features, including intricate secret passageways that served both as shortcuts for the servants and means of escape during sieges. Elizabeth memorized the map. She soon put her newfound knowledge to use. She used the secret passageways to travel from one part of the castle to another. Kereshtur was as complicated as a French cake. It had been built, rebuilt, and added to since the fourteenth century. Its galleries, towers, battlements, palisades, walls, gatehouses, and barbicans were connected intricately to one another. On the ground level were the cellars, granaries, and kitchens, with their great boxes, barrels, casks, and household utensils. There also were the barracks, the garrison, the armory, and the stables.

Above that were the great chamber and a chapel that
rose through several floors and could be reached by
Lady Bathory and the noble family from the upper
floor, and by their servants from their own quarters on
the second level. Chambers, spiral staircases, and fireplaces were built into the thick walls at various times
and had fallen in and out of use throughout the centuries. The privies had been tunneled into the rock and
ended in the dark and swift waters of the Vah River. An
invading army had once used these tunnels to climb into
the castle, so the places where they descended into the
river had been surrounded by retaining walls.

Elizabeth's wanderings ended one day in a room attached to the garrison, where she witnessed the ques-
tioning of a thief. Andrei de Kereshtur in his *Chronicles*
recalled this incident in detail under the heading "My
Lady saw the judging and punishing of a thief."

The thief was a ditchdigger, coal hauler, and occasional horse groomer named Brunos. He had stolen two
swords from the garrison while the soldiers slept. Brunos camped on a pile of straw in a barn next to a stable
of carriage horses. He had covered the swords with
straw and gone to sleep on top of them. In the morning,
when he went to fetch a pail of water, one of the grooms
picked up some straw for the horses from Brunos's bed
and uncovered the swords. When they brought him before the garrison commander, Brunos confessed everything. He wanted the broadswords, he said, because
they were so shiny. He wanted to "see his face in them."
The commander, attended by his lieutenants and a
number of soldiers who were milling about polishing
boots and weapons, gave a huge hoot of laughter. The
company joined in until all were laughing madly. Some
had tears in their eyes. But Brunos, his face covered
with coal powder, bits of straw, and plain dust, did not
laugh.

"Why did you . . . want to see your face in the swords?" the commander demanded.

"Because," Brunos replied gravely, "I have never seen my face, my lord . . . save for its reflection in moving water."

The commander then asked him why he didn't ask one of the maids of the court ladies to let him see himself in a looking glass. Brunos said that he didn't know any maids but that he intended to meet one after he ascertained if he looked suitable enough to make an approach.

"And what if you didn't look suitable?" asked the amazed commander. The merriment increased.

"I would have used the swords to cut my body and die," said Brunos.

There seemed little need to torture the man, though it was customary to torture suspects; Brunos had already confessed and would be put to death anyway. But the young Countess Elizabeth, who had been sitting in the shadows of the room without anyone noticing her, decided to intervene. She startled everyone when she stepped forward and asked, "Shouldn't the thief be tortured?"

"Of course, my lady," replied the surprised commander, "but you must not watch his punishment."

One of the soldiers escorted Elizabeth out through the visible door (ignorant of the secret passage through which the girl had arrived) and delivered her to Lady Klara, who was sitting before a large mirror in her room. Aunt Klara was beautiful and smelled divine and liked to stare at herself in the mirror all the time, even when she was speaking with someone. Consequently she didn't pay much attention to her niece. She listened to Elizabeth's adventure, making faces at herself and fiddling distractedly with a silver box fitted with tiny doors. Elizabeth was soon able to slip away. She found her way secretly to a balcony just above the garrison where they were torturing Brunos. His screams gave her an odd feeling of dread mixed with delight, as if they were some kind of music. When she had asked that Brunos be tortured, she had little idea of what *torture* meant. She had heard the word used many times, in all sorts of ways, from Darvulia's shouting at Teresa to "quit torturing me" to Hebler pontificating gravely on the "ennobling effects of torture, which, by imitating the fleshly torment of our Lord Jesus Christ, purifies the victim for the judgment."

Andrei de Kereshtur said that Elizabeth may have decided then that the only way to understand the true meaning of things is to watch them in secret.

She confided to me many times that the truth of a thing was to allow it to unfold as though no one was watching. She gave the example of seeing the court singer, Melotus, practicing his melodies alone. When she watched him at work in his room through a small fireplace, he produced divine poetry. This was not the case when he sang for the court. And another example was looking on the torture of the thief Brunos, who "might have held back his screams if he knew I was looking."

When the soldiers came dragging Brunos's broken body through the door, she saw his face clearly. His eyes were wide open, two iridescent blue stones. His mouth, a swollen purple rose, was moving, articulating something that didn't leave his throat. The soldiers stood Brunos upright against a wooden post and tied his hands and feet to it. The two of them then crossed in front of Brunos's face the two broadswords he had stolen. The thief looked quickly at his reflection, and then his face vanished as the broadswords cut clean through his head. His face, cut in half, fell to each side of his neck like petals of a flower about the stem.

Elizabeth stayed in her niche after the soldiers left, watching the body. She was not sure why she watched. Andrei de Kereshtur said, "My Lady had the habit of sitting very still long after a performance had ended. She also liked to stand watch over a bird or a rabbit she had shot, long after the creature pierced by her arrow quit quivering. She suspected that most conclusions were 'false endings,' as in certain popular plays or fables."

When Elizabeth had watched long enough and was ready to quit her observation perch, two crones dressed in black from head to foot appeared in the courtyard, glancing furtively about. Quick as lightning, one of them withdrew a knife from her cloak and skillfully cut the thief's hands from the wrists. The other one took the blade when the first one was finished and cut open the wet rag in front of the crotch. With a swift stroke she sliced off the thief's penis, which had hardened at the moment of death. Elizabeth saw but a swift glimpse of swollen purple flesh before this too disappeared under the crone's cloak.

This scene took place in full daylight, but so very quickly that Elizabeth wasn't sure she hadn't dreamt the whole thing. A few moments later, two peasants came pulling a cart, untied the corpse, and loaded it unceremoniously, without seeming to notice its handless, emasculated state. Nauseated and excited, Elizabeth ran up the stairs to collapse into the arms of her aunt Klara. She told her what she had seen. When Elizabeth got to the part about the penis, Lady Klara was convulsed by laughter. She laughed so heartily that Elizabeth could not help joining in, though she failed for the moment to see the humor.

Lady Klara removed a Harlequin doll from the table

under the mirror and stuck it in front of her dress. "She cut off his thing, this thing?" she said, making exaggerated gestures with her hips, pushing the doll forward like a penis.

Since Elizabeth did not seem to understand, Klara asked her to sit on the bench next to her. Aunt Klara lifted her voluminous skirt and revealed her petticoat. She then turned toward Elizabeth and straddled the bench. Holding her skirt up with one hand, she pushed her undergarment aside with a satiny rustle. Elizabeth had never before seen a grown woman's genitals from this close. She was fascinated. There was a great chestnut beard around the jagged red lips of Aunt Klara's vagina. Klara asked Elizabeth to position the Harlequin between her legs. The girl did, sensing the great heat of her aunt's loins as she nestled the doll in that great hairy forest, trapping him there. Lady Klara then lowered her dress like a curtain over the doll. With her dress down, she did not look as if she had a doll between her legs. Elizabeth imagined Harlequin coming to life down there and pushing those red lips open to go inside. She was jealous of Harlequin for the opportunity to explore. Her aunt asked her to sit on her lap. Elizabeth did, wiggling uncomfortably when Harlequin poked her between her skinny buttocks.

"Do you understand now?" Lady Klara asked, flushing deep red.

Elizabeth didn't. But she planned to.

A half century later, Notary de Kereshtur hadn't forgotten: "Elizabeth's aunt Klara enjoyed holding a Harlequin doll between her legs. She told Elizabeth this was her male part."

When Elizabeth told him all that had transpired—from her intervention to the Harlequin—the scribe felt both astonishment and discomfort. The discomfort, he realized, had to do with how little he knew about these things. He was a homely boy who had been born with a little hump. He could have hidden his hump under a specially tailored cloak, but he did not want to. The hump did not bother him. He felt that it gave him a kind of distinction. He liked also the fear he evoked in the superstitious staff and peasants. He'd heard that hunchbacks from the villages were forced to live by themselves and that people brought food to their hovels in the forest in exchange for the privilege of rubbing the hump, which was said to bring luck.

Elizabeth had of course already inspected his hump, after a great deal of coaxing and foot stomping on her part, and she had declared herself satisfied. She liked it. She had worried, she told him, that his hump might be hollow. In that case, he would be able to hide things from her in there. After squeezing it, prodding it, and even poking it with the pin of her brooch (Andrei screamed and did not like this a bit), she decided that the hump was full and thus not a threat to her, because nothing could be hidden in it. Andrei sighed a great inaudible sigh of relief. He never wanted to be the subject of Elizabeth's curiosity. He would be plain as daylight to her at all times. He would record her stories, encourage her to talk. He would be her mirror. Andrei resolved to remember all the things she told him. His friend had an uncommon destiny that he, Andrei de Kereshtur, could already hear, as he could hear the wind outside above the roar of the collapsing logs in the fireplace.

The two children sat quietly together many times, reading books or simply staring out the big castle windows at the rolling hills with their villages and churches spread out like a tapestry. They saw the peasants toiling in the field and watched the cows and the sheep graze. The peaceful landscape gave no indication of the upheavals that had racked it for centuries. There were no great armies clashing beneath the walls. The rebuilt churches barely gave any indication that they had recently been burnt to the ground. Jagged ruins here and there were being quickly overcome by clinging vines. The peasants moved slowly, as if they had forgotten the Turkish army that had rolled over them only two years before, leaving fire-blackened dirt in its wake. They had survived by hiding in the forest, in caves, and in tunnels carved underground centuries before. It seemed that Elizabeth Bathory and Andrei de Kereshtur, born the same year, anno Domini 1560, had been blessed to live in a peaceful age. But this was an illusion. The immutable order of things deemed war inevitable, disease a fact of life, and God the only salvation. Their world was momentarily static, privileged, and tied by unbreakable bonds of blood to the great Bathory estate. They were only children, but they already knew that the defense of their world would entail great suffering in the years ahead and that nothing would unfold as expected. It was less than a year before Dozsa's rebels would murder Elizabeth's sisters before her eyes.

Still, during that winter of peace in the waning days of their childhood, many wondrous things happened to the children. Elizabeth rarely saw her sisters, who occupied a different wing of the castle, tended by their own maids. One day, Elizabeth accompanied Andrei and his father to the city of Pest to purchase a book. Elizabeth went despite being forbidden by Preacher Hebler.

Pest was a noisy and exciting town with great big houses and carriages stuck in mud. The bookseller was a Jew living on a crowded street where all the houses seemed built on top of one another and leaned at perilous angles. The street was full of donkeys laden with all kinds of merchandise, and prostitutes stood in every doorway, breasts exposed, striped cloth around their waists, the emblem of their profession.

Elizabeth was delighted, but Andrei kept his eyes to the ground in mortified dismay, while his father did not seem to notice. Neither Andrei nor Elizabeth had ever seen a Jew before, so they were both rigid with fear when the elder notary introduced them to an old man with a long black beard, curls around his ears, and two bright, piercing black eyes that seemed to penetrate to the depths of their trembling souls.

The Jew's name was ben Lebus, and in addition to trading in books he read fortune cards and did a bit of prognostication. Andrei had been told by Hebler that Doctor Luther hated Jews because the Jews had been punished by God, and that it was up to good Christians to erase them from the face of the earth. When Andrei asked how this might be accomplished, Hebler, his eyes blazing with fury, said that "we must burn their synagogues and kill them in the flesh, especially the converted ones who hide under the Christian cloak, erasing all the debts that they have bewitched us into contracting."

Andrei didn't know why his father consented to sit down, accept a mug of hot wine, and have a long conversation with the Jew ben Lebus. But Elizabeth felt quite thrilled by the adventure. She believed that Hebler was an infallible gauge as to how things really stood. Whatever he hated was good, and vice versa. Before any book was even brought out, the two men engaged in a long discussion of history, man's fate, and God's hidden design. The talk lasted way past the setting of the sun. Candles were brought in. While the children listened quietly in the deepening shadows, the men discussed the science of the Kabbalah and the ten sephiroth, which were ten circles of fire that lived inside every human body. These circles of fire were different aspects of God, and they corresponded as well to a myriad of things on earth and in the stars, which all contained sephiroth that mirrored the divine ones. Andrei's father argued that if God were ten aspects—instead of three, as in the Trinity—the work of keeping track of them would occupy a man's entire life, so that he would have time for nothing else.

"That's precisely it!" ben Lebus shouted with satisfaction. "A man shouldn't have time for anything else! Everything else a man does, like stealing, killing, cheating, persecuting the Jews, shitting in the water he drinks from, is not worth doing. Better that a man contemplate the sephiroth!"

"Well, then," the elder de Kereshtur shouted back, "are you saying that the Father, the Son, and the Holy Ghost are entirely too simple and thus too liable to being ignored? That's blasphemy, Jew, and I will not have it!"

And so it went, for hours.

Now and then Elizabeth would catch a glimpse of the fascinating world outside the door. At one point she grabbed Andrei by his sleeve and they sneaked out. They were immediately surrounded by a swirling mass of beggars, who pointed to their deformities and cried for alms. They had no money, so they pushed their way through and walked on until they found themselves in a kind of . . . moving field. To their horror they realized that they were walking on human bodies that were lying there one on top of another. Holding Andrei's hand, Elizabeth broke into a run as the moving field became a forest of skeletal limbs thrust at them, tearing at their clothes. Pieces of flesh hung from the skeletons as they moved weakly. The children had wandered onto a field of sleeping lepers. Andrei had seen but one leper before, bathing in the moat outside the castle wall, and had dreamed about him for two weeks. But Elizabeth had never seen one. A kitchen boy had once given her a stack of uneven-sized parchments to write some letters on. After she finished writing the letters for the boy, she asked him what kind of parchment it was. "Dried leper skin," the boy said, laughing when Elizabeth turned pale. "They sell strips of skin in the leper fields," the boy explained. "You buy them by the gross." Now here she was, surrounded by a writhing mass of human paper, more paper than she would ever need in her entire life, even if she were to write as much as Andrei, her notary. Elizabeth had a vision of an immense library, with shelves higher than the highest tower of Kereshtur, containing all the writings in the world penned on human skin.

The children were saved by a whore, who snatched them into her hut. Lowering his eyes in shame at the sight of her naked breasts, Andrei thanked her. But Elizabeth looked straight at her large, womanly breasts and asked her whether she let men bite them for money. The whore laughed and said that she would do anything for money. Elizabeth liked her, and when the woman returned them to the hut of ben Lebus, Elizabeth whispered to her that she would repay her one day. The men had not even noticed the children's disappearance: they were absorbed in examining a book so old it was falling out of its leather binding.

The Jew, ben Lebus, noticing them, laughed. "Your son," he told the notary, "is going to be a great writer. He will learn the difference between a leper's skin and parchment. He will also learn the difference between a man and some zealot's idea of a man." His deep gaze then alit on Elizabeth, and he was quiet for a moment. "Your daughter is also a remarkable child. She will be spoken of for many years after you and I have become spirit." He then became very sober.

Andrei remembered the remarks of ben Lebus for many years. Elizabeth told only Darvulia what had befallen her. Darvulia said that the old Jew was a wise man and that she must never say anything to Hebler about him, because Hebler was a zealot. "But that's the same word ben Lebus used!" exclaimed Elizabeth. Darvulia said that certain words were very powerful. As for Hebler, she'd made him a special place in her heart where it was pitch dark. Every time Hebler looked at her, she put him in that dark place and he got lost. It would be best, from this time on, if Elizabeth hid all her thoughts from Hebler. When Elizabeth said that she was afraid that Hebler might wrest things from her anyway, Darvulia gave her a little pouch full of poppy seed, which she said was the herb of forgetfulness. Even if she unwittingly told the preacher something that mattered, the preacher wouldn't be able to remember it.

About the time Andrei de Kereshtur had recalled all these things to himself and had succumbed to a sweet melancholy mood verging on sleep, the carriage came to a sudden halt. Elizabeth pulled back the curtain to see what was the matter. Swarming from everywhere like some sort of succubi were hundreds of lepers with out-stretched hands. Elizabeth laughed.

"What is it?" asked Teresa.

Elizabeth showed her. "Oh, my!" Teresa exclaimed. "Where did they come from?"

"From our past!" said Elizabeth, noticing Andrei's astonishment as he watched the familiar sight.

The coachmen whipped the beggars out of the way after Darvulia showered them with small copper coins. Pleased with herself, Darvulia smiled and produced a fragrant herb tied in a small bundle from under the folds of her dress. "Before you meet your future husband, Franz Nadazdy, rub this on your hand, then sprinkle some in his wine. It's adoration pollen. He will adore you forever and forever, and he will be chivalrous and write poetry to you."

Elizabeth took the herb and put it under her own dress. She knew that what Darvulia had just said about Franz adoring her was highly desirable, but she wasn't sure what it meant. Would it be like the *Adoration by the Magi of the Baby Jesus* that was painted on the ceiling of the chapel at Kereshtur? Would Franz adore her the same way, offering gifts and falling to his knees? Would a halo surround her head? She was a child, after all. She had read chivalric romances, knew verses from *Tristan and Yseult,* had heard hundreds of songs of love and longing, had even seen (unobserved) bawdy plays performed by the Gypsies for the garrison. She had all on her own discovered the meaning of the word *buggery.* But she had no particular meaning or feeling to attach to the word *marriage.* Elizabeth understood, of course, the political and financial considerations that had led to her engagement. She had known ever since she could walk that marriage was something a girl's parents arranged in order that the family might benefit from added wealth or political power. She knew also that she was living in perilous times and that it was necessary for families to make alliances against common enemies. What bothered her was the physical aspect of this business. Was he going to touch her? Did she have to touch him? She crumpled Darvulia's herb in her hand. It smelled strongly of summer. In the corner of the carriage, her notary was pretending to sleep.

Your Honor, what follows is the true description of what took place during the first days of my return to Hungary. I will be scrupulously honest about the details, but just in case my memory has weakened, I refer you to a journal I have kept, which you are free to open and read when you are considering my punishment.

"Proceed, Mr. Bathory-Kereshtur. Or should I say Count?"

You may not, Your Highness. This is America.

Klaus Megyery's house squatted like a frog on old Judenstrasse, with its rows of narrow fifteenth-century doorways and high walls. All three of us had grown up on this street: Eva at number 9, Klaus at number 22, and I at number 11. I knew the feel of its rounded cobblestones under my bare feet. I had made music running a stick along the iron bars of the fences on my way to school.

Jews had lived in these houses for two centuries, until they were expelled in the seventeenth century and their houses were given over to petty imperial officials. They returned after their emancipation in 1848, only to be expelled again, this time forever, during the Second World War. During the war, SS officers were garrisoned here. After the Communist takeover, old aristocrats expelled from their baronial mansions were allocated apartments here. A few Jews returned also, stubbornly refusing to abandon the empty shell of their long history. In its way, Judenstrasse was the embodiment of our saddest history.

By the time I came around, the houses had been divided into small apartments, just the way they had been four hundred years before. Only, instead of bearded Talmudists, watchmakers, or antiquarians, these rooms were now filled with the silent footsteps of fallen aristocrats who moved discreetly through the fog of history, hoping to attract no attention.

Number 11 Judenstrasse, where I grew up, slumbered in the snow behind locked iron gates. On the other side was the courtyard with the woodshed on the right and the curving staircase that led to our third-story apartment. I was scared stiff of that woodshed after dark. Ghosts lived in there. My father told me that during the war three Jews had been shot in there. Their blood could still be seen on the cobblestones. There was one stone in particular I was most careful not to step on. One summer, barefoot, I stepped on it by mistake, and something sticky clung to the bottom of my foot. I screamed in terror. I took great pains to avoid this stone: I was convinced that if I stepped on it some more we would all be shot. I was afraid of death.

I looked up to the window where the dreamy and fretful child I'd been used to sit gazing aimlessly. A shadow moved behind the muslin curtains. Someone was watching me. For a moment the figure peeking from behind the curtains looked like my mother. Of course it wasn't. She has been dead for over a quarter of a century now.

Number 9 Judenstrasse hadn't changed either. Eva had only lived here for a brief time when we were both ten or eleven years old. Later she moved to one of the new apartment buildings in a suburb of Budapest, one hour's trolley ride from here.

Filled with memories like a harp full of music, I walked toward the figure standing before the gate at number 22. Shaky Stringbean was waiting for me outside the massive door with a large key in his hand.

I recognized him immediately. The ax-shaped face,

the furry eyebrows, the swollen lips, the caved-in chest. And those ice blue eyes with their faraway look that had carried a message all the way to America. Klaus was dressed in a funereal black suit like an undertaker.

I made a gesture to embrace my old pal, when he did something completely ridiculous. Klaus Megyery bowed deeply, took my hand, and kissed it.

"Count Kereshtur," he said.

It was so incongruous, I burst out laughing.

Megyery gave me a pained look. "Laugh," he said, "but there are certain things bigger than both of us."

"War," I said. "Famine. American Airlines."

Klaus opened the gate with his ancient key. We crossed the courtyard and climbed the staircase with the polished walnut railing. I felt instinctively for the letters I knew I had carved there ages ago, one afternoon when Eva and I waited for Klaus to come back: *E&A*. I didn't find them.

Back then, Klaus lived with his mother, a large woman who had decorated their small rooms with lithographs of the pope and many portraits of saints. She was gone, and Klaus Megyery's sitting room had undergone a nationalist change of taste. It was covered by Hungarian carpets. On the walls the lithograph portraits of saints had been replaced by lithographs of Hungarian kings, who stared fiercely over one another's heads. A censer, two peeling wooden angels, a squashed knight's visor, a mace, and a rusted pair of bellows occupied the windowsills and a small table.

"Did you loot a museum, Megyery?"

My pal looked alarmed. Maybe he had.

"Only kidding," I reassured him.

I inhaled deeply the musty air. It was a familiar smell. History and fake history. The cooking smells and stinks of generation after generation. Decades of pov-

erty and Communist communal kitchens were merely
the latest layer.

"Klaus, have you seen Eva?"

He seemed to have been expecting this question.

"When I wrote to you in New York, I hesitated to
tell you the news. Eva is very ill. But her daughter, Teresa, is working with us. She and my son Imre are both
involved in Saint Stephen's Knights. She knows that you
were a good friend of her mother's and can't wait to
meet you."

"What is wrong with Eva?"

"She's been in Horoarspital a long time now. She
remembers nothing, recognizes no one, doesn't speak.
Teresa visits her every week. They sit outside. Teresa
talks, Eva looks straight ahead, no expression. But the
strange thing is . . ." Klaus stumbled. "The odd thing is
that . . . she hasn't aged a day since she was hospital-
ized. Her hair is shiny, she has healthy, glowing skin
. . . She looks as young as her daughter. The doctors
say it is a form of autism."

This is what I pieced together from Megyery's
patchy account: Ten years before, Eva ceased speaking.
She closed up like a shell. No one knew why. She had
been married and divorced, had given birth to Teresa,
and had remained, at least to a distant observer like
Klaus Megyery, pretty much the same—a vivacious
woman with striking red hair and black eyes who moved
her hands a lot when she talked. She talked a lot. How
well I remembered! She was always moving; her nervous, skinny legs swung back and forth all the time. The
only way to still her was to kiss her. It was hard to
imagine this Eva suddenly withdrawing into silence and
stillness.

I must admit that, horrific as this news was to me, I
was a little happy that, despite (or perhaps because of)
her condition, Eva had remained suspended in time.

The passing of time had altered her looks but little. She was still a young woman. I resolved to see her as soon as possible.

Klaus was eager to discuss business.

"The time has come, dear Count, to claim back our country. The time has come for you to claim what's yours."

"What is mine?" I asked.

"Becko, Becs, Bicse, Borsmonstor, Csejte, Nagy-ecsed, Fuzer, Kapuvar, Nemet-Kereshtur, Kosztolany, Leka, Poszony, Postyen, Sarvar, Sirok, Vag-Ujhely, Varanno."

Megyery recited the names of these places as if they were his grandchildren.

I was only vaguely familiar with the names.

"Castles and territories of the Bathory branch of your family. We will pass a new law giving back everything that rightfully belongs to its owners."

I could think of a hundred quick reasons why such a claim was absurd. "My father," I said, "was a mining engineer. My mother was a printer. Our family hasn't owned any of those places since the nineteenth century or before."

"That's the beauty of it!" Megyery exclaimed. "We'll rid the country of Communists, socialists, capitalists, and Jews! After that, God willing, greater Hungary will be ours once more!"

Looking into the swollen orbs of my old pal, which gleamed with what I felt quite sure was sheer madness, I considered briefly whether I should get up and never return. On the other hand, my journalistic self advised me: let's see what this is all about. Everything was strange, even that little phrase *God willing* which sounded so alien on Megyery's lips. He had also invoked

God in his letter. I had no idea where this new piety came from. God was not someone we had mentioned very often when we were growing up. My father's Catholic religion and my mother's Protestant faith had an underground life, if any. There was the unspoken assumption somehow that religion had been important to our subjects and, perhaps, to our ancestors. We had won, however, a kind of exemption from it. Now and then, at the high holidays, led by my severe grandmother, we would kneel in church and sing. I would fidget until it was time to go. Megyery had no religion at all: his father was a Communist bureaucrat. Officially everyone was an atheist. Old people went to church and kissed crosses and invoked God. The young hadn't for a long time. God had been banished, first by the Fascists, then by the Communists. People my age and younger had been stripped of God, defoliated like sprayed trees.

"The problem, Klaus, is that I am not sure who this Count Kereshtur is . . . I'm Drake, an American."

"I expected as much," Megyery said. "After all those years in America . . . Pepsi, 'He's a Jolly Good Fellow,' Trident chewing gum, Campbell soup . . . See, I am not ignorant. But there is nothing you can do about it. In your veins runs the blood of the Bathorys. We will *teach* you to remember who you are!"

"Who's 'we'? Saint Stephen's Knights?"

"Of course. My son, Imre, and Teresa, Eva's daughter, have kindly agreed to put themselves in your service. They will teach you what you have forgotten, guide you back to your roots, show you the history of your family . . ."

Now, this was interesting. The child of my old love and the son of my oldest friend. In my "service." I didn't have an heir myself, a fact that made me occasionally wistful. But I had "subjects," so to speak.

"This blood of mine," I said, "isn't it the blood of

virgins murdered by Elizabeth Bathory? Aren't you afraid to entrust your children to me?"

Megyery waved his hand impatiently and tried some humor of his own: "I may not like it, but it's the twentieth century. Show me a virgin in Budapest and I'll show you a unicorn. Those stories about Elizabeth Bathory . . . I don't believe them. Spread by the enemies of Hungary. Elizabeth Bathory was a bit mad, certainly. But she did not kill virgins for their blood. That's a capitalist exploitation story for their—what do you call it?—mass media . . ."

"That's what I work for, Klaus. The *Chronicle*. Western mass media."

"We will—how do you say it?—debug you! Imre and Teresa will debug you!"

He meant *deprogram,* Your Honor.

I wanted to rush quickly to Horoarspital to see Eva. But Klaus advised me, quite rightly, to see Teresa first. She might be able to shed some light on her mother's condition. Teresa was in the countryside for another day, but Imre, Megyery's son, was eager to meet me that same day if I didn't mind.

I didn't mind. Sitting in Megyery's patriotic den with its familiar smell had given me intense and unusual energy. I was most curious to see what kind of spawn had issued from such a strange bird. Megyery himself had, of course, told me nothing or almost nothing about his own intentions or motives for working on behalf of the royalist cause. He was not a nobleman, and as far as I knew, he had never held the aristocracy in high regard. His sympathies were with Fascism, which was not a promonarchist movement. His son was another story, though. Raised and educated during the Communist regime, he must have been a swirling mass of confusion.

Imre Megyery came to my hotel that evening. He was a thin and awkward young man. He had modishly long hair that reached over the collar of his blue-jean jacket. Nonetheless, he exuded an air of formality. He wore a pinstriped shirt with a tie under the informal jacket. Not quite twenty-three years old, he had recently graduated from Matthias Corvinus University with a degree in nineteenth-century history.

We took a walk along the Danube. Couples strolled along the river under the evening lights. Imre and I walked together over the streets of my childhood, and I abandoned myself to a rather giddy flow of exhilarated talk. I was happy to rediscover Budapest in the company of someone who was as young as I'd been when I left. Perhaps I talked so much that Imre could not get a word in edgewise. In any case, I had no reason to think badly of the young man who had been entrusted with such a strange mission by my childhood friend.

We sat on the steps at the back of the Matthias Cathedral. "I saw an angel here one evening," I told him. "It was as close to me as you are. It had a sad face with round black eyes and powerful big wings that he kept folded when he looked at me. He was both male and female, I think, though angels are supposed to be genderless."

"Perhaps he was a poor secret policeman following you in such a disguise," said Imre.

"That was a distinct possibility in those days."

I noted that Imre didn't believe in angels. He also did not mention God, although, hierarchically, God the Father must have been important to the scheme of things for Saint Stephen's Knights.

We strolled past the former headquarters of the Communist Party, where an enraged cultural commissar once shouted at me to lower my defiantly raised collar when I came in with a group of young Communist

Youths to be commended for something or other. Perhaps the commissar was aware of my unhealthy social origins and had singled me out. In any case, he made me lower my collar, a gesture that I purposefully made to look as if I was lowering the flags of nobility before the new peasant order.

"The Communists were terribly formal, Imre. They always wore suits and ties and were always looking to improve their manners. They were all peasants with dreams of petit bourgeois propriety . . ."

"Perhaps," said Imre, whose tie must have felt suddenly uncomfortable. And then he added something strange: "You seem to have had a lot of problems with authority!"

Coming from one so young, of an age when authority cannot help but be the enemy, Imre's statement was truly startling. "Well, yes," I said. "Don't *you* have a problem with authority?"

"No," said my friend's son, "I respect authority. I respect the authority of my father, my church, my military leaders. I expect that one day others will respect *my* authority."

"You must be an ambitious young man."

"Perhaps," he said.

We walked in silence for a time. I *did* have a problem with authority. My father had been only a shadow for me. I had loved him, but I mostly felt sorry for him. The official father of our country when I was growing up was Stalin, a Russian. I felt little for him. I despised the police. I had contempt for my teachers. Other men who might have once impressed me had simply been silent. Somewhere along the way, my inner conviction that I was a Jew had somehow become wedded to the word *anarchist*. And *anarchist*, as far as I knew, meant someone who did not recognize authority.

We walked into the old Printers' Guild building,

where my mother used to work, to see if any of the old printers were still there. We found Herr Meyer, an old German typesetter, who remembered me. The old man was nearly blind and worked in the bindery, sorting paper on the night shift. He said that lead had killed nearly all the printers but had taken only his eyes. The old presses dated back to the sixteenth century; they might have been the very ones to print the vernacular Bible of Janosz Silvay, the book that brought the revolution of Martinus Luther to Hungary. The old man touched my face and said to say hello to my mother. I didn't have the heart to tell him that she was dead.

With Imre in tow, I stared into the grimy windows of shops and looked at my face between the peeling signs. Not much had changed. I remembered the bare shelves of my childhood, the desolate emptiness of markets. I had grown up in a world devoid of material things, a defoliated, despoiled world. For all of that, or perhaps because of it, the light of the spirit shone sometimes through the barrenness like moonlight through the branches of a leafless tree. It had been winter for much of my childhood. The trees were perennially leafless. No wonder that history—cursed, bloody European history —poured through every opening like water through a sieve. There was nothing solid to keep it dammed, no marble slab to shut closed the mouth of its grave.

Next morning, Imre came by early. Stimulated by his remarks about authority—and feeling slightly guilty—I decided to visit my father's grave at Lamosz Cemetery.

The month before the Soviet invasion, we gymnasium students went on strike. I led some of my striking classmates to this cemetery. We strolled among the rich mausoleums in a state of woeful disrepair, reading the inscriptions. Here was true Hungarian history, not the garbage we were taught in school. I pointed out the graves of my ancestors, feeling for the first (and perhaps the last) time in my life that I was inspiring others. We searched for history among the listing angels and broken urns of the past and felt the cleansing power of truth. The group I led, which included Klaus Megyery, learned more history during these few visits to Lamosz than we had during years of Comrade Hebler's monotonous recitations.

In 1956, my father's grave had not been among those we visited. My father died in 1965. I had long been in America by then, and the news did not reach me for a whole month, because my mother's letter had passed through the hands of censors and had been purposely delayed. My father died suddenly of a heart attack during one of his evening poker games. My first thought was to wonder what hand he had been holding. Kings and queens, no doubt. I was already thinking like an American.

My mother died one year later and was buried in her hometown, Sarvar, by her own request. I could only wonder at the bitterness that caused her to be buried three hundred kilometers away from my father.

It was a gray winter morning with a hint of snow as Imre and I trudged up to the hilltop cemetery. Above the gate, two baroque angels spread their iron wings. A lone flower vendor stood behind a peeling cart. Buying flowers seemed like a good idea, but what had looked like a profusion of flowers from the other side of the street turned out to be a sorry arrangement of dusty silk and plastic bouquets with wire stems. There wasn't a single fresh flower in the bunch.

The vendor explained that he had once sold fresh flowers, but that the cemetery was so sparsely attended that his wares faded before he sold them. At first he had only a few artificial flowers, but his customers, such as they were, preferred them to the fresh ones. In the end he had decided to sell only artificial blossoms, and so far no one had complained.

I laughed but didn't complain either. I bought a dozen plastic daisies that looked like the ones embedded at the bottom of my bathtub in my first New York apartment. In fact, I remembered that they were actually called "bathtub daisies."

Well, Father, here is what the world has come to. You never told your son where he truly came from, so he's back now, bringing you the blooms of his American bathtub. By the time you died, our history had already turned into some terrible imitation of itself. Nobles had become civil servants, warriors had exchanged their spurs for felt slippers, and plastic flowers took the place of fresh ones.

I tried to explain this irony to Imre, but he looked baffled. The young Hungarian admired my devotion, partly because I had spent the equivalent of two months of a Hungarian salary on plastic flowers for my father. He saw no irony. He probably told himself that his work of reconnecting the estranged noble to his roots was already bearing fruit.

Once the exclusive preserve of the aristocracy, the cemetery was overgrown and forgotten. Our family crypts occupied an entire corner next to a crumbling wall. We hacked our way through vines and bushes. Powdery snow fell on us from the disturbed branches. The frozen ground gave way here and there to mud. We tripped over fallen stones all but sunk into the earth.

At last we stood before a black marble mausoleum. The wolves' teeth at the center of the Bathory coat of arms greeted me with all the familiarity of childhood. Pulling hard, I pried the iron gate open and entered the frozen world of my predecessors.

Layered as in a Bavarian cake, the tombs of my ancestors awaited me. At the very bottom lay two knights carved from stone, their hands crossed on their chests over the hilts of their swords. Count Franz Nadazdy and the palatine Thurzo were buried side by side there under their effigies, as if they had been man and wife.

Above them lay the gray-veined white marble bodies of two noble ladies with their arms crossed over their bosoms, their long hair carefully combed over their bare shoulders. Lady Thurzo, a virtuous and faithful woman, lay side by side with Lady Elizabeth Nadazdy-Bathory, the wicked Blood Countess. The sculptor had rendered them equally beautiful in stone—as if awaiting the resurrection. I brushed some leaves and branches from the effigies and looked at the names etched there, the same as my own, and felt nothing.

My father, Julius Kereshtur, MINING ENGINEER, was buried to the left of the main crypt. A square gray stone with his name and profession and the words *aliis vixit* ("he lived for others") marked his grave. The lie made me smile. My father had not lived for others. He had lived only for himself. I laid the bathtub daisies at the foot of the stone and turned away.

The dilapidated cemetery squatted under the dark purple sky like a flayed skin. I had once considered being a surgeon. Human skin reminded me of parchment.

What was I doing here? I felt no sorrow, compassion, or regret. My feelings were as dead as the slabs of stone that secured the remains of my ancestors.

The dirty light already filled every nook and cranny of the pointlessly huge room when the cheerful knock at the door brought me wincing out of a nightmare. My iron bedstead was being tossed by a storm in a yellow sea. An empty bottle of Jack Daniel's on the nightstand reminded me that I had toasted the entire gallery of my galloping ancestors until nearly 4 A.M.

Teresa stood there, an undeserved vision of sweetness and light, in an open pea coat with an embroidered peasant scarf around her neck. She looked so much like her mother, my heart stopped. There was the red hair, the black eyes with the gold sparkles in their depths, the crooked smile . . . yet she was only a girl.

I kissed her long, impatient fingers smelling faintly of tobacco and felt time stand still. The touch of my lips to her warm, young skin brought back Eva.

No, you old fool, she is not Eva. This is 1993, not 1955.

Not embarrassed in the slightest by the rumpled state of my pajamas, my unshaven face, or my bloodshot eyes, Teresa said that she would wait outside the door while I dressed. A quick glance at the Jack had clued her in.

It was breakfast for me and lunch for her at a small restaurant. I ordered a bottle of red. After two glasses I was infinitely more capable of benign attention. I turned the beam of it toward the girl, who did not, after all, resemble her mother all that much.

Teresa told me about herself. She didn't know her father very well. Eva had divorced him when she was only three years old, and he had left the country and was now an agronomist in South America. Her mother had told her about me, she said, and she had often found it strange that the men Eva loved all left the country. One other boyfriend of her mother's left Hungary only two months after they began living together.

Teresa had spent all her summers at her grandmother's in a small village in the south of Hungary. She too, like Imre, had studied history at Matthias Corvinus University. That is where they'd met. She had joined a resistance group shortly before the fall of the Communists. Imre had been the group's leader.

Three Gypsy violins wailed across the checkered tablecloths, making it difficult to hear. At the end of each song, one of the Gypsies came to the tables, and the patrons slapped banknotes to his sweaty forehead. Spicy smoke from frying meats drifted past. There was something intimate about this ancient Budapest restaurant, like the smell of one's family. People had eaten here for one whole century, lived, and died, left their scrawl on the wooden tables, the benches, the scratched plates, bent forks. Over steaming dishes of paprika-red stews and eye-stinging soups they had fallen in love, parted, argued politics, betrayed one another. All this human activity had created a unique aura, a mixture of lassitude, sentiment, passion, violence. This was national life at its best, and it all somehow became concentrated in the slender girl before me, the daughter of the woman I once loved. Teresa exuded the essence of Hungarian life, in the best sense.

Her speech was colorful, laced with phrases learned from her grandmother. I could hear both the country accents and the wisdom of folktales in her voice, which became happier and more careless the more wine she drank. But sad notes crept into it now and then, particularly when we talked about her mother.

They had just become close when her mother fell ill. She now visited her every week at the hospital and they sat together.

"To tell the truth, I don't know what my mother thinks. I talk to her. Sometimes we hold hands. She does not speak. I tell her about my life, but I don't know if she hears me."

"She hears you," I said. "The Eva I remember heard everything, even when she seemed to be far away."

Teresa looked at me quizzically for a moment, then

took me in with her deep eyes. "You really did love my mother . . ."

"Yes," I said. "Why do you doubt?"

"There is a story my grandmother told me. I hope you won't be offended . . ."

"No," I reassured her. "Go ahead."

"The story goes that there are certain women who are immortal. They are a species of witches, vampires, called *virkolak* . . . You can tell them because they have red hair and three nipples, one just below the other two, above the navel. They are born this way, but they don't know who they are. One day they stop speaking and become still as statues. They remain like this for many years, sometimes forever, until a man who loves them shows up. When he comes he must sacrifice something that is dearest to the *virkolak* . . . After that, the woman comes back to life."

"What happens to the man?" I asked, trying to smile.

"No one knows," Teresa said, and laughed impishly.

It wasn't very funny. Eva had, indeed, three nipples, one above the navel. But then, of course, her daughter must have known this.

"Do you believe this story?"

"Oh, I believe in living for the moment," she said, and drained her glass. After a pause she added, "And for Hungary!"

I drained my glass too.

I learned also from Teresa that although Imre might be considered what people call a boyfriend, he was more like a friend and someone she respected as a future leader. She was more attached, in truth, to one of her professors, who was more of a mother to her than Eva had ever been. Her name was Lilly Hangress.

I was startled at the mention of this name. I knew

who Prof. Lilly Hangress was. She had written a biography of my ancestress Elizabeth Bathory.

Professor Hangress, Teresa told me, was the daughter of the prime minister of Hungary's first Communist government. On her mother's side she came from one of Hungary's most distinguished Protestant families. At the university she had been surrounded by a coterie of young girls, who cooked and did her laundry for her. Several of them, including Teresa, boarded at her large apartment. When Teresa first became attracted to Professor Hangress's subject, she had been put to a series of tests to prove her loyalty. One time she was locked in the professor's study for a whole day and night and not allowed to leave until she finished translating an entire Latin text of the letters of Saint Catherine.

Teresa laughed when she told me this, but at the time she had been unable to sleep for a week. Many of the girls in Lilly Hangress's entourage had rings under their eyes from lack of sleep. She was an exacting but lovable mistress.

"A little like Elizabeth Bathory," I said.

"Maybe," said Teresa, "but she didn't kill any of us."

Professor Hangress's book on Bathory had been badly received by the critics. The historian had sought to debunk most of what had previously been believed about the Blood Countess. The conclusion of the book was that Bathory had been innocent, the victim of a particularly skillful witch-hunt.

"Is that what you believe?" I asked Teresa.

"No," she said, "I think that Elizabeth Bathory is protected by many Hungarian historians because of some secret. From what I have read, she was a true monster. If anything, she did not receive the punishment she deserved."

I didn't quite understand. Did she mean that her

crimes were being kept secret because they reflected badly on Hungary?

"Yes, but not because of her crimes. Every nation has criminals. It's something else. Another secret." Teresa laughed. "I don't know it. Maybe the countess really found out the secret of eternal youth. Maybe she killed young girls and found out something that works to keep one young forever."

"You'll never need it," I said gallantly, and felt immediately stupid. I have always disliked the easy flattering manner of European men.

The splintered gold light of the lanterns in the old Pest restaurant played on Teresa's face. I became unaccountably sad watching her. "Nothing in Hungary is a mere historical curiosity!" I said, refilling her glass. "If Bathory killed all the virgins in your villages, virginity must be a curse."

Teresa shrugged. "There is something about Countess Bathory that speaks to us now. Maybe it's all this nationalism, with its sixteenth-century symbols, all this medieval kitsch . . ."

That was smart. And tactful. Despite my light head, I knew myself. I had an indefinite dread of young women. Literal age had perhaps less to do with it than a certain provocative girlishness—barely conscious sometimes—that distressed me. It was here, present in Teresa, as palpable as the cigarette smoke in the air.

In truth, my ancestress interested me less than Teresa's mother. But this was a painful subject for her. And yet it seemed to me that even when we were speaking about the ancient countess or about her history professor, we were still, somehow, speaking about Eva.

Nonetheless I pursued the subject, if only because it made me seem like a good student of Teresa and Imre's reeducation program.

"How can I find documents about Elizabeth Bathory?"

"That should be easy. I work part-time at the national archive. Come by tomorrow morning and I will help you find all that you want to read."

I told Teresa a little unessential bit about myself, about my newly found nostalgia for the Budapest of my childhood, about my obscure desire to resolve something in my past. And then I asked her about the Megyerys and Saint Stephen's Knights.

"Politics!" she said contemptuously.

"I had thought that politics is the reason why you admire Imre . . ."

"Oh, no," she said. "I admire him because he will make a handsome leader. They will put him on stamps and coins. I couldn't care less about his *programs* . . ."

"Do you love him?"

Teresa gave me a brief coquettish glance, lit a cigarette, and blew two smoke rings before she answered.

"He is a terrible lover."

I was flattered by her confidence, but it made me anxious.

"Tomorrow after I come to see you at the national archive, I am going to visit your mother. Is there anything I should know?"

"Take her a shawl. She is always cold, and she always loses her shawls. If you are the one . . ." Teresa stopped and regarded me probingly. "Maybe she'll come back and live forever."

After our repast, tipsy and quite unsettled, I took her home in a taxi. Teresa lived in a monstrous Stalinist-vintage building that had once served as a training school for cadres of the state security police. It reminded me of the Hungary of my youth, a uniformly depressing place. After she got out of the taxi I watched her being swallowed by the dark mouth of a creaky steel gate.

The Hungarian State Archive in Buda is an immense building occupying several city blocks, a massive and forbidding fortress in the bowels of which lie the records of centuries of imperial and royal history. Sieges, occupations, wars, and politics have unsettled this building time after time. The pockmarks of bullets and the small craters of cannonballs dot its facade with an intricate map, a true guide to Hungarian history.

It wasn't far from here, Your Honor, in Moscow Square, that my pals and I listened to the roar of Soviet tanks climbing the hill. We had been up all night stuffing rags into the mouths of bottles filled with gasoline. In our imaginations we had seen the tanks burst into flames, the soldiers surrendering. But when the metal monsters roared into view, their massiveness frightened us. But we felt heroic. We had been trained to recognize historic moments and told that these moments would give birth to true heroes. We wanted more than anything else to join that selfless, idealistic parade that made Hungarian history worth recalling. Those hundreds of heroes, fighting lost causes, called from their romantic aeries with golden trumpets . . .

When one of my Molotov cocktails made contact with a tank and burst into flames, I felt an undescribable mixture of happiness and abandon. The blue-and-red flames licked the side of the steel beast for a moment and then went out, leaving only a dark stain. The next moment it began raining bullets around me, a rhythmic rain like hail on a tin roof. I rolled on the cobblestones, away from the fire, feeling as if I were flying. I imagined that I had big, clumsy wings I still had to master. Just as I was about to open them wide and begin to soar, I brushed something warm and wet. I stopped only long enough to see what it was: the severed, bloody hand of my friend Gabor. I recognized it because I had admired his black walnut ring many times. Gabor himself lay dead a few meters away. My wings folded and disappeared. I wasn't flying any longer. I was simply fleeing. Fleeing from Soviet bullets and my best friend's hand.

This took place in the square in front of the national archive, close to the recorded deeds of Hungary's other heroes. Their ghosts must have looked out the windows. It must have been like looking in the mirror. After all, modes of dying are quite similar, notwithstanding my ancestors' efforts to expand the repertoire. Some of the pockmarks on the facade of the national archive had come, no doubt, from the burst of Russian fire that killed Gabor, severed his hand, and broke my wings.

The archive looked peaceful now, but I knew that the documents stored within had been invoked and used to justify and to continue the violence that periodically and inevitably shakes my little country. The papers lying in deceptive repose there on their shelves and in their cabinets have been moved, sealed, carted away, hidden, found, returned, displayed, waved before mobs, kissed by winners and losers. Some of them had traveled to Vienna, Prague, and Moscow before returning home to continue their subterranean work.

Behind the sculptured doors with their huge brass knobs were tomblike rooms lit only by the dim light that managed to sneak in through the stained-glass windows, now uniformly gray and dirty. Lugubrious-faced gnomes in soft slippers moved noiselessly through ceiling-high stacks of ledgers and wooden drawers. The interior of the archive, with its gloomy frescoes and reliefs depicting great moments in Hungarian history (coronations and humiliations), had the structure and consistency of a nightmare. This was the style of building inside of which the clerk Franz Kafka once worked, extrapolating from its bowels a vision of an infinitely depressing world of connecting passages, mirroring rooms, and infinite hallways. The Austro-Hungarian bureaucracy had been a punctilious, record-keeping world. Whatever the horrors, no matter how great the outrages, records were kept!

Happily, I bumped into Teresa before the building could swallow me in its web of horror and madness. She was on the grand staircase to the third floor. We nearly collided as she flew down breathlessly with a sheaf of papers under her arm.

Teresa wore a flower-print dress and sandals this day. Her shoulders were tan, and there wasn't a trace of makeup on her mischievous face. She didn't look so much like Eva now. She looked like a delinquent adolescent, the kind of girl that hangs out with boys and smokes cigarettes while skipping history class.

I liked her very much, all for herself. Her bright energy seemed distinctly out of place in the funereal environs of the national archive. But she had "temporarily bad news" for me, as she put it.

She had been unable to find any records pertaining to Countess Elizabeth Bathory. She had made careful notes, using Hungarian books of archival data concerning the countess. One of these books, written by her teacher Lilly Hangress, noted the Elizabeth Bathory "inquest records" in "Thurzo archive, f. 28," meaning the file containing folio 28 of the Hungarian palatine's papers. She had also noted the archival numbers for Elizabeth Bathory's letters to her son; numbers for her mother-in-law Ursula Nadazdy's letters; numbers for the correspondence between the palatine Thurzo and King Matthias II about the Bathory case. None of these things were where they should have been.

Teresa led me to the room containing the records of

the latter part of the sixteenth century. A languid assistant with the demeanor of one who had not slept in ages —or who, *au contraire,* had spent four decades sleeping —guided us softly (he was wearing paper slippers) through the layers of ledgers until he found the catalog of the Thurzo archive. Written in the spidery writing of another era, it pointed the way to another ledger. We floated from ledger to ledger until we came to their apparent end, but there was no mention of Countess Bathory.

"The Jews," whispered the languid employee. "They've hidden everything!"

"Why?" I said.

He gave no answer, only a look that said, "If you don't know, you must be a Jew." Oh, I'd forgotten.

We undertook a circular journey through several assistants in different rooms, always with the same result. All the archive assistants shrugged their shoulders helplessly with a look of sorrow in their eyes, behind which I caught both a glint of incomprehension at my American impatience and hidden amusement at my predicament. Teresa always introduced me as Drake, an American journalist, but it would have made little difference if I had told them my given name. The inertia of the bureaucrats steeped in the long siesta of Communism, combined with willful meanness and perhaps deliberate obstruction, was permanent. As in a fairy tale, we kept returning and advancing deeper and deeper into the bowels of the Hungarian archives, slaying soft paper dragons, never getting anywhere.

Finally Teresa said that she knew a better place than the archive for traces of my famous ancestress. This disappearance of documents was a mystery that she intended to pursue in the next few days. Meanwhile we could be better employed. It was already past lunchtime when we left the gloomy building.

It was a beautiful sunny day, though cold. We walked among the oblivious tourists training their cameras on pigeons atop the statues of knights. The saints perched on the spires of the church looked fixedly at one another over the heads of the throng. The imperial eagle of the Hapsburgs loomed over one of the buildings in the square. Budapest wears history the way a dandy wears clothes. I was glad for the moment to be just a tourist, with a beautiful girl at my side.

While sipping a cup of sweet Turkish coffee and peeling an orange, I felt something draw me to look up to my left. At first I saw only the rays of the sun setting fire to the gold dome of a building standing there detached from the others. Then as my eyes adjusted, I spotted it: above the wooden doors secured by iron belts, the Bathory dragon was swallowing his tail, looking at me.

I laughed out loud.

Teresa asked me what was funny. I pointed to our coat of arms and said, "I will never be alone in this country!"

And, seemingly to confirm this, Teresa led me directly to the Thurzo Museum, site of my adolescent agony. This is where she intended to show me traces of my famous ancestress.

The museum was much busier than it had been in my day. Schoolchildren led by fresh-faced young teachers went noisily through the galleries, pointing with glee to the naked angels on the ceilings and the breasts of Madonnas.

The torture room was their favorite, though. They laid themselves down on the racks; they rattled the rusted chains jutting from the walls; they tried to lift the crushing ball. More than one of them tried to fathom the iron maiden, who stood closed now, her mechanism jammed. An overpowering smell of rust came from her.

Teresa explained everything enthusiastically. I didn't have the heart to tell her that I knew everything in here like the contents of my living room. How could I have told her that the rusting iron maiden being climbed by schoolchildren had once pierced her mother's flesh, mixing her blood with my sperm?

Since my day, the Thurzo had added only one section of possible interest to me, a room dedicated to Stephen Bathory, prince of Transylvania, later king of Poland.

Stephen Bathory intrigued me because there was a family resemblance between us. The large portrait of the Transylvanian in the Thurzo had the intense black eyes of all the Bathorys, the characteristic drooping mustaches, and the elongated skull that I had always thought held some unknown information, like the locked memory of a computer. One day I was going to find it. Perhaps it contained nothing more than my misplaced affections. The first thing women notice about me is this extension of skull that hangs like a ledge at the back of my head.

Stiffly dressed in chest armor and tights, with his hand on a huge sword, Stephen stared at me with a look of supreme disdain, extreme nearsightedness, or artistic clumsiness. "OK," I told him, "*you* should try living in New York!"

Stephen Bathory, prince of Transylvania, Elizabeth's cousin, collected chamber pots. Eccentric like all the Bathorys, Stephen had been fond of these vessels, some of which were mislabeled variously as soup tureens, cooking containers, or ceremonial cups. One of them stood on lion paws, with grotesque faces carved on its sides. A fine porcelain pot displayed five painted heads of idiots, a classic illustration of excessive tempers. I tried to imagine what it must have been like to squat on such a monster and to see the huge bumpy foreheads, the receding chins, and the oversized ears of these medieval fools between one's legs.

One of Teresa's college projects had been to catalog these objects. "The whole country was turning into shit," she explained, "and here I was cataloging chamber pots. It was a political commentary, but they couldn't arrest me for it."

What do you know. She had her mother's sense of humor. I laughed. "Which one's the best?"

Her favorite was a transparent glass urn with delicately painted nude figures of chunky maidens with animal heads. "This one," she said, "I used one time when we received a package of toilet paper from my father in South America." For most of the Communist era, toilet paper was an unattainable luxury.

Documents in the Stephen Bathory collection included a log of expenditures for the year 1593, wherein it was revealed that the purchase of ten Arabian horses had cost the prince forty ducats. Gifts in the amount of thirty ducats had been dispatched to King Matthias, Pasha Bey of the Turkish Porte, Emperor Maximilian, and Ladies E. Bathory, Susanna Forgach, Ilona Thurzo. Wine in the amount of six hundred liters had been exchanged with the Polish ambassador for an unspecified quantity of weapons.

Among letters written by Stephen Bathory to his noble cousins in Hungary was a brief message dispatched by Stephen to Elizabeth Bathory in 1610, during the time of her imprisonment. He urged his "dearest cousin" to bear "the blows of fortune" with grace because the time would soon come when "injustice will be punished and righteousness set to rights."

The letter was in Latin. Teresa translated it and told me that it was a well-known but controversial document. Some scholars had taken the business about "righteousness" being "set to rights" to mean that Stephen and

Elizabeth hatched a plan to help her escape justice. Others, however, did not think that an offer of asylum was meant. They thought that the sympathy offered therein was merely formulaic, following the courtly customs of an age rich in polite subterfuge.

"She could have escaped anytime she wanted to," Teresa said. "She stayed because she believed that she had been unjustly treated and that the truth would help free her."

I wasn't sure what truth we were discussing. From what I knew, Countess Bathory had been imprisoned within her castle at Cahtice by her cousin, the palatine Thurzo, pending investigation of allegations against her. If she had planned to escape, it would have proven her guilt. Stephen would have had little interest in helping her to escape. On the other hand, they may have shared certain secrets that Stephen wanted to keep.

I was impressed by Teresa's knowledge of the Thurzo Museum and asked her why she had specialized in early modern history.

"Lilly Hangress. I adore her."

"Why did Imre choose the nineteenth century?"

"Oh, that's another story," said Teresa. "I will tell it to you if you promise never to let him know that you know."

I promised.

"He fell in love with Nietzsche and Wagner, you see. His infatuation began on his eighteenth birthday when his father gave him two books and a record album, Nietzsche's *So Spoke Zarathustra* and *The Will to Power,* and Wagner's *Ring* cycle. He listened to the *Ring* cycle while reading these prewar editions and experienced, so he says, a sublime intoxication that raised him immediately above his unsuspecting contemporaries, who often mouthed the name of Nietzsche in the cafés without having read a word by him. If he didn't understand most of what Nietzsche wrote, it was no great deal. The name alone and the fact of possessing the forbidden treasures were sufficient to erase the shame of adolescent acne and a certain slowness of wit that left him in the shadow of some of his brighter classmates."

I laughed, but Teresa said: "There is more. His ecstasy of plunging into the forbidden texts was not diminished by the fact that the bookplates in these books from his father read *ex libris Rosenthal.* Imre thought that was a small mystery, compared to the exalted grandeur of reading, which became even more majestically elevated by Wagner's tragic strains."

As Teresa told me this I could see Imre Megyery, fueled by the will to power and charged by the intensity of Nordic myth, rising from his father's worn fauteuil to challenge destiny head on. Though it could not have been clear to him what that destiny was or when it would arrive. What *was* clear was that both books and the *Ring* album had belonged to Rosenthal, whoever *he* was.

The mystery was solved, Teresa told me, some months later when his father, who brought home more books and records belonging variously to Rosenthal, Perlmutter, and Bernstein, explained that a campaign was under way in the Party to purge some of the "Trotskyite," "cosmopolitan" elements who had escaped detection so far. That all of them were Jews was not surprising. As his father said more than once, everyone had had it "up to here" with "the treachery of Jews."

Teresa said that Klaus once showed both of them where "up to here" was by passing his hand over his throat like the blade of a knife. That such a gesture should have been made once more on old Judenstrasse did not surprise me. As long as there were going to be Jews on Judenstrasse, men like Klaus Megyery would extort them for everything. Before killing them. That a young man like Imre would accept such doings was no surprise either. He respected authority. He respected his father. What did surprise me was that Teresa told me these things matter-of-factly. History, to her, contained nothing unusual. Horrific, perhaps. Astonishing, no.

"You know," I said, more testily perhaps than I intended—after all, it wasn't her fault—"more than one million Hungarian Jews were sold to the Nazis for trucks during the war. Of that one million, fewer than ten thousand survived the death camps. What was once a thriving Jewish community in Budapest is now reduced to the ghostly presence of a mere few hundred."

"Those few hundred," said Teresa, "must have been cosmopolitan Trotskyites!"

Such cynicism was hard to swallow. It didn't jibe with her otherwise innocent attempts to appear sophisticated and at ease in the world. Perhaps it wasn't personal. Easy, flip cynicism was a mark of her generation. It was an overreaction. But in Americans it was brought about by ignorance of history. In Europeans it was a bitter thing.

Teresa sensed my displeasure before I even said anything.

"I'm sorry," she said. "Sometimes I forget that not everyone knows Imre."

That was true. Still, I found it difficult to see how Imre Megyery, a young man born and raised in a world without Jews, could be a full-fledged anti-Semite. The poisoned flower of this hatred was only partly his father's work. The muddy grounds it sprouted from layered his very soul. I regretted now having felt warm toward him. I resolved to look him straight in the eyes when I next saw him, to express the revulsion I felt.

Teresa and I walked through the museum in silence for a time. It was just about when I had made up my mind to leave that we came before a life-size portrait of

Elizabeth Bathory. She loomed suddenly from between two windows, rigidly held within the folds of a court dress. Her face was white and flat like a sheet of paper, but her black eyes were filled with cold fire.

Elizabeth Bathory's eyes, which even the bad Genoese painter could not help but render with feeling, constellated the famous *Chronicles of Andrei de Kereshtur,* often giving the impression that they peered from the pages. Andrei de Kereshtur's *Chronicles* began: "Arpad, the first Hungarian king, Elizabeth Bathory's ancestor, was said to have set fire to his enemies simply by looking at them." And they ended: "Dorothea, her maidservant, confessed that 'all she had to do was look at me with her eyes and I was without will of my own.' Darvulia, her wet nurse, admitted that she had been fascinated by Elizabeth's eyes 'since she was an infant at my bosom.' Forgive me, Lord, for what I have written down, because I, Andrei de Kereshtur, humble clerk of the Bathorys, have loved my Lady's eyes and feel them upon me even as I write, fierce like Arpad's. Rest her soul, Lord Jesus, and gently close her eyes."

I knew that all biographers based their opinion of Elizabeth's beauty solely on this painting. Despite the poor execution, Elizabeth's eyes burned urgently across the ages, filled with a plea that moved me. They sat in a face that was badly rendered, atop a body clad in a stiff and unrevealing dress. But those eyes, focused directly on my own, were devastating.

If the flesh into which they were set had had any artistic life to it, the effect would have been profound. The painter had known that his humble gift was unable to render the entire person before him, so he had concentrated on her face, giving it a pleasing oval shape that accentuated the power of her eyes. Her lips were thin and tightly drawn, her nose was slightly flared in displeasure. Only her pearls were rendered with care, shining from the surface of the canvas with a radiance of their own.

The itinerant Genoese who made his living traveling from castle to castle painting highly flattering portraits of nobles must have heard stories about the famous Hungarian countess. By 1603, when the portrait was painted, rumors of the dark doings of Countess Bathory of Hungary had reached as far as the Turkish Porte.

A clerk in the vizier's office negotiating the release of Kharmal Bey from the Bathory dungeons wrote confidentially to his superior: "If monetary negotiations fail, we may turn to the crimes of Nadazdy's wife, Elizabeth, and spread them through the villages in the hope of an uprising."

If the Genoese had heard of his subject's gruesome reputation, he gave no hint of it while painting her body. But when he painted her eyes, he must have looked into them. What he saw there, whether they represented his fear or something unfathomable in his model, had come through the centuries.

By 1603, few girls dared to present themselves at Castle Sarvar, Castle Kereshtur, Lockenhaus, or any of the other fortresses of the Bathorys. Rumors of evil doings were rampant. The Genoese must have known that she was immensely rich—he hoped to be handsomely paid for the portrait. He must have known also that she was one of the most powerful women in Europe, the financier of many of the king's and the emperor's war campaigns. He would not have been surprised by the extent of her power. Elizabeth Bathory was a powerful woman in a time of powerful women. She was a contemporary of Queen Elizabeth. Educated in the highest traditions of the late Renaissance, she was the absolute ruler of her domains, which were situated at the center of Christian Europe. If it was true that she tortured and killed, bathed in blood, and ate the flesh of young girls, these charges had to be carefully considered by those who would judge her. Her castles had strong garrisons of hundreds of men who were sworn to defend her. Her corner of Europe was soaked in the blood of countless commoners who had not done the bidding of their nobles. Death was the common punishment for almost any infraction, even petty theft. Peasant rebellions were suppressed so severely that they passed into folktales because straightforward accounts were too gruesome to tell. The intervening centuries since her death in 1613 were not considerably gentler, despite the flourishing of learning, art, writing, and music that we now know as Western civilization.

My ancestress had lived in the same Europe where four centuries later one could hear the music of Wagner floating over the gas chambers of Nazi death camps. High European culture was in no way an impediment to the physical crassness of torture and butchery. Perhaps they were of one piece: they needed each other to exist. Looking on her now, I felt convinced that my ancestress held keys to much more than the simple question of beauty.

I felt Teresa's warm touch on my shoulder. Just in time.

"What do you think of this portrait?" I asked her, startled from my deep reverie.

Teresa said, fearing perhaps to offend me, "Only a great lady would wear such a dress."

I said: "Only a very bad painter would render such a dress while avoiding the person inside it. Elizabeth Bathory is not inside her portrait. She has escaped, my friend. She is in the world somewhere, murdering virgins and poisoning the souls of innocents like Imre Megyery with hatred greater than anything I can imagine. Our job is to find her."

"Our job? I don't understand."

"I am speaking metaphorically, of course. We must destroy what she *represented* . . ."

But I wasn't at all sure that that's what I had meant. For a moment I had truly meant the person Elizabeth Bathory, not some metaphor based on her deeds.

"I don't believe you," said Teresa.

I looked into her suddenly frightened eyes. "Isn't it funny? Your job is to find the aristocrat in me, and mine is to kill it—as soon as you find it, naturally."

I was convinced at that moment that this was my mission.

But I was troubled by something that I could barely articulate even to myself. The eyes of the lady in the portrait had come briefly to life, and they had felt more familiar to me than my own.

I took Teresa's arm and left the Thurzo. I asked her if she wanted to come with me to visit her mother.

"No," she said. "You go. Maybe you're her knight."

Horoarspital is as gloomy as its name, Your Honor.

Visiting hours were between four and five in the afternoon. It was five-thirty. But I bribed an attendant in a dirty gray coat to let me in. I was shown past dingy doors along a long hallway. The attendant unlocked one of them with a key. I turned the knob and found myself face to face with the love of my life. She was sitting on the edge of a narrow bed, looking at the door as if expecting me.

It was true. The woman before me was considerably younger than she would have been had time taken its toll. While not quite the skinny girl that lived in my memory, life had not treated her badly. It had rounded her face a bit, given some weight to her breasts, loosened her always ready shoulders. Still, this was undeniably Eva, my adolescent love.

But she was also not Eva. I closed the door behind me and sat on the edge of the narrow cot, facing her. She regarded me without expression, a cloud on the sky of her inner vision. But I felt within my violently beating heart that somewhere within that familiar form was my girl. Her eyes looked on me without surprise, steadily, but I thought I saw behind them a quick white flash, as if someone was signaling with a handkerchief from the depths of a well.

I put out my hand and took one of hers, which lay limply in her lap. She let it fall inside mine like a dead bird. I rubbed the tips of her fingers to elicit some recognition. Her hand became warmer, but her fingers did not tighten their grip. Only her gaze, steady and serene, continued to rest upon me as if I were not real but wholly contained within her mental universe.

I looked deeply into her eyes, but for the longest time they reflected nothing except my own image. My Eva, the lively, nonstop-talking, chain-smoking Gypsy, was hiding somewhere in this eerily preserved body.

"Eva," I whispered, "come speak to me. I have missed you very much."

Hoping for a glimpse of that flash I had first seen in the depths of her pools, I whispered to her some of the things that I had been telling her in my mind for years.

I told her how in 1956, in the refugee camp in Austria where Mari and I spent six months before being allowed to emigrate to the United States, all the talk had been of return. The feverish, sleepless, half-starved inmates spent days and nights fantasizing about the glorious return after the American intervention that everyone believed to be imminent. I lay on my bunk in the communal dormitory listening to bloodthirsty scenarios of vengeance and dreams of power. My bunkmates talked of going back to kill Communists and Jews—no matter that there were many Jews among them—about burning down the houses of party officials, making bonfires of the red books, cleansing the Pannonian plain of foreign vermin, returning Hungary to its noble destiny, its former greatness, et cetera, et cetera.

I had at first been carried away by such talk, but as the days dragged on and it became apparent that no American intervention was in the making and that even our acceptance into the U.S. was by no means a certain thing, I began to wake up as if from a dream. I started to doubt not only the bloodcurdling rhetoric of my countrymen but their sanity.

Worst of all, I found it difficult to talk to Mari, who, like the others, raved enthusiastically about the great days ahead. Her naïveté wouldn't have bothered me so much if she had shown me some affection. But the entire time we shared a bunk in Austria she refused to let me touch her. "They will hear us," she would say, drawing away; no matter that all around us, couples made love noisily and in as uninhibited a manner as if they were alone in a field of flowers.

How I missed you, Eva, at those times! I imagined your lithe, Gypsy body trembling with impatience, and I berated myself for choosing the wrong girl.

I whispered these and other things to the statue before me. Now and then in the course of my incoherent babble I thought I saw my girl's white handkerchief signaling me. I did not notice that it had gotten dark. I drew Eva's pliant and unresponsive form to me and wept softly into her hair. I babbled on and on about my longing for her.

I am not exactly sure when I put my arms around her and felt the points of her breasts. They burned into my skin. My weeping and compassion changed to desire. I pulled her hospital gown over her head. She neither assisted nor resisted me. I took off my clothes quickly, as if I were in a dream. I watched Eva's naked body in the dim electric light coming in from the hallway. I saw with great clarity her third nipple, some seven inches above her navel, almost under her left breast. She reclined at my urging when I took her in my arms. I lay on top of her and entered her easily. All of my years of desire, my memories, my image of our youth, came flooding irresistibly through me. I thought that I felt something tug at me from within her, and I released everything in me. But at that moment, the joy that should have been mine wasn't: I felt chilled, as if I had just sent my sperm across time to someone else. And her eyes opened wider and I saw, in the semidarkness, the flashing of a malevolent brilliance that I recognized. I had seen it earlier: it had been in the eyes of Elizabeth Bathory's portrait at the Thurzo.

Someone else lived inside Eva now, someone who had snatched my seed. Wherever Eva was, this had not been the way to find her. I withdrew quickly. The woman on the bed lay there, spread obscenely, regarding me steadily with that maddening gaze. Forgive me, Your Honor, but this is the first time that the thought of murder came to me.

I felt guilty and ashamed. I wiped her with a corner of the sheet on her own bed. I tried to tuck her in but succeeded only partly. I wanted to get out of there as quickly as I could. I was afraid of my own murderous impulse, and I was terrified of the woman on that hospital bed. Just before fleeing, I touched her cheek. It was cold, like the marble of my ancestors' tomb.

I am not quite sure how I succeeded in getting dressed and returning to the Gellart, where I drank myself silly once more.

SARVAR CASTLE WAS VERY DIF-
ferent from Kereshtur. Everything exuded
an air of cared-for elegance. The flagstones in the floors
of the salons were polished shiny. Italian paintings hung
in galleries. The portraits of the Nadazdy family
stretched along the main gallery leading to the chapel.
Marble satyrs and nymphs after the Florentine fashion
crouched in niches along the grand staircases. Well-
maintained tapestries hung over the balconies encircling
the main halls. They depicted the triumphs of Thomas
Nadazdy in diplomacy and war. The Nadazdy coat of
arms was woven into the tablecloths and embroidered
on the servants' spotless livery. It was also carved in
stone over fireplaces and gates. It shone in polished
gold from the doors of the carriages. Everywhere Elizabeth went, doors opened silently and servants stood at
the ready. This was a well-maintained and carefully supervised household. It would be difficult for her to get
away as she used to in her carefree days at Kereshtur.

Her intended husband, Franz Nadazdy, was at
school in Vienna, where he would stay until the end of
the year. Elizabeth was disappointed. She would have
liked to meet right away the man to whom she had been
pledged. Meanwhile, she would remain under the tutelage of her mother-in-law. Ursula Nadazdy received her
the morning after her arrival. By then, Elizabeth was
ready, having slept, bathed, and put on her prettiest
gown. The audience was formal. Ursula asked her many
questions, which the girl endeavored to answer modestly. Her future mother-in-law was most interested in

the state of her education, which she seemed to find unsatisfactory. When she heard that Elizabeth had not yet learned to play an instrument, she exclaimed, "But, dear, you must begin tomorrow!"

Elizabeth looked doubtful but expressed a possible interest in the harp.

"The harp it shall be!" said Ursula, broaching no further discussion. Ursula was proud of her open mind concerning the instrument of Elizabeth's choice, but she didn't think that the girl had quite grasped the importance of her concession. Ursula had been endeavoring to distance her household from the overly seductive practices of the Roman Catholic church, including its too rich music. While it was still fashionable to employ skilled Italian musicians—Ursula herself employed an Italian harp teacher—the preachers were doing their best to eliminate them and to replace their music with the wholesome new forms recommended by Dr. Martinus Luther. Doctor Luther had denounced the elaborate musical services of the Roman church, substituting hymns, harmony, and singing in unison for the canon style refined beyond the understanding of the people. The good doctor of theology from Wittenberg had nothing against the harp per se, but when he wrote his famous hymn "A Mighty Fortress Is Our God," he imagined that God lived in a castle free of Italian harpists.

Elizabeth was not afraid of her severe mother-in-law-to-be with her fervent educational ideals. She considered herself quite well educated. She had not learned to play a musical instrument because she had disdained all the weak womanly arts customary for young noble girls. Under Silvestri's tutelage she had learned how to read music and had considered geometry and the music of the spheres. These philosophical considerations on the nature of sound seemed to her to transcend the trivial practice of music itself, which was better left to talented serfs, actors, mimes, and singers. For the very same reasons, Elizabeth also disdained knitting, embroidering, and reading romances out loud. She could discourse on Aristotle, but she had little patience for the shameless romances of the minnesingers. For practical skills she had chosen archery, jousting, and sword fighting. She felt quite angry with herself for politely playing along with Ursula when, in truth, she couldn't care less about playing music.

After the regal departure of Ursula Nadazdy, Elizabeth reconnoitered her surroundings. Ursula's spies were everywhere. She hoped to find a map of Sarvar soon in order to learn its secrets. She thanked God for her faithful Darvulia, for Andrei, Teresa, and Lena, and swore to be good to them. She shared a room with Teresa, but Darvulia and Lena had been sent to the servants' quarters in a different part of the castle. She did not know where the notary and the monk were lodged. Before going to sleep, Elizabeth also made a vow to get Darvulia back near her, in the same room, and to find quick and secret ways to reach all her servants.

The harp that Elizabeth was going to learn to play had its own room. She wore the white lace and silk dress she had found laid out for her that morning, a gift from Ursula. The harp room had hundreds of angels flying through it, on frescoes, on tapestries, and on all the embroideries covering the chairs and the window seats. The ceiling had been painted a pale blue like the sky, and plump angels frolicked on the clouds. Ten human-sized painted angels occupied the entire wall behind the splendid harp, which, polished and tuned, smelled of lemon oil. The harp looked as if it was waiting for the angels behind it to take turns at its strings. The angels themselves, their hefty, richly feathered wings folded, were engaged in various tasks. One was playing the tamboura; another already had a small harp between its long-fingered hands; one clasped a book; another blew into an S-shaped trumpet; another beat a small drum . . . Elizabeth had never seen so many angels together at once.

"You are an angel among angels, Signorina!" a musical falsetto trilled behind her.

Elizabeth turned to encounter the elegant and trim figure of Maestro Gozzoli, her harp teacher. Benezzo Gozzoli was a Genoese who had come to Hungary in search of his father, the philospher-alchemist Silvestri Gozzoli, who was said to have found the philosopher's stone. Benezzo was not moved entirely by love of his long-absent father, though this is what he told everyone. In actuality, he was on a mission from the Genoese despot Torrini to find out if Silvestri had indeed found the philosopher's stone and, if he had, to bring him home presto to make gold for Genoa, which was his citizen's duty. The mines of Hungary produced so much gold it was generally believed in Europe that an alchemist had succeeded in finding the stone. Nearly every ruler of the day had dispatched spies to the Pannonian plain to discover the mysterious alchemist.

Benezzo found not hair nor hide of his father but continued his search. Meanwhile he earned a living teaching the harp to Hungarian youths, all of whom, male and female, he liked to hold very tightly while guiding their clumsy digits across the heavenly strings. This method had gotten him into a bit of trouble the year before with the young Franz Nadazdy, who did not like being held very tightly and who, furthermore, had neither aptitude nor sympathy for the harp. When Bennezo's arms encircled him Laocoönlike, young Franz simply elbowed the Italian in the stomach so hard that the afflicted harpist could not eat for several days and avoided all human company as well. He certainly avoided Franz, who made a point every time he saw him of caressing the hilt of his sword in a manner both obscenely suggestive and threatening. He was relieved when the boy was sent to school in Vienna.

Benezzo expected no such treatment from the slight girl with the big black eyes. She looked like an angel with the eyes of a Madonna, he explained to her while holding her elbow at a painful angle. There wasn't enough flesh on Elizabeth's bony person for Maestro Gozzoli's taste, so he stayed at what was for him a quite respectable distance while he taught her. But he feared her dead-earnest manner, which she displayed as soon as he called her an angel among angels.

"Maestro," she said, "I have studied angels with the monk Silvestri and I know many of their varieties . . . from cherubim to archangels . . . They are nasty creatures, suspected by many to have brought us the Black Death. Lucifer is the greatest angel, and the rest are his minions!"

Elizabeth smiled her most angelic smile and folded her hands on her lacy white lap. The Italian's face reddened slowly as the full import of what the little girl had said took hold of his mind. The blasphemy bothered him, but he had been startled mostly by *Silvestri,* which was his father's first name. Elizabeth told him that this Silvestri was a learned monk from Florence. Benezzo didn't think that the monk was his father, but he resolved to look into it.

Elizabeth's blasphemous remark on the subject of angels did bother others. After the harp lesson, a rail-thin man with a nose like the beak of a bird of prey appeared in the harp room. The Italian made himself scarce quickly. The man, dressed all in black, looked like a twin of Preacher Hebler. He introduced himself as Pastor Ponikenuz and begged the countess's forgiveness for the intrusion. She granted him pardon, and he came to the point of his visit.

"We do not put much store in the gold-winged angels of the pope. They could never do the Lord's work so laden with gold . . . It is doubtful whether they can even fly, but . . ." Pastor Ponikenuz paused, coughed, and laid a hand on Elizabeth's shoulder. "We must respect the angels of the Lord, because they are not only around us but within us. There are seven angels in every man's body, counting and judging every deed and every word he speaks. When you die—and make no mistake, Countess, you will die one day—they will fly out through the seven openings of the body, carrying their ledgers to God, and by these ledgers you will be judged."

Ponikenuz let his fingers flutter in the air for a moment before letting them come to rest again on Elizabeth's shoulder. The preacher's hand was cold, and she could feel the chill through her dress.

Elizabeth was sufficiently familiar with this view of angels from her lessons with Hebler, who also preached the doctrine of individual responsibility. But she had also heard other opinions. Endeavoring to present a studious and faithful countenance, she replied: "This is undoubtedly so, Pastor, but there are angels outside us as well. At Kereshtur Castle there are angels in our fountains. An angel the size of a small shoe perched on my mother Anna's shoulder when she gave birth to me. Everyone saw it. It is said that every hollow place houses an angel. Once an angel was caught in one of our tapestries. He caught his foot in the gold thread and couldn't get out, but the monk Silvestri unraveled all the thread and freed him . . ."

Ponikenuz raised an impatient finger. "Foul superstition!" he shouted. "The point is, my daughter, that angels are symbols of our duties to God. The rest are demons, spirits, unholy vapors . . . You and I will talk every day after your music lesson. I am going to have a book of the writings of Dr. Martinus Luther on the subject of angels brought to you. You must read it every day, alongside the Bible, until all thoughts of dark angels flee your mind, leaving you clean for the work of the Lord!"

With this admonition, the skeletal bird left the room. Elizabeth heard what she thought was the flapping of dry, black wings behind his back.

Elizabeth wondered how it was that her remark about angels, which she had made to the harpist, had traveled so quickly to reach the ears of the preacher. There had been no one present except her maid Teresa, whom she'd instructed to wait on the other side of the door. Perhaps Teresa had overheard her and repeated the remark to some other maid who then relayed it to the pastor. Elizabeth became convinced this had to be the case. She grabbed Teresa's arm so hard it hurt. She dragged her servant at a frantic pace toward the place she believed their quarters were. Teresa swore up and down that she hadn't heard anything. If her maid was right, Ursula must have had spies listening through secret openings in the room. It was possible. But Elizabeth, still furious, continued to berate her maid.

Teresa was bewildered and alarmed, not so much because her mistress suspected her of carrying tales—she hadn't—but because she felt guilty. In fact, she should have been accused of neglect instead of spying. While her job had been to wait for the countess outside the harp room until the lesson was finished, she had allowed herself to be persuaded by one of the cook's assistants to help pluck a large peacock in exchange for one of its gorgeous feathers. The peacock would be the glazed and decorated centerpiece of the evening meal, but not before its tail was removed in vivo. Peacock feathers had to be plucked this way because they lost their luster once the bird was dead. While Teresa held down the huge kicking bird with her body, lying on it, really, the cook's assistant pulled out its beautiful feathers one by one. It was difficult to know at what point Teresa began feeling an odd sensation about her ankles, then higher, all the way to her upper thighs and between them. Unable to let go of the furious bird imprisoned by the weight of her body, she suffered the odd tickling, protesting only a little less than the peacock. The bird bit her arm and then nearly plucked out one of her eyes. She was scratched and bleeding, but the infuriating tickling went on. By degrees, however, the sensation became not only tolerable but pleasurable. The soft plume that the cook's assistant was deftly maneuvering between her legs made her mad with impatience and pleasure. She let her weight down even harder on the bird while opening her legs just a little for the feather's maddening work. Teresa could barely remember at what point the bird stopped breathing, but it was shortly after she squeezed its neck spasmodically two or three times between her legs.

Teresa was still under the spell of her encounter with the peacock and its feathers as she listened to her mistress's accusations. She threw herself to the ground and began to kiss Elizabeth's lace slippers. Elizabeth stopped, astonished, and took this act of contrition to be proof of guilt. She grabbed a handful of her maid's red hair and yanked. Teresa sprang back to her feet.

"So it was you, unspeakable tincture of nightshade, who repeated what I said about angels!"

Teresa vainly protested her innocence again. Elizabeth, possessed of a strength she didn't know she had, dragged her down a narrow stairway, calling her a poisonous weed, a stinking fish, and a rabid rat all the while. She also administered rather ineffective blows to the maid's bewildered person.

The two girls found themselves at the bottom of the stairs in a round, empty chamber with only one small window near the ceiling. There was barely any room inside, and Elizabeth chased Teresa around with increasing fury until she collapsed from exhaustion. Only then did she look around.

"Where are we?"

Teresa had no idea. The room resembled an empty well. The only objects not made of stone were two iron rings set way above Elizabeth's head and the smoky glass window. While Teresa explained tearfully why she couldn't possibly have been the one who betrayed her to Countess Nadazdy, Elizabeth tried to remember what it was about the empty round room that seemed so familiar. It reminded her of one of the secret passages at Kereshtur. She felt certain that this room must lead to others. She missed being able to slip unobserved from one end of the castle to another to watch the uninhibited lives of her subjects in their rooms. She had to find a map.

At dinner that evening, Ursula gave no indication that she knew anything of Elizabeth's blasphemy. In truth, she was not overly concerned with angels, not even with Lucifer. At the moment, practical considerations were more urgent. There were several guests at the table, including a distant relative of Elizabeth's, an eccentric count from her father's side of the family, just returned from Vienna with unsettling news. He explained that the Turks were gathering forces for a second attempt at conquering the Christian world, but Emperor Maximilian was not preparing an adequate defense. He was preoccupied with his loss of control over the western provinces, particularly the German cities that were succumbing one after another to the teachings of Luther. He seemed unaware of the threat from the east. Hungary was on the front lines of the eventual Turkish assault, and the king's treasury was nearly empty. All the nobles had to unite under the king's banner and fight for Christianity. Now—as at several times in the past two centuries, only more so—the fate of the Christian world was in the hands of the Hungarian knights.

After the count delivered this dire news there was a debate about which fortifications were directly in the path of the Turkish force and had to be reinforced. Ursula thought immediately of Cahtice and Lockenhaus and decided to recall Franz from Vienna to supervise the building of new walls. It was becoming imperative also to raise a new army, a difficult endeavor given the near-open rebellion of the overtaxed burghers and the discontented landholders.

Having finished the discussion of these grave matters, the count begged Ursula to allow Elizabeth's poet, Melotus, to tell a story. The request was granted, and Melotus strode in hugging his lyre.

The glazed peacock Teresa had helped to pluck rested resplendently at the center of the banquet table, his iridescent green-and-blue feathers arranged elegantly about the platter. Teresa, who stood behind Elizabeth ready to do whatever she was told, shuddered involuntarily, imagining which of the plumes had played between her legs that morning. The blue eye in one of them winked at her.

Melotus, greedily eyeing the peacock being distributed on the guests' plates, began by paying elaborate and flowery homage to all the ladies present. He compared Ursula to the sun, held by God in his hands as it warmed every heart in the universe. Her breath was a field of flowers that made every knight within breathing distance into a love slave ready to put his sword at her disposal . . . Ursula cut him short with an impatient wave of her hand, so he turned his fat, moonlike face toward Elizabeth, plucked a string of his lyre, and said, "The crystal goblet full of light that is the Grail stands poised over your lovely head, my lady, ready to pour its drops of fire, beauty, and immortality on your lovely tresses." That was quite a lot, but Melotus had more metaphorical arrows in his quiver. "The ancient goddesses of love have gathered in the forest to weave an enchanted life for you, my lady, and when their weaving is finished the goddesses of wisdom will add their gold thread to the pattern."

At this point Elizabeth, mimicking Ursula, waved her hand in the air to silence him, and everyone laughed.

When at long last Melotus told his story, it contrasted most powerfully with the lightness of his flattering introductions.

"Not long before King Stephen saved our souls by committing them to Christ, the castle of a pagan chieftain stood where Castle Sarvar now stands. This chieftain had seven daughters so beautiful they had to be kept in a seven-sided dark room, because if he let them out, they would eclipse the light of the sun. Because this room was dark, the girls never saw how beautiful they were.

"Once, when the chieftain was away at war, a young man changed himself into a bird and flew into the daughters' room. He brought a torch and a looking glass with him. While the girls stared dumbfounded at their beautiful images in the looking glass, he impregnated them with his seed. Then he flew away.

"When the chieftain returned from war, he found all

his daughters heavy with child, staring helplessly at themselves in the looking glass. The chieftain flew into a terrible rage and swore to kill the man-bird who had ruined his daughters.

"He went to a witch and made a deal with her. If she would bring him the young man, the chieftain would give her one of his daughters as well as her child to do with as she pleased. The witch made a net of her hair and trapped the bird-man when he returned to consort again with the girls. She brought him snared in the net before the chieftain, who cooked the man-bird in a pot. He then let his daughters out of the dark chamber, set the table with seven gold bowls, and had them eat their seducer.

"While they sucked on his bones, not realizing it was he, a flock of black ducks landed on the girls and snatched them by their hair and flew away with them. They flew over a lake and dropped the terrified girls into the living water, where they immediately turned into seven black swans. Their human skins drifted on the water and caught on some rushes at the lake's edge. The witch gathered the skins and took them back to the chieftain, who was mad with grief. She blew over the skins until they became a bowl of living yarn. The witch wove this yarn back into a girl.

"The chieftain was very happy, but the witch said, 'This is the girl you promised me. You still owe me a child.'

"The chieftain didn't know where to find a child, so he offered to impregnate the remaining girl himself. But the girl, whose name was Beautiful Braid, closed her knees to him.

"Finally he gave her a looking glass. Entranced by her own beauty, she submitted to her father and became pregnant. She gave birth to a daughter, who flew away and married the sun. The chieftain died of a broken heart. The witch kept the girl in a stone cell, angry that the promised child had escaped her. In the land where they lived grew lilies shaped like tears.

"Soon after these events, King Stephen came and delivered all the souls to Christ. When all the souls surrendered to Christ, the lilies that were tears became splendid with the joy of redemption. A joyful house—the house of Nadazdy—took root there, and nothing was remembered of the old sorrow except this sad tale."

The assorted company, who had hoped for something more fashionable, a chivalric romance of the Round Table, perhaps, or the story of Tristan and Yseult, was not happy with this folktale. Melotus was quickly sent away without as much as a slice of the now depleted peacock, and acrobats took his place.

Elizabeth was not displeased with the story of the seven sisters. It filled her with wonder and disquiet. How could one girl be woven from seven? Could Darvulia take seven girls and make one? Elizabeth looked about her and imagined that the dining hall had become a loom. She pulled the drunk count, the unsmiling Ursula, and the serving girls like threads into her weaving. She swayed back and forth, pulling them across and up, changing them. She felt a little drunk, as if the cider in her cup had turned to wine.

But she felt uneasy too. Why were the girls "ruined" by consorting with men? She had seen peasant girls beaten and sent back to their villages for dallying with soldiers and grooms, but no one had ever told her that they'd been "ruined." She had never been forbidden to "consort" with anyone. Why were the girls so helpless and obedient? Where was their mother? Why had they been left in the care of such a mean father? She thought of her own father, George, who was like a gentle clown in the shadow of her mother.

It troubled her also that the girls could so happily eat their lover. What did he taste like? What did George Dozsa's flesh taste like to his followers? She tried to think of herself eating a roasted piece of Dozsa, his hand, perhaps. She shuddered. For that matter, what part of Christ's body did she eat at communion? Hebler had insisted that communion *was* Christ's body, and Silvestri, for once, had not objected. The wine that was his blood was easier to swallow. She had no fear of drinking blood; she had often sucked her own from nicks and cuts. But flesh was another matter. To eat the liver, where the soul was, might not be bad at all. But other parts—Christ's baby penis, for instance, which she had seen often in churches . . . or the penis of Christ on the cross, lying under its cloth between the bare legs with the crossed ankles—that was another matter. Perhaps she could just drink the blood. Above Ursula's head was a black crucifix on which a suffering Redeemer offered the wound in his side to feed the faithful. In her mind, Elizabeth kissed the wound in the side of Christ's body and bent her head to drink from it. Saint Catherine had. It tasted sweet and sour like wine, and it filled her with the music of boys' voices. It was Rudolf's choir! Drinking the blood of the Savior caused one to hear the choir of Prince Rudolf!

Did the girls' skins that had drifted off contain their souls? She found it strange that their skins had come off so easily. She had often wondered about this: How is it that our souls are so tiny and our bodies so big? Why was there so much room between the soul and the wall of skin that surrounded it? She had somehow conceived of the idea that a person grew up by having her soul expand so much that it touched all the surfaces of her skin. But then why weren't grown-ups more soulful than children? She fancied sometimes that she could see whether or not someone's soul had touched all that person's skin. Teresa's eyelids and cheeks, for instance, were fully alive because they had been touched by her soul. The backs of her hands were untouched, though— they looked lifeless. Darvulia's breasts were definitely touched by soul. Elizabeth had seen the witch's nipples rise by themselves, emitting tiny flashes of light.

When Elizabeth looked at her future mother-in-law, she saw no part of her skin touched by the soul. If any soul substance reached the surface, it was well hidden by the folds of her impeccably starched dress or the coils of her coiffure. Her own mother, yes, had only patches of soul-touched skin, and, furthermore, they changed day to day. Sometimes her hands were marvelously alive, particularly when she was so angry she looked as though she might strike someone. At other times her hands were dead but her lips were full of life. Elizabeth wanted her own soul to touch every part of her body with its fire, so that it would be impossible for any part of her to become loose and lifeless. She did not want to look into the mirror one day and find that she had become wrinkled and soulless.

Elizabeth felt quite sure that even the girl who'd escaped the witch and the father to marry the sun was not quite safe. What if a stranger came one day while her husband the sun was on his rounds and gave her a looking glass? Would she forget herself and suffer the wrath of her husband?

Elizabeth loved looking glasses. She had three of them. The day would come when she would be the mistress of her own fortune, and on that day she would cover all her walls with looking glasses. The thought of looking at herself in several mirrors at once gave her a strange shiver, as if a butterfly were walking up her silk stocking.

* * *

Teresa had been battered so grievously by the peacock and by Elizabeth that it was difficult for her to conceal her bruises. She had almost succeeded, dressing very carefully so as to cover the ugly marks, when Elizabeth called her name. Elizabeth was propped up on her pillows, watching her maid walk gingerly about.

"How long have you been awake, my lady?" blurted Teresa. She hoped that her mistress had not seen the purple bruise on her left breast.

"I want to see your whole skin," said Elizabeth.

At first Teresa pretended not to understand. Then she fell to her knees begging Elizabeth not to think that her bruises were the result of an amorous tryst. "They are not even caused by a beating of the kind my husband, may he be soon struck by a horse's hoof, used to give me . . ."

Elizabeth told her that she did not care where her bruises came from; she simply wanted to see her whole skin. Teresa stripped away garment by garment the outfit she had so carefully contrived to conceal her bruises. Off came her voluminous skirt, then her corset, then her petticoat, then her pantaloons. At last she stood naked and trembling before the young countess. She was a well-made young woman with firm breasts, full hips, and sturdy buttocks. She covered her breasts with her arms to hide the purple swelling that throbbed on one of them like a dark flower.

Elizabeth studied her dispassionately, then asked her to turn around. Teresa did. There was another swelling on her hip; her back was intricately scratched.

"You look like a tablet of heathen writing," laughed Elizabeth. She asked her to stretch out next to her. Shaking with fear, her maid lay on her back next to her mistress and shut her eyes tight.

There were three things about Teresa that intrigued Elizabeth: her breasts, which unlike her nurse Darvulia's did not hang down to her belly button; her bruises; and the red hair that sprouted in luxuriant abundance between her legs and under her arms. Elizabeth had none of those things. She bent over Teresa and pinched firmly one of her nipples until she cried out.

"I don't have these," she said imperiously.

Teresa swore that it wouldn't be long before her mistress, who was endowed by God with everything else, including wealth and power, would get nipples just like those, and probably bigger.

Next Elizabeth grabbed as much of Teresa's red bush as her hand could hold, and she yanked, repeating peevishly the fact that between her own legs no such growth was yet visible.

This too, swore Teresa, would come in time.

Elizabeth was inclined to believe her. But she wasn't through with her. She poked one of the maid's bruises and once more demanded to know when such would also befall her skinny little body.

"That," shouted Teresa, "is nothing to wait for! My lady should lie on top of a peacock as it's being plucked!"

That was not an entirely satisfactory answer, so Elizabeth whacked her once more across the bruise. Teresa shrieked again and swore never to get herself in a situation where a bird got the better of her. Could she get dressed now? Elizabeth did not deign to answer. She pulled her own cotton nightgown over her head and stood there in all her fleshly insignificance, comparing the shine of her skin with that of Teresa's. Teresa's skin, with all the plucking and whacking it had suffered, was pretty shiny. Elizabeth was not sure how much of that burning pink glow was soul and how much was simply pain. Perhaps pain brought the soul to the surface. Elizabeth pinched herself a few times, looking for some plumpness. She found just a little on the inside of her thighs. It was not easy being thirteen years old in a world full of well-rounded women. She pointed to those vaguely plump areas inside her thighs, very close to the pencil-thin line that sketched her future womanhood.

"Pinch me there," she ordered her maid.

Teresa wouldn't dream of it. It was bad enough being bitten by a peacock, but pinching the sacred flesh of her aristocratic mistress was more than she could endure. She would rather die than hurt her mistress, she wailed. Teresa put her hands together and prayed to her mistress, as if she were the Virgin incarnate, to please forgive her, but she couldn't bring herself to cause her pain.

Elizabeth promised that she would not punish her and that, anyway, she had no choice in the matter, because Teresa was but a lowly fly that she could squash with a flick of her wrist. However, given the fact that she had been disobedient, she should now go ahead and bite her instead.

Teresa lowered her face, her disheveled red hair spilling all over it, between her little mistress's thighs and nibbled a bit. It was so light a bite that Elizabeth kneed her sharply in the cheek. Teresa was becoming desperate. Crossing herself, she entrusted her soul to the Lord. Perhaps, she told herself, it is not my mistress's flesh that I am biting but a loaf of sacred bread. And since, after all, she had not yet had her breakfast and was fairly starving, she bit hard on the meager flesh until a small bruise blossomed there.

Tears sprang to Elizabeth's eyes, but she endured the pain silently, thinking of her horse, Luna, whom she loved more than anyone in the world.

After commanding Teresa to make yet another bruise on the opposite thigh, Elizabeth allowed her to rise and to dress and sent her off to fetch breakfast. While she waited for the maid to return, the countess sucked on the flesh of both her arms and raised a fair number of welts that stung most remarkably throughout her breakfast of roast mutton, white bread, and quail eggs. She drank down two whole cups of hot goat's milk.

After Teresa helped her dress, Elizabeth did not go to her music lesson as she was supposed to. Maestro Gozzoli be damned. She went to look for her horse. She found the silver-haired mare standing in a corner of the stable while Ursula's grooms busied themselves combing and talking to her mother-in-law's prized Arabian horses. Elizabeth kissed Luna's head and looked into her eyes. The great, dark eyes were sad. She did not look well taken care of.

Elizabeth whirled around furiously and grabbed a giant mustachioed man by the belt of his leather breeches. He turned his startled eyes on the enraged being tugging at him. "Hairy scum!" shrieked Elizabeth. "When is the last time you combed this horse?"

Not used to being spoken to roughly by a mere child, the master of the stables, Groom Master Ficzko—for that's who he was—nearly knocked her to the ground with the back of his hand but checked the impulse when he noticed the child's finery. "And who might you be?"

"I am the one who's going to have you skinned and fed to the dogs," replied Elizabeth, "unless you leave whatever worthless task you're involved in and feed, comb, and pet my Luna at once!"

There was just enough conviction in the girl's voice to make Ficzko take a step back to have a better look at her. "How did you get those bruises?" he asked, noticing the blotches covering her thin arms.

"Each one of these marks," replied Elizabeth, "will be worth ten lashes of the whip on your back unless you do what I just told you!"

Ficzko smiled a crooked smile, bowed deeply, and begged her to let go of his belt. She did. He didn't know just who she might be, but something about her manner suggested that the child would soon blossom into a young lass, and he was a lover of young lasses. He picked up a bucket of soapy water and a brush and went over to Luna. Ficzko soaped the mare and began to stroke her vigorously with his brush. Elizabeth liked the brisk way he groomed her horse. As she watched Ficzko work, her bruises tingled with a pleasurable heat, and she wished that the brush would stroke her as roughly as that.

After Luna was washed, brushed, and fed apples and boiled chestnuts, Ficzko helped Elizabeth mount, help she did not desire or need, so she kicked him in the chest with her foot when his large callused palm encompassed her rump and shoved her upward.

Elizabeth rode around the courtyard, observing the orderly life at Sarvar. She nearly rode out of the castle through the open gates, but the bridge was drawn up over the moat just as she readied to cross. Nonetheless, she wandered about long enough—in addition to missing all her lessons—to cause everyone to worry.

Elizabeth's escapade strengthened Ursula's resolve to take the girl's education more seriously, so that such incidents might not take place again. A young lady with a rigorous course of studies would not have time for such foolishness. In addition to the absolutely essential academic curriculum, plus manners and etiquette, Ursula planned to teach her daughter-in-law the intricacies of administration. Ursula had run the affairs of her estates for more than half her married life, and she suspected that Elizabeth would have to also. The fresh round of wars about to break out in the region made it a certainty that Franz would be spending all his time on military campaigns. It was not easy for a woman to wield power over a vast household and over castles spread a great distance apart. She had to prove herself worthy of respect, and she had to show from the start that she was competent and resolute. She could not afford to shirk her duty to punish, or loosen her financial grip. She had to also be consistent and to cultivate skilled advisors dedicated to her. These advisors were most important, and the mistress had to do whatever was necessary to keep them devoted, including, if it couldn't be avoided, some flirtation. Within the bounds of common sense, of course. "There are always those," Ursula said, "drunk on the perfume of their first reading of Boccaccio who would let the perfume of their lady mingle with their sanity. They must be brought to their senses gently."

Elizabeth's day now began at 6 A.M. She was awakened by the tinkle of Teresa's small silver bell and given her breakfast in bed. Teresa put before her a warm glass of fresh milk, mutton roast, two slices of white bread with jam, and a pear or strawberries. Elizabeth rarely touched anything but the bread and took two or three sips of milk. Teresa then removed the tray and set to combing her mistress's hair. Elizabeth came slowly awake under Teresa's brush. Her hair was long and curly, chestnut colored with more red than brown, and often unruly. Elizabeth reached for her silver-backed looking glass and stared long and sleepily at herself. First she saw her sleepy face with a pouting little mouth in the middle of it like a tiny frog on a lily pad. Her face was still round like a child's, but she thought she could see it lengthening to an oval. She then watched her eyes open wider and wider until they became almost as big as the whole looking glass. Elizabeth made them grow so big that they chased the rest of her face away and took over the whole silver pool. It now looked as if the mirror were floating on two deep black pools. She could see the looking glass reflected in the black pools of her eyes, which reflected two other pools and another looking glass, and so on and so on. She then lowered the looking glass to her chest and peered attentively at the front of her nightgown. It puffed up a little. She was quite certain that there was something there that hadn't been there the night before. She shifted so that her nightgown would lie flat, but the slight bulges remained.

Teresa's proud and stupid face hovered near hers to let her know that her hair had been brushed, swept up, and beribboned. It was time to wash. She let Teresa unfasten the ribbon on her nightgown and pull it over her head. Elizabeth looked down expectantly and what she saw took her breath away. Plainly visible to her was what undoubtedly had to be breasts. She thrust her chest out hoping that Teresa would notice, but Teresa looked indifferently at Elizabeth's momentous new protuberances and noticed nothing. Was Elizabeth dreaming? She touched her nipples and felt quickly under them. There was no doubt about it; something was under there.

Next to the bed was a steaming copper bath; it had been brought in at dawn and filled with hot water. Using Teresa's bruised shoulder for support (it hurt, but Teresa decided to bear it stoically), Elizabeth put in first one foot (and said, "Ouch!" which pained Teresa because she thought that if anybody ought to say "Ouch!" it ought to be herself) and then the other. Then Elizabeth sat on a small stool, and the water came up to her waist. She studied herself in the looking glass while Teresa scrubbed, washed, and rinsed her. The glass fogged, and Elizabeth wiped clear two little holes and trained them on her chest. Looking back at her were the full, firm breasts of a young woman standing naked before her husband, Franz. Franz looked adoringly upon the undeniable fullness of his bride's breasts and fell to his knees, reciting a poem in praise of them:

> *Twin moons of a dream star*
> *they are*
> *my beloved!*
> *Islands rising from the foam of an emerald sea*
> *Allow me to kiss them and press them to me!*

Feeling the blood rush quickly to her face—this, combined with the hot water, was making her feel faint —Elizabeth quickly lifted the steamed mirror. She wiped it again and examined her lips, which were pretty full, though not as full as she would have liked. She opened her mouth and let her tongue dart in and out, first flat, then folded like a little scoop. Her tongue was a fish that had been hooked from inside her by a wily fisherman who perched in her throat. The fish struggled to escape from the hook. It was a terrible struggle. "Ach! Ach!" Elizabeth made some dreadful choking sounds that caused Teresa to drop the silver pitcher she was using to pour warm water on her mistress's back.

"What's the matter?" she asked, alarmed.

"The little fish wants to go back to the sea!" groaned Elizabeth, pushing her tongue out of her mouth as far as it would go.

Teresa had no idea what her mistress was talking about, so she resumed her task. Next Elizabeth cleared another little hole in the steamy mirror for her nose. Pert, arrogant, with thin, flared nostrils, it was the very picture of aristocratic displeasure. It would be possible, thought the girl, to express the entire range of human emotions through the flaring and unflaring of her nostrils. She wondered what would happen if she decided to stop speaking altogether and expressed herself solely through her nose.

"*Have you any idea of the number of documents a castle's mistress must read and sign in one day?*" asked Ursula.

Elizabeth's nose twitched slightly, meaning both "no" and "who cares?"

Her future mother-in-law then said, "*The castle is burning. We must run quickly!*"

Elizabeth's nose twitched in supreme disdain of such earthly disasters. "*If we must run we will run, but in a dignified and graceful manner!*" her nose admonished her elder.

Yes, Elizabeth decided, this nose could do the job.

She then examined her throat, which was long and white, pretty and tender. Today she would wear a gold chain with a black stone to underline her graceful neck. Poets will sing of this neck, she decided, and then it was time to stand up and let Teresa's hands wrap a large towel around her.

Most days Elizabeth preferred to dress like a boy, in a short tunic with tights. Today for some reason she wished quite the opposite. To Teresa's astonishment (and displeasure), she demanded her most feminine finery. She let Teresa help her put on a silk undergarment and a blue satin dress, silk stockings, and blue shoes with tiny gold flowers on them. Around her neck Elizabeth fastened a gold chain with an onyx. On her head she set a small gold circle with tiny precious stones.

Teresa had to admit that her mistress looked very pretty indeed, and she wondered what had come over her. Elizabeth always hated womanly clothes, and she made quite a fuss when the occasion called for complex formal garments. Could it be, Teresa asked herself, that her little mistress was fancying someone? She wracked her brains for anyone her capricious little lady might conceive any sort of feeling for. There were two little baronets at the castle, the Szigedy twins, but they were only nine years old and Elizabeth had already expressed annoyance that the two boys were in her classes. Besides, they were too young. Teresa did not think that any of the servant boys would inspire Elizabeth, because the young countess was a terrible snob who had declared on many occasions that the lower classes smelled terrible. (Teresa could not see the face of the handsome groom Ficzko flash briefly through Elizabeth's mind.) The only other possible candidate for Elizabeth's affections might be her harp teacher, the Italian. Teresa considered the exaggerated and effeminate manners of the Genoese and suppressed a smile . . . There wasn't much man in the harpist . . . For the life of her, she could not fathom why Elizabeth was dressing up, and anyway, she wished Elizabeth would just get on with it, instead of staring at herself in the mirror for long moments after putting on each garment. Teresa had been urgently summoned that morning to the fish-salting room by the cook's assistant, who promised to show her how to make the brine for which Sarvar Castle was famous. And Elizabeth was already late for her music lesson.

At a little after eight o'clock, the beautiful countess floated into the angel room. "Grazia di Dio!" exclaimed Signor Gozzoli. "The heavens have been ravished! The light of paradise has been stolen! Make room, Beatrice and Laura! Make room for Elizabeth!" Elizabeth let Benezzo prattle on for an unseemly long time before she made the short, dismissive gesture she had learned from Ursula. The harpist shut up, but he kept shaking his head and rolling his eyes in disbelief, silently imploring the angels to be his witness. Elizabeth was amused, and feeling quite lighthearted, she not only completed her harp lesson without having to repeat herself, but she actually played a melody, showing anyone who cared to listen that she could master anything.

Even Pastor Ponikenuz, whom she saw next, couldn't help the small appreciative twitch that had quite a hard time rising from his arid soul. He had been determined to subject his charge to a large portion of the corpus of Aristotle's writings and to demand that she translate one hundred pages plus commentary within the week. If she failed, as he had no doubt that she would, he would ask for special permission from Ursula to beat the little bitch with his own hand. But now, looking at the lovely image of feminine purity before him, he had some doubts. He wasn't sure if it was wise to beat his future employer and patron. Women, Ponikenuz knew, had only one-third of a soul, just enough to power their devotion to children. But even this small portion had to be monitored and shaped, or it would degenerate into a lusty swamp that was the devil's favorite dwelling place. The only way to discipline such a meager endowment was to cram it full of Latin, theology, and grammar. He had noticed in Elizabeth a remarkable gift for retention of things that interested her. It was possible that she had a prodigious memory, but on the other hand, this may have been only a gift for mimicry of the kind to be found in monkeys.

Pastor Ponikenuz had a monkey, Isabel, a gift from the great Melanchthon, who had received it from a traveler to the Indies. The pastor spent many delightful hours watching the monkey imitate his gestures. He was fond of the beast but was somewhat ashamed of his weakness for it. Ponikenuz thought little of other creatures of the flesh, all of which, particularly humans, he found to be too riddled with sin to be worthy of anything more than his pedagogical severity.

The Szigedy twins, in the pastor's opinion, were devils of the first magnitude. They were lazy, badly behaved, and had no aptitude whatsoever for the life of the spirit. They were typical self-important aristocrats, proud little peacocks stuffed full of power, whose minds, if you could call them that, were inhabited only by sport, hunting, horses, and dreams of war. Their pockets, which Pastor Ponikenuz often made them empty, always contained miniature soldiers and weapons. No matter how many profound subjects the pastor brought before them, it was all for naught. Once he had confiscated a little drawing they were making inside their syllabus. It was a naked female walking between rows of swords. After chastising them severely, he ordered them to kneel on kernels of corn until evening.

For all that, the empty-headed twins were perfect specimens of their class and in that sense easy to understand and to guide. God put his church on earth precisely for this sort of people so that he may rule through them. Elizabeth, however, troubled him. She could dutifully memorize and recite her lessons, but there was always something offhand about her manner when she was finished. She looked as if she had doubts about the righteousness of the teaching or, even worse, thought the teaching was a mere trifle compared to some other thought that Ponikenuz could not fathom.

Today's lesson was on punishment. The pastor lectured the children on the fallen nature of humanity and on the necessity of punishing the natural inclinations of children until they were made humble and brought to understand the teachings of the church and the lessons of Christ. He enumerated the varieties of punishment proportionate to each infraction. Impertinence toward teachers and elders called for abstinence from food and drink for a whole day. Beating with the rod was an appropriate response to purposefully misinterpreting the teachings of Christ. The worst punishment of all was banishment from company for a period of time. This punishment, which resembled the one meted by God to Adam and Eve, whom he banished from paradise, was reserved for infractions of a sexual nature. These infractions and the resulting punishment would grow more serious as a person matured, the greatest danger occurring around the ages ten to fourteen. Pastor Ponikenuz looked significantly at Elizabeth. "Have you any thoughts regarding the matter of punishment?" he asked her.

"Only that Saint Anselm, when he was an abbot in Normandy, took the view that punishment of children was not a good thing."

Surprised, the pastor cleared his throat and asked Elizabeth to elaborate on this wholly extraordinary proposition, bringing to it arguments and facts, not just hearsay.

Elizabeth replied that "Saint Anselm"—who succeeded Lanfranc as prior of Bec in Normandy and later became abbot—"had been speaking with the abbot of another monastery, who complained that the boys in his charge were growing worse and worse even though 'we never give up beating them day and night.'

" 'You never give up beating them?' asked Saint Anselm. 'And what are they like when they grow up?'

" 'Stupid brutes,' the abbot replied.

"Anselm then spoke sternly to him: 'From men you have reared beasts . . . Now tell me, my lord abbot, if you plant a tree shoot in your garden and straightaway shut it on every side so that it has no space to put out its branches, what kind of tree will you have in after years when you let it out of its confinement?'

" 'A useless one, certainly, with its branches all twisted and knotted.'

" 'And whose fault would this be except your own for shutting it in so unnaturally? Without doubt, this is what you do with your boys. At their oblation they are

planted in the garden of the church to grow and bring
fruit for God. But you so terrify them and hem them in
on all sides with threats and blows that they are utterly
deprived of their liberty. And being thus injudiciously
oppressed, they harbor and welcome and nurse within
themselves evil and crooked thoughts like thorns, and
cherish these thoughts so passionately that they dog-
gedly reject everything that could minister to their cor-
rection. Hence, feeling no love or pity, goodwill or
tenderness in your attitude towards them, they have in
the future no faith in your goodness but believe that all
your actions proceed from hatred and malice against
them. The deplorable result is that, as they grow in
body, so their hatred increases, together with their apprehension of evil, and they are forward in all crooked-
ness and vice.'

"Saint Anselm went on," said Elizabeth, "to compare the teacher's role with that of a goldsmith, who
shapes his leaves of precious metal with gentle skill
rather than with blows."

When Elizabeth had finished delivering this extraordinary rebuff to Ponikenuz's entire pedagogical philosophy, she became aware that she had gained the
unconditional devotion of the Szigedy twins, who had
left behind whatever thoughts they were harboring and
had been listening to her with their mouths open. Pastor
Ponikenuz himself experienced such revulsion when she
was speaking that he became convinced she had been
possessed at just that moment. In truth Elizabeth, in
search of an old map of the castle, had picked a volume
at random in the library. It happened to be a life of
Saint Anselm, from which she'd read and memorized
the above conversation, after which she'd closed the volume as casually as she'd opened it and had forgotten all
about it until this moment. The entire time she related
the conversation of the two abbots, she had been won-

dering about her budding breasts. Were they real? Had she been hallucinating? She felt the overwhelming need to touch them in order to test the insights of that morning. When she finished her story of Saint Anselm, she brought her hands together to her chest in prayer. Yes, there was definitely something there. Swept by intellectual adoration, the Szigedy twins watched her touch her chest and were beside themselves with joy. They began to leap up and down, shouting, "Tree shoots! Tree shoots! We are tree shoots!" Pastor Ponikenuz brought the rod he always carried down hard on a stand holding the open Bible. The rod broke; the stand collapsed; the heavy leather volume toppled to the floor. Happily for everyone, the noon bell began to toll.

Next day, Elizabeth came to with a start, as if she had been slapped. The slap came not from a human hand but from a bottle of salts that Darvulia held under her nose. She had been undressed and was lying on two velvet pillows. She felt alternately as though she would faint again or be killed by the sharp pain. "I am being killed by my curiosity!" she told Darvulia. Elizabeth was sure that this agony was retribution for the restlessness of her mind. It was simply not ladylike to be so free and so curious. Perhaps Pastor Ponikenuz was right after all. She did not possess the necessary humility to be a wife, and now she had to die.

Darvulia laughed and, sitting next to her on the bed, crushed dried sage with mortar and pestle. "You are so right, my lady. This is punishment all right, but not for your thoughts. It's punishment for all of us poor womenfolk's thoughts. Our thoughts got so free, God decided to punish us all, no matter that some of us have freer thoughts than others. He made it so in his everlasting glory that every twenty-eight days, we get to feel so much pain, all thoughts are chased away from us, and what thoughts we thought we had, we repent and suffer for. What's happened, my lady, is that you are no longer a child . . ."

Elizabeth stared in horror between her legs, where Darvulia had thoughtfully placed a white cotton towel. Three bright red roses bloomed there. They had come from inside her. The longer she stared at her blood, the more faint she felt. She saw the white towel with the three roses fluttering like a pennant from the parapet at Sarvar. Below the castle walls two armies were engaged in mortal combat. The blood of the combatants flew dark and heavy from their pierced armor into the castle moat, which turned bright red. Nothing Elizabeth had heard about this event had prepared her for the actual moment. What did it matter to her now that Christ himself had honored her with a perpetually renewing wound? She felt as heavy as a boat laden with corpses and as light as candle wax dripping quietly over the edge of its holder. Waves of hot and cold washed through her small body, tossing it over the waves.

Elizabeth drank the brew Darvulia mixed up for her, but even though it made her sleepy, she could not sleep. What did it mean that she was a woman now? The women she knew, from Teresa to Ursula, were coarse. Not their manners or their speech, but their skin. Perhaps, thought Elizabeth, what makes their skin come to life is not the soul . . . Perhaps the soul fills each body to the rim and sheds its beneficent glow upon the skin. She had seen how babies glowed at birth, how their pink skin shone as if the soul sat in every part of it . . . Perhaps what made women coarse was the loss of soul, which seeped out through the blood . . .

Terrified, Elizabeth looked down again. The three roses had now linked up and had become a single, monstrous red sun. Darvulia held her head in her hands and sang an ancient women's lullaby that must have come from before the days of Noah's flood:

Pluck your silver from the moon, my sweet,
scoop the light from the star's eye,
the world will redden soon and fall
from God's hand like a fine ash of time.

Time! Elizabeth woke startled from the trance into which Darvulia's singing had put her. What would happen to her time now? Every twenty-eight days now she had to be held to the horror of her body! She realized now how free she had been. She did not like this at all. She wanted to be a little girl again, free to run through the halls of Kereshtur with breathless Andrei in tow. The thought of what it might be like if this terrible thing were to happen to her during a public function, or at a great dinner, or during an audience with the king . . . made her break into a new sweat. She now remembered the reproach of her mother, Anna Bathory, when she had once surprised Elizabeth dreaming away in her favorite window seat watching the clouds roll in from the Carpathian Mountains: "You're killing time, Elizabeth!"

She had not known what Anna meant, but she had caught the trace of regret in her voice. Anna probably wished she could kill time in the same way that her little daughter did, daydreaming. But that wasn't it at all, Elizabeth realized. She had not been killing time at that window. She had been experiencing eternity. Time had not even entered her mind. Killing time was her mother's problem—as it was, indeed, the problem of all aristocrats who lived in big castles with much time to kill. Only during war or great celebrations did time acquire any meaning. Otherwise it just got killed. Only children, who did not live in time, had no fear of it. "Has my eternity died?" Elizabeth asked softly.

Darvulia did not answer for a long time. When she spoke, her voice was deep and different, as if it was coming from another being. "One eternity died so another could begin. You are now relegated to the world of women and the suffering of the flesh. The souls of the dead and the unborn will now begin to fight over the right to penetrate your womb, which is being laid open to them. The strongest and cruelest will win and make their way to the world through you. Out of the misery of your flesh and blood you will forge the fire of another eternity for yourself, an eternity of the night. The eternity of day has died so that the eternity of night can begin. You will now join the sisters of the moon, who meet to share the blood and the flesh they shed on the ground, and out of our common flesh make wings for themselves to fly to places no men are allowed to go."

When the deep voice receded, Elizabeth was seized by a terrible sadness. It was true. She had now joined the world of women through this blood, which separated her forever from the world of men. There had been times when she had felt at one with her friend Andrei the scribe, as if she had been a boy too, or rather, as if they had both been made one body. Now, if she wanted to be a boy, she had to hide the dark stain of her shame.

When she next opened her eyes, Darvulia had placed a fresh towel between her legs. She had taken the blood-soaked towel from the bed and had wrapped something in it. The object inside, whatever it was, was soaking up her blood. She asked to see it, but Darvulia refused to show it to her. She said that it was a little doll that needed to drink all of Elizabeth's first blood. After lying wrapped in the towel for a fortnight, it had to be buried at the time of the full moon in a Christian cemetery. Darvulia began singing again, this time to the doll inside the towel.

Elizabeth now remembered the little mandrake man that Himlat had given her in the forest after her sisters had been murdered. She kept it at the bottom of her jewel box by the mirror. She asked Teresa to fetch it. "I too have something to wrap in a towel," she said. When the new towel was also soaked, Darvulia wrapped the mandrake man in it and laid it alongside the first one. She also marveled at Elizabeth's knowledge of these things.

Teresa came and went carrying pots full of steaming water, which she placed at the foot of the bed. Darvulia dropped strong-smelling herbs in the water; they made Elizabeth both sleepy and dreamy. She saw in her half dream the lying-in chamber where her mother, Anna, suffered the pain of her childbirth. She screamed alongside her mother while watching herself being born. There was blood everywhere. Her mother almost died. Elizabeth then saw both Darvulia and Teresa become transparent, as if their skin had become glass. She looked inside them and saw the blood flowing through the veins and their tributaries, a flowering map that was alive and moved without surcease.

It so happened that out of sympathy for her mistress, Teresa had also begun menstruating. She had not even been aware of it in her rush to help Darvulia ease the pain of her mistress's first blood. But now, as she put down another pot of steaming water, she became aware of the trickle of blood down her thigh.

"Look," she cried. "I am getting blood too!"

Elizabeth looked to see Teresa holding a red finger in the air. Something made her want to taste it, and before the astonished servant could cry out, Elizabeth stood in the bed and took Teresa's finger in her mouth, biting sharply down. The pain and surprise on Teresa's face almost made Elizabeth laugh. At that moment she forgot her suffering. Still not letting up on the finger, she bit until she felt the crunch of bone. The blood from Teresa's finger mixed with the blood from between her legs tasted rusty and sweet to Elizabeth, like an old key. Like an old key, she thought, remembering the pleasurable taste of her wet nurse's keys when she had been a baby. Whenever Darvulia had taken her breast out of Elizabeth's mouth, Elizabeth had taken hold of the big keys and sucked on them. Later, when Elizabeth was three or four, Darvulia had given her an old key to play with, and she had spent hours sucking its pleasant rusty iron. This was what Teresa's blood tasted like. An old key. This was the last thing that passed through Elizabeth's feverish brain before she fell fitfully asleep, a big, old key that had once opened the door to some forgotten chamber.

When Elizabeth was asleep, Darvulia carefully removed the third towel from between her legs and wrapped it around the bit of flesh from Teresa's finger that Elizabeth had spit out. She then put some potion on the maid's finger and tried to console the girl, who couldn't believe what her mistress had just done. Teresa stared at the flesh hanging from the end of her right-hand pointer and shook her head in disbelief. A big salty tear fell on the open wound, and she began crying even louder. "Why do these painful things happen to Teresa?" she wailed.

Darvulia patiently wrapped a small bandage around the wound and said nothing. She had her suspicions about both why such painful things happened to Teresa and why Elizabeth had bitten her finger. Painful things happened to Teresa because Teresa was made out of the kind of milky flesh that people liked to bite. Darvulia knew that Teresa had been bitten many times by men, who it seems just couldn't help themselves. Teresa had been made to be bitten. She was a loaf of fresh bread.

As to why Elizabeth had bitten her, that was another story. A long time ago, Darvulia had been told by an older and wiser witch that the Bathory child was going to surpass them all in dedication to the craft. Elizabeth was destined to give the three wolf teeth on the Bathory coat of arms new meaning and substance. Darvulia felt that she had been chosen to teach the new woman in the ways of the night and magic. She had had to wait patiently until the first blood. But now Elizabeth's true education was going to begin.

The first blood brought Elizabeth fully into the fold of the worship of the goddess of the night, who had three faces—of a young woman, a woman giving birth, and an old woman. For each of these faces there were rituals to be performed, dances to be danced, herbs to be gathered, sacrifices to be made. Darvulia had worshiped the aspect of the young woman and that of the mother, but now she was ready to assume the face of the old woman, the teacher. She had been taught by her mother, who learned from her mother, who had received the knowledge from women going back to the first Eve, Lilith, who had been twice banished from paradise. Lilith's banishment had been first for the sin of knowledge and then for the sin of pride when she refused to regret her first sin. Eve, on the other hand, had repented for the sin of knowledge and surrendered herself to man.

Darvulia had already told Elizabeth the story of Lilith, but like all her stories, it came wrapped in the cloak of adventure and imagination, and she doubted if Elizabeth had fathomed its true meaning. Elizabeth's mind had been trained this far by men, whose powers rested in logic, grammar, and geometry. The time had come to begin the training of her emotions, the channeling of her female powers to the precise ends of the magical arts. These ends were various, but they were all grounded in the real world. She would teach her pupil to cure illnesses, to make others unknowingly bend to her will, to draw power from rain and wind, to use the rays of the moon to heal her own womanly soul, and to fly.

Darvulia laughed softly to herself, thinking of the foolish preacher and all those bookworms that crawled about Sarvar. All their talk of manners and astronomy! Their willing pupil was about to undertake a completely different education. For all that, she had to give Ponikenuz, that dried-out beanpole of a preacher, a little credit. His thin nose had discerned something in Elizabeth that was beyond his grasp. His suspicion had settled like a mosquito on something more than his usual distrust of womankind in general. His bloodsucking trumpet sensed the rumbling of greatness in Elizabeth's yet-to-be-born womanly soul. Darvulia knew that he would not easily give up his prey. He would dog them for a long time.

"*A*m I to understand," asked the judge, "that in addition to whatever horror lies ahead, you are also confessing to rape?"

I have undertaken a truthful account, Your Honor. It is up to you to decide what crimes lie within it. From my point of view, it is all a crime. There is nothing I have done in my life that has not been a crime. It is all punishable. I was born an aristocrat in Hungary when it was a crime to be an aristocrat. I fought against the legal government. I escaped illegally across the border. I have lied on my U.S. residency application form. The women in my life have long thought that I should be put away. If you are in a hurry, Your Excellency, I can try to reduce the narrative to the evidence and hope for the best.

"That is not necessary, Count Bathory-Kereshtur. The court finds your narrative highly instructive."

At lunch next day I asked Teresa to introduce me to Professor Lilly Hangress. Naturally I did not tell her about my unfortunate visit with Eva. She did not ask. In retrospect, I find this curious. Perhaps I should have wondered about it at the time, but I was too caught up in my guilty conscience. In any case, my intention in asking Teresa to introduce me to Professor Hangress was to try to right something. I wanted to get back to the course set for me by Klaus Megyery, which was for me to recover my sense of being Hungarian and an aristocrat. I wanted to follow a set course because my own initiative had been such a tremendous failure, I felt devastated. There was also, I must add, the professional assignment from the *Chronicle* to document the changes in Hungary.

"She is hard to find," Teresa said. "When someone calls her, her maid always says, 'Professor Hangress is at a funeral.' That is always her excuse. Lilly is always at a funeral. If she went to as many funerals as she says, she'd have no relatives or friends left. Call her. Say my name to her. But do not mention my mother. For some reason, she gets very upset when I mention Eva."

I had no such intention.

No one answered when I knocked on the imposing door bearing the professor's name and title in raised letters on a bronze plaque. A white-haired savant in the next office informed me that Lilly Hangress had gone to a funeral in the country and was not expected back until the mourning period was complete. He then added, with an evil chuckle, that "mourning in Hungary can take anywhere from three days to three years, since it is the most important vacation a Hungarian could take."

I laughed, remembering Teresa's warning. I was familiar with the phenomenon. During the communist era, when no one worked for forty years, mourning took most of that time. Clearly there had been lots of things to mourn in Hungary. And more were on their way. I remembered the uncanny number of "deaths" that had been used as excuses by both students and teachers during my years at the gymnasium. One by one, my classmates and my professors had "killed off" their aunts, uncles, grandfathers, grandmothers, brothers, sisters, and then their mothers and fathers. Often they "killed" the same people several times, forgetting that they had already used their deaths once. Amid so many phony deaths, a real one usually went unnoticed. When one of my classmates' parents or siblings really died, no one believed them. The grief-stricken child would wander about the halls red-eyed until he would be sent home, where often he or she did not want to be. I wondered if this was a phenomenon peculiar to the Communist Hungary of my youth, when people's appetite for living was greatly diminished, or whether it was a universal phenomenon.

I left my name and number. A few hours later, Professor Hangress called and agreed to meet me for dinner.

I had expected a nicotine-stained, badly dressed, frumpy Communist bureaucrat. But Lilly Hangress was austerely elegant. She was about a slender inch or so taller than me. Her black hair was cut short, leaving her long graceful neck free but for a familiar-looking gold chain with a small black stone at the end of it. She wore a waist-length ermine fur over a long black dress that moved easily with her body.

When the maître d' at the Neptune removed her coat, she took him in with a severe glance. She was in command of her surroundings. The ornate restaurateur practically tripped over himself walking away from her backwards. She was at home in a world that knew the rules of social etiquette and was aware of social distinctions. Forty years of Communism had not erased the elaborate social codes of the Austro-Hungarian Empire. Without speaking a word, by simply allowing her coat to be removed, Lilly Hangress had managed to communicate her superior standing to the entire restaurant.

The Neptune, suggested by Doctor Hangress over the phone, was one of Budapest's snazzy new nightclub restaurants, a fin de siècle salon made surreal by fish-tank floors and walls, in which swam exaggerated tropical creatures bursting with color. In pointed contrast, the opulent chandeliers and velvet draperies announced a wholly different era. Oddly enough, the exotic fish and the chandeliers seemed to arrange themselves to frame Lilly Hangress. They seemed eager to. Goodness, I thought, she commands the furniture!

The professor shot me a quick ironic look as if she had read my mind.

Clusters of silver-finned, wide-eyed fish darted under my feet to gather at the points of Lilly's high heels. Perhaps it hadn't been such a good idea, in my emotionally tenuous state, to dine with someone as powerful as my table companion.

I looked around the restaurant but found nothing reassuring. At the next table, two handsome Argentine or Brazilian men sat with a bevy of gorgeous models around bottles of champagne. An elderly gent with a monocle bowed slightly when I noticed him. A brass bar was visible in the wavy mirrors. That was hope: a drink.

"Quite an extravagance in landlocked Hungary!" I commented.

"This is you and me," she said abruptly.

I didn't understand.

"The chandeliers are me, the fish is you. America is surrounded by oceans, is it not?" Her voice was smoky and deep, redolent, it seemed to me, of a deeply lived essence.

"English menu?" asked the waiter, holding a thick velvet-bound book toward me.

"No, Hungarian," I said, to his evident disappointment.

The candles in gold candleholders on every table added to the underwater shimmer of the place, as did the discreet Gypsy orchestra tucked in a velvet box at the far end of the huge aquarium.

I winced slightly when the 1938 Tokay that my dinner companion ordered was brought to the table. I wouldn't have dreamt of approving or disapproving such a thing, so I asked Lilly to do the honors. She did so with little hesitation. She smelled the cork, tasted the wine, and declared it "fine."

Just how fine I found out later. Four hundred bucks for a liter of wine is a lot of money, even in New York. I didn't want to seem crass, so I said nothing. Besides, 1938 was the year when I was born, and I was just a little curious to taste what kind of sun, wind, and grape had been captured in that bottle.

When Lilly saw my face, she laughed. "I drink this stuff like water," she said, in some kind of fake American accent that sounded pretty droll.

I laughed with her.

How did I expect to understand a sixteenth-century countess whose purveyors emptied the seas for pearls if I worried about the price of a bottle of wine? A process of dreadful contraction must have taken place over the centuries, transforming the extravagance of my ancestress into my penny-pinching anxiety. Even my father had been more generous than I was. Largesse was an aristocratic trait that I clearly lacked. Perhaps I really was an American after all. A Puritan. A sober New World denizen.

"I have read and admired your book on Elizabeth Bathory," I lied. A habit of flattery, which I had never had before, seemed to have clung to me since I had come to Budapest. "I have a philosophical interest in Bathory," I continued, making matters worse.

"Such as?" she asked curtly while opening the more modestly bound (velour) Hungarian menu.

I waxed somewhat lyrical, unable to stop myself, or inspired perhaps by the shimmer of the Neptune, which was concentrated in the woman before me.

I said that I had always had an intellectual interest in the complex connections between beauty, blood, magic, religion, and nationalism. "I also believe," I gushed with unaccustomed enthusiasm, "that certain ideas born during Bathory's time continue to fascinate. Beauty. Blood. Magic. Religion. Nationalism. They are all words capable of provoking an emotional response. Even the dramas being lived by Eastern Europeans now seem to be rooted somehow in Bathory's age . . ."

I would have gone on if I hadn't noticed the index finger of her right hand moving across the rim of her wineglass, wringing a small song from it. She wasn't paying attention. At a neighboring table, two elderly gentlemen dressed in prewar gabardine had fallen utterly silent and were staring at my dinner companion.

"What are they looking at?" I asked.

"At someone in their minds. What men are always looking at."

I doubted it. Lilly Hangress looked stunning. Her black dress was stylishly cut, showing her form in the best light. The gold chain with the black stone lay between the rounded whiteness of her breasts like the tear of a dark angel. Two small diamonds in her earlobes refracted light from the mirrors. There was only the slightest suggestion of makeup on her high cheekbones. Her eyes had been exaggerated with a bit of kohl. They looked immensely deep.

I was beginning to feel troubled by my inability to make myself interesting. From the brief biography at the back of her book, I had surmised that Lilly Hangress must have been roughly my age, but she looked much younger, like a woman in her mid-thirties.

She held her glass for me to pour wine, and for a moment I found myself gazing at a most beautiful arm, a sculptural object that ended in the perfect hollow of her armpit. There was something theatrical, flirtatious, and somehow perfectly appropriate about the gesture.

"Was Elizabeth Bathory beautiful?" I asked.

For the first time since the evening began, I made a natural connection, one that sounded neither pompous nor forced.

"If you believe in fairy tales. In fact, no, she was not beautiful. Think about it. If she was beautiful, would she have been obsessed by beauty? A beautiful woman gets whatever she wants. If she had whatever she wanted, would she have been a cruel and capricious woman?"

I disagreed. "Bathory did what she did in order to preserve her beauty," I said vehemently. "Why would she have bathed in blood if there was no beauty to preserve? All the writers agree that it was fear of old age that prompted her crimes."

"All of them but one. She never bathed in blood. There is no evidence in any of the documents that she bathed in blood. That is one of the fairy tales that causes sensation-seeking foreigners to wander about Hungary. Think. One may drink blood, in the belief that it's an elixir, or suck it, in an excess of passion, but bathe in it? The sticky mess. The quick coagulation. What other fairy tales have you brought with you?"

"She may have had an illegitimate child before she married Franz Nadazdy." I had read this in a badly faded German pamphlet.

"There is no evidence of that. It's stupid. Think. She married Nadazdy in her early teens. When did she have an illegitimate child?"

I decided that Lilly Hangress's favorite words were *stupid* and *think.* I went on.

"She was a witch."

"She did not practice witchcraft. There is no evidence."

"The evidence was excised from the trial documents," I said.

"There was no trial!" Lilly Hangress stared triumphantly at me across the table. Her eyes were black with little flecks of gold. But for all their resemblance to Hungary's other deep black eyes, she was wholly within her gaze.

I was astonished. The entire case that posterity had built against Elizabeth Bathory was based on the testimonies of numerous witnesses.

"No," Professor Hangress said firmly, "those witnesses did not testify at any trial. They testified at preliminary hearings. Interviews. The so-called inquests of 1611 and 1613."

"Why then were most of the interviewees executed, and why was she condemned to perpetual imprisonment in her own castle?"

I knew one or two things. After all, it was *my* family.

"No one was executed as a result of statements about Elizabeth. Some of these people were executed for crimes they confessed to . . ."

"But weren't these crimes committed while helping Elizabeth Bathory to torture and murder girls?"

"Yes, but she was never officially charged and never punished."

"But she was imprisoned . . ."

"For her own protection. The family held the hearings and confined her to her castle to protect her from a trial by the king's court. There are numerous letters from the king asking the palatine Thurzo to summon a royal tribunal to try Bathory. The palatine never allowed it. He protected her because, if she had been tried, she would have been beheaded."

"How did the palatine keep the records of the hearings from the king?"

"He deposited them in his archive, in the Thurzo archive."

I was beginning to feel an increasing sense of eeriness. We were playing some kind of game of hide-and-seek. I had searched the Thurzo archive together with Teresa, and we had not found the documents under the archival numbers in Lilly's book. Had she hidden them after completing her study?

I became certain that there was much more to Lilly Hangress than met the eye.

She looked to the bottom of her wineglass as if there was a hint to be found there, and said: "I will tell you something I have discovered. Listen well. History is an underground river that flows underneath the present. Everything that ever happened keeps happening below us. This river empties into the present now and then. That is when catastrophe occurs. Historic catastrophes are sometimes caused by someone inadvertently digging too deep into the past and reaching the river of history."

Lilly Hangress closed her eyes for a moment.

"But," I said, "a river flows from somewhere to somewhere. It cannot *repeat* events . . ."

"This river," said Lilly, "flows simultaneously backward and forward: it has no source and no exit. It is formed by the debris of time, it is *made out of unfinished history*. As we hurtle forward in time, this river fills with the unconcluded events and unfinished forms we leave behind. And yet, because it moves, it is also *present* right under us . . . we can never move faster than it does. It is in our best interest to keep this river underground. We historians are always in danger of opening vents . . ."

"Is this," I asked, "the river Lethe, the river of oblivion?"

"Well, no, it is the opposite of Lethe; this is the river Retentio, the river of memory."

I was baffled. "But what purpose does it serve? Can we never escape history?"

"The purpose," said Lilly, "is a mystery, but I suspect that it exists because we never finish anything. Everything we abandon before we can bring it to a conclusion continues to live until it is played out, until the story is finished. *All strains will be played out.* Everything that exists obeys a narrative imperative; it has a structural logic. When this imperative is frustrated, the object continues an underground existence. It will live out its structural destiny *on its own*, without us. The underground river of history is made out of all the unfinished stories of all the human beings who ever lived. The inconclusive bits that form its raging waters rush back and forth in an effort to complete themselves. They cannot, without us, reach closure, which is why they are so pressurized, so agitated, so mad . . . If they reach us, catastrophe occurs."

"This is an unusual perspective," I admitted.

"Well," Lilly said slowly and without a hint of the amusement that had attended many of her remarks, "you have a part in the drama. It is destiny."

"I intend to search for it then," I said, not quite sure what she'd meant.

"Is anyone assisting in your research?" she suddenly asked.

I told her that I was being helped by Teresa, one of her former students, who had helped me track her down.

This confession may have been a mistake.

"What did she say about me?" asked Lilly.

"She said that you are an exacting teacher, particularly in the area of translation. She said that your students had to translate or perish."

I thought that this brief summary would obscure all the other things Teresa had told me.

"What else did she tell you?"

"Nothing."

"If you must know about this nothing, I will tell you," said Lilly. "My husband was Jewish. He was a Nazi hunter."

"Was?"

"He is dead."

"I'm sorry."

"Anyway. He was never here; he was always hunting Nazis in Brazil, in Germany, in Paraguay, in America . . . Here at home I had to deal with tremendous lack of discipline. My children were terrible. My students were worse. In the seventies and the eighties, everyone in Hungary became cynical. Understandably so, perhaps. Everyone did whatever they thought was expedient and best only for themselves. At the university no one enforced rules, and no one learned anything. In 1983, I took matters into my own hands. I organized a study group of girls outside the university, a Socratic school for women only, based on translation. My girls translated day and night until history became part of them and oozed out of their pores like sweat. They lived with me; they ate with me; they studied and translated with me. When they were bad, I punished them."

"How?" I was quite astonished.

"I know what you are trying to find out," said Lilly quickly. "I was writing on Elizabeth Bathory at the time. I did want to know what would compel a woman surrounded by young girls to act the way she did."

"You didn't kill anybody, did you?"

Lilly laughed. "I was interested in my reactions. I wanted to know the quality of my anger among all these girls. It was an experiment."

"An *erotic* experiment?"

"Why not?"

I couldn't think of a good reason. I thought of Teresa, who couldn't sleep for fear of her teacher, and of the dark circles under the other girls' eyes. I became slightly aroused despite myself. Lilly noticed.

"My experiment was not intended to excite men." I could feel the warmth of her skin. *"I* am intended to excite men."

"You'll have to forgive me. I'm a bit of a monk," I lied.

"There are monks and monks. Many of them have been consumed by lust. Which kind are you?"

"Andrei de Kereshtur comes to mind."

"What do you know about Andrei de Kereshtur?"

"Not much. Only that he was Elizabeth Bathory's chronicler and worshiper. Perhaps this is my job too."

As I said, I knew one or two things. But in truth, I had only heard about the *Chronicles of Andrei de Kereshtur* the day before from Teresa, who had promised to ferret a rare copy out of the national archive for me. In fact, she was supposed to have been working on it right at the time Lilly and I were dining.

"That is your job," she admitted. "But you have another, a more important one."

I was astonished. "What is it?"

"You will know when the time comes."

I was intoxicated more by the mystery of Lilly Hangress than by the heady Tokay.

After dinner we took a cab through the crooked streets of Budapest coming to life in the evening. Trams and buses went noisily by, and neon lights sprouted everywhere. Art nouveau gas lamps from another century still threw their ghostly lights onto houses hidden behind snow-covered lindens.

She lived in a 1940s deco-style villa surrounded by a wrought iron fence smothered by snowy vines.

Next day there was an agitated crowd milling about the entrance to the Gellart hotel. Imre Megyery stood at the center of a small gang of skinheads who were listening to him respectfully. He was a head taller than all of them and looked incongruous in his suit jacket amid all the leather. He broke off when he saw me and came over.

"Strange bedfellows!" I said.

"Not bedfellows. Foot soldiers. How do you say in America? Muscle!"

"The future SS!"

"More like the SA, actually," said Imre, refusing to take my bait.

"What's with the crowd?"

"There are rumors of a coup. I came by to make sure that you are close by. Today may be our appointment with destiny."

"*Our?* I still have no idea what my role is."

"It should all become quite evident."

At this point Teresa joined us, her cheeks flushed as if she had been running. A few snowflakes were melting on the collar of her peacoat. She carried a bulging briefcase. The three of us went upstairs to my room. Teresa threw a sheaf of papers on the bed and sat down. Imre remained standing, keeping an eye on the mob outside the window.

Teresa had undertaken a search at the archive among the legal documents of King Matthias II's reign. She looked through everything the king's justice machinery had chewed up from 1611 through 1613 and found all manner of things, from charges that led to thieves' heads rolling in the public dirt, to the indictments of witches, which had resulted in their flaming in the squares, to terse dispatches ordering deserters torn apart by four horses, in addition to a number of hearings ending in common hangings—but no records of Elizabeth Bathory's inquests. The records of the most notorious case of the early seventeeth century seemed to have been carefully excised from Hungary's national archive.

But then she tried another path. Teresa opened King Matthias's correspondence, and there, among thousands of letters, she struck pay dirt. She found two folios containing (1) an exchange of letters between King Matthias and George Thurzo, the palatine, concerning Elizabeth Bathory, and (2) an unknown portion of the manuscript of the *Chronicles of Andrei de Kereshtur, Concerning Her Ladyship Elizabeth Bathory*.

The exchange between the king and the palatine was in Latin, with additional letters by Elizabeth Bathory's pastor Ponikenuz in Hungarian and Latin, some addressed to the palatine, others written to the king. The *Chronicles* of de Kereshtur were in old Hungarian, with occasional portions in Latin and Slovene. Teresa had commandeered the archive's lone copying machine, had cheerfully slapped the ancient parchments with their fragile handwriting on top of the glass, and zapped them. We were now looking at her haul.

I opened a bottle of Unicum, a black liqueur made from five hundred bitter grasses that I had purchased across the street when they told me they were out of Jack. The Xeroxed documents were all over the bed, in addition to a long yellow tablet on which, in longhand, Teresa had begun to translate. I lounged next to her with my tumbler and listened to her try out the translation.

A letter from Pastor Ponikenuz to King Matthias accused Elizabeth Bathory of witchcraft. He said that he had been on the verge of "making the woman confess, but in further proof of witchcraft, she made me forget the accusation proffered by me."

This was quite startling. Lilly Hangress had told me that there had been no accusation of witchcraft. Was it possible that the eminent historian had not seen this letter? Teresa's unusual search may have yielded an unknown document—and a whole new light on my ancestress's activities.

Ponikenuz went on to tell the king that as soon as he had left conversing with the countess, he remembered the specific details of the accusations, because he'd witnessed one of the outrages himself.

"Hidden by the wall of the cemetery, we watched Darvulia, the Bathory woman, her maid Teresa, Katalin, and two of the village wives beat a cat to death with their bare feet. Then they brought a bundle, inside which something made such noises my heart was gripped by fear. If this was a child it was not a human child. They passed the bundle around talking to it."

Ponikenuz was close enough to the ceremony to overhear the spell the women used. He wrote down the spell in the original tongue in which it had been delivered. Since none of us knew what language this was, we left this part untranslated, although Teresa and I mouthed the words together:

AKAELOS KALENDRIA FUISOR
RAMZET HALBUR KOLEMZI KRAH
RAMEZAH HOLRAB ARK AMARGO
PALER KMOSTREH HALBERUT

"Given hints from conversations overheard by our informants, this spell was for the purpose of stopping the ravages of time, which the countess, though still of a tender age, had begun to fear," speculated Ponikenuz.

Our awkward recitation made the room all of a sudden very warm.

"It must work," I said. "The spell."

Teresa laughed. "They've never gotten the heat right in this country. It's either too hot or too cold."

It was a different sort of heat, though.

Ponikenuz concluded his letter with an appeal to have the countess investigated. "Only the learned minds of Your Majesty's judges together with the best theologians in the kingdom could force the secret doors of such an evil mind to open."

Ponikenuz undoubtedly considered himself one of the "best theologians." He said that he "had authored over twenty pamphlets."

Translating this letter took the better part of an hour, because Ponikenuz's handwriting was hard to decipher. He slipped quite often into old Hungarian and Slovene. Teresa said that this was not unusual. The literate people of the time, mainly clergy and high aristocracy, wrote Latin as easily as Hungarian and mixed the two quite often, particularly in correspondence.

Imre had remained standing by the window for most of that time, participating only now and then in our enthusiasm for the old documents.

We had been downing Unicum throughout the translation, and as the pastor's charges against the countess became more vehement, I couldn't help staring at the nervous and intelligent toes of Teresa's bare feet. They were more like fingers than toes, long and flexible. She punctuated her reading with stretches, arches, and flexes of her toes. I wanted to put them in my mouth. She still looked very much like her mother at that age. I felt a surge of shame at the thought of Eva. But it did not prevent an equally strong surge of lust.

I touched her hair. "AKAELOS KALENDRIA FUISOR," I said.

Snow started falling thickly outside the window, and Imre could not see the crowd anymore. He said, "I'll be back," and dashed out the door. After the slam it got very quiet in the room. From somewhere in the building came the distant plaint of a Hungarian folk song on the radio. We looked at the snow for a dreamy moment and then began reading de Kereshtur's *Chronicles*.

For the first time since arriving in Hungary, I began to see just how real Elizabeth Bathory had been. And I began to glimpse also the extraordinary presence of the chronicler himself. I felt the way I did when I first read Bernal Díaz's *Conquest of New Spain*. That book, written in simple soldier's prose, had cleared away centuries of cobwebs from the confused understanding of the Spanish conquest of the New World. Andrei de Kereshtur was a contemporary of Bernal Díaz. They shared a disdain for fabulation and a love of facts. For that reason they were both believable, though both stories remained full of mystery.

Despite his care for the facts, the Bathory family notary was unabashed in the defense of his friend and patron. He wrote down all that had been said about her, even the horrific things that must have chilled his blood, but there shone throughout the story a love so profound it elevated his prose from mere chronicle to something on the order of a grand love story.

Watching Teresa bent over her own writing, I felt

great affection for her. And sorrow for Eva, her mother, who stared mutely out the window of her tiny cell, empty of her own self, frozen in a body nearly as young as her daughter's. And shame for my weakness.

I was only too aware that shadows haunted the world. These shadows nestled in hollows and drew strength from innocence. I disliked feeling so much. Things had ended badly every time I surrendered to emotion. I would have liked to live in the Megyerys' hard world of men, but I didn't believe in it. After each of my exhausting surrenders to pure feeling, I retreated to my world of one, my kingdom of misanthropy. I feared affection for others in whatever form, but especially here in the former utopian camp. Here the world didn't respect my misanthropy: no matter what I did, it drew me in. Now I had reached a crossroads. I'd come to Hungary to find my childhood and found, instead, an adult role assigned to me, as if I had never left. It was amazing. My birthplace had gone on reserving a niche for me. And now that I had returned, it placed me in it naturally, without hesitation.

When the door chime rang, the sound lingered in the air. A stray musical note fell on the carpet like a snowflake.

It was Imre. I had forgotten all about him.

Watching him stand there in the doorway, hair full of snow, a frown on his face, I remembered. There was a coup in progress. Or maybe not.

"The government has fallen," Imre said. "There is a constitutional crisis. The president has resigned. There is a big mob in front of the palace. My father thinks we should move fast. He is convening all the peers. You must come to Judenstrasse now. Everyone will be there."

In the lobby of the Gellart Hotel, the inmates were watching a small black-and-white TV. An obviously disturbed announcer was appealing for calm. The president had resigned and the prime minister was about to announce the formation of a new governing coalition. Outside the Parliament building, the restless mob was shouting slogans I couldn't make out.

"The television station is under attack by Fascists," someone commented. An image of Imre's skinhead friends flashed on the screen.

"Who are these peers?" I asked Imre.

"Your peers. The Nadazdys, the Rakoszis, the Thurzos, the Ecseds. They have traveled a long way to be here."

When we reached the street, we were met by three skinheads with blackjacks in their hands. One of the creatures wore a mud-spattered leather overcoat and hobnail boots.

"Yours?" I asked Imre. "Do you think they should allow wild animals in front of nice hotels?"

"We thought it safe if, for your own protection, you were accompanied by some of our friends."

"You are joking. What are these imbeciles supposed to be protecting me from?"

Imre waved his arms vaguely, indicating a host of threats.

A familiar-looking black car with its door open waited for us. I remembered the make and the style well. The old secret police used to drive cars like these.

"Just like in the old days, eh, Imre? But then you were too young to know what your father did. You just read the books he brought home."

I was furious. The imperious bastard was actually ordering me around. But it was useless to argue. The booted subhumans were close enough I could smell them. Garlic sausage and unwashed armpits. Sour wine breath. I was furious because of Imre's manner. I didn't mind going to the meeting. I just didn't like being *escorted* there in such a fashion.

Judenstrasse sported more leather-wrapped skinheads on the corner. They leaned against walls and doorways, picking at bad teeth with bits of wire or fingering some primitive weapon under their coats. They formed a kind of gauntlet all the way to Megyery's door. Counting the ones in the car, there must have been twenty of these vomit-spattered baby Nazis.

"What do you call this scum?" I asked Imre.

"Your honor guard," he said, without apparent irony.

"We must be in hell," I said.

The peers looked as if they'd sprung out like newts from the behinds of Bosch monsters. Crowded in Klaus Megyery's shrine to Hungary's past, a dozen men and four women perched uncomfortably on fauteuils and divans sipping black Turkish coffee. Stacked on a table in the middle of the room were plates overflowing with tiny rolls of stuffed cabbage, rolled slices of ham, black glass containers of sour cream, potatoes fried with parsley, fish balls, pickled tomatoes, and an assortment of other rolled foods I vaguely remembered but had forgotten the names of. Imbedded in each cabbage, ham, fish, and vegetable roll was a toothpick with the flag of Hungary.

No one appeared in any hurry to pull the patriotic toothpicks out of the food. Everyone had a glass of wine in hand, however. The cigarette smoke was thick.

When I made my entrance there was a polite buzz, and several elders half rose in muttered greeting. The room smelled of mothballs and sauerkraut.

I bowed sarcastically and swept the scene with my gaze as if I was looking over ripe cheeses brought over for my inspection and approval. It was apparently the correct approach, because the faint buzz acquired respectful weight.

Most of the assembled wore eyeglasses with heavy bone frames, except for Baron Thurzo, who wore a gold monocle that hung on a thin chain from his vest pocket. My father's old chess companion must have been in his late eighties, but he looked exactly as he had during those long-ago dark silent evenings. His austere profile turned to me and something akin to a smile broke briefly on his thin lips. The last Thurzo shook my hand limply, but the touch of his clammy skin sent a shiver through me. He meant nothing to me, but an inexplicable rage rose in my soul nonetheless.

"Why didn't you and my father talk during those chess games?" I found myself asking.

Baron Thurzo bowed his head to the side a little and said, "In those days, dear Count, we simply existed. Speech was not an option."

I wasn't sure I understood, but the baron lapsed into the primal silence again.

They were dressed for the most part in worn suits of good material, like a group of old-fashioned professionals. What distinguished them from any group of professionals, however, were their eyebrows, noses, and lanky frames. I had never seen so many profuse eyebrows at once. Luxuriant, tufty growths that sprouted angrily below resolutely furrowed brows, these eyebrows communicated a sense of purpose and a fierceness that were terrifying.

Their noses also had a labored look, as if they had been crafted over an anvil by a metalsmith. Some noses were as thin as a sheet of gold, while others drooped to a sharp beak almost to their chins.

Baron Thurzo's nose jutted straight out of his face like a hound racing from the gate. When he leaned for-

ward, I backed involuntarily away for fear of being overcome by it.

Clean shaven for the most part, the men's faces were
ashen gray, while the women had powdered theirs to the
point where they did not look like flesh at all but some
sort of old fabric. Their heads were elongated and listed
slightly either to the left or to the right, as if the weight
of history had skewed them.

I was among my own kind.

I shook the hands of the descendants of Hungary's
aristocracy, names as old as my own and as old as Hungary itself: Baron Thurzo, Countess Forgach, Count
Ecsed, Baron Bocskay, Count Windisch-Graetz, Gyula
Poszony, Lady Francesca Nadazdy, and others whose
names whooshed by like wind through barren trees.

Shaking their hands while they bowed stiffly, I experienced a mixture of panic and wonder. I sensed the
extraordinary effort that had been expended over the
centuries to maintain these bloodlines, the unyielding
pressure to make the right alliances, the cold calcula-
tions of inheritance and possession. The exaggerated
chins, the protuberant noses, the misshapen crania were
the result of wars, cruelty, inbreeding—but also passion,
illicit liaisons, religious conversions, mystical revelations. Whatever history had thrown at these survivors,
pitting itself against the wills of individuals, had translated into their flesh. Each hair in those tufty eyebrows
was a flaming stalk under a witch or a whiplash on a
rebel back. The eyebrows in particular looked to me like
the redhot signatures of overdetermined wills that had
leached slowly out of the bloodlines over the merciless
centuries.

To think that I was one of them! Everyone in the
room was some degree of myself. Our ancestors had
been so thoroughly mingled, I had the feeling that all of
us in Megyery's living room were a single organism, like

a giant fungus or a cloned forest. The mad history of this aristocracy, with all its excesses, crimes, and heroic deeds, was concentrated here like an essence about to be released.

No, I thought, a thousand times no. I must not let this noxious concentrate escape from the glass jar of Megyery's apartment. Do anything. Set us on fire. Our ancestors had fought and murdered one another, married and forged alliances, founded countries. At their best—but only for selfish reasons—they patronized art, literature, and music. But their worlds had to be overthrown by revolutions, because there was room in them only for themselves.

I imagined the tangled lines in the room as a twisted whip with many strands, caked stiff with old, rusted blood.

Klaus Megyery, like some kind of demonic conjurer, was getting ready to lift this whip from its hook and wield it with unforeseeable results in the unstable new world of Hungary.

Blow up this room, I prayed again to no one in particular, and all that's left of Hungary's attenuated past will blow away like a dandelion!

I was surprised that so many descendants of the old lines could still be found. I knew that some lines had been extinguished before the eighteenth century, but in one stubborn form or another, here they were, weak chins, bushy eyebrows, beaky noses.

"Ladies and gentlemen," Klaus intoned, "as we meet, Hungary is undergoing a great crisis. We must seize the moment! The confusion engendered today will cause the people to turn for help to our great past. You represent that past in its purest form!"

It wasn't quite Lenin speaking from atop the locomotive at the Finland Station, but the room grew quiet. Listening to my decidedly plebeian secret-policeman friend speak, it occurred to me that this whole scene was a charade. There was no effort to restore the aristocracy. This was a bogus monarchist movement. Indeed, there was no monarch. Klaus himself was no royalist: he had always been a nationalist, first of the Communist variety, then of the orthodox Fascist kind. He was using this motley crew for purposes even he may not entirely have known.

What sort of role was I playing in this strange play? Perhaps this was a plot to destroy rather than restore what remained of Hungary's melancholy past. After all, what was easier than disposing of all these mothballed aristocrats after bringing them together in one room?

But looking again at the enthusiastic and overall insecure mug of my old pal, I wasn't so sure. I didn't believe him capable of anything so complex. The skinheads were not hard to understand: he had recruited them with bottles of cheap wine and sentimental songs. Klaus was carrying out his mad scheme on instructions from his old police bosses, but his delusions may have been sincere.

The peers also looked painfully uncertain. These people had already been destroyed by history, not once but several times. What was the point of bringing them together, only to get rid of them again? They had been irrelevant for a long while now.

Only a truly deluded mind could conceive of returning twentieth-century Hungary to the hands of this inert group. Whatever worth they had was probably in their modest professionalism. Baron Thurzo was a banker in Finland. Count Ecsed was an engineer in Canada. Countess Nadazdy, who was also a Bathory like myself, was a Los Angeles divorcée who dabbled in real estate.

Megyery put on a scratchy record of the Hungarian

Royal Anthem, and everyone stood awkwardly. After refilling the wineglasses, Klaus continued.

"My lords and ladies, knights of Hungary, peers of the kingdom, I am your humble servant. The Knights of Saint Stephen, an organization to which all your graces belong by virtue of your titles, is working to restore the monarchy in Hungary. We want to bring about a Hungary true to its noble origins, purged of the foreign elements that have polluted it for most of this century . . ."

Megyery went on in this vein without being interrupted, until there was a dreadful choking sound, and everyone started in alarm.

Count Windisch-Graetz had been surreptitiously swallowing a cabbage roll during the speech, and part of it had lodged in his windpipe. Moving past the helpless faces around me, I put my arms around the count and performed the Heimlich maneuver. A chunk of gristle shot out of his mouth.

"No need to thank me," I murmured when the embarrassed count mumbled his gratitude in German.

"Where did you learn to do such a thing?" Countess Nadazdy asked. "Are you a doctor?"

"No, no. It's the Heimlich maneuver. I learned it on *Sesame Street,* an American children's show."

Megyery resumed speaking, but the nearness of mortality and the sordid nature of the actual world had touched the room, and ideals didn't seem quite as lofty anymore.

"Where are the active, er, political, other members of the Knights of Saint Stephen?" Baron Thurzo asked. "Why are they not here?"

I looked out the window and saw the leathery swarm of my "honor guard" passing the wine around. It occurred to me that they might be the sole "active members" of Saint Stephen's Knights.

Klaus answered the baron politely but quickly. "We thought it best if your graces met first amongst yourselves in order to discuss some of what's being proposed. Our membership consists of an executive council of ten, of which I am the secretary, and a general membership of eight thousand. Your graces are the supreme council. A formal session of the entire group will be scheduled when your graces can agree on a time."

Klaus then proceeded to explain the extremely complicated business of primogeniture, which had to be clarified before the present company could begin to consider the candidacy of the next king of Hungary.

The trouble was that most everyone in the room had a claim, because there was no direct descendant of the Corvinus line. It had to be more or less a matter of agreement between ourselves.

As their graces pulled one flag after another out of the national hors d'oeuvres and downed their wine as quickly as the glass could be refilled, it became apparent to me that the sorry crew didn't have the slightest idea who ought to be king, although it was apparent that some of them had given the matter some thought.

Particularly articulate on the matter was a Count Rakoszi, who like myself was descended from Transylvanian princes and numerous illustrious royal servants. He produced a kind of chart, using flags plucked from cabbage rolls to trace some of the main lines.

I kept both my silence and my distance from this display, because almost everyone else had crowded around the table and there wasn't any room. I could see Baron Thurzo's suit-jacket sleeve dip into the mayonnaise as he jostled for a better view of the flags.

It was thus with some surprise that I heard my name called and was asked to advance forward.

According to the toothpick chart, I was slightly ahead of this Count Rakoszi for the throne of Hungary.

The whole solemn business of staring at a bunch of dirty toothpicks with grains of rice and meat juice sticking to them in order to ascertain my rights to the kingdom was more than I could bear. I could feel my face widen into an unseemly smile that threatened—I could feel it—to break into laughter.

Fortunately, Count Rakoszi said, quite reasonably, that no toothpick chart could settle anything and that a rigorous charting based on the *Almanach de Gotha* and Hungarian genealogies had to be drawn by specialists in the field. Nonetheless, he insisted that he had given the matter much thought and that he would be very surprised if the specialists' conclusions did not coincide with his own. The likeliest candidate was doubtlessly Count Bathory.

This proclamation was greeted by the others with what I thought to be sighs of relief.

"So I'm the king of Hungary now!" I said in my best New York accent. I felt like the hero of a bad Hollywood picture. The cab-driver prince.

No one laughed. I assumed that the peers didn't watch many movies.

"I resign," I added, "because of my great love for a commoner." This quip did get some smiles.

"Well, I would not hasten to do that," said Count Rakoszi. "There is a way to go before we can be certain."

I looked closer. In addition to all the pronounced physical defects of good breeding, the count exuded dark mass. He would be a formidable adversary if he ever entertained the idea of challenging my claim to the throne.

The subject of the succession dominated the rest of the proceedings. With hands over well-tailored lapels the peers reaffirmed their patriotic nostalgia, but not one of them declared any readiness to return definitively. They had families, jobs, and interests elsewhere in the world, where they had been scattered for more than half a century.

Nonetheless, one by one, they found an occasion to bow when I looked in their direction. After a time I felt as if I deserved these bows. I didn't think them strange. I did not even flinch when Klaus, who should have known better, tried to kiss my hand again. I let him. The wet hairy sensation of his face pressed against my hand seemed exceedingly familiar. But not from this lifetime.

As the wine warmed them, my relations began to take on more and more the characteristics of hunting dogs. I had the brief impression that I was watching a kennel of high-priced mutts.

I was brought out of my canine reverie by Klaus, who was—once more—talking. He declared that there was no need for their graces to return definitively. It would suffice that they pay symbolic visits to their ancestral holdings in order to claim them. The Knights of Saint Stephen would see to the practical details of taking actual possession. More important than the question of return was the business of agreeing on a monarch.

I adjusted the crease of my pants and recrossed my legs. I must confess that in the presence of so many of my addled peers I began to feel sort of normal. I am an adaptable creature. What I usually experienced as normal, that is, my life in exile in New York, may in fact not have been normal at all. Logically, this indolent kennel was a lot more normal. Here I was among my own, creatures with similar features, discussing matters our parents, grandparents, and ancestors had shared. Our common pasts reached farther back than the memories of most Americans. How could I have more in common with my apartment-house neighbors in New York than with these shareholders of my own history?

There was an easy familiarity in the national murmur of this moth-eaten gathering. Lands that had once belonged to us had been taken from us. Those lands must surely share some of our physical characteristics as well. Forts on hills shaped like the noses on our faces doubtless still kept vigil over nationalized farms whose furrowed fields were our very skin. What could be the harm in at least visiting some of these sights that "belonged" to me, whether I claimed them or not?

Megyery handed out mimeographed sheets listing the former domains of those present.

He's not doing this for me, I reminded myself. He has other—unknown—reasons. Still, I took the blue dittoed sheet—a reproduction process all but extinct in America—and felt its cheap paper with a certain feeling. Not rational, I know.

In the course of this extraordinary meeting, Teresa and Imre had disappeared. During a lull in the din, I heard the sound of crying from another room. I got up and walked out in search of the sound, which became louder. I opened the door to what I assumed was a bedroom.

Standing by a small bureau by the window, an angry Imre towered over Teresa, who sat crying on the bed.

"What's wrong?" I asked.

Teresa wiped her eyes with the back of her hand.

"Nothing," she said.

"What's going on?" I glowered at Imre.

"Nothing," he said.

"Nothing," reiterated Teresa.

Whatever this "nothing" was, it upset me. I suspected some kind of jealousy fit. After all, it was only natural.

"Come and join us!" I said imperiously, perhaps even royally.

Obediently the two young people followed me into the room.

The meeting broke up inconclusively, having accomplished a generalized state of nostalgia, like an evening session at the Golden Paprikash in New York. I had seen enough teary-eyed Hungarians bemoaning a past that didn't exist and beauty that existed only in memory to recognize the ersatz brew.

Still, something in me, if not all of me, was anxious and even curious about the future.

Klaus begged their excellencies to remain in Budapest for the next few days. The political map was changing from hour to hour. Another meeting was possible early next morning.

Klaus asked me to stay. The rest took their leave, bowing to me as they crowded the exit.

"I can't stay long, Klaus. I have to get to the streets to file a story for my newspaper, if it's not too late."

"Your Highness," Klaus said without a trace of irony in his voice, "you must remain here. We may need to present you to the nation on television sometime during this night."

A shiver ran up my spine. Klaus's punks *were* poised for a takeover of the TV station, just as I had suspected. I had to play along. And I had to get away.

"Fine," I said, "but I must return to my hotel briefly to get some things."

Megyery agreed.

Imre and Teresa accompanied me. The black car was waiting outside. The three of us sat uncomfortably in the back seat without talking. Teresa's warm thigh rubbed against mine, but I couldn't help noticing that her other leg was pressed against Imre's.

At the Gellart I asked my companions to wait while I went up to my room. Just when I got to the elevator, I turned and said casually to Teresa, "Shouldn't you get the materials for your translation?"

Before Imre could object, Teresa sprinted to my

side. The elevator door opened. We stepped in, leaving Imre behind in the lobby.

"We have to get out of here," I told Teresa, who looked red-eyed and upset.

She agreed, but without much enthusiasm.

On the second floor, the elevator stopped and a portly gentleman got in. We got out.

We followed the stairs down to the basement level. The dim storage area was filled with ancient Hapsburg furniture. A complex maze of pipes snaked overhead.

I pushed open another door and we found ourselves inside the famed Gellart Hotel steam baths. Rows of naked men with imprecise outlines slept in the steam with disintegrating newspapers in their hands. We slipped and skidded along the wet floor to another exit. At last we were outside in a small alley. None of Megyery's boys were there.

Hand in hand, Teresa and I hurried away from the Gellart toward the Danube. When we had jogged a safe distance, we stopped in a café about half a mile from the hotel.

"What do we do now?" asked Teresa.

"Now we rent a car and visit my ancestral holdings."

I had with me the list of Bathory castles and lands that Klaus had given me. Also an American Express card, a passport, and a small tape recorder. But more important, for the first time since arriving in Hungary I had a reason to act: I wanted to get away from the politics of the moment in order to find my history. And I had the perfect companion: a young historian who knew more about my ancestors than I did. Of course, in my arrogant new sense of purpose I assumed that Teresa was interested in the same thing. I even assumed—oh boundless conceit!—that she might be romantically interested in me. After all, she was my first love's child—and I felt proprietary.

We pored over a Michelin map of Hungary. Teresa marked the sites with a Hungarian-made red Magic Marker that bled on the pillow between her thumb and forefinger. The most important places, Sarvar and Kereshtur, were within a day's drive from Budapest.

F RANZ NADAZDY RETURNED FROM Vienna to marry Elizabeth Bathory in the middle of October 1574. The autumn rains had already begun, soon to turn the whole Hungarian plain into a field of mud.

Franz had not finished his studies, but the likelihood of war compelled Ursula Nadazdy to act. Turkish campaigns usually started in late spring, so the Nadazdys had but a few months to fortify Sarvar and to raise an army strong enough to withstand the advances of Murad's well-trained and battle-toughened soldiers. The Hungarian nobles could count on little outside help. It was every castle for itself. King Matthias of Hungary was in debt to his own nobles, and his relations with Austria were strained.

The gradual sinking of the Austrian emperor Maximilian into the religious quarrels of the German lands, added to his heir's madness in Prague, had thrown all of Europe into an uncertain and depressed state of mind. Reports of Prince Rudolf's pranks at Hradschin Castle in Prague were on everyone's lips. Jokes, caricatures, and crude pamphlets had already sprung up among the people, portraying the next emperor as a lizard or pig-headed demon. Nor did those who had personally met him have anything good to say. "He smells like sulphur and acts like a rabid dog," Ursula Nadazdy claimed after a visit to Prague. Most likely he had just been rubbed with some putrid ointment by one of his alchemists and was having one of his notorious convulsive visions.

The Counter-Reformation, begun by the pope in Rome to counter Luther's revolution, added to the confusion of the nobles on the threatened first lines of defense against the Ottoman Empire. The Nadazdys and the Bathorys were Lutherans, but this had always seemed to them to be strictly a matter of choice having nothing whatsoever to do with their military alliances within the Christian camp. Branches of the Bathory and Nadazdy families were Catholic, as was Stephen Bathory, the future king of Poland.

The addition of religious argumentation to the already complicated business of interfamily relations did not bode well. Ursula was determined to take matters into her own hands at Sarvar. After the wedding, which would bring substantial revenue for defense, she intended to send Franz on a diplomatic mission to the Turks to see if any separate deals could be made with the sultan. She did not confuse the interests of Hungary with those of the empire, or the interests of her faith with her need for self-defense.

Franz rode through the castle gates on a white Arabian horse, ahead of his servants. He was followed by a carriage filled with gifts for his mother and fiancée. Despite his youth, Franz was a connoisseur of beautiful objects.

He brought Ursula twelve gold plates and cups made in Florence, inscribed "For Ursula Kaniszay-Nadazdy, than whom none is fairer. In loving affection, Her Son."

He gave his future wife a Spanish-crafted pendant made of gold, enamel, diamonds, rubies, and pearls, and a gold cup with hunting scenes engraved in filigree enamel.

He had also brought books for the Sarvar library, including incunabula illuminated by Austrian and Italian monks. One of these, inscribed to his mother, was the *Mirror of Gold of the Sinful Soul,* a Latin devotional that Ursula had often quoted from memory. It had been taught to her in her childhood. For his future wife he had purchased a doeskin-bound parchment edition of Boccaccio's *Tales from the Decameron.* Franz, who prided himself on his Viennese sentimental education, hoped that Elizabeth would be every bit as graceful as the protagonists of that great story, while at the same time showing the acumen that a lady of her caliber must necessarily possess in the trying days ahead.

He did not have much insight into the character of his fiancée beyond the rather brief descriptions in his mother's letters, which parsimoniously praised Elizabeth's aptitude for memorizing the Latin classics and her progress in learning the harp. There had also been an allusion to Elizabeth's "becoming lost in her tender youth during Dozsa's revolt and seeing terrible things, because of the negligence of her servants and the inadequacy of her guard." Franz didn't know what to expect, but he trusted his mother.

The bells of the church rang on first sighting of the young Count Nadazdy. Ursula and Elizabeth, clad for the occasion in high-collared ruffled gowns, led the local nobility, churchmen, and maids in welcoming Franz at the gates of Sarvar. The young man looked magnificent in his light armor; the setting sun struck the gold cross engraved on his breastplate.

Franz Nadazdy smelled strongly of horse. Elizabeth drew in his scent with a long breath even as she curtsied. She loved the smell of horse almost as much as she loved her horse, Luna, whom she had brought with her.

Franz was broad-faced and broad-shouldered, every-thing about him suggesting dense muscle and disci-plined strength. He was also shy. He took her hand but held it only for a second—long enough for the mildly fragrant oil of Darvulia's herb to seep from the skin of Elizabeth's hand into the skin of Franz's. His skin, made rough by sword-fighting and archery, felt like bark and leather together. Elizabeth was pleased. Many times when she would find herself alone—a hard feat these days—she would rub herself against the bark of trees in the castle park. She also had many dolls made from leather and bark that felt just like her fiancé's skin.

When they sat down to dinner that evening under Ursula's watchful eye, Elizabeth caught Franz looking at her furtively over his soup, then quickly lowering his eyes. She looked straight back at him. She liked the way his strong neck strained against the lace collar. His eyes were black and cruel despite their apparent shyness. The candles flickered when he spoke. He had a clear loud voice and expressed himself eloquently but without frills.

At the feast that followed, Franz regaled the com-pany with tales of Vienna, some of which made the women blush. He told of a particular escapade when he and two of his companions had disguised themselves as beggars and gone into the markets by the Danube to look unobserved on the life of the poor.

In one of the sorry taverns by the river they watched two Hungarian merchants behaving abominably toward a poor widow traveling with her young daughter to west-ern Hungary, where they had been promised employ-ment in the household of a wealthy lady.

One of the merchants had thrown a silver coin at the woman's feet and, urged on by his drunken companion, made indelicate suggestions. He said, among other things Franz would not repeat, that if the widow would pick up the coin with her mouth she could earn another by entertaining them in their room later. The poor daughter, who could have been no older than Elizabeth, burst into tears as her mother, compelled by need, abandoned her dignity and knelt before the fat velvet-clad merchant.

She had begun to lower herself to the floor when Franz and his friends advanced on the merchants. Franz's friend Thomas pulled the woman to her feet, while another put a protective arm around the child. Franz himself kicked the silver coin away and watched it roll under the feet of the drunken patrons, many of whom dove for it.

Franz then demanded that the merchants beg forgiveness of the ladies. The men laughed, and one of them made an obscene gesture with his hand.

Franz threw open his beggar's cloak and drew his short sword, which he brought down on the merchant's hand. He severed it at the wrist while it was still making the obscene gesture. (Franz didn't tell the ladies that he had placed the hand, still making its obscene gesture, in a glass container that he had proudly brought back with him.)

The other merchant rose drunkenly to his feet, only to meet Franz's blade at his throat. The tavern fell quiet. Once more Franz demanded of the two boors that they beg the ladies' forgiveness. Sensing that things were not going their way, the two merchants, one of them holding his blood-gushing stump in the air, fell to their knees and kissed the dirty floor. Franz then allowed them to seek a physician. The tavern owner gave everyone free ale and roast venison.

"What happened to the women?" asked Elizabeth.

"My lady, I did not take the liberty of asking after the name of the noble they were going to serve. I compensated them with a gold florin each for the indignities they suffered."

Franz did not mention that after drinking many pots of ale, the three young men took a room above the tavern to sleep it off. They did not trust themselves to return to school in their condition.

Not long after they retired, the mother, whose name was Jo Anna Tohka, came to their room to show her gratitude. In fact, she also came bearing a business proposition concerning her daughter, Dori, who was a virgin. Although she was certain that her daughter's virginity was of great importance to her future husband when, God willing, she was going to find one, the mother was not averse to allowing the noble and brave young men who had saved her from shame to take Dori's virginity in gratitude, and for another gold florin.

She herself, in her capacity as mother, would stand by to make sure that the performance of this major occasion met all their expectations. She was also willing to assist any of the young men who did not gain complete satisfaction by giving him the additional pleasure. And this would cost another florin. She offered either to come back with her daughter to their room or to entertain the gentlemen one by one in her own chamber, which happened to be next door.

Franz was elected by the others for the privilege of deflowering the virgin whose honor he had defended. Franz entered the darkened chamber next door and found the girl dressed in a modest white linen dress, which her mother pulled roughly over her head. Franz was no novice with women, but until now they had all been grown wenches with profuse hair on their mons veneris and under their arms. He had never seen such unbroken smoothness, from which only two tiny budding breasts protruded. Spurred on by thoughts of Elizabeth, of whom he dared think rather sacrilegiously at this moment, he lay on top of the trembling young girl and parted her thighs with his hand. He probably could never have entered the maiden if it had not been for her mother's helpful guidance. With the aid of a salve that Jo Anna applied to his virile member and to her daughter's small passageway, he managed to effect a slight entry. After some effort, encouraged by the girl's helpful hand as well as by the mother's well-placed caresses and occasional obscenities whispered into his ear, Franz found himself halfway inside. Soon the supine child cried out something Franz didn't understand and pulled him closer. He found himself entirely inside, and there was a great deal of stickiness all around, which Franz assumed to be blood, though he didn't look. He did not ask his companions how they fared when they visited the widow and her daughter later that night.

In the morning, the women were gone. Franz suffered from a terrible headache, partly from the ale, partly from fear of having contracted some disease of common women. On the other hand, he felt rather proud to have taken a virgin, an activity that had been quite common among his ancestors, who took their droit du seigneur seriously. Theoretically, Franz still had that right as a feudal lord, but he doubted that the fanatical Lutherans with whom his mother had surrounded herself would condone such a thing.

Naturally he spoke none of this out loud, but Elizabeth, with uncanny intuition, sensed that the story of the two women did not end so abruptly. Susanna Forgach had been invited to Sarvar for the celebration of Ursula Nadazdy's fiftieth birthday, and Elizabeth thought she would ask her about the fate of the two women.

Elizabeth had been preparing for her wedding night in her own way. She had discussions, with some practical illustrations, about marriage, milk, men's seed, the menstruum, and other preparatory subjects.

The first and briefest conversation had been with Ursula, whose views Elizabeth was already familiar with. The only surprising thing Ursula had added was that she believed a young woman should breast-feed her first-born herself, and not deliver it to a wet nurse as was the custom. Elizabeth, who had still not thought very deeply about the matter, nodded her head in agreement. The thought of giving birth was far from her immediate concerns.

The better discussion, with practical illustrations, was with her aunt Klara. Klara described most graphically to her young niece what takes place in the marital bed. Her description went beyond everything Elizabeth knew, and she had thought herself pretty knowledgeable. Klara described the man's sexual organ as a kind of war club that bludgeoned a woman into a stupor from which she did not recover until she gave birth to a baby.

By way of illustration, Klara showed Elizabeth a thick rounded club of well-polished wood that had been carved in the shape of a phallus. The object had two leather straps attached to one end. After Elizabeth had run her hand over the surface of the object, which was at least twice as thick as her wrist, Klara told her that she would teach her the effects and the form of the sexual act.

Clearly, since Elizabeth's main asset was her virtue, Klara was not going to subject her unnecessarily to the pain she would inevitably experience later. Klara herself would allow Elizabeth to subject her to the action of the wooden phallus.

The two women shed their clothes on Klara's bed, before the mirror. Elizabeth admired Klara's well-shaped figure, her full breasts, her rounded hips. But she could see clearly now that her own breasts were not far behind. Even Klara took notice.

"Look at the poppy cakes!" she exclaimed, and

kissed Elizabeth's tiny nipples, to Elizabeth's embarrassment.

Klara tied the wooden phallus to Elizabeth's skinny middle by one strap. She passed the other strap between the girl's legs and tied it to the first. Elizabeth considered the heavy, cumbersome wooden club hanging between her legs and was amused.

"How can men walk about with such ridiculous dangling objects between their legs?" she asked. "Don't they fall over? How do they keep their balance?"

Elizabeth took a few clumsy steps and pretended to fall. When she moved, the strap tightened and hurt her a little, but not in an unpleasant way.

Klara lay down on the canopy bed and opened her legs to display herself to Elizabeth, who had only just begun to grow soft down on her pudendum. Elizabeth was familiar with the look of a grown woman's aperture. She had already seen Klara's, and she had investigated Teresa's many times. Aunt Klara's was very different from Teresa's: the lips of her vagina were swollen and greedy, and her "little man in the boat," which was but a small pea in Teresa, looked like an angry purple string bean.

Elizabeth lay on the soft pillows of her aunt's breasts, feeling like a tiny ant crawling on the body of a giantess. With her left hand, Klara took the wooden phallus and inserted it inside herself. She then instructed Elizabeth to move her hips up and down so that the monstrous wood would go back and forth.

At first, Elizabeth's clumsy movements distracted Klara, who kept trying to adjust her niece's skinny buttocks at just the right angle. But eventually Elizabeth established a rhythm and penetrated her aunt deftly. At least she thought so, judging by Klara's sighs. Elizabeth found that she enjoyed hearing Klara sigh with pleasure, although she had a brief moment of doubt when she considered that she might be hurting her. But instead of restraining her, the thought that she was causing Klara pain actually inflamed the young countess, who began rising higher and falling in harder. The little strap between her legs was giving her excruciating but pleasurable sensations. Aunt Klara's sighs were growing louder, and Elizabeth began whimpering herself. When their combined song reached a crescendo, Aunt Klara, streaming with sweat, reached up and squeezed Elizabeth so hard she knocked the breath out of her.

The two women lay there quietly for a time, feeling each other's heart beat violently.

"Now the difference," began Klara educationally, "between what you did to me with the polished penis and what Franz will do to you with his living one can be very great, one way or another. It may be very great in a disappointing way, or it may be even greater in the greatest way. I certainly hope the latter, for your sake."

When Elizabeth told Klara that she had a great desire to insert something in herself right away, her aunt wagged her finger disapprovingly. "Your virtue is your seal of honor. Don't forget that. There are ways, of course, to give yourself satisfaction without piercing the veil that men prize so much."

To exemplify what she meant, Klara asked her to lie on her back and spread her legs apart. If Teresa's little "man in the boat" was the size of a pea and Klara's the size of a string bean, Elizabeth's was a tiny pebble. Klara put her mouth on her niece's finely drawn pink little opening and kissed the pebble.

Elizabeth was familiar with the surge of pleasure that followed and the small beads of moisture that formed. She had been fond of touching her little pebble since she'd been five years old. But unlike her skinny fingers moving the little hood about, Aunt Klara's tongue was hot, wet, and firm.

Elizabeth abandoned herself to her aunt's ministrations and drifted off on a pleasurable reverie. She saw the quick, bright eyes of her fiancé, Franz, and his well-filled velvet tights. She put her arms around him and unhooked his sword. Franz took her in his arms and she felt his polished wooden phallus between her legs. The next moment, however, his wooden manhood became a round Gypsy roast and it was seeking her anus instead of her maidenhood. Franz slowly turned into the Gypsy who was killed for her, and she quickly chased away the image of the barefoot musician pierced by the iron maiden. Next, for some reason, she saw a dead horse lying in a field with his belly split open. She couldn't help but notice the dead horse's erection. It was long, thin, and had a brown wet knob at the end, on which a swarm of greedy flies had settled and were sucking.

As the pleasure emanating from her throbbing little pebble increased like a wave under Klara's skillful tongue-lashing, Elizabeth invoked her friend Andrei in order to rid herself of the unpleasant vision of the fly-ridden horse cock. Andrei's gentle countenance immediately sprung to her mind's eye, holding a glass vial with a milky substance in it. Elizabeth took the vial from him and drank its contents. Immediately she became long and transparent like a dragonfly, and she fastened her lips to Andrei's small hump and began to suck greedily. She now knew what the flies on the horse felt, and a great deliciousness spread through all her limbs as she sucked the nectar from Andrei's hump. She shuddered as the last drops of milk slid between her legs and were swallowed by her Aunt Klara.

Elizabeth looked at her aunt, who was sprawled at the foot of the bed bathed in sweat, with her eyes closed and an expression of happiness on her face, which was covered by her undone hair.

Elizabeth leapfrogged over her aunt and went to the

looking glass. A bluish light was playing about her face as she looked in the mirror. She thought she heard the hum of dragonfly wings.

When Klara came to, Elizabeth told her the curious reveries she had experienced during her pleasure. She had been distressed, she said, not by the rather unappetizing but by no means off-putting images of the dead horse, but by her husband's strange insistence in searching out her back door rather than her God-given entryway.

Klara pondered this and frowned. "It is true," she said, "that some men prefer that. The advantage of that mode of loving, known as Turkish, is that you will be spared pregnancy, which, as you know, is mostly pain and sorrow, and it never stops. If your husband prefers the Turkish way, you are a fortunate woman."

Elizabeth wasn't sure about what she desired. Also she could see no earthly way in which that tiny back hole could accommodate something as large as the polished penis.

"There is only one way to find out," said Aunt Klara, "but I am rather exhausted myself. Is Teresa hereabouts?"

She was. The maid ran in out of breath when she heard her name called. She had been sitting on the lap of a halberdier charged with guarding the ladies' wing.

Elizabeth explained succinctly to her that they needed a subject for demonstrating the Turkish way. Without much complaining (Teresa was used by now to her mistress's odd demands) the girl unfastened her shawl, stepped out of her dress, and wiggled out of her petticoat. Among other skills she was learning, Teresa had mastered getting in and out of her clothes in a shake of a lamb's tail.

Teresa lay obediently on her stomach and Klara straddled her, having attached the large wooden phallus still wet from her juices. Klara attempted to carefully guide the wide rounded tip into the maid's anus but was met by stiff resistance. Teresa had also begun screaming from the moment it became evident what the demonstration would consist of.

"This is intolerable, you stupid servant girl," shouted Klara. She took Teresa's shawl from the floor and lifted the girl's head by the hair. She then put the twisted shawl in her mouth and tied it behind the back of her head. Teresa's muffled screams were all but inaudible now.

The second attempt failed as well, so Klara rubbed some ointment from a jar on the wooden club and inserted one, then two fingers into the maid's stubborn behind. With great difficulty, Aunt Klara managed to insert the club inside Teresa. After a number of difficult thrusts, Teresa quit wiggling so much, and her muffled screams became subdued. With increasing force, Klara moved in and out of the maid, until she felt that her niece was satisfied in understanding the Turkish way. When she withdrew the club, there was blood on it.

Teresa ran out of the room rubbing her behind. The halberdier was waiting on the other side of the door, but she didn't even glance at him as she ran teary-eyed to the privy to relieve and wash herself.

Elizabeth and Klara had a good laugh at the expense of the silly goose. They called Klara's maids and asked them to draw a bath. They took their bath together and splashed about like two children while the girls soaped and scrubbed them.

After dinner, Elizabeth and Maestro Gozzoli performed on the harp while the Szigedy twins who were being educated at Sarvar sang an old song about the tragedy that had befallen Hungary at the battle of Mohacs.

Then Franz recited with great feeling his own rendering, from an Italian version, of an eighth-century Anglo-Saxon poem called "The Wanderer":

The memories of my heart lie in heavy chains
While far from my kinsmen I wander
Driven by grief from my homeland . . .
If only I could find once more
Someone to show me kindness in the evening
Someone to pour my ale
Or should I dare dream of her fair face
In the long ago?

So sadly did Franz Nadazdy recite this that his listeners all had a feeling of melancholy, and perhaps a premonition of the sorrows of the war that lay ahead.

To dispel the gloom, one of the local nobles called on Melotus to recite an epic, but the assembled company protested all at once, which made Melotus run out of the room, while everyone laughed. The problem was that the singer's stories had gotten so strange as to be almost senseless. Everyone hastened to tell young Franz about the kind of stories Melotus had been reciting since Elizabeth came to the castle. He now sang of virgin girls who lost their skins on lakes and became swans; of ladders made from the hair of maidens beheaded by Turks, who sold their headless bodies to sky monsters; of cities made of red-hot iron where dwelled the spirits of Arpad's nobles; of gardens where trees were really young maidens rooted weeping to the ground . . . Melotus, who had once recited Dante's *Inferno* in Italian, who could render the French verses of *Tristan and Yseult* and declaim the *De Rerum Natura* in Latin— Melotus, Hungary's most erudite poet, had become utterly . . . Hungarian. It was as if a beautiful garden cultivated by refined hands had suddenly reverted to nature. Melotus had abandoned the well-polished parables of the classics for barbarous and barely understandable tales of bear paws hidden in honey pots or of the waters of life and death. Either Melotus was going mad or, as someone suggested, all the stories began climbing into his head at once and he mixed them up.

Elizabeth kept silent during this exchange, because she did not think Melotus's stories strange. They had a charming effect on her imagination that, hours after Melotus had finished, helped her wander through his magic worlds. She found deep meanings in his tales, which were more like riddles than stories. She loved best his stories of magic kingdoms where no one aged. They touched something in Elizabeth's soul: not something that was growing like her young breasts, but something that sat hidden deep inside her already grown, waiting to be revealed. And there was something else she did not yet dare articulate. She felt Hungarian to the core. She loved the stories of her people and the customs of simple folk. She had gone in disguise among villagers many times. She loved the shades of red in the embroidery of girls' blouses and the riotous colors of their festivities. She thought paprika a spice superior to cardamon and believed the Hungarian language to be capable of as much subtlety as French. Had she given her opinion on this last subject, she would have been laughed out of the room. Hungarian nobles still wrote to one another in Latin, believed Italian to be the language of poetry and French the language of drama.

Pastor Ponikenuz, who did not like the frivolous direction the evening was taking (he also did not like the torrid glances that the engaged couple kept exchanging), proposed a serious topic of conversation: the education and duties of a young woman. He was taking quite a chance here, as he became well aware when Ursula shot him a look full of disapproval.

226 · *Andrei Codrescu*

"Nonetheless," he insisted, "since this great celebration is for a young man who will soon be married to a young lady, the subject is of great importance."

Since he had brought up the subject, the pastor offered the opinion that more important than a woman's education was that she be well mannered, clever, prudent, and capable, that she be a good manager of her husband's property, house, and children. In short, she should be exactly like Ursula Kaniszay-Nadazdy, who was the ideal prototype of all well-born women.

Drawn into the subject against her will, Ursula retorted that she appreciated the good preacher's praise and agreed with him that, in these days of danger and war, a woman should be able to rule. It was all to the good to be pleasant, to dance gracefully and to appreciate poetry, to entertain graciously, and so on, but a woman should also be able to keep track of the business of her estates, to know the difference between good and bad wine, to have a practical regard for the qualities of her servants, and not to allow the flattery of preachers to overtake her own good common sense.

Everyone laughed at this, but Ponikenuz, his severe and thin person stung to the quick, replied that while this might well be true, a woman should not be overly concerned with rhetoric, but rather with probity and prudence, and that it was not unbecoming for a woman to be silent. What was foul and abominable was to be wayward and behave badly. A woman's treasures were chastity, silence, and obedience, qualities that his mistress, rarest among women, possessed in quantity.

Franz interjected that he knew of no greater woman than his mother and that what made her great was not being skillful, happy, friendly, and obedient, but that she was firm and could run the vast Nadazdy estates as well as his father, God rest his soul. And furthermore, he did not want his own wife to exhibit solely those qualities that the church found so desirable, but he desired in her a thirst for knowledge, a love of books, and an enjoyment of those things that make life pleasant: dance, poetry, appreciation of beautiful objects, and even a good working knowledge of military strategy and weapons.

Elizabeth considered silently how she measured up to the ideals of her future husband. She found, to her satisfaction, that she could not quarrel with any of his desiderata. She thirsted for knowledge, but not solely for the knowledge to be found in books. She was not quite sure what direction this desire would take, and she wasn't sure whether her inquiring mind would find any answers satisfactory. She felt within herself the flame of burning curiosity that was not easily satisfied, and she suspected that such curiosity was not entirely benign. She remembered the fury she had felt before she had been able to ascertain whether her friend Andrei de Kereshtur's hump was hollow. She had had to pierce the hump with her brooch to reassure herself that he was not hiding anything from her. She had found herself unable many times to contain her anger at knowing a word but not its meaning. *Buggery* had been one such word, and she had not rested until she found its meaning, though that knowledge cost a poor Gypsy wretch his life. As for the other qualities Franz was looking for, she was sure she possessed them aplenty as well. Deep in her reflection, she heard her name.

"And what does Countess Bathory think of the subject?" came Paster Ponikenuz's unpleasant, high-pitched whine.

"The countess," she replied, "is terribly anxious to acquire all the qualities that the present company thinks desirable, and then, when she has acquired them, she would like to live where she can put them fully into practice without having them enumerated and discussed as if there were no other subjects in the world."

This was the second time in one evening that the good pastor had been reproached. Rebuffed by both mistresses, he thought longingly of his monkey, from whom such impertinence would not be possible. He began to conclude that in addition to having only one-third of a soul, women possessed a potent meanness that, at its most manifest, was a form of devil worship.

Elizabeth Bathory and Franz Nadazdy were married on May 9, 1575. Elizabeth was fifteen years old; Franz was twenty-one.

Feverish preparations were made to ensure that the union of two of the greatest families in Hungary would be properly celebrated.

Andrei de Kereshtur in his *Chronicles* spared no detail of the splendor. Elizabeth's parents, Baroness Anna and Baron George Bathory, arrived at Sarvar three days before the wedding. De Kereshtur described the splendid event from the moment of their arrival, dwelling long and lovingly on everything, including the foods for the wedding feasts, which had been obtained by raiding the forest, parks, ponds, warrens, rabbit runs, and dove cotes.

With the gluttonous glee of a starving monk, Andrei described the gleam of large pots filled with mortresses and quenelles, the seemingly endless rows of meat and fish pies, pastries, and fritters. He pondered the making of sauces from herbs, wine, verjuice, vinegar, onions, ginger, pepper, saffron, cloves, and cinnamon. He spoke of the gallons of mustard in clay pots arrayed on long wooden shelves. He was particularly taken by herring flavored with ginger, pepper, and cinnamon but did not slight the barrels full of mullet, shad, sole, flounder, plaice, ray, mackerel, salmon, and trout. There were even sturgeon, whale, porpoise, pike, crab, crayfish, oysters, and eels, brought at great expense from France.

Andrei listed "a mountain of bread loaves" and so many barrels of wine that "they stretched farther than the eye could see." In a rare moment of relaxed writing, the usually spare chronicler described the bleating of whole flocks of sheep waiting to be turned into roasts, the squeaking and squawking of fowls waiting to enter the finest molded aspics of the century, the grunting of piglets to be roasted on turning spits, the flocks of partridges dedicated to the enhancement of soups with their rich underwing flavor, and the sizzling and bubbling of sauces, glazes, and aperitifs. An artificial river of wine had been created in the great hall and made to flow between raised banks of stacked apples, pears, plums, and peaches. A river of ale flowed at the opposite end of the room, mainly for the lower nobility and burghers.

Grooms, smiths, laundresses, pantlers, butlers, stewards, dispensers, cupbearers, fruiterers, slaughterers, bakers, brewers, wafer makers, sauce cooks, poulterers, cofferers, carters, and clerks were brought from all of the Bathory and Nadazdy estates to help.

In addition came musicians of every kind, from harpists to organists, bringing harps, oliphants, psalteries, vielles, glockenspiels, mandolins, and bells. Singers, actors, acrobats, jugglers, puppeteers, and clowns from all over Christendom brought their skills.

An enormous variety of soothsayers came, from astrologers to tea-leafers. All these professionals had their own boys and girls in attendance.

The hundreds of guests arriving day and night with their retinues of servants had to be accommodated and fed, their horses had to be taken care of, and all their other needs seen to.

Ursula wanted to make sure that the wedding of her

son would surpass in splendor even the coronation of Stephen Bathory as prince of Transylvania. She wanted to send a twofold message throughout the kingdom: that the Nadazdy and Bathory estates had been united into the single most powerful fiefdom in Hungary and that the glory of the Protestant faith was second to none. For this latter reason, she had invited the greatest scholars and preachers of the Lutheran and Calvinist faith and had them seated in places of greater honor than the pope's prelates and envoys, who also came in numbers.

The Holy Roman Emperor, Maximilian, was ill and could not come. He sent his son Rudolf instead.

Rudolf arrived with his usual choir of sodomites, his odd-smelling chemists and bath makers, and three splendidly attired regiments of horsemen, many of whom were his frolic mates.

Elizabeth had been looking forward to the prince's arrival because she hoped that her friend Johannes might be among the retinue. She was told to her disappointment that Johannes was showing great promise in the fields of mathematics and astrology and had been sent to study in Florence.

As Rudolf's massive entourage entered the castle, there was discussion (and worry) about the size of the prince's armed guard, in view of the presence of King Matthias II, who was at odds with the emperor.

Franz took care to house Rudolf's soldiers in a rather remote area of the castle where his own garrison could keep them under observation. The old donjon had recently been renovated, and it had the added advantage of being surrounded by a small moat of its own, as if it were a separate castle. Two drawbridges led over the moat. Franz had the moat flooded with river water to the very top, and he stocked the water with stinging eels.

* * *

King Matthias was already very drunk when he arrived, three days before the wedding. He walked everywhere with his gold goblet in his hand, his long cloak sweeping through the halls as all fell to their knees and bowed until he passed.

Most of his wandering had to do with Franz. For no reason that Franz could discern, King Matthias had taken a great liking to him. "He is our only friend," the king was often heard to say. This was not a good thing for Franz Nadazdy, who began noticing other noblemen's narrowing eyes whenever they were discussing their common interests. Franz tried to reassure them—in vain—that he was not the king's man. He even gave them to understand that he considered the king a drunken fool, but no one believed him.

Matthias, meanwhile, tried to have Franz at his side at all times. It was only with the greatest difficulty—by pleading the taxing duties of his role—that Franz escaped the king in the days before the wedding. Of course, Matthias immediately forgot Franz's excuses and proceeded to look for him, shouting to anyone in his path that Franz was his only friend, that the bowed heads before him were but "empty gourds on a field of traitors." The restless king paced the corridors like a ghost, stumbled over things, walked into privies, poked his nose into kitchens and ladies' chambers.

In addition to shielding Franz from him, the castle attendants had the doubly difficult task of keeping the king from bumping into his archenemy Rudolf, who, happily for everyone concerned, came out only late at night, long after the king had been felled by food and drink.

The day before the wedding, King Matthias stumbled through the doors of Elizabeth's rooms, which had been left unlocked by Teresa, an unbelievable oversight.

A great deal of activity was going on. A swarm of seamstresses, hatters, veilers, cutters, ironers, shoemakers, and assorted other attendants revolved around the young bride, fitting her for her nuptial dress.

The place was a madhouse, and the king went unnoticed until he had advanced almost to the center of the swarm, where the pale, delicate, and naked young countess sat on a blue velvet stool before the mirror.

When Elizabeth's servants recognized the king, they fell to their knees on the floor and bowed like a wheat field bent by a strong wind.

Elizabeth, who had been looking at herself in the mirror, was left sitting on her stool while her servants lowered themselves all around her. She did not know what had happened, so she swung around to castigate the wretches who had so suddenly abandoned her, and found herself face to face with King Matthias II of Hungary.

Now, Elizabeth was faced with a great dilemma. There was no question as to the proper thing to do. She had to curtsy and then fall to one knee before her sovereign. Elizabeth became terribly conscious of her nudity and of the humiliating ritual that she was duty bound to perform. How could she rise, let alone move? Defiance and humiliation raced through her body like two burning flames. But she could not see any way in which she could avoid her duty.

For his part, King Matthias had become paralyzed by the sight of the girl's perky little breasts, whose pale nipples looked at him without fear. When he was able to tear his eyes from her nipples, he raised them to her face and was smitten by the flawless oval of that visage and by the angry bow of her lips. But it was when he saw her eyes that the king fell deeply in thrall, like a nocturnal fish caught by the light of a ferryman's lamp. Those eyes were black, deep, angry, and layered, like the soul of Hungary. These, the king told himself, are the eyes of Hungaria herself. He recognized in their depth something profoundly national. These are heraldic eyes, he told himself; I must bow before them. At the same time, Matthias became aware of the girl's humiliation. He had surprised her at her toilette, which was very bad form, even for a king. He had to beg her forgiveness.

At the very moment that the king, overcome by the mystical emotion of beauty and by the need to apologize, threw himself down before the naked girl, Elizabeth herself, determined to do her duty, flung herself off her stool to kneel before her purple-robed king.

The king's bald dome with a simple gold circle around it met Elizabeth's flying dark tresses in midair; they collided and fell inelegantly, one on top of the other.

They rested like this, sprawled on the floor, breathless and aware of their absurdity, but no one dared to help them, though scores of servants lay stock-still all around.

Finally Elizabeth gathered her slender corpus from the folds of the king's robe and curtsied properly, even as a swelling the size and color of a cuckoo's egg began forming above her eyes.

The king himself dragged his blubbery flesh with some difficulty from the floor and rose to one knee. One of his hands shot up in the air, and his cupbearer instantly put a goblet of wine into it.

"My dearest lady," spoke the king on one knee to the kneeling, unclothed flower before him, "I kneel to you, whoever you are, because you are Hungary. I beg your forgiveness, great lady. If you be the daughter of a great noble, even if he is my enemy, I will make peace and beg for your company. If you are one of the traitors' children, I will behead them and keep you as a sign of divine providence . . ."

Matthias II rambled in this manner for the duration of two goblets of wine, until his knee, overcome by royal weight, began to hurt.

With great difficulty, and only after listening politely to the king's ramble, did Elizabeth succeed in speaking. She explained that to her everlasting regret, shame, and embarrassment, she was not available to him because she herself was the object of the entire event. She was Elizabeth Bathory, the bride of Franz Nadazdy. She also begged the king to retire so that she could get dressed.

The king was not distressed by this news for very long. Rising to his feet, he impulsively took a gold ring with several large diamonds from his index finger. Grabbing Elizabeth's hand, he placed it on the fourth finger of her right hand. The ring, so much bigger than her finger, rolled off and fell to the floor, and was quickly out of sight.

None of the prostrate servants dared retrieve it. With the exception of the large seal-of-state ring with the royal coat of arms, the vanished ring had been the king's largest.

Later, when dozens of servants searched in vain for the vanished ring, popular superstition held that a black-winged angel had been seen descending to catch the rolling ring of Matthias II and flew off with it.

But at the time, the king rose and said good-bye to the kneeling maiden with a great flourish of his sleeves and with wine-sour breath.

As soon as the door closed after His Majesty, Elizabeth flew into a rage. Taking hold of anything likely to make an impression on flesh, the shrieking bride-to-be lashed out at her servants, many of whom would sport fresh gashes, scars, and swellings for weeks.

The worst of it befell Elizabeth's own maid Teresa,

who had been charged with locking the doors. Teresa had had the big key to Elizabeth's private chambers hanging from a belt around her waist. She had fully intended to lock the chamber as she had been told. Unfortunately she had run into the cook's assistant, who did not care a whit that Teresa's brutal husband had arrived with the party from Kereshtur. In fact, Teresa had been avoiding her husband all day and was persuaded by the cook's assistant to accompany him to the making of a walnut sauce only because the sauce kitchen was in a very remote part of the main castle kitchen. Indeed, the place was so far that Teresa nearly turned around several times for fear of the lost time. When they arrived at the place where the huge copper vat sat over flames, the cook's assistant pulled her behind some tall pots filled with shelled walnuts and lifted her skirt. In a desperate attempt to shorten the torture, Teresa turned around when the cook's assistant tried to prod her from behind, as was his wont.

"I want you to do it like a man," she said. She then lay carefully on the hay-strewn floor, lifted her dress and her petticoat, spread her legs, and pulled the clever cook on top of her. The young man did as he was told and, as Teresa had anticipated, lasted but a brief moment before spending himself.

Teresa leapt to her feet and ran back to lock the doors to her mistress's chamber. She was too late. She entered the room at the worst possible moment, right after the king had left.

Pausing from the pelting of her servants with sharp objects, Elizabeth spun furiously and sprang on Teresa. The others, taking advantage of their mistress's distraction, quickly ran out. Elizabeth tore Teresa's clothes as if they were spiderwebs. Then she scratched her flesh and bit her on the shoulder so hard that a piece came off, and Elizabeth chewed on it while beating her. She swallowed some of the flesh and spit the rest in the girl's face. Her phlegm was thick and bloody.

Teresa was never so terrified. Fearing for her life, the girl put her arms around her mistress and pulled her down on top of her. She also spread her legs very wide, as she had done only a few minutes before.

Elizabeth, interpreting this activity as unheard-of defiance, an impertinent attempt at self-defense, brought her little fist square between Teresa's thighs, hoping to hit her hard. On impact her fist met the slippery substance of the cook's assistant's secretion. Believing that Teresa had wet herself, Elizabeth pushed her fist as far as she could inside her servant, and aided by the cook's assistant's substance, she managed to bury her arm halfway up Teresa's vagina.

The oddest sensation took hold of Elizabeth: her anger was replaced by an intense curiosity. She wanted to know what was inside Teresa that made her so crazy. She wanted to look inside her. She opened her fist inside and fanned out all her fingers, touching the opening of Teresa's womb. She needed a light to see inside, a torch. Her fingers did not tell her enough. But Elizabeth was exhausted. Her tantrum had utterly spent her. She withdrew her hand and lay gasping on her back, while Teresa, bathed in blood, sweat, and sperm, sprang from the bed and disappeared from sight.

At the feast given by Ursula in her honor that evening, Elizabeth wore a veil. It covered the swelling on her forehead and the purple blotches her anger had brought up on her face. She sat very still through the many love songs composed in her honor by singers who performed them feelingly, accompanied by harp, lute, and vielle.

She was aware of the king's burning eyes fixed on her from the high place at the end of the table where he sat and of the equally piercing fire issuing from the eyes of her fiancé, Franz.

The story of what had happened that day had spread quickly through the castle and had reached Franz's ears almost immediately. He had quickly gone to Elizabeth when he heard about the terrible embarrassment but had found his fiancée's doors locked. The woman who guarded Elizabeth's chambers would not let him pass. From inside he heard what sounded like the crying and laments of a deeply wounded creature. They did not sound human. He had been on the verge of bursting through the door, but he was reassured by Elizabeth's women that what he was hearing was simply the sound of a woman's deep grief, a time when she could not be disturbed.

Franz left reluctantly, still unaware that the story of Elizabeth's humiliation, which was making the rounds of the palace, held a grave political challenge.

It was Count Thurzo who took him aside an hour before Ursula's dinner for Elizabeth and explained to him what everything meant. Franz Nadazdy was faced with a great test. If he did nothing to express his displeasure at the king's behavior, his enemies, who already believed that he had given his entire loyalty to Matthias, would become convinced of it and would henceforth treat him like an enemy of the nobility. If he expressed his displeasure to the king, it might lead to the king's withdrawal from the wedding and Franz's ostracism. There was also the matter of Rudolf, whose interpretation of the insult was not yet known. But it would not be beyond Rudolf to dream up some kind of advantage for himself out of the situation. Tensions were building by the moment.

With little time left to spare before dinner, Franz went to see the king. He found him slumped on a Turkish divan, drinking. Franz bowed, but Matthias waved impatiently to him and made room for him to sit on the divan.

Franz explained his position frankly, without mincing words. He added only that he hoped, for the sake of their friendship, that Matthias had simply been drunk and did not know that he'd attempted to place a love ring on his bride's finger.

Matthias regarded his young friend with a puzzled expression on his face during the recital of his situation.

"But . . . ," the puzzled king said, "I do not see your dilemma."

"My dilemma, my lord," Franz said impatiently, "is that you have stood before my naked wife-to-be and courted her. Now the whole nobility stands poised to see what happens next."

"What happens next?" asked the king.

"This is what I would like to know," Franz said.

"I am your king."

"I have no doubt of it, my sovereign . . ."

"Well, then," Matthias II, king of Hungary, said testily, "I will take your wife for myself on the first night of the wedding—*jus primae noctis*—and you can have her for a hundred years thereafter . . ."

Franz paled. Droit du seigneur had not been invoked in Hungary for two centuries. But he could see that Matthias was serious.

The day of the wedding began with the sound of the horn calling the guests to breakfast. Most of the servants had been up before the light of dawn, but the nobles were groggy and tired because they had been up late.

Elizabeth had barely slept, and when she finally did, she slept fitfully and had bad dreams. She dreamt that she had a secret pet, a mouse with two tails. Her mother-in-law had somehow discovered her secret and was trying to take it from her. Elizabeth moved her two-tailed mouse from room to room through secret passageways, only a step or two ahead of Ursula. In the morning she was exhausted.

After she heard about the king's request for *jus primae noctis,* she had sequestered herself in her chamber with her friend Andrei de Kereshtur, and they had spoken late into the night.

Elizabeth told Andrei that she would rather die than lie down with the king on her wedding night. She also confessed to him her reluctance to lie down with anybody now, including her husband, Franz Nadazdy. She believed that she loved him, yes, but that doing with him what servants do to each other did not appeal to her in the slightest. She was being only partly disingenuous, and her friend knew it.

He told her about certain erotic practices of the Cathars, who increased their love of God and their wisdom by practicing a wide variety of sexual exercises. The men withheld their seed during lovemaking, while women increased their ecstasy by means of bondage and pain. The Cathars also increased their spiritual understanding by inflaming themselves with images of the beloved until all the sexual energy was sucked upward to the top of their heads, where it blossomed in flowers of light.

Andrei had been practicing this "inflammation," but it hadn't been easy, because he'd had to reach even into his dreams in order to avoid nocturnal emissions. Otherwise he was still a virgin.

"That is all very well and good for you," Elizabeth said tartly, "but what do the Cathars say about the rest of us, who are not monks? I need to escape from the king's trap. What good is a flower at the top of my head going to do me?"

Andrei suggested that the Cathar love lessons applied to her situation. If she did indeed have to sleep with the king, she should imagine Franz in his stead. At the moment of the king's emission she should say slowly the words "I transform your seed into the seed of Franz." When next she would be making love with Franz, she should take his seed and say, "I take your seed and transform it into God's golden light." This would effectuate the attraction of only the best souls to her womb if she were to become impregnated.

Elizabeth said that there was no question of saying anything, because she wasn't going to sleep with any of them but would kill herself instead. But even if she didn't kill herself—and here Elizabeth allowed for a thoughtful pause—she would rather give herself to someone else first, so that neither one of them could have the honor of deflowering her.

Andrei de Kereshtur blushed very deeply. If his mistress was considering offering him the prize that she would deny the others, he did not see how he could refuse. Yet he felt himself completely unworthy. He was also sure that, faced by the nakedness and willingness of his beloved Elizabeth, he would not be able to reproduce what came so easily to him during nocturnal emissions. When Elizabeth made a movement with her hand, as if she was going to touch him, Andrei jumped up in the air.

Elizabeth laughed. "What is the matter, my bookish friend?"

Andrei explained with uncharacteristic hesitation and halting speech that he had gone back to see the Jew ben Lebus, who lived next door to the kind prostitute who had saved them from the lepers. He'd talked to ben Lebus about angels and had received a great deal of information about their activities, including the names of specific angels that attended him personally in order to guide him in his work. These angels demanded, above all, purity.

Ben Lebus had also sold him a book on *aurum potabile,* the substance sought after by alchemists, despite Andrei's protests that he was not interested in alchemy. On his way back to the castle he stopped to thank the prostitute for her kindness once more and she invited him to partake of her flesh. He'd been tempted and had gone as far as to remove his belt, but then he felt as if a tiny being, one of the angels mentioned by ben Lebus, a succubus of sorts, entered his body just below the heart and began gnawing it at the place where he felt lust. He was quite sure that if he'd gone through with the abandonment of his senses, the succubus would have eaten his heart.

Elizabeth listened with evident amusement to this story and then told him that when she mentioned giving the prize of her virginity to someone else, she had not been thinking of Andrei. She had been thinking of Ficzko the groom, who had been caring for her horse, Luna. Ficzko was a vigorous man with a brutish disposition, the worst of all men.

Instead of relief, Andrei felt hurt. He only half listened to Elizabeth tell him about Ficzko, his strength, the firm manner in which he had brushed Luna, the feeling of his callused palm on her tiny rump when he helped her mount . . . but as her story went on, Andrei became fascinated and . . . aroused. Now that he knew Elizabeth had not chosen him for her defloration, he felt a painful throbbing in his loins. He was certain that if Elizabeth asked, he could now perform the deed with the utmost authority.

Elizabeth looked at him in astonishment. He had not been listening. She had just asked, "If the king impregnates me, will my son have a claim to the throne?"

"Forgive me," said Andrei.

Elizabeth repeated her question.

Andrei thought so, most definitely.

Elizabeth's mood changed. She decided that her son, the inevitable result of her union with Matthias, would become king. Andrei didn't know how his mistress had arrived from Ficzko's hand on her rump to acceptance of the inevitable, but he attributed the missing steps either to his inattention or to the mystery of female logic.

Together Elizabeth and Andrei carefully went over the lines of succession in the royal family and the places where the Bathory line intersected the royal line. It was more than possible for her son to assume the throne. It was a certainty.

Elizabeth now abandoned herself to imagining her night with the king and what was required of her to insure that the king's seed took root.

Andrei's reading of alchemical literature came in handy here. He explained to his friend the necessity of increasing heat during the unfolding of the *process*—the love act, in this case. Elizabeth had to go to the king's bed properly heated, that is, in a state of sensual excitement. During the act proper she had to think of increasingly more exciting things in order to increase her heat and the king's pleasure.

Together they made a list of these things for Elizabeth to memorize in proper order. First, she was to think of Ficzko the groom roughly combing her hair with the horse brush while she sat peeing on his phallus, which was spurting man milk. Second, she would think of penetrating Aunt Klara with the wooden phallus while Lena whipped Teresa in such a way that her blood spurted all over Elizabeth's body. Third, there would be seven Gypsy men buggering Rudolf's choir of blond boys, while Elizabeth whipped them. The list of thoughts necessary to heat Elizabeth properly continued to grow, as did Andrei's excitement.

The two adolescents continued to elaborate on the heating process so long that the heat in Elizabeth's chamber rose noticeably. Elizabeth said that the heating of her body with such thoughts would have another good consequence, namely that of easing the pain that the king's phallus would inevitably cause her. She reasoned that since the king was greater than all the nobles in the kingdom, his phallus would be proportionally the biggest. She had seen the penises of servants. By comparison, a count's phallus would probably be a hundred times larger. The king's could barely be imagined.

Andrei, who up to this point had been heating up right alongside the bride, felt himself become inconsequential. He was only a scribe. He wasn't even sure that his phallus was as large as the servants', though he knew that in the order of things, a scribe was high above their status.

Elizabeth also thought of this. Laughingly, she asked, "And a scribe's phallus, how does it fare?"

Andrei's throat suddenly became dry, and he found himself unable to utter a word. Elizabeth looked significantly at the tiny—and becoming tinier—bulge in his tights and demanded that he show her.

Andrei tried desperately to change the course of her thoughts.

"Would it not be extraordinary," he said, "if you were not deflowered by either Franz or Matthias II but by a lowly groom who smells of horses and hay?"

Elizabeth laughed, seeing through his transparent diversion. Her desire to see the scribe's phallus abated. She felt very sleepy of a sudden. She also felt her anger returning.

"If I don't kill myself tonight, I will grow old. That will be worse."

Sympathy welled deep within the soul of her scribe. He wanted Elizabeth to remain forever just the way she was now.

"I will be a successful scholar," he cried from his heart, "and I will find the formula to keep you forever young. Others have found it before me."

"You must promise me that you will suceed, scribe," Elizabeth said gloomily. Nothing was bleaker than crumbling away like the crones that danced by moonlight in the cemeteries, calling for the angel of darkness to smooth their flesh.

Andrei fell to his knees and kissed the hem of her dress. "If I do not succeed in this life, I will in a future one!" he promised, He meant it.

Elizabeth believed him. But she was suddenly sad nonetheless.

She sent her notary away and abandoned herself to her dreams, in which all her feelings and the excitement of her impending deflowering gave way to anxiety about keeping her mouse with two tails safe from her mother-in-law.

Franz Nadazdy held a number of emergency meetings. He met first with the captain of his guards, Aloysius. They devised an elaborate plan whereby, on the evening of the wedding, if the king still insisted on his *jus primae noctis,* Franz's men would cause a clash between Rudolf and Matthias's guards. During the wedding dinner, at a sign from Franz, two of Franz's men, dressed in the uniform of Rudolf's guards, would attack Matthias's soldiers. In the ensuing melee the king would be wounded in such a way that sexual performance would henceforth be impossible for him.

Franz Nadazdy also met with Prince Rudolf, who was in the thrall of some kind of drug and barely understood him. Nonetheless, Franz managed to communicate to him that the king's soldiers had been overheard talking about a night raid on his quarters.

Rudolf regarded Franz as from a great distance, as if he were some sort of ant crawling over a page in a book. (This is, in fact, what he saw.) He listened to Franz's words, which sounded to him like rows of disciplined ants headed for the imperial flower at the top of Rudolf's skull.

"I can't let your ants suck the nectar from my flower!" shouted Rudolf.

Franz said that he had never intended such a thing, that the emperor's flower was safe at his castle, but that he ought to watch his back nonetheless. After he left, Franz posted four of his men by each drawbridge and gave them orders to draw up the bridge as soon as Rudolf's troops tried to cross the moat.

Franz carefully avoided the king all day, while the king, quite naturally, looked for him everywhere, loudly proclaiming his friendship.

Quite by accident—or so it seemed to Franz—he ran into Darvulia, one of Elizabeth's servants. The woman approached him urgently and begged to speak with him.

Franz had never met Darvulia, but he felt greatly at ease with the woman as soon as he lay eyes on her. She whispered that she must speak with him privately. Franz followed Darvulia to a small chamber near the great hall. The woman said that she understood the distress of the young man and that she would protect him as well as she had always protected her young mistress. She told him not to fear the king's demand.

Darvulia gave Franz some simple instructions and handed him a small vial. For some reason, this modest encounter reassured the young count more than all the elaborate plans he had been making. He had always trusted instinctively in the wisdom of women.

The church services began in the afternoon. Richly clad clerics wrapped in clouds of incense passed through the crowds that filled the church.

Elizabeth entered the church veiled, resplendent in her white dress fringed with gold lace. Following her were all the nobles of the Bathory clans in their splendid vestments bearing the family's coat of arms. The equally resplendent Nadazdys poured in, followed by religious luminaries brandishing psalters and holding family relics.

King Matthias and Prince Rudolf sat on equally high brocade-covered platforms to the right of the altar.

Outside the church, astrologers and soothsayers did a brisk business predicting futures based on the propitiousness of the hour. Everyone agreed that the moon was in a most favorable position.

Among the common folk who had crowded outside, the talk was all about the beauty of the young countess and the bravery of the young count. People marveled at Elizabeth's dowry, which included castles and lands in addition to chests of gold and precious stones, tapestries, paintings, and statues. But there could also be heard, just below the loudly offered praises, talk about King Matthias's extraordinary invocation of his droit du seigneur. People feared that terrible things were in store for Hungary.

There were also some who gossiped about Elizabeth's cruelty to her servants, about her escapades when dressed as a boy, and other things that had been whispered about. It was said that she had raised taxes on her estates at Kereshtur and elsewhere at the request of Lord Thurzo. There was talk of a new war with the Turks, a war so terrible it would lay Hungary waste.

In attendance, besides the Christian dignitaries, was a small Turkish legation led by Kharmal Bey, whose acquaintance would prove important to Franz in the coming years. The pasha was treated with courtesy. The people were encouraged by the sight of the Turks, because they knew that as long as the Turks were among them, they wouldn't be attacking.

Franz Nadazdy and Elizabeth Bathory were linked in marriage at five that afternoon. She retained the name Bathory because it was of higher rank, while Franz added her name to his.

Flowers and gifts covered the entire front of the church. When the newlyweds stepped out into the sunlight, the crowds let out a great cheer. From the carriage pulled by twelve brightly decorated white horses they showered the people with coins. The poorest serfs, the sick, the afflicted, the widowed, the half-savage stretched out their hands and were rewarded with silver. Among the throng Elizabeth recognized for a brief second the wizened faces of her forest friends. She threw them a whole purse full of coins. They waved and cheered her with the greatest fervor.

The newlyweds would have been happy, if not for the kingly cloud hovering over their heads. Neither Franz nor Elizabeth wanted the carriage ride to end. But it did eventually, and the great feast began.

Toasts of good wishes and long life were offered in seemingly endless rounds by the nobles of the realm. Festive songs were sung between toasts. Custom held that the king be the last to address the newlyweds after all the toasts had been offered. It was widely expected that at that point King Matthias would invoke his seigneurial rights.

Franz was prepared, as soon as the king looked as if he was going to speak, to give the signal that would spark the armed hostilities between the royal and imperial garrisons. At the moment the signal was given, someone would rise from the table and warn the king. Franz hoped the king would then give up speaking and order his men to arms instead. The plan depended on extremely fine timing.

Elizabeth was possessed of contradictory emotions. Her last night's plan to give birth to the next king of Hungary had paled in the light of day. She admired her handsome husband, his vigorous youthful looks, and his easy command of people's allegiance and sympathy. She did not want this night of her life to belong to the foul-smelling, flabby old king. She decided again to kill herself instead.

Meanwhile, one of the Nadazdy butlers brought the king a very special bottle of wine. He opened it with great flourish and sat it before the besotted sovereign.

"From the Nadazdy vineyards!" he declared grandly.

The king, who rarely drank anything but his special reserves, sniffed contemptuously. But Franz spoke up at this point: "You must honor your friend and drink his wine!" he shouted.

Matthias looked at Franz carefully and then remembered. Yes, Franz was his friend, his only friend! He held up his goblet, and Nadazdy's butler filled it to the top with ruby wine. The king drank it all and flung his cup behind him.

He stood up to make his toast. Franz prepared to raise his arm to signal his men. But as quickly as he had risen, the king fell back stiffly and was barely caught by his attendants. Darvulia's potion had been swifter than Franz's complicated plan.

The king not only slept without stirring the entire wedding night, but he had a vivid dream of possessing the young countess. In fact, the dream was so vivid the king believed that it had been real. He was convinced that he had made love to Elizabeth Bathory. If there was any seed of doubt in his mind, it had to do with the fact that he had performed with rather uncharacteristic energy and vigor. The king couldn't remember when he had last felt so potent. He was quite sure that he never had. But there is always a first time, Matthias told himself, and this is the first time for me. And for her, he chuckled to himself.

Elizabeth and Franz's *nuit d'amour* unfolded to the plucking of strings and the tumbles of her prenuptial gift. Players were arrayed around the nuptial chamber to fill the atmosphere with sensual madrigals. The musicians had been instructed to play from the moment the newlyweds entered the chamber until the moment they left it. After many hours, their fingers began to bleed, but they did not stop. The music became sweeter and more poignant as the blood seeped down the lute, mandolin, and violin strings, staining the white robes of the performers.

Franz's prenuptial gift to Elizabeth was an Abyssinian dwarf acrobat named Ibis. Ibis counted among his many unusual endowments a long, twirling tongue, which he used like another limb. He spoke several European languages in addition to his native speech but could only pronouce the words very slowly, one at a time, because of his great tongue.

Elizabeth thought that she could *see* the words as they rolled down the middle of Ibis's tongue. She thanked Franz and said, "He is ideal for the recitation of poetry!"

Ibis was adorned with a gold collar studded with precious stones and attached to a gold chain. He had gold circlets around his ankles. Elizabeth was to discover later that Ibis also had three small diamonds set into the foreskin of his black penis. Franz had left nothing to chance. He adored his young wife.

Later that night Elizabeth discovered that Ibis was trained in giving pleasure. His long tongue had been trained to perform certain activities that few mortals were capable of. This too was Franz's gift.

In order to introduce his wife gently to the pleasures of sex, of which he was convinced she knew nothing. Franz had brought a number of incunabula to the nuptial chamber. These were manuscripts of famous romances illuminated with scenes of idleness and sensuality. They depicted the protagonists of the *Decameron*, the knights and fair ladies of the *Roman de la Rose*, and the lovely figures of Beatrice, Laura, and Yseult.

But so as not to lose sight of the other side of the coin, Franz had also brought a book depicting horrific scenes of adulterers condemned to hell. He had been advised in this regard by his mother, Ursula, who thought that sensuality must be prudently hedged by warnings about transgression. The damned in these pictures were preyed upon by unearthy beasts that fed on their nakedness. The men's phalluses were erect and enormous, pointing to the precise nature of their sins. The women's breasts were immense, with protruding nipples on which sat a host of demonic beings sucking milk and blood. The women's vaginas were open for the beaks of hungry birds who fed inside them. Flitting succubi with intricate wings buried their plumed narrow heads into the piss holes of the men. Buttocks were flayed by masked demons. The devil roasted choice parts of men and women on fires whose flames were slow tongues. A profusion of wounds flowered on the flesh of the damned like the intricate thread of a tapestry.

Elizabeth was struck by how formal human flesh in a state of suffering looked. She said to Franz while turning the heavy pages of the incunabulum, "This artistry has no smell . . ."

Franz gazed with admiration at his beautiful young bride. She smelled of nard and sandalwood, and she had loosened her long chestnut hair, which hung to her waist.

For many hours before the wedding, Elizabeth had been carefully ministered to with warm baths spiced with rare salts and had been lovingly rubbed by Darvulia with oils guaranteed to inflame and arouse a man's senses, but mostly his sense of smell, which Darvulia said was "the king of the senses."

Franz now inhaled deeply the clever work of generations of women skilled in the art of attraction.

He was certainly aroused and inflamed, but he had been told by Melotus, the court poet, that a maiden needs infinte tenderness and patience on this most important of nights. It had been Melotus who suggested showing her erotic pictures to awaken her passion. He had also suggested reciting ribald poetry to her in order to make her laugh. Laughter, maintained Melotus, is the key to possessing a woman. Failing that, crying would also do, because it is a known fact that emotion in a woman is her body's way of assenting to surrender.

Franz knew a few ribald songs, but he thought that they were too ribald for his wife, although they had often been performed in the castle late at night. He knew, for instance, all the words to the dialogue between the knight errant and the fair lady:

"Have you any hair between your legs, lady bright?"
"None whatsoever, handsome dark knight!
But why do you ask? To excite my wrath?"
"No, my lady, I know grass does not grow on the
well-trod path!"

Franz knew that while these pleasant ribaldries were perhaps appropriate for late-night drinking, they were not the kind of things he now needed to whisper to his bride.

He showed her pictures, as Melotus had advised, but instead of speaking rhymes he stroked her hair and spoke to her about her beauty. He told her that he had carried her image in his heart ever since she had been spoken about when she was only a small girl. He told her that the coming wars would require his presence much of the time and that she was going to be the absolute mistress of their combined domain.

"Everyone," said Franz, "will owe you obedience!"

Elizabeth looked at him surprised. It had never occurred to her that someone might not owe her obedience. Since she had been an infant tied to her crib she had believed that her wish was everyone's command. She told Franz that while she knew she herself owed obedience to her husband, her church, and her king, she knew also that those who must be obedient to her far outnumbered those three.

"Obedience is not enough," she sighed.

Now it was Franz's turn to be surprised. "What might you mean, my beloved? If they do whatever they can to obey your wishes, what more can you want?"

Elizabeth was not concerned with wishes that were carried out. She knew that her inferiors did what they could and that if they didn't, they were punished. What concerned her were the limits of what she could ask for.

"But you can ask for *anything!*" cried Franz.

"Yes," Elizabeth said, "but don't you see? I am limited to what they can do . . . I cannot ask them to obey the commands of my imagination. I cannot ask my servants to ascend to heaven to bring me a golden apple, as they do in fairy tales. I cannot ask my horse to fly. I mean, I can ask, but will they obey me?"

Franz conceded this point to his young bride and kissed her round little shoulders, from which the muslin robe had slipped. He then said that anyone as pretty, as charming, and as intelligent as she should have no trouble at all getting people to fly.

"Oh, I can get *people* to fly, all right," said Elizabeth. "It's my horse I was thinking about."

Franz relegated this remark to the tender blossom of poetry that was opening its petals between the two of them. He gently pushed down her robe and gazed entranced at the two perky buds atop her tiny mounds of snow.

"Why should you want that they obey you in ways they cannot?"

"Because," said Elizabeth, moving closer so that only a thin pane of warm air separated them, "if they will not obey an impossible command, I will never know if they truly obeyed me or only went through the gestures. What is possible never contains sufficient proof of being *totally* engaged . . ."

Franz now lowered his head and kissed Elizabeth's nipples, which did their utmost to transcend the possible and push past his lips.

Elizabeth had become aroused by the possibilities of absolute obedience. As Franz gently suckled her breasts, she began making a list of commands that she would issue to test the loyalty of her subjects. She would ask them to bring her the mirror on the surface of a lake. She would ask them to open their chests and give her their hearts. She would ask them to make gold out of wool. She would demand that they build tall cabinets with thousands of drawers out of thin air and that birds fly out of every drawer when she said so. She would command them to bring her goldfish that were half women to swim in water in her room. She would ask for everything her imagination and memory could conceive of.

Franz told her about a weary traveler who was passing through a dark forest and looking for a soft, mossy spot where he could rest.

Elizabeth knew where that mossy spot was, and she lay on her back. Taking hold of Franz's large square hand with heavy rings on every finger, she guided it to the soft, mossy spot between her legs. A thin film of girlish wetness met Franz's hand.

Elizabeth lay on her back with her eyes closed, reciting her list of impossible demands. Living water from a rock. Molten gold pouring on flagstones. Strong winds for Luna. A moving carpet of flowers to sit on while flying above the forest. A speaking bird that would bring her news from everywhere.

She let her legs be parted and felt a sweet weakness spread heavily through her limbs. Streams of honey. And then her world of wishes and commands went dark as the wet snout of a fat piglet entered her. It hurt, and she could not expel it. She pushed with all her strength to expel it, but it pushed its way in firmly, brooking no dissent. She threw her entire body from side to side to get it out, but it only entered deeper the more she flailed.

Franz's body lay on hers, and she was unable to command it to lift. She started screaming. The piglet bore in deeper and deeper, until it filled her with pain. Elizabeth had never felt so helpless in her entire life, not even when she had been tied to her crib. Even when tied to her crib she had been able to lose herself in the murmur of Darvulia's voice telling her stories that she lived and participated in. But this bondage was inescapable. There were no words, and the insistent boring of the moist piglet chased away all thoughts of escape. Elizabeth tried in vain to remember her list of commands.

She tried, also in vain, to remember the "heating" list she had made with Andrei the scribe, but she could not form a whole thought. She called with all her might on her great memory to bring her something from the past she could take refuge in. Nothing presented itself. All was replaced by an insistent, painful hammering at her womb that made its own wordless music.

When Elizabeth, exhausted by all her attempts at escape, surrendered to the demands of the piglet attached to Franz's heavy blanket of flesh, she was flooded by an unbearable itch that made her quake with impatience. She cried Franz's name as loud as she could, charging it with all the impatience she was capable of—which was quite considerable—and Franz, who was still considerate even in the throes of his passion, obliged his young bride by allowing the fountain of his man milk to rise and flood her.

Elizabeth had never been so humiliated in all her life.

Trembling, sweaty, bloody, rumpled, her face tear-streaked, she said, "Franz, my husband, you are the only one I will owe this kind of obedience to. My church and my king will never compel me to such obedience!"

Franz, shaken himself, was pleased with the oath his young bride had just taken. He had been quite pleased also with her submission and with the way her resistance had turned to weakness, and then to complete surrender. He felt very much like a man. A wave of affection for his young wife swept through him. He would bring her gifts from everywhere. He would make sure that she was obeyed.

In Elizabeth, something like iron began to harden. It was her resolve never to allow such helplessness again. In spite of her horror at having had to let go, she felt an odd sort of gratitude to the man whose breath was still unquiet next to her. She also felt little rivulets of milk growing cold over quickly drying blood between her legs. She shifted uncomfortably.

"What is it, my beloved?" asked Franz.

"Between my legs," she said. "Flowing springs . . ."

Franz smiled, delighted. He had been waiting for this moment. He clapped his hands, and Ibis, the Abyssinian dwarf, tumbled in. He did a somersault from the door all the way into bed.

"Clean her, Ibis!" commanded Franz.

Before she could express her surprise or her opinion, Elizabeth felt the dwarf's deft tongue begin to lick her clean between her legs, removing blood, sperm, sweat. Ibis untangled her soft down, smoothed it, and combed it with his tongue. It all felt very warm and dreamy. Elizabeth listened to the sweet strings filling the air around her wedding bed with harmonies and fell asleep to the gentle lapping of the dwarf's tongue. She thought she was floating on a wave in an azure sea.

The newlyweds lay in bed until noon the next day.

The string pluckers' fingers had become tattered rags of flesh, but they continued to issue the sounds of love and sweetness to which they had been bound. Some could not bear the pain and were replaced by others. (Later in her life, in a grotesque parody of her wedding night, Elizabeth would order an entire orchestra to play until the flesh on their fingers was entirely gone. To insure their compliance, the musicians were chained by their ankles to the wall.)

Elizabeth's women hovered anxiously about the nuptial chambers, listening to every sound, feeling compassion, pity, weariness, affection. They strode in with breakfast at the first sign of stirring from within, and they returned with wine, bread, viands, and fruit so many times before lunch that Elizabeth had to order them to stay out until she called for them.

Every time Darvulia came in, she sprinkled fresh flowers about the room and around the bed. One time she came in carrying a golden bowl full of rose petals that she tossed over the lovers. She also made sure that no one but her removed and returned the porcelain chamber pot with its painted angels.

Darvulia became terribly cross with Ibis when she saw that the dwarf had been called to her mistress's bedside before her. She smacked the dwarf with the chamber pot when she saw him next. Ibis did a somer-sault over her head and climbed on her back. Darvulia elbowed him sharply but couldn't dislodge the strong little devil.

It took four women to take him off Darvulia's back and to hold him down long enough for her to empty the entire contents of the chamber pot on his head. Ibis stalked off, dragging his gold chain and mumbling terri-ble curses in his savage language.

Franz dreaded rising from his young bride's bed. Outside the chamber wrapped in the cocoon of sweet song were King Matthias, Prince Rudolf, his men-at-arms, his mother Ursula, and all the rest of those he had magically left behind for the space of several hours. But he knew that sooner or later he had to rejoin them.

He drew himself up from the bed and said to his wife: "We must return to the clothed world!"

This gave Elizabeth an idea for testing the limits of obedience. She told Franz that perhaps this return could be made less unpleasant if the clothed world were un-clothed. They could ask all those who owed them obedi-ence to unclothe themselves.

Franz laughed and though that this was a splendid idea. Furthermore, it would disarm all the heavily armed men who were so worrisome to him.

They fully realized that Ursula, the king, the Lutheran pastors, and the Catholic monks would have to be exempt from this command.

Elizabeth sent away her women when they came to dress her, and Franz did likewise with his men servants. When they emerged from their wedding chamber, the two newlyweds were as Adam and Eve in paradise. Everyone lowered their eyes in shame. Standing hand in hand in the doorway, first Franz, then Elizabeth announced the command of the day. The command then traveled from mouth to mouth.

In the name of the Lord's paradise, which was built in innocence, and in honor of the successful consummation of the wedding of Franz Nadazdy and Elizabeth Bathory, it was decreed that "everyone under the roof of the castle, excluding King Matthias, Prince Rudolf, Ursula Nadazdy, and clerics, would go about naked for a whole day."

The guests and servants were bid to go about their duties as if they were in paradise, where there was neither sin nor guilt. The men were asked, but not commanded, to lower their eyes before the ladies, unless they felt that they could gaze upon them in all innocence. (And, if not, they were bid to pretend!) Servants were commanded to lower their eyes at all times before the nakedness of their masters. Slaves were commanded to look only at the feet of free men and nobles.

Outside of these minimal aspects of courtesy, the court was going to be fully naked.

The order went out quickly and without possibility of redress. Franz's soldiers made sure that everyone was undressed before they themselves took off their armor, weapons, and cloth.

Prince Rudolf's soldiers objected strenuously at first and appeared ready to resist with arms, but then their commander, Rudolf, found the idea irresistibly charming and not only orderd them to undress but undressed himself. His pale body, looking very much like a prematurely faded eggplant, was seen drunkenly weaving through the naked mobs like an odd purple devil in a painting of the Last Judgment.

King Matthias, who had slept long and woken up convinced he had possessed the beautiful Elizabeth Bathory, opened his eyes and saw that all his servants were naked but going about their chores as if they were not aware of this fact. They brought him his breakfast and they prepared his bath.

The bewildered king stuck his head out the door and saw his guards lounging naked about the hall. He closed the door softly and went back to bed. He decided that he was dreaming. He became more convinced than ever that he had made love to the young countess but was now asleep and having a curious dream in which everyone was naked. He would just lie down until it went away.

May 10 is known to this day in Hungary as Naked Day or the "day of the pinching of the maidens." It is customary on this day for maidens to go shopping to the market without a stitch of underwear beneath their skirts. The soldiers mill about the markets and pinch the girls on the bottom, a habit tolerated only on this day by Hungarians, who despite the red paprika that runs through their veins, behave most decorously.

Even Andrei de Kereshtur, so punctilious in other matters, passed quickly over the events of May 10, 1575:

A kind of madness seized the castle. The young, servants and nobles alike, seem to have been overjoyed after their initial embarrassment. Older servants were secretly pleased that their masters were no better than they under their fancy clothes. The misshapen cried and hid in dark corners. And Elizabeth saw that class and rank had nothing, absolutely nothing, to do with the size of a man's manhood.

The clerics were so shocked by the young people's foolish decree that they decided to put the best face on it, lest they be accused of collusion with Satan. They declared the nakedness an atonement for the sins of the people. And then they made a huge list of sins that the naked residents were supposedly atoning for: concupiscence, avarice, sloth . . . The monks painted huge banners with those words on them and had them flown from every parapet. Pastor Ponikenuz retired with Ursula Nadazdy and Count George Thurzo to her rooms and did not emerge until everyone was properly dressed again.

Hungarian historians have for the most part shied away from this odd day in their history; but there are those who claim that on that day the inhabitants of the castle experienced ergot poisoning from rye flour. In Hungary there were periodic outbreaks of this affliction, which caused hallucinations and odd behavior. It is amusing to note that May 10 passed into folk history without much note in the chroniclers' scrolls.

Elizabeth Bathory had every reason to expect that she would reign over a court of fun and games. Her wedding had been wonderful in all respects, and the wild frolic afterwards proved that Franz was spirited, unconventional, and daring. She admired those qualities. Her own qualities—curiosity, memory, firmness, command—complemented his.

She had escaped the clutches of aging King Matthias II, who left the castle after kissing the hem of her gown and looking up at her like a puppy in love. Elizabeth didn't quite understand, since she had been sure that he would be angry when he woke up. King Matthias also acted most humbly before Franz Nadazdy, whom he continued calling as before "our best friend." The king gave both Franz and Elizabeth a slew of new presents after the wedding—including a castle and three villages —in gratitude, he said, for their "adherence to the ancient traditions of Hungary."

Franz was as thoroughly confused as Elizabeth. Perhaps the king was mad after all.

Your Honor, I now ask for the full attention of the court, because what follows is fraught with ambiguity, lapses from reality, and crime. What follows is my attempted flight from my destiny, a flight that continues. It can be argued that the more I tried to flee from it, the closer it came. This may be improper, but I am begging the court to help me understand my own story. And then to punish me.

"Not only is it improper," said the judge, disciplining a strand of hair that had escaped her severe judicial chignon, "but helping you to understand can be construed as putting thoughts in your head, which is the equivalent to putting words in your mouth. The court is only interested in the truth."

Of course.

My escape partner, Teresa, knew about a car rental agency on Rakosi Utka. It was one of Hungary's new private businesses, and it was not easy to find. It was located at the end of a medieval courtyard in a cul-de-sac. A tire-shaped sign announced its existence in English: SLUGGER—THE HIGHWAY & THE INFO SUPERHIGHWAY —RENTALS & SALES. In Hungarian, just below the tire, was written quite mysteriously: YOU BETTER BE TRAVELING.

"Is *slugger* a Hungarian word?" I asked.

"No," said Teresa. "I thought it was something from your sport, baseball."

The door chimed when we entered. A muscular man in an uncomfortable blue serge suit lifted his eyes from the console of a computer behind a plain wooden counter. The room was utterly bare. There was no literature. There were no posters on the walls, no price lists, no pictures of the rental cars.

"A bit bare"—I grinned—"for a new capitalist business."

"The trimmings are unnecessary," he said with a New York accent, "when your services are of our quality."

"We would like a car for the highway," I said, "but I'm curious, what does this *info superhighway* signify?"

He patted the console of his computer. "We sell information too."

"What kind of information?"

He shot Teresa a quick glance, leaned over the counter, and whispered conspiratorially, *"Any kind."*

He added quickly that six months previous, he had arrived from Brooklyn to open a car rental franchise for Hertz. He had teamed up with a Hungarian who used to work for "them"—he winked—and who had access to "their whole goddam archive."

I knew he didn't mean Hertz.

Using local capital, he and his partner acquired six cars and a computer, and now they were in both businesses: cars and info. They had access to all "their files," and in addition they ran a service in the Internet enabling people to add info to existing files, as well as verify the information they had bought.

"You mean to say that your files are *growing?*"

"The ones in demand are."

That was quite amazing. After the Communist secret police were ordered to quit spying on people—or so they claimed—here was a capitalist entrepreneur who had found a way to continue their work! Not for ideological reasons, of course, but for money. It was amazing and, quite clearly, useful. Slugger explained that every new business in Hungary was in fact a double business. Even little grocery stores doubled as pawnshops or laundries or social clubs or real estate agencies. The reason for this doubling was twofold: the only people with money were either ex-secret policemen or Communist party bureaucrats, and there were gangs composed of rival ex-secret policemen and CP bureaucrats who offered protection in exchange for using businesses as fronts.

"And, of course," added Slugger, "if you don't speak two languages, you can't do business. Double your pleasure, double your fun. Now what can I do for you?"

"Suppose I need the scoop on someone," I said.

"Five bucks a page, you wait right here."

"Klaus Megyery."

Teresa had evinced some anxiety at the revelation of this strange little business, but she relaxed when I asked for Klaus's file.

"And we want a car too, of course."

Slugger went to work.

It was harder than he had anticipated, because Klaus's file was not quite as evident as some of the others.

"You're sure he exists?"

I vouched for it.

Slugger dug around for a while, then said, "Aha!" and sighed. "It'll cost you more. Around twenty a page."

The problem was, he explained, that Klaus was one of "them." You could easily get the files "they" had assembled, but getting files on "them" was a much harder job.

"Go ahead."

"I'll need a small reference, something from his past."

"Comrade Hebler," I said.

Leave it to a Brooklyn boy who'd been hacking since five. Slugger came up with Klaus's file after some fancy footwork in the digital outland. His dot matrix printer happily spewed out about two hundred pages of raw Megyery data. Only, his code name was King.

A cursory look—I planned a detailed study later—revealed that Klaus Megyery, aka King, had been working for the secret police since we were both in high school. At that time his job had been to keep an eye on . . . me! My name jumped out of the stack of papers like a silverfish. I guess we did go back a long time. I raced through the stack. One of the last entries had him assigned to the formation of a security detachment that would appear to be a "spontaneous return to Hungarian Fascism . . . with all the outward symbols, including the Arrow Cross, but resembling in a general way its counterparts in Great Britain and Germany." In other words, the skinheads. Hungarian skinheads were the creation of Klaus Megyery and the Hungarian secret police. How charming.

"Do you take American Express?"

"Of course," said Slugger.

"Then get me another thousand bucks' worth on Bathory-Kereshtur."

This time it didn't take very long. I was floating right above ground in info land. I gathered the stack and handed it to Teresa. I envisioned a quaint motel room by the side of an old castle where Teresa and I would study my file by candlelight. Outside, the moon would be full.

Slugger now turned to the other side of his business: five of his cars were gone, leaving only a shabby little Opel. This mildly dented tin can was in a garage behind the bare office. While he passed a greasy rag over the hood, Slugger claimed that it was suited for any kind of excursion.

"You are not escaping from Hungary, I bet," he said suspiciously. "It would be a terrible time to leave now. These are great days. There is even talk of a Hungarian king."

When I handed him my American Express card, he said, "So you're the guy with the last file. You are trying to get away, aren't you, pal?"

I assured him that we were simply going on a pleasure trip.

"Well," he said, handing me the form to sign, "I can't guarantee that ten minutes from now someone won't come in here asking for the same file. We're a business, you know."

I considered this.

"Suppose you add another five hundred on the bill for services rendered *confidentially,*" I said.

Slugger tore up the form and took a fresh one out. "Some information is one time only," he said.

The sun came out briefly and washed the old buildings with harsh winter gold. But a light springlike fragrance emanated from Teresa. I maneuvered the jalopy over potholes and barely managed to avoid pedestrians. It was a relief to reach the less crowded outskirts of the city. Soon the Opel whizzed past the blackened hulks of factories outside of Budapest.

I looked intently at the landscape that had in some way shaped me, but the dreary industrial ruins evoked nothing. An older world was coming to life inside me. Castles had once stood here, not mounds of rusted wire and smoldering tires. An oily pond with a floating barrel on it became a moat with a black swan. I saw aristocratic ladies in great gowns, knights standing on ramparts, a peasant girl pouring water from a pitcher on a lady's fine hands . . . Leaning against me, Elizabeth Bathory thanked me for retrieving her pearls. The coachman, a nasty brute named Ficzko, whipped the horses. For our love games later that evening we had retained a virgin from Lakesvar.

I brought myself back with a start.

We were passing through a tunnel. Teresa said she'd heard that a dog had once been brought to this passage and had died from the pollution. She had heard this from the owner of the dog. Her voice brought me back fully, behind the wheel.

"I am sorry," I said. "I had a vivid hallucination of Elizabeth Bathory at her court."

"Hypnagogy," said Teresa. "It happens to me all the time."

The sky was the color of ashes. As we reached the countryside, my spirits lifted. We drove past rolling hills with snowy haystacks set on them like white lambskin hats. The Pannonian plain stretched before us, an unbroken expanse of snow. Little clean villages with black church towers rose from the whiteness. Crooked-toothed peasants leaned on their walking sticks before the village taverns, watching us pass. Vineyards planted since the days of the Roman Empire climbed in snowy rows on the sides of the hills.

The sweep of the snow-covered land became hypnotic, and I again began hallucinating scenes of life at a great sixteenth-century court. These imaginings were so vivid, they didn't seem merely to be suggestions derived from reading de Kereshtur's *Chronicles* or revisiting the Thurzo. They seemed printed right on the inside of my eyelids. I saw a pretty girl, a maid of Countess Bathory. She approached me and whispered something in my ear. Her breasts, squeezed tight by the laces of her bodice, brushed my face. I concentrated hard but heard only the hum of the engine. I glanced at Teresa. She was looking out at the snow, a faint smile on her lips, as if she was listening to a distant music.

"It was very selfish of me," I said, "to only get my file and Klaus's. We could have had hours of reading pleasure with yours and Imre's as well."

I realized that I hadn't asked for either Teresa's or Imre's file because it hadn't occurred to me that they had one. They were so young!

"It is doubtlessly full of lies," said Teresa. "Everyone in Professor Hangress's entourage had a file. It was de rigueur. I don't want to see mine."

I had the distinct feeling that Teresa didn't want *me* to see her file. The mention of her file had clearly unsettled her. Perhaps she wasn't so young after all.

"Everyone in Hungary must have a file."

"Why, yes," said Teresa. "Everyone in the *world* has a file. Americans don't?"

I admitted that this may indeed be the case.

"It must be part of this doubling," I said. "Everyone is who they appear to be, and then there is this double, who is in the file. In English, *file* is an anagram for *life.*"

I wondered who my double was, lying there in the backseat, ready to spring out of the file.

After three hours we crossed the border into Burgenland. It was evident that we were in another country. The relaxed Hungarian landscape gave way to a clean severity. Burgenland, where Franz Liszt was born, had been part of Hungary until 1918, when it became part of Austria and its orderly Germanic rhythms. Austrian haystacks were rigorously symmetrical, each hay straw in its place, the cords of wood before houses stacked in order, no log longer than another, no stack higher than the other. The sky too had a crystalline crispness, as if a giant hausfrau had taken her broom to it and gotten rid of every speck of dirt.

"These were the Bathory lands from the ninth through the nineteenth century," Teresa explained. "Ten centuries of rule by one powerful family."

"Wonderful," I said. "And now let's throw everybody out and take our lands back. Isn't that the general monarchist idea?"

"No need to throw them out. Just show them their files, then watch them run. We'll attach delicate chains to the ankles of those who won't leave and we'll use them to pull our chariots."

Teresa had a complex imagination.

We came to a hilly village dominated by the spire of a Lutheran church. The cobblestoned street was deserted. A red sign in the main square indicated in German Gothic writing that THE HAND was located within.

My village, my street, my tavern, I said to myself. The count is back, I told the unaware village; there is a new salt tax. I saw myself in a horse-drawn carriage, pulling before the tavern. The clientele came tumbling out to flatten themselves in the snow before my horses. We parked in front of the place, but the peasants stayed within.

The tavern was dim, with wooden tables. Several hefty blond Burgenlanders sat drinking beer. The tavern keeper, a rotund man with inflated red cheeks, came out from behind the bar. We ordered a round of the local brandy.

The men in the tavern looked familiar. I thought I had seen their square jaws, blue eyes, and broad shoulders before. It was as if someone or something inside me recognized them. They were familiar to a presence that was taking residence in my mind—someone with his own sentiments and memory. It was disquieting.

When we finished our brandy, I asked the barman in

English for directions to Kereshtur Castle. He told us, and then I asked him why the tavern was called The Hand.

"It's an old story," the barkeep said. "A long time ago, there lived a very cruel countess at Kereshtur. They say that her lover, who was her coachman, fell in love with a barmaid at the inn in the village. The coachman gave the girl a ring that the countess had given him. He was mad with love, so he told his mistress that he would have the girl's hand no matter what.

"The countess kidnapped the girl, beat her with a whip, and cut off her hand. She gave the hand to her coachman, who knew by the ring whose hand it was.

"He killed himself. He was buried together with the barmaid at this place where the tavern is. For many years their ghosts cried every night so the townspeople couldn't sleep.

"One day about a hundred years ago, a package came to the post office here in the village. It was addressed to 'the lovers of Castle Kereshtur.'

"The postman left the package on the grave of the two lovers: next day it disappeared and the ghosts were quiet.

"My great-grandfather built The Hand here. It's a nice tavern, *ja?*"

The men at the tables, who had been listening raptly, rapped their mugs on the tables. *"Ja, ja,* a nice place, *ja, ja."*

Ja, ja. Of such "nice places" is my dominion built.

The directions were simple. Follow the road past the church for six miles.

About a half mile from Castle Kereshtur, the Opel gave an ominous sputter and went dead. I popped open the hood with a knowing frown, but I had no idea what the mechanical innards meant. The mechanics of the beast were a complete mystery to me. Teresa looked inside too and shrugged. We laughed.

Vast fields of snow stretched on both sides of the road. Looking about her at the snowy fields, Teresa said, "I have been here in the summer. These are fields of rye then, with red poppies in them."

We could see Hungary on one side and the beginning of the Austrian pre-Alpine country on the other. The ruins of Castle Kereshtur were outlined just below the low gray sky. There was not a car or a house in sight. I made a snowball and rubbed it against my face. It was bracing. My heritage. The Bathory lands. Snow as far as you could see.

We set out on foot for the castle. The packed-snow road must have been trod in its time by the armies of three empires. Soldiers of dozens of nationalities marched into these fields to their perdition. The silent environs belied their history. The ground under our feet was soaked with blood.

Teresa walked ahead of me.

I suddenly remembered. She was a young girl in the year 1590, walking up to Kereshtur, intending to enter the service of Countess Bathory. After working for five years, she would obtain a dowry that would enable her to get married. This is what she had been told at the inn by the fat innkeeper, who steered travelers to the castle. She walked hopefully, suspecting nothing of the life that awaited her.

At the castle she will be bathed and scented and presented to her mistress in the evening. She will be given strong drink and made to dance. After that, Bathory will order her to undress . . .

Teresa suddenly turned around, as if she had heard my thoughts.

"Are you watching my very beautiful ass?" she asked.

I told her what had sprung to my mind's eye.

"Yes," she said softly, "I remember. There is a young man there too, watching her undress. The countess will order him to make love to her. And then . . ."

Teresa shuddered and closed her eyes.

"What then?"

"Her maids stretch the girl on a rack and begin to torture her. She will make the man ejaculate at the moment of her death."

Teresa sounded very convincing. A chill went through me.

"You have great feeling for Elizabeth . . ."

"Not for Elizabeth . . . for her victim. I don't know Elizabeth. She was Lilly's subject, not mine."

"We are both very good at imagining things. Let's look at this rationally, though. We both know too much nonsense. Bathory is a monster in the popular imagination. It's not hard to imagine her wickedness . . . but the popular imagination may be more monstrous than the real person. It is the popular imagination that allows monsters and heroes to appear. Hitler was a pitiful little man. Look what the German people allowed him to grow into."

"Elizabeth was no Hitler," Teresa said, quite judiciously. "Her sphere was domestic. Hitler was rejected by his family; he turned himself into a monster."

"Ah, psychology, the poor offspring of fear," I said. "When cruelty became internal, psychology was born. The monsters came inside. Out of the cold . . . Never mind, my dear friend. We are all monsters to those who do not love us."

This was one of my cherished notions. Once upon a time, people were epic, fruitful, action minded. They did things that had consequences. But little by little in the course of history they had been forced to internalize their deeds. Now they are guilty of everything and capable of nothing. I was myself feeling lighter and lighter, as if I were being forced out of myself, evicted from that little messy nest of feeling wherein we all dwell now.

Teresa fell silent.

The snow started falling hard, sticking to our hair. I was feeling a kind of sleepy beatitude, as if I were in two worlds at once, the silent, snowy one about us and a summer world of another century, with poppies nodding in the breeze. When I closed my eyes I saw fields of rye grass dotted with bright red poppies.

The ruins grew as we neared them, overtaking the road and the low sky. Jagged walls of fallen towers rose from snow-filled courtyards. Snowy vines wrapped themselves around mysterious shapes. The once vast fortress was surrounded by a thick chain-link fence padded with windblown snow. We found ourselves right next to the padlocked gate.

"So this is where my ancestors lived their uncertain lives," I mused. "Not much here now." But I understood the snowbound ruins: they were as indistinct as my feelings. The history of my family was beyond recognition.

I wiped the snow from a sign hanging on the gate. Written in black Gothic letters was this warning: "This is Castle Kereshtur. It is slated for renovation in the year 1999. It is not safe to walk near it. Please keep your distance, traveler."

We walked around the fence, hoping to find a place where Burgenland children, like children everywhere, might have made a hole to sneak through and play. But there was absolutely no chink in the smooth expanse of the chain. The ruins inside the circle of wire were inviolate and foreboding.

"History is gloomy," said Teresa. She lay down on the snow with her arms spread, sinking into the soft comfort of it.

I looked at the depression her body made and felt that she would sink deeper and deeper until she vanished. I remembered making such impressions in the snow when I was a child. We called them angels. Teresa, you are an angel, I thought as she lay still, her eyes open to the menacing sky. Once I loved your mother, but she is gone now to some place we cannot reach her. Regret and remorse flooded me.

It is all too easy to lie down and give in to history, I told myself; the river Retentio comes up from beneath and snatches those who give in. I remembered what Lilly Hangress had told me.

The ruins must have been resisting the pull of that terrible river. They pushed up, jagged, incomplete, stubborn. Everything felt suddenly unmoored; the large snowflakes drifting down from the sky covering Teresa, the fields buried beneath, our words . . . the poppy fields I kept seeing in my mind. And as the snow kept falling, the ruins of Kereshtur became heavy with darkness. These stones hold evil, an inner voice warned me. If so, it was too late to run: this evil was in me, no matter who I thought I had become.

I tried to make myself enter into the core of this evil, perhaps put a face to it. But there was also an *absence* here. Through the persistent poppy fields under my eyelids and the falling snow, I tried to summon the mistress of Kereshtur Castle, but all I could intuit was a void, a dark deep well inside of which sat *nothing*. The poppies finally went away, leaving *nothing*. Elizabeth Bathory was something that was disturbingly *not there,* though she was doubtless also present, like the impression of Teresa's body in the snow.

"You'll freeze to death," I said. "Let's find an inn."

Teresa didn't respond. Her stillness scared me. I bent over her and put my lips to hers to feel her breath. Suddenly she opened her eyes and laughed.

"You thought she got me, didn't you?"

It was not necessary to ask who it was got her. But I was unpleasantly struck by her prank. I tried to rise angrily, but Teresa held me.

"Make love to me in the snow. Pretend that I am my mother when she was young."

I did not want to. I did something as unexpected as it was shocking. I slapped her across her cold cheek with my open fingers. The imprint of my palm burned red on her skin.

"I'm sorry!" I genuinely was. I don't know what possessed me. I had never struck a woman before.

My surprise grew when Teresa laughed. She leapt to her feet and started taking off her clothes. She ran along the fence, shedding her clothes. I followed her, picking up her parka, her sweater, her shirt, her jeans, her underwear.

I shouted at her to stop.

And then she did. By this time, she was completely naked, standing in the cold, almost as white as the snow. Only, her whiteness was interrupted at random by the black, purple, and yellow flowers of variously shaped bruises. She had been beaten.

I was more astonished by these than by her nakedness.

"Who did this to you?" And then I guessed. "Imre?"

"No. They are the stigmata of our Lord Jesus Christ."

Teresa lowered her eyes. Imre had beaten her. I was furious. I coaxed her back into her clothes, item by item, and we started quickly back toward the village.

The old man looked like a black question mark in the snow. I had seen him from a distance but I had first thought he was a scarecrow. He stood squarely in our path.

"Finally," he said, offering the root of a grizzled hand. "You've come."

"Yes, we have, and now we're going back," I said, taking Teresa's hand. "Is your name Finally?"

He paid no attention to my irritated reply.

"You *are* looking for the inn at Castle Kereshtur, are you not? Well, you have found it. Since the renovations began ten years ago—or was it one hundred years?—I have had, as you can well imagine, little business. But now you've come. I'm glad, I'm glad!"

The little man hopped and skipped with glee ahead of us. He had a barely noticeable hump under an old gabardine coat. It was not an unpleasant deformity.

"I never thought another guest would come. I've been ready to sleep for a thousand years for a hundred years, if you pardon my pun. But I am not allowed to until I have enough guests. Follow me. Follow me. My place is warm."

The promise of a warm place just then, perhaps also a drop of brandy, sounded good. Teresa expressed no opinion. We followed the bent back of the old man across a snowy pasture, then up a little hill.

On the other side of the rise, a small stone house with a wooden porch stood alone in a white field. A curl of smoke hung like a question mark in the air above it. The smoke resembled the shape of the man himself.

"The Inn of the Question Mark," I whispered to Teresa.

"What did you say?" asked the elder, whose hearing was apparently better than his eyesight.

"Everything is shaped like a question," I confessed.

"Everything *is* a question," he said.

"How did you know we were coming, old man?"

"They told me at the tavern."

A little chime sounded when he opened the door. We found ourselves inside a nearly dark room filled with bric-a-brac. Floor, tables, walls, and windowsills were completely obscured by leather-bound books, glass containers, copper implements, and hundreds of keys hanging from hooks. Jars full of coins kept down loose manuscript pages. A Saxon tile stove gave off steady warmth and a little light.

"It's been so long," the innkeeper said, "since anyone came."

I call him the innkeeper, Your Honor, because that was how he introduced himself. But when we entered his domain of dusty junk, I couldn't understand where his guests might repose. What furniture there was, was completely buried under various objects. Feeling his way like a blind man through this chamber, he finally swept some hefty books from what appeared to be a narrow sofa and bade us to sit. I did, but Teresa remained standing, looking at him with a puzzled frown on her face.

"I could swear I've seen you before, old man."

"How beautiful you are, my dear. You always were. Always. They say beauty is subject to fashion, but it's a lie. Beauty is the same always. The only eternal principle. It's been my misfortune to live long enough to read the ravings of idiots since the so-called Enlightenment . . . Darkening, more likely . . . they lost beauty. Now we will find it again. You are here."

All the while he kept up this patter, the old man busied himself, sweeping things out of his way. Some of the glass containers set randomly on the floor contained disquieting shapes. Floating in liquid in one of them was, clearly, a fetus of some kind, a monstrous thing with four hands. I now noticed that on the walls, objects I had first taken to be bundles of dried flowers actually had the texture of skin. One looked much like a seven-fingered human hand.

Noticing my gaze, the man said, "The debris of research. They make the atmosphere authentic, don't you think? After all, this is the inn of Castle Kereshtur."

He disappeared briefly and then came back with two delicate, nearly transparent porcelain cups and a kettle of hot tea. He poured it into the cups. I put my hand gratefully around the fragile object and let the steam warm my face. But Teresa made no gesture to touch the tea.

"Drink, dear. Do not be afraid. Your beauty will outshine the heavens. Certain things are eternal. Take these keys, for instance . . ."

He removed a string of heavy keys from a hook and dangled them in front of Teresa. She burst into tears.

"Now, dear, sit down. Drink your tea."

Obediently, Teresa sat next to me and took the tea-cup.

"Forgive me," I said, baffled by what had just taken place, "but are there any other rooms at this inn? The house seems awfully small."

The old man made an alarming sound, as if he were being choked, then small dry ripples of raspy sound came out of his mouth. He was laughing.

"Rooms?" he said several times, choking with eerie dry laughter. "Rooms? There are hundreds of rooms, my friend! Hundreds! When you are ready for bed I will show you rooms! There are so many rooms! And they are ready for you! The rooms!"

I had begun to think the old coot quite demented, so I let him spend himself in hilarity and decided that we were going to get out of there as quickly as possible.

Teresa was still crying. I became angry at the old man, who was still laughing. "What's going on? Why are you making her cry? What are those keys?" I was suddenly alarmed by that key chain, still hanging from his gnarled fingers.

They reminded me of the heavy keys that Klaus Megyery used to open the medieval gates of his house. Those iron bars with teeth polished by time had seen and known more than I could ever hope to. Of all the odious things attributed to Elizabeth Bathory by witnesses, perhaps the most puzzling had been the one testified to by her maid Jo Anna Tohka, who claimed that "Her Ladyship with her own hands had keys heated redhot and then burned the hands of the girls with them. The same thing happened with gold pieces that the girls had found but had not given to Her Ladyship." I had read this in the *Chronicles of Andrei de Kereshtur*. In fact, Teresa had just translated the passage.

"Look," I said to the old man, "I don't see any rooms. Also, your patter is getting tiresome. Whoever it is that you are waiting for, it's not us. Living near the ruins of Kereshtur has obviously had some strange effect on your sense of humor. I don't know. I can be charitable and pretend that I know what you're talking about, but we only came here to get warm. Now we will leave."

Still, I made no move to get up. The pleasant warmth was just beginning to seep under my clothes, together with the lovely black tea.

"Among other things, good manners have fled the world, my child. You must speak kindly to me, my son. I know that you are scared of our old Europe, with all its locks, secrets, heavy keys . . . In America everything is open, clear, not brooding, historical, layered. But you are back now."

"I know these keys," Teresa said softly. "They were the keys to Elizabeth's rooms, to the pantries, the kitchens, the washrooms, the linen closets. They were very heavy."

She reached forward and took them from the man's hand.

He patted the back of her hand. "She loved you," he said.

"And I her," said Teresa, speaking in a small, child-like voice.

I asked meekly, of Teresa, "Who are you talking about?"

They both answered at once.

"Elizabeth," said the old man.

"Lilly," said Teresa.

"What are you," I said, "some kind of psychic?"

That startling, sudden laughter welled up again. It sent chills through my whole body. It was deep, insane, but also, somehow, *knowing.*

"Don't you understand yet?" he said when his fit of hilarity passed. "I know everything. I am more than four hundred years old. I can read minds, leaves, winds, ripples of water. I would have long ago become leaf, wind, or water myself, but I made Elizabeth a promise. I told her that she might live again, at a future time, and that she would be beautiful then. The time has now come for her to collect her promise. You are the son that bears both our names. The key is in your blood."

That's what I *thought* I heard him say. But in all fairness, with the din of the Saxon stove, the wind outside, and the old man's undefinable accent, I wasn't sure.

Teresa, who had been playing absentmindedly with the string of keys, dropped them suddenly to the floor. It broke the spell.

"You are raving, old man!" I was angry.

At this time, Your Honor, I did not believe in magic. Elizabeth Bathory, my ancestress, had been a witch all right, but that had been then and this was now. She had clearly unhinged the old innkeeper across time. He lived in the shadow of her castle and had surrounded himself with her objects. He had looted them. But magic like ideas of eternal beauty had fled the world. The telephone was our magic.

"Do you have a telephone?"

He laughed again.

"Our car," I explained lamely. "It needs repairs. And we have our things in there." I was thinking of my files.

"And so it does." Our host stood up suddenly, as if he had unfolded from where he had coiled inside himself. He was strangely tall. His eyes filled with fire. Age seemed to drop from him like a skin.

"Your journey is not yet ended," he said, "but it is nearly over. Prepare yourselves. You may take the keys, darling. And you, Count Bathory, must begin to assume the authority that is yours. I am getting impatient. You may not wish to see my rooms now, but you will. You must. I am tired of living. You must bring my promise to fruition. I will see my beloved Elizabeth one more time, and then another cycle begins. Good-bye."

Dismissed summarily, Teresa and I found ourselves outside in the snow. As we walked away from the stone house, I turned back to make sure that it was really there. It was. What's more, Teresa had the string of keys hanging from her wrist.

"What was he?" I said anxiously. "A mad archivist? Was that really an inn?"

"If you want my opinion, I think he was Andrei de Kereshtur, Elizabeth Bathory's notary." Teresa said this flatly, without any emphasis, as if she were noting the weather.

"Surely you are joking."

"Why? He knew all about us. He knew your name. He knew about Lilly."

"You mean Elizabeth."

"No, the one I love. Lilly."

We walked in silence then, while I feverishly tried to understand. I had no trouble with part of what had unfolded. The old man, like most psychics, tea-leaf readers, and soothsayers, had a gift for personal insight. He had uncovered something I had not known: Teresa's relationship with Lilly Hangress. It was clearly more than a teacher-student relationship. Elizabeth Bathory was Lilly Hangress's subject. Therefore the two were easy to confuse. But this is how far my reason got. The old man had known also who I was. That was harder to fathom. Perhaps someone at The Hand had seen the registration in our stalled car.

"Teresa, is it true about the keys? Did Elizabeth burn the hands of girls with keys?"

"Lilly said that this, of all that Elizabeth Bathory did, was most telling. These were the keys of domestic life. 'This is your pitiful life!' she shouted at the girls whose hands she burned. 'Your life will end when I place my domestic keys over your palms!' The keys of domesticity erasing the keys of God . . ."

I was shocked. Professor Hangress had translated the terror of such cruelty in the simplest, most domestic terms, to her students.

"The metaphysic of domesticity . . ." I mumbled, "the triumph of reality, the revenge of the hausfrau . . . Was she just a domestic Fascist then? Someone cruel enough to harness a fantastic imagination to the service of the unimaginative?"

"There is no 'just' anything. There is no trivial situation, no harmless activity. Remember, Elizabeth was not beautiful. Beauty is an ideal. She had to combat this ideal with all her strength. She had an imperative to deromanticize."

"How could this be? She surrounded herself with beautiful things. She loved pearls and jewels. Painters made her frescoes. Musicians composed. Poets sang. The feminine shapes she destroyed were chosen for their beauty . . ."

"We always destroy what we love," Teresa said simply.

I did not know the girl walking beside me in the snow of Austria. Who was she? Innocent, young, almost virginal one moment, cruel, analytical the next . . . and Lilly's lover! Perhaps I *should* have gotten her file.

"Who are you, Teresa?"

"The victim," she said, "always the victim."

She had said this so matter-of-factly that once more I felt the chilly wings of something inexplicable brush me. There was only the merest sadness in her voice, a trace. Otherwise, it was just a fact. The victim, always the victim. And there were the bruises to prove it.

I vowed to myself to protect her. My heart beat violently. If I do fall in love now, I will let it be. I was going to interpose myself between Teresa and whatever victimized her. I had a purpose.

But then I stopped myself. Protect her from what? Who wanted to harm her? The old man? I could wrap one hand around his withered neck and choke the life out of it with one squeeze. Imre, who had beaten her? I would show the little punk what I had learned about boxing. I would humiliate him. Lilly? My inner ranting paused for a moment. The face and body of Lilly Hangress, bathed in the light of chandeliers at the Neptune, presented itself to me, half mocking and inquisitive. The beautiful Lilly Hangress. She would be a formidable adversary. But why would she harm Teresa? Weren't they lovers?

I N 1576 SHORTLY AFTER ELIZA-
beth's sixteenth birthday, the Holy Roman
Emperor Maximilian died after a twelve-year reign and
was succeeded by his son, Rudolf II (1576-1612). That
same year, Ursula Kaniszay-Nadazdy passed away suddenly and was mourned by all the Christian world. Some
of these mourners secretly wept for sorrow at the ascension of the madman in Prague as well. Rudolf was emperor for most of the rest of Elizabeth Bathory's life.
She outlived him by only one year.

Andrei de Kereshtur wrote in his *Chronicles*:

After the ascension of Rudolf, every man appeared to
have acquired a double of himself. Men of honor betrayed their friends as if they were not themselves.
People professed things that they did not heed. A
man's beliefs were not the same in his heart and his
mouth. Even the weather, beginning that year, was
strangely at odds with itself. Blue skies could be seen
side by side with rain. It snowed and rained at the
same time. Falling stars came all the way to earth and
then changed their minds and went back into the sky.
Astrologers read the stars in contradictory and con-
fusing ways. Saturn, the lord of Capricorn and Aquar-
ius, reigned over Rudolf's zodiac.

Rudolf's Saturnian person was best described by
Johannes of Hasfurt: "Saturn is cold and dry. The
Saturnian individual has a broad and ugly face, small
eyes downcast, one larger than the other and having a
spot or a deformity; thin nostrils and lips; connecting

eyebrows; bristly black hair, shaggy and slightly wavy; uneven teeth. His beard, if he has one, is sparse, but his body—especially his chest—is hairy. He is nervous. His skin is fine grained and dry, his legs are long, his hands and feet deformed with a cleft heel. The body is not too big, honey colored, smelling like a goat . . . In his complexion coldness and dampness prevail."

A better description of our emperor could scarcely exist. I thank the stars for my hump, which puts me out of reach of his lust. Otherwise, Rudolf is indiscriminate and will take anyone for his lust as he sleeplessly roams the galleries of the castle.

Shortly after Ursula Nadazdy's death, the Turkish offensive began in earnest. Franz Nadazdy was gone for a full year. Elizabeth glanced often at his handsome figure above the fireplace, with its fierce mustache, the shoulder-length black hair, the piercing eyes. She didn't need the life-size portrait to remember him. She carried his image within.

In her mind's eye she saw him laying siege to the Turkish Dombra Fortress at the Danube River. The Turkish army defending the pass to Dombra had been vanquished. Five thousand Hungarians and eight thousand Turks perished in the clash. Franz Nadazdy captured Kharmal Bey, who commanded the Turkish army, and had him taken under guard to Sarvar to be held for ransom.

In her mind, Elizabeth saw Franz, his armor covered in blood, steering his horse on the field of corpses.

She willed him to think of her perfumed body stretched before the mirrors. Elizabeth lay still in her husband's mind, surrending to him.

His horse stepped on the corpses of disemboweled Turks. One of them was still moving, but Franz did not lean over to lop off his head. He led his horse instead to step on the insolent face.

Franz would have liked to unfasten his armor and to lie down among the corpses, who were no longer corpses but the bodies of his wife reflected in the Venetian mirrors of her boudoir.

That evening he ordered a raid on a nearby village and had wenches brought to his tent after they had been bathed and perfumed.

Elizabeth saw him lying with them, still as a corpse, letting their hands knead his tired flesh.

Afterwards she watched him hand them over to his soldiers.

Tired of her barren imagination, Elizabeth ordered Darvulia to bring two of the new girls to her chamber.

She ordered them to be undressed and made them lie next to her under the canopy embroidered with gold lilies. She commanded them to be still as corpses.

The countess lay still between them and, once more, conjured her husband to take possession of her body. She felt her soft skin toughen, her plump thighs harden, her silky down become coarse. She had nearly succeeded in bringing her husband into herself when one of the girls moved.

The illusion emptied from her as quickly as water running down a drain.

Enraged, Elizabeth leaned over to her writing table and seized the first object, a gold letter opener. Striking angrily, she plunged the letter opener into one of the girls. Her blood gushed up over Elizabeth's breasts and face and over the body of the other girl.

Elizabeth wiped the blood from her eyes and told the other girl to drag the dying body of her friend to the window and to hold her there in her arms like a baby.

Darvulia, who had been the only one of her maids to witness the scene, pulled the terrified girl from the window before anyone could see her from the courtyard below. It took all Darvulia's strength to wrench the wounded friend from the girl's arms. But when Darvulia tried to bind the wound, it was too late. The girl was dead.

Elizabeth had removed herself completely from the scene and was combing her hair in the mirror as if nothing had happened.

She did not see Franz in her mind's eye any longer. She tasted the girl's rusty blood on her lips and couldn't remember what the taste reminded her of.

During the months after her mother-in-law's death, Elizabeth had to make important decisions. For the first time in her life, her book-learned knowledge was insufficient. Her reading of Tacitus gave her no clues as to which border forts needed immediate attention before the Turkish onslaught.

The rough advice of her captains was more valuable than the writings of Aristotle, but even they contradicted themselves, leaving the decisions to her.

Before a selected group of burghers to whom she had to explain the necessity for new taxes, she spoke as eloquently as if she had been taught by Tertullian. The burghers were not enthralled by the countess's fine rhetorical skills. They were representatives of ancient guilds, long inured to the fine rhetoric of nobles. The meister of the Weavers' Guild, Heinz Odein, told her plainly that new taxes would be firmly rejected by the guilds.

Her well-wrought phrases met the same fate before the heads of villages, who told her, speaking for small landholders and free peasants, that "you can squeeze a stone until it becomes sand, but our peasants have been sand for so long, you won't get a drop out of them."

The revolt of George Dozsa was still fresh in the minds of the aristocracy, and the landholders knew it. She discussed the situation with Captain Moholy, her mother's old lover, whom she had put in charge of her garrison. Moholy was fiercely devoted to Elizabeth and feared no one.

He told her that although things were in some respects worse than they had been during the Dozsa revolt, the spirit of revolt was lacking. He advised Elizabeth to bribe the peasant leaders, which she promptly did.

It was not so easy to bribe the representatives of the guilds, who knew only too well what was at stake. With them she negotiated the new increases and settled for less than she had been asking.

Her tenure as chief administrator started propitiously. She began to enlarge her female staff. She put her friend Andrei de Kereshtur in charge of the record keepers and notaries. De Kereshtur took to his task energetically and competently. He also began to print books on the old Sarvar presses.

She also made sure that her two ecclesiastics, Hebler and Ponikenuz, did not run much into each other. Ponikenuz officiated at Sarvar, while Hebler remained at Kereshtur, where he intrigued mightily against the aging monk Silvestri, who had set up a laboratory and engaged in scientific researches. Hebler was convinced that the devil was being summoned by those researches, but there was little he could do for the moment, when even the Holy Roman Emperor was involved in similar work.

Elizabeth's aunt Klara Bathory traveled often with her to Kereshtur, but also to Lockenhaus, Cahtice, and Vienna, to oversee the managers of her estates. Elizabeth's traveling entourage usually consisted of Klara,

Teresa, Darvulia, Lena, Helena Jo, and occasionally Piczka, a foulmouthed buffoon who amused her greatly.

Her coachmen and guards were devoted men who were asked, now and then, strictly for the amusement of her women, to join the ladies in their carriages to make love to them. Elizabeth was fond of the rocking motion of her coach, which induced amorous feelings in her.

When Elizabeth arrived at one of her castles, it was customary for Her Ladyship's personal staff to await her by the castle gates. After settling in, she hurled herself into a flurry of activities.

Hundreds of girls were hired during this period of Elizabeth's life. There were questions about the need for such a large retinue. Ponikenuz grumbled in a letter to his fellow cleric Hebler: "They run about like a flock of geese, chattering and getting in the way. They are less useful than geese, though, their main purpose being, it seems, to hold up Her Ladyship's mirror and tie her bows."

Ponikenuz didn't know how right he was. The girls not only held Elizabeth's mirror, they *were* her mirror. She watched her reflection in their youth as if to measure the increments of time that grew between them as she aged.

Andrei de Kereshtur noted that "My Lady's girls were like the sand in an hourglass; she watched time seep out of them."

One time when a new girl was brought in at Kereshtur, Elizabeth waited for her dressed in wide Turkish pants, reclining on Turkish pillows, and drinking thick, sweet Turkish coffee from a porcelain cup. The girl was barely fourteen, covered by a clean white linen dress, barefoot, with a thick braid of hair down the middle of her back.

She was shy and kept her eyes to the floor.

"What do you believe in, muffin?" The countess

could be quite affectionate when it suited her. Darvulia testified that "On good days, my Lady was kind and loving; she called everyone by endearing names such as *muffin, cinnamon, jewel, sweet poppy,* and this made everyone be devoted and pleased by her, and work so much harder to see her in such mind."

"I believe in God the Father, Christ the Son, the Holy Ghost, the Blessed Mother, and the host of angels . . ." whispered the girl.

"Louder! I can't hear you!" Elizabeth's voice rose sharply.

The girl repeated what she had said, reddening.

Elizabeth sprung to her feet and slapped her.

"I asked you what *you* believed in, not what your idiot village priest told you!"

Tears were streaming down the girl's face while she tried hard to think what it was that she really believed in.

Elizabeth slapped her several times. Her rings left impressions on the girl's wet cheeks.

"I believe . . ." she whispered, "that dogs and cats tell people to go to war . . ."

Elizabeth burst out laughing. She asked for an explanation, and the girl haltingly described her belief that domestic animals, especially cats and dogs, were sent into people's houses by wild animals in order to provoke them to make war on one another. They did this because there were too many people and they were eating all the animals. Dogs and cats were spies defending the animal kingdom by making people kill one another instead.

This was so unexpected that Elizabeth laughed until tears ran down her own cheeks. All her anger drained away and she dismissed the girl with a wave of her hand after directing Darvulia to employ her in the sewing shop.

The terms of the girls' engagements were originally for five years of service, at the end of which Elizabeth undertook to provide them with the dowry necessary to get married. Darvulia supervised the new girls. Some of them proved to be good learners, diligent, uncomplaining.

Two of her favorites, Selena and Jo Anna, impressed the countess with their beauty but also with their eagerness to serve her.

Selena, who was fourteen years old, was a spirited and pretty girl with red hair, tall for her age. Jo Anna was somewhat older, a black-haired siren with a half-lidded, sleepy look who moved like a serpent. Her annoying habit was to slip unobserved into a room and stand still until she was discovered and made to slither away.

Darvulia, who was fond of finding the animal nature in people, nicknamed Selena Squirrel and Jo Anna Snake. Elizabeth, though Darvulia had never told her this, was She-Wolf. Teresa was—what else?—Goose, and Dorothea was Cat. For Aunt Klara, Darvulia had had to devise a whole shameless new animal called Heat-Leopard.

The females who made up Elizabeth's staff were supplemented by Aunt Klara's two girls, Maria and Sara, two moist-lipped teenagers who always looked slightly disheveled, as if they had been working long hours in a sunless cave. In truth, they worked nights in the fanciful caves of Klara's imagination, which would rarely stop long enough to sleep. Darvulia nicknamed them Chipmunk One and Two.

Elizabeth could barely manage the flood of increased activity required of her. A spate of visitors arrived at Sarvar to make the acquaintance of the new mistress. They came from all corners of Hungary and Transylvania, bearing gifts and tales, trying to make themselves gracious and memorable to the girl who was richer than the king.

They brought her fancy birds, peacocks and pheasants, rare spices and fruit from New Spain that had been traded by Italians in the markets of Transylvania, glassware made in Venice by artisans who blew spun glass as light as gossamer, gold cups crafted by German goldsmiths, cloth woven by Flemish weavers, and prayer books copied by monks, who illuminated the first letter with rare inks.

Her cousin Stephen Bathory presented her with a strange and wondrous animal brought by Spanish sailors from New Spain. It was a wildcat that had been trained by humans since its birth but that nevertheless had a great many dangerous instincts. The cat was called a jaguar and it was worshiped as a god in many parts of New Spain.

Indeed, as Elizabeth looked at the splendid animal pacing inside its strongly barred cage, she felt a shiver. There was so much strength in the easy loping of his body that she was seized by envy. She felt a deep kinship with the ferocious-looking animal. Gazing into the slivers of light that sliced the dark pupils of its eyes, Elizabeth had foreknowledge of a deep connection between them.

She named the jaguar Night Snow because it looked to her like glinting snow under the moonlight. Elizabeth fed him raw meat herself, because none of her staff dared go near the big cat. When he stopped growling at her approach, she had his cage set at the foot of her bed. Some nights she pulled the quilts and comforters off her canopied bed and slept naked on the floor next to Night Snow's cage. She often had dreams of running alongside the jaguar across the valleys of savage mountains.

In the mornings after these dreams, Elizabeth felt

thirsty and brilliantly lucid. Her body was growing stronger in imitation of her cat.

It wasn't long before Elizabeth opened the door of the cage. The magnificent animal walked out slowly, paced about the room, and then leapt with an effortless stride on Elizabeth's bed, where it lay stretched and at ease. Elizabeth put out a hand and stroked his back. Night Snow licked her hand.

From that time the jaguar slept in Elizabeth's bed, to the terror of her maids, who never quite got used to it. When she had visitors in her chamber, she put Night Snow in her cage, but she rarely bothered to lock it.

The animal's evident good nature eventually reassured most of those who had some kind of contact with the young mistress, but no one relaxed completely. Teresa was so afraid of it that she'd had Darvulia rub her with bitter oil of nutmeg, which the cat frowned on.

When Elizabeth found out about the nutmeg, she had Helena Jo and Darvulia hold Teresa down while she rubbed honey on her maid's legs and breasts. They held her like this for Night Snow, who leapt onto the bed and licked her. Teresa fainted when the cat passed his tongue between her thighs.

Elizabeth Bathory continued to uphold the reputation for enlightenment that her mother-in-law, Ursula Nadazdy, had been known for. She continued to invite scholars and artists to the castle.

In 1583, the famous philosopher, astronomer, astrologer, and theologian Johannes von Kepler came. The visit of the great Kepler had been arranged through complex diplomatic maneuvers by Elizabeth's aunt, Countess Klara, who had traveled to Castle Hradschin in Prague and had prevailed on Emperor Rudolf II to allow Kepler to journey to Hungary.

Johannes von Kepler arrived in a toylike carriage and had difficulty getting out the door. He was a tall man, bent slightly at the neck, which made him look like a question mark. Indeed, he spoke mostly in questions: "Am I to understand that I am indeed in the presence of the gracious Bathory? Am I not pleased to meet you, Lady Bathory?"

Elizabeth was certainly pleased to see him. She had recognized him from the moment he stepped down from his carriage. The renowned scholar was no other than the frail Johannes of her youth who at Stephen Bathory's coronation had allowed himself to be buggered by a Gypsy for her sake.

Kepler blushed deeply when he saw the mistress at Sarvar, and bowed so low that his ermine cap brushed to the ground. Elizabeth graciously gave him her arm, and together they entered the great hall, where a splendid reception took place.

In a letter to Rudolf in which he, quite naturally, whispered not a word of their previous acquaintance, Kepler wrote that he found his hostess "gracious, beautiful, and uncommonly intelligent." At the table, he directed all his words to her, ignoring the flirtatious wit of the distinguished ladies assembled in his honor.

The countess and the astrologer sat on the raised platform at the head of the table, gazing at each other like falcons on the high branches of a tree. Andrei de Kereshtur stood by the side of his mistress, ready to supply her with facts should she find herself at an intellectual impasse during the conversation. But Elizabeth only glanced at him once with the look of someone consulting a mirror in passing. Kepler took no notice of him either.

Plate after plate of roast venison garnished with dill, pheasant in aspic, and beef tongue studded with whole cloves of garlic passed by the philosopher, who ignored them. But he downed his goblets of Tokay wine as quickly as the servants could fill them.

Kepler discoursed on Pythagorean astral music, the beauty and harmony of the heavens, and the divine qualities of numbers.

Andrei noted the rapt attention in Elizabeth's eyes, the glitter of her pearls streaming down between her breasts to her waist, the whiteness of her high collar. Kepler was gaunt and taut, with the nose of a bird of prey, dressed in the black habit of a monk whose only concession to worldliness was a large sapphire ring on the pointer of his left hand. But his long black hair was curly, making him look feminine. The fashion of those days considered such girlishness highly desirable.

Kepler was then in the process of calculating the horoscope of Jesus Christ, which he subsequently published in 1602 under the title *Concerning Certain Fundamentals of Astrology: A New Brief Dissertation Looking Toward a Cosmotheory, Together with a Physical Prognosis for the Year 1602 from the Birth of Christ, Written to the Philosophers.* It was not clear to Andrei how much of Kepler's cosmo-theory Elizabeth understood, but the sparkling evening, followed by the musical recitations of the poet Melotus, was exceedingly pleasurable. Andrei was left intellectually aroused and hungry to find and to devour all that the erudite Kepler had referred to.

The countess too was left in a state of pleasant excitement.

Kepler had come from Prague with a twofold mission. He was prepared to take delivery of five hundred casks of Hungarian wine from the Nadazdys on behalf of a friend of his, the wine merchant Terrimini. His other mission, which was covert, was to gauge the depth of the Protestant faith of the Hungarians in order to ascertain what it would take to bring them back to the fold of the Holy Roman Church. He was himself being watched by the Inquisition and had been told that he must make a gesture that would redeem him in the eyes of the Holy Father. He carried with him a reliquary containing the tip of Christ's index finger and a letter in the handwriting of Catherine of Siena. The jeweled reliquary and the letter displayed together were said to restore faith in the lapsed and to convert heathens on the spot.

Kepler didn't quite believe this, but he had employed these objects with great results, so he kept his doubts to himself.

During the interminable meal, between discourses on the planets, Kepler embarked on a halfhearted apology for the Holy Father in Rome. He displayed the reliquary and fell to his knees with his eyes closed after begging everyone to kneel and kiss the tip of the finger of our Savior.

When he opened his eyes, he saw that none of the ladies present had fallen to their knees. On the contrary, Elizabeth fixed him with an icy stare and told him that Luther had spoken against the practice of collecting pieces of our Savior.

This was one of the few times that Pastor Ponikenuz, who had held himself rigidly at the lower end of the table and nervously stuffed himself in order to keep himself from shouting, felt admiration for his mistress.

Kepler defended his treasure with some obtuse argument and produced the letter from Catherine of Siena. He read it weeping, with a shaken voice:

Jesus made of his blood a drink and his flesh a food for all those who wish it. There is no other means for man to be satisfied. He can appease his hunger and thirst only in this blood . . . A man can possess the whole world and not be satisfied (for the world is less than man) until blood satisfies him, for only that blood is united to the divinity . . . Eight days after his birth, Christ spilled a little of it in the circumcision, but it was not enough to cover man . . . Then on the cross the lance . . . opened his heart. The Holy Spirit tells us to have recourse to the blood . . . And then the soul becomes like a drunken man: just as the more he drinks, the more he wants to drink, so the more the soul bears the cross, the more it wants to bear it. And the pains are its refreshment, and the tears that it has shed for the memory of the blood are its drink. And the sights are its food.

The words of Saint Catherine impressed Elizabeth, who already knew that Catherine had been given a ring fashioned from the foreskin of the Lord Jesus by Jesus himself when she had sucked the poison from the wound of a dying man during the Black Death.

Elizabeth believed this, but still she could not bring herself to kneel before the jewel-encrusted reliquary.

Kepler had also brought with him an early draft of an essay concerning the composition of blood and its relation to the flesh. He read this treatise also to those assembled at Elizabeth's table, making each sentence a question and stopping often to address his dinner companions: "Whatever participates in matter, insofar as it participates in it, is cold by its nature? And whatever is hot by potency, has this nature from an animal force, either implanted or generated?"

After he read this, Kepler turned toward Elizabeth and asked impatiently, "Given this principle, fair lady, is a human being hot, cold? What is it?"

"He is hot when he is being buggered, and cold immediately afterwards," she would have liked to reply, but instead she merely took in the beanpole figure of the philosopher, who looked so different from the waif-like boy she had met so long ago, and said, "A human being is that which steams the mirror. Therefore, a human being is a cold agent that causes glass to sweat."

Kepler, taken only slightly aback, as if he had divined her unspoken reply, bowed his head and declared questioningly: "If reflection had the power of reaction, are human beings who are reflections of God not also hot? Are we not the mirrors of God? Do we not steam when he contemplates his divine figure in us? And when He finds that we obscure his image, what does he do?"

He had addressed this question to another member of his audience, but Elizabeth answered him anyway. "He smashes the mirror, which brings him thousands of years of bad luck."

Johannes von Kepler turned his whole body toward Elizabeth, twisting violently on his seat. His collar twisted with him, traveling to the back of his head. He glared at her for a moment, then resumed reading his text. "It has been proven by experience that all things swell with moisture as the moon waxes and subsides as it wanes?"

Kepler asked many questions about the influence of the planets on human affairs but took care not to appear that he had studied occult matters. He also praised his hosts questioningly and directed interrogatively that his "dissertation" be printed next day in a limited edition of two for Lady Bathory and himself.

Andrei de Kereshtur went to work right away and stayed up most of the night setting the lead type unto paper until he had in his hands the printed pamphlet of Kepler's thoughts. Only, he made three copies instead of two, keeping one for himself to underline and criticize at leisure.

At long last, after dinner, Elizabeth and Johannes retired to the rose salon at her apartments to speak unencumbered.

"I knew you right away," said Elizabeth, "and was

glad to see you. I had thought at one time that you despised me, because you did not come with Rudolf to my wedding . . ."

Kepler looked at his hostess with a glint of amusement in his gray eyes. "Our childhood adventure has contributed greatly to the path of study I have chosen."

Kepler explained that he had launched his researches into the patterns of the stars in the belief that every human event, no matter how small, whether past or present, was reflected therein. He wanted to see if the incident at Stephen Bathory's coronation had been foretold. Indeed it had, he told her.

Elizabeth qustioned him about her own life, but here the philosopher begged her indulgence and said that it was unwise to reveal such things, even to one as dear to his heart as Elizabeth.

Instead he broached the more philosophical aspects of their lives.

"Is a philosopher himself not a mirror of nature?" he asked. "And given that fact, is it not true that the greater a philosopher he is, the greater the quality of the nature that he need reflect? And the highest nature being beauty, is it not a great privilege for him to reflect the great beauty of Elizabeth Bathory?"

Elizabeth assented easily. Emboldened by her assent, Johannes then asked if he could count on her patronage should he find himself in difficulty. Once more, Elizabeth assented.

Finally he offered the question: "If the fair lady believes in the strength of the best mirror, would she not care to strengthen her beauty with the mirror's seed?"

Elizabeth replied that, regardless of her belief and despite the obvious charms of the philosopher, she had pledged her virtue to her husband and could not traffic in any other seed. This was a lie, but the truth of the matter was that she felt no attraction whatsoever for the astrologer. In addition, she doubted his ability to carry on such an operation, since she was quite certain that the buggering of his youth had taken him into a direction that had little to do with women.

Johannes sighed, then protested vigorously that he had not been propositioning the great mistress. He had meant only the "seed of his belief," which was contained in the reliquary containing the finger of Jesus. He begged her once more to kneel before the holy jewel with him and to kiss the diamond on its lid.

Elizabeth allowed that she would. She knelt before the reliquary, which Kepler held with both hands like a chalice, and kissed the large diamond on its lid. When her lips met the stone, she felt the desire to bite through the gold casings all the way to the piece of bone inside. She wanted so much to feel the crunch of bone between her teeth that she bit her own lip instead, drawing blood. A drop of this fell on the diamond.

Kepler raised the reliquary to his lips and licked the drop of Countess Bathory's blood. Elizabeth flushed red when the philosopher licked and then sighed as deeply as if he had just entered her body. How strangely different we grow from the children we once were, she sighed to herself.

Kepler's visit had an unexpected consequence. When he was introduced to Benezzo Gozzoli, Kepler asked: "Did I not meet your father?"

Benezzo put his hand to his mouth in astonishment. He confessed that he had been looking for his father throughout Hungary but could not locate him.

"How could you not locate him?" said Kepler. "Did I not meet him in Prague where he was visiting our holy emperor? Did he not become a monk and change his name, giving up the earth with its vices, temptations, and fleshly incitements? Is his name not the monk Silvestri?"

Benezzo confessed that he had not known of his father's conversion, only that his father had put himself in the service of a Hungarian noble in some unknown capacity.

"Was it not to save his soul?" wondered Kepler, who saw in this area a fruitful beginning to his own enterprise. "Is it not the work of every son of our Father to help bring others to the foot of the cross?"

"But where is my father?" asked the tearful Benezzo.

"Don't I seem to know that he was with my Lady Bathory's household? Was his holy name not Silvestri?"

It was Elizabeth's turn to be astonished. Silvestri was the harpist's father? Could a great, wise man like her teacher be the source of this insubstantial ball of musical fluff?

Benezzo, who had found out so casually about the secret object of his search, fainted. He had to be revived and carried back to his room, where, in the days to come, Elizabeth visited him and promised to bring Silvestri to Sarvar.

After Kepler retired for the night, Elizabeth could not sleep. Her childhood memory aroused her. At the inquest conducted on January 11, 1611, by the lord palatine's high commission, Selena recalled that on the night of Kepler's visit, after the company had retired, "Her Ladyship singed the private parts of a girl with a burning candle."

The great Kepler had been sublimely inspiring that evening. Elizabeth recalled the philosopher's every word as she tossed and turned on her bed. For Kepler the stars made mathematically perfect sense. The universe was an intelligible and harmonious musical instrument played by God. Every single human action was reflected in the celestial harmonics, which contained past, present, and future. The birth of Jesus Christ was announced by a great celestial conjunction, whose meaning Kepler had been able to read and interpret. In the process he had also provided a method for such reading that would stand future generations in good stead. The stars were "arranged by God," and everything on earth, not just the "great conjunctions," could be read in them as easily as one read the pages of a book, if one knew how to read. The stars burned brightly in celebration of God's perfect mathematics.

This, for Elizabeth, was a reassuring thought. It made her feel a kind of peace, and gratitude. If human affairs were so firmly inscribed in God's book, what was there to do but await their unfolding and chart their course?

Kepler's discourse had excited her like music, making her feel erotic, exhilarated, swollen with sensation. It was all she could do while the philosopher had spoken to keep her hands folded quietly in her lap. Her pent-up desire—Kepler talked for hours—surged through her body, leaving her no recourse but sensual excess.

She rose from her bed and played for a while with a strand of pearls. She had thousands of pearls. They hung out from overstuffed jewelry boxes, they were draped lavishly over the bedposts. Her greed for pearls was known throughout the Christian world. "We are emptying the seas for you, my lady," her purveyor had once assured her.

Elizabeth emptied some of her boxes and laid the long strands of pearls on the silk sheets. She stretched on top of them and rolled over them, feeling the firm white globes push at her philosophically incandescent flesh. She thought of the many brute women of her castle who were lying with their men at that moment. Her stomach tightened with envy and jealousy.

Elizabeth felt no longer young. She became easily bored and angry. The mind was not enough. She pushed down hard into her pearls and rolled on them like a boat on uneasy waves. She then called for her trusted Darvulia, ordering her to bring one of the new girls hired that morning.

A pale, fretful teenager, already shaking in fear of her formidable mistress, was brought to her. The girl was trembling like a leaf as Darvulia's skillful hands undressed her.

The weight of her age came bearing down from the malicious heavens when Elizabeth glanced at the tender down between the girl's legs. Her own down was rapidly coarsening, its once silky fibers growing tough like horsehair.

Her job done, Darvulia withdrew. Elizabeth ordered the girl to spread her girlish legs wide. Elizabeth studied intently the pencil-thin line of the girl's opening. A virgin.

"Oh, stop shaking, stupid creature! You are no better than a rabbit or a squirrel. Be grateful I'm not serving you to the pigs!"

It was all so dreary. She thought about God's candles, Kepler's astral music . . . She reached for the candleholder at the side of her bed and lowered the candle flame to the soft down between the girl's legs.

Her own thoughts became briefly and pleasurably feverish: she smelled the singed girlish pelt, the sting of cooking flesh. Power and contempt surged through her blood. She saw that Night Snow had become aroused as well and was softly licking himself between his lithe thighs.

When the girl fainted, becoming as still as a sheet of music on a stand, Elizabeth lost interest. She nearly set the draperies on fire with the candle before she set it down.

Darvulia tiptoed in discreetly and took the creature out of the room to rub some healing ointment on her. She would doubtless live, though the strength of her mind after this would be another matter.

After burning the girl with the candle, Elizabeth slept and dreamt that she was crawling on her knees toward the Crucified One in order to drink blood from the wound on his side. The blood flowed copiously, but no matter where she moved her mouth to receive it, it flowed past her. Rage suffused her. Her Savior was denying her the solace of his life elixir. She rose into the air until she hovered over the crucifix. She opened her legs over the holy cross and let her menstruum flow out of her unto the upturned face of Jesus Christ. Elizabeth felt in her dream the force of her dripping blood. But her rage did not abate. The all-forgiving Savior gently took her blood in his mouth. "There is no end to my forgiveness," he told her. Elizabeth felt damned: there was no forgiveness in her at all. Neither was there mercy, tenderness, or pity. Where those feelings had once been, there were only scarred craters, pits of darkness. Rage gave way to sorrow, but only for herself.

Elizabeth woke up crying. She fully expected to find herself in the ice-cold hollow of her tomb. Instead, Teresa was standing solicitously over her.

Elizabeth motioned her to come close, to whisper perhaps the shattering words Christ had spoken to her. Teresa bent her ear to her mistress's face. Elizabeth bit hard on the tender drop of pink flesh lowered to her. She swallowed greedily the blood that gushed from it. She had intended to whisper Christ's message to Teresa or perhaps cry on her cheek, but the sight of that helpless flesh was irresistible. Besides, she told herself, considerably cheered up, Christ may refuse me his blood, but Teresa's is so much sweeter. It's free of all that preaching crap.

Kepler left before dawn that day, while Elizabeth dreamt her tormented dream. He inscribed Elizabeth's copy of his essay: "If God has so much trouble with his children, how can such beauty as yours, my Lady, not move him to Mercy?"

Elizabeth read the inscription with amusement. She left the book open and leaned on her elbows to contemplate herself in the looking glass. On the surface of it, she was becoming more visibly beautiful. But she knew that her fine silken down was coarsening, that the once thin lips of her womanhood had swollen and grown greedy in their search for pleasure.

The looking glass told her that her features were most becoming in the elongated oval frame. Her eyes looked no longer too big for her face. Her mouth with the thin but moist lips gave no hint of the extraordinarily long words in Latin and German that she was capable of pronouncing. Her perfect ears had the smoothness and color of mother-of-pearl. The poultices that Darvulia was applying to her face made her skin alive and healthy. Her pretty neck made the young knights sigh, and her long fingers flying over the strings of the harp caused many of them to swoon as they listened. All of it pleased her but did not deny her inner knowledge that these visible displays were but the outward signs of the decline that had already begun. And Franz was still at war. Always war. Always no Franz. Always more war.

The visit of Johannes von Kepler troubled Pastor Ponikenuz, who suspected that some of the Catholic's idolatry might have impressed Lady Bathory. Ponikenuz resumed teaching theology to Elizabeth with greater ardor, attempting to add some charm to his colorless exposition. Pastor Ponikenuz knew that his teaching held little warmth, so he made an effort to draw some from the depths of his parsimonious nature.

He went so far as to bring his cherished monkey, Isabel, to show his young mistress, convinced that the well-known instant sympathy of women for animals would better dispose her toward him. Pastor Ponikenuz felt for his monkey the absolute maximum of affection he allowed himself toward any living creature, and while this feeling could not properly be called love, which Ponikenuz considered a weakness, it was nonetheless his only allowance for sentiment.

During the many hours that Ponikenuz spent in the monastic spareness of his room reading books, he always felt the reassuring presence of his pet, who perched on his chair looking over his shoulder, almost as if it too was reading. Occasionally the pastor read aloud some particularly inspiring thought of Martinus Luther's, and at those times, Isabel seemed almost to comprehend. He would have never admitted it, but the animal had become in many ways indispensable to him.

He had not been wrong. Elizabeth took pleasure in the creature and patted its head. The monkey leapt on Elizabeth's shoulder and put its little face next to hers. It was such a spontaneously affectionate gesture that both teacher and pupil smiled for a moment. It was the only time they felt close.

The monkey would not leave its perch on Elizabeth's shoulder when the day's lesson was over. Elizabeth suggested that Pastor Ponikenuz allow her to keep the animal until next day. This request filled the cleric with anxiety. He said that he would gladly leave the animal with her but that he was the only one capable of feeding it, so he didn't think this was very wise. He hastened to add, however, that if his young mistress wanted to walk as far back as her chamber with the monkey on her shoulder, he would follow, and then they would part.

Elizabeth walked, with the preacher following behind her. When they arrived before her doors, she said that she would like the little creature to meet her exotic fellow being from that far part of the world where such wonders lived.

Ponikenuz agreed and followed Elizabeth into her rooms, where a scene of utter tranquility reigned. Teresa and Darvulia were engaged in wiping clean one of Elizabeth's dozens of gold-framed mirrors. Night Snow was lying peacefully asleep on Elizabeth's bed. A shaft of bright sunlight came through one of the stained-glass windows, bathing the jaguar in golden light.

Feeling unusually contented, Elizabeth sat on her bed. The monkey leapt suddenly off her shoulder in terrible fear, startling Elizabeth, who stood bolt upright.

The monkey's leap ended short. He landed right between the jaguar's padded paws. Opening his eyes lazily, Night Snow considered the creature for a moment as brief as a musical note. He lifted his paw and brought it swiftly on the monkey's head. Even if anyone could have moved, it would have been to no purpose. Before the immobile witnesses, the jaguar brought the monkey before his face and, looking into its eyes, snapped off its head like an apple from a branch. He bit deeply and with evident pleasure into the creature's head and licked his gushing brains clean.

Elizabeth saw the pastor's face turn to stone as he watched the cat leisurely finish off his last link to the weakness of sentiment. Elizabeth's two women had frozen before the mirrors they had been wiping.

Elizabeth's first impulse was to apologize to the pastor, but when she saw his face she knew that nothing she said now would matter at all. When she saw Teresa's and Darvulia's faces, however, she felt an inexplicable wave of warmth that was partly lust and partly hilarity. Elizabeth then did something she did not herself expect: she laughed.

Pastor Ponikenuz ran out of the room.

After the departure of the great Kepler, despite all the excitement that followed, Elizabeth felt that she was insignificant, possessed neither of greatness nor of wit. She attributed this in part to being a woman. She began to dress more and more in men's uniforms, trying as she had done in her childhood to pass unobserved among the members of the guard. But no amount of makeup or binding of her breasts sufficed to hide her feminine curves and manner.

Elizabeth took a steady lover.

One day when she felt like riding her aging mare, Luna, she had unexpectedly come upon Ficzko the groom making love to one of the scullery maids. She was seized by jealousy.

The girl ran off when Elizabeth made her appearance.

Confused, Ficzko rose from the hay and began to draw his trousers back on. Furious, Elizabeth asked him to remove them and to lie still on his back. She then climbed on top of him and took him, still wet from the scullery maid's juices, inside her.

The next few times, she ran into the groom accidentally and made love to him wherever they met. After a month, Elizabeth began choreographing their encounters with precision.

Her jealousy was a strong feeling that did not subside after making love, so Elizabeth began to intuit that jealousy was a force that had to be used in order to make her feel passion.

She ordered the scullery maid to be brought to her. Selena and Dori stripped the girl and tied her arms and legs to the bedposts. Elizabeth stabbed the girl below her breasts with a pair of scissors. Blood gushed from the wounds. Selena collected the blood in a chamber pot.

When the girl's screams started annoying her, Elizabeth stabbed her in the throat and cut her vocal cords. Her maids, possessed by frenzy, also stabbed and cut the girl long after she had died.

They collected three chamber pots full of blood. Elizabeth's heart raced furiously the whole time, but after Selena and Dori removed the body and cleaned the room, she became extraordinarily calm. It was like the aftermath of a storm. Elizabeth felt more peaceful than she ever had.

The countess enjoyed her anger. She did not want to kill again but could not help toying with the powerful jealousy that welled inside her whenever she thought of Ficzko with another woman.

She tested herself by asking him to make love to a girl while she watched. As her jealousy mounted, Elizabeth bit her own lip until she tasted blood. She stopped their lovemaking before Ficzko spent himself. She ordered him to enter her and spend himself there.

This was repeated often in the course of time. Each instance, Ficzko withdrew just before consummation and finished inside Elizabeth. Slowly Elizabeth began to realize the nature of her arousal. It had little to do with Ficzko. Her excitement fed almost exclusively on her jealousy.

Elizabeth was intrigued by the power of these plain girls to arouse her. She began toying with them in other ways, to see what made them tick. She ordered that the hair on the head of all the new girls coming to the castle be shaved. She then had ropes made from it to test its strength. "Hair is strong," she explained to her maids. "It is easy to see how in the old days a knight could climb to a tower on a maiden's braid . . ."

She had these ropes hung from her bedroom window and then she asked Ficzko, her lover, to climb them to where she waited for him naked and lit from behind by a wall of candles.

Another time she had a robe made from the shaved hair of servant girls, and she wore this without a stitch of other clothing beneath, allowing glimpses of her breasts and mons veneris through the loosely woven hair as she went about her duties, conferring with her administrators, instructing clerks, and bargaining with tradesmen. If she caught anyone looking too boldly at the partings in her robe of hair, she spoke harshly and demanded both an apology and a compliment on her fashionable garment.

"Saint Cecily," she sometimes said, "went about bare with nothing but her tresses to cover her, and yet we venerate her."

There were bare-shaven girls all over the castle, who hid their humiliation under kerchiefs and other head coverings. But they were rarely left alone. The countess, after removing her dress at night, wanted what was left of the poor creatures for her nightly amusements. Most of the shorn victims were too young to evince any pubic hair, but when the countess discovered an exception— either in the form of soft down or more luxuriant growth—she asked that it be cropped. She then had mustaches or fine beards made from it, which she wore on her face when she bit on the girls' tiny breasts or on their thin nether lips.

Dori would later testify that

there was perhaps nothing more frightful than seeing my Lady bite the poor lips of a girl's cunt with her face covered in the beard of the poor girl's own down. When the girl's blood came spurting over her face, my Lady screamed with pleasure and cried, "Forgive me God!" Sometimes she asked me to suck a poor girl down below and to put my whole hand in her.

Despite such entertainments, Elizabeth conducted the day-to-day business of her estates with unparalleled energy. Early in the mornings she went to the chapel, where she suffered the sermonizing of Pastor Ponikenuz, whose unvarying subject was the weakness of the flesh.

Before noon she met with Jacob Silvazy, the administrator of Sarvar, and went carefully over the expenditures and needs of the household for the following week.

For three more hours she wrote letters to the administrators of her other estates, at Kereshtur, Cahtice, Lockenhaus, and Vienna, instructing them in various matters and answering their questions.

Captain Moholy of her horse guards demanded to see her about increasing the size of the guard at Kereshtur from five hundred horsemen to seven hundred. She approved it.

A representative of King Matthias had been waiting patiently for the countess all morning. He had come with a request for a loan from His Majesty the king, whose treasury was broke after the last war. She approved this too, but not before castigating the king's representative for his shamelessness in requesting a loan so soon after she had given him one.

She remembered all that she was told, even the smallest numbers and all the names, and was diligent in applying this knowledge to the affairs of the estates. In

addition to administering the vast Bathory estates, su-
pervising the staff of her many castles, she dealt daily
with merchants, negotiated with representatives of the
guilds, kept a tight rein on thousands of disgruntled
peasants and serfs, dispensed justice, and generally tried
to maintain her authority.

Among her duties was the overseeing of punishments. The official administration of justice at her
courts was not unusually cruel. Whippings were quite
frequent for small theft, but only one hanging was recorded at Sarvar for the entire decade from 1578 until
1588.

The business of daytime required efficient and so-
ber-minded servants, but the activities of the night also
had their own equally efficient staff.

At the time of Kepler's visit, Elizabeth's court num-
bered twelve poets and singers, who wandered the halls
and camped in the inner courts singing of their "divine
love" for their patron and mistress. The chief poet of
Elizabeth's court, Melotus, had become weak with age.
Younger bards supplanted him. With tresses that
reached past their shoulders, they caressed their mandolins as if they were women. One of them, the singer
Palosz, was famed for the greatest number of euphe-
misms for female genitalia, including Elizabeth's favorite, "the gentle, always rocking pearl."

Andrei de Kereshtur was not fond of the poets. He
wrote that "the poets made the most noise of all and
created unpleasantness among the noble ladies in Elizabeth's entourage." He found the relentless frivolity of
the poets unnerving. The agitation of the women was
incessantly fueled by the little florets of language the
poets were strewing about. The pressure to perform to
the standards of the poets' courtly ideals was great, if
"earthly beauty is the manifestation of divine beauty,"
as Melotus's confreres never stopped proclaiming. But

Andrei knew well that while the poets extolled divine beauty, they were "testing" the poor flesh of earthly beauty for the "glow of divine fire" with tools tempered not in spirit but in lust. This testing rarely failed to uncover the "divine fire"—which usually resulted in a poem—and it released other feelings as well, jealousy foremost among them.

There was so much jealousy among the women and girls at Sarvar that Andrei de Kereshtur could rarely fall asleep without having to listen to the anguished howl of the hurt and wounded who prowled the halls looking for their unfaithful lovers. It was particularly bad when the moon was full.

The poets often suffered from this affliction as well, which caused them to spill forth poems shrilly cursing their rivals, showering invective, and invoking demons.

Lust, love, and jealousy were inseparable at Sarvar Castle. The castle inhabitants were not in the least embarrassed by physical ardor. During all the times that he had difficulty falling asleep, Andrei de Kereshtur heard these cries of rage and passion within the castle. He always believed that they were cries of joy or laments of hurt pride. It never occurred to him that these sounds might also be caused by the agony of girls being drained of blood in Elizabeth's chambers. Later, when his turn came to testify, he denied indignantly the charges against Elizabeth. "Even a monk knows a cry of love from a cry of death," he said.

The poets were supplemented by other workers of the spirit. Castle Sarvar accommodated eight astrologers, who saw the affinities and sympathies of celestial bodies operating within human bodies. They produced daily horoscopes for Elizabeth.

Three alchemists, who had been students of the monk Silvestri and were now supervised by Andrei de Kereshtur, who also dabbled in the black art, occupied a remote wing of Sarvar. They specialized in the secret attractions, passions, mergings, consummations, effervescences, boilings over, and explosions of substances they mixed together in erotically shaped alembics.

The odd smells issuing from their quarters caused Ponikenuz to howl with rage. His protests went unheeded, but he continued complaining in letter after letter to church authorities and to the king. He also preached against these workers of Satan in the village church, where he found sympathetic ears.

A number of philosophers and theologians with rather vague job descriptions came from far places to read and write at the renowned library at Sarvar. The whispering of their goose quills over parchment could be heard all the time.

Other visitors to the castle included magicians and witches, whose trade was in human excretions, body parts, fetuses, ecstatic drugs, and intoxication.

Mixed among these earnest workers one could also find a transient population of charlatans, thieves, purveyors of novelties from newly discovered worlds of New Spain, and visionaries of all kinds.

The female household kept growing. In addition to the women in Elizabeth's entourage with well-defined jobs, there were relatives and children of the staff and many country relations who were looking to marry. There were maids who sold what they couldn't give away to the perpetually aroused soldiers of the garrison. Dressmakers, hairdressers, decorators, masseuses attended the bodies of their betters, particularly Elizabeth's. She demanded attention without surcease.

There was little privacy for anyone, with the exception of Lady Bathory. Her rooms were situated on the highest floor of the castle. Five of her seven halls had private fireplaces. She slept in her canopied bed but was separated from her best maids only by curtains.

Even as she made love to Ficzko, her trusted maid-servants busied themselves around her with chores. Her jewels and clothes were continually being handled, polished, caressed, folded, and stretched by busy young hands with smooth skin.

Our flight, Your Honor, was but a day old, and there were already hints that the usually firm shell around reality was beginning to crack, allowing glimpses of a host of impatient demons. We saw now a claw, now a tail, now a red eye. It wouldn't be long now before a whole slew of the damned would bust its way through. What's more, our car was dead. The Opel lay there on the snow a mile from the village like a dead mule with its legs up in the air.

After escaping from the eerie babble of the innkeeper at Kereshtur we walked back to the village and arrived frozen at the spot where we had originally obtained directions.

The Hand tavern was more crowded now. The same burly men sat drinking at the long wooden tables, but in addition, a whole crowd of younger men had arrived. Many of them had hair cropped very short, while others looked familiar to me. They wore the skinhead uniform: leather jackets and heavy boots. One or two sported tattoos on their shaved skulls.

Teresa walked in ahead of me. Two schnapps-sotted boys at the bar whistled when they saw her. Then they elbowed each other and mumbled something in impenetrable Burgenland dialect. I thought I heard "Get thee here, wench, for a soaping!" or "Take a bath in beer!" It was all very rude and almost amusing. But I was not amused. I was tired and hungry and sick of skinheads.

Did all the skinheads know one another, or were they just rising spontaneously from the dirt like killer spores? I couldn't tell them apart from the Hungarian ones, which was probably the idea behind the uniform. They wanted to appear identical, a great army of disaffected young with a penchant for violence. Then I remembered: the Hungarian skinheads had been invented by the secret police. So much for "disaffection." If they were disaffected, it was probably over their pension plan.

The steam in the tavern fogged my eyeglasses, so I took them off. When next I looked at the drunks, they had fallen unaccountably silent. I followed their collective gaze and saw that they were looking at Teresa, who sat at the bar perfectly still, like a statue. The good boys of Burgenland had fallen as quiet as children facing an inexplicable sight.

The barkeep said, "So you're back from Kereshtur?"

"Something wrong with our car," I said.

"Some of these boys will help," he promised.

I had three brandies in quick succession. Teresa had two. And then I saw what they were looking at. When Teresa had removed her peacoat, she had pulled her blouse low, and one of her breasts was all but popping out. This would not in itself have so impressed the denizens of the tavern. But the ugly black-and-yellow bruise on it did. Several of them stared at me in mute reproach. Others, however, looked amused.

I confided to the bartender that we had somehow lost the suitcase with our clothes and that we needed some dry replacements. He had a couple of sheepskin vests in the back and he sold them to us. The black fur collar was too tight for me, but Teresa's fit perfectly. We looked like two shepherds now, ready for the mountains.

Several men—but none of the skinheads—rose and walked back to the car with us. One of them carried a lantern that threw feeble light on the snow. I could see the round peasant face of the man behind the lantern. His eyes were small and suspicious, set deeply in his beer-sodden flesh. Surely he had been among those whose daughters had gone to the castle, never to return. More than four hundred years had passed, but the man's face looked as if it had come unchanged through time, filled with a brute, stone cold suffering.

This man and those walking with him didn't need the lantern to see by. The snow fell on them, but they knew this road as if it were carved on the soles of their boots. It was carved also with a whip on their backs. But they walked without guile, with broad steps.

They pushed the car and it started.

I tried to pay them but they refused. When they left, they took their hats off to Teresa, and speaking only to her, advised us to drive only as far as the next village, where there was an inn.

"Why did they refuse money?" I asked once we were safely ensconced in our bubble of warmth. The heater worked.

"Because they wanted the wench."

"And you are her?"

"The wench is not offended," Teresa said cheerfully. "They were a good-looking bunch. I am sure that I was a pretty jolly wench in a different life."

I was happy to see her come back to her young self. After the encounter at Kereshtur, I feared that she might withdraw suddenly like her mother. Dear Eva. Where had she gone? Where, for that matter, had *we* gone? Where were we? The dark road shimmered in our headlights like a long memory lapse.

We drove in silence for a time.

"What happened to my mother's rival, Mari . . . your wife?" Teresa asked unexpectedly.

What hadn't? In America, everything changed. In those first years, I'd had a series of humble jobs. I had been an attendant on the eighth floor of the New York City morgue, a flower deliverer in Manhattan, and a button puncher in a Korean sweatshop. When I worked at the morgue, it amused me to imagine what the other morgue attendants, a pretty phlegmatic bunch who treated corpses as if they were furniture, would have thought if they had known that I was a Hungarian count. I had no difficulty with the dead bodies, either, not even those maimed by bullets or scarred by accidents, and at the time I marveled and even congratulated myself on my sangfroid.

One time, however, I lost my composure. A young woman had been brought in, beautiful in all aspects but for burn marks on her cheeks and breasts. Someone had branded her with hot irons before killing her. I looked at her until I felt the ground give way under my feet. I quit the next day.

The Korean sweatshop boss for whom I worked next would not have been surprised to find out that I was an aristocrat. The Korean was himself a prince exiled from his country. This was America; one was what one did. In the evenings, at the Golden Paprikash, my fellow émigrés laughed heartily at my adventures in the minimum-wage world. Some of them, who had university degrees, did pretty much the same things, but some had already begun going to American schools, setting up businesses, prospering. There were opportunities that I ignored. I was not interested in prospering.

My wife, Mari, who had never been terribly animated, became even more listless. She resisted all my entreaties to go out, staying in bed all day instead, reading novels and eating chocolates. Her full though not unpleasant figure started bulging here and there.

I begged her to come out with me, make friends, study, go to school. But she stubbornly closed herself in her bed world.

Thinking that my lack of ambition somehow caused hers, I enrolled in an evening course at Columbia University. We had very little money. In the end, it was the fact that we could not afford the Swiss chocolates that were her favorites that got Mari out of the house.

She started working at the Hungarian Secret, a beauty parlor owned by the wife of one of my friends. The salon, on East Eighty-second Street, claimed in its advertisement to possess the kind of Hungarian beauty secrets that had made Helena Rubinstein, a Hungarian Jewess, famous. The middle-aged uptown matrons who frequented the place enjoyed lying on massage couches, their faces covered with yoghurt and cucumber slices, listening to Razzi, the owner, tell them preposterous stories about miraculous cures and beauty potions distilled from the magic mud of Pannonia.

But while they enjoyed Razzi's ministrations, they did not particularly like Mari, who was sullen and scornful. The meager tips and small salary she earned were spent almost exclusively on Swiss chocolates.

By the end of our second year in America, Mari could not fit in any of the clothes she had. Little by little she swelled and grew until the girl she had been stretched grotesquely into a shape I could barely recognize. I blamed myself for a time, thinking that her listlessness was due to a lack of sensual eagerness on my part.

After a while, I stopped coming home. I spent the nights at friends' houses or with women I met at restaurants and bars in the Little Hungary section of New York. One day when I came home in the morning dazed and still drunk from the night before, I found a note on the bed: "I ran away with a fat man. Have a nice life."

The first half of the note was factual. Mari had moved in with the Polish butcher who sold us sausages at Kowalski's, a shop on our street corner. I decided at that moment to become a vegetarian. I never again ate meat.

The second part of her note did not prove to be so factual. I did continue having a life, but I wouldn't call it nice.

I didn't tell Teresa any of this. I said only, "We were divorced two years after we went to America. She got fat, and I wasn't very good for her."

The snow seemed to be coming down even harder as we rounded a bend in the road. We had been climbing for the past half hour. I could smell the pines through the snow. We were at a much higher altitude. Our feeble headlights didn't help much. I saw only an impressionistic white fabric dancing inches from my face. I didn't know how much longer I could keep driving.

And then I didn't have to wonder any longer. I struck the windshield with my head. Teresa lifted surreally from her seat and landed on me. The car shuddered and I heard things break. It felt as if we had hit a wall. The sticky mess on my lips was definitely blood. Mine or hers?

It took a few moments to ascertain whether we were still in one piece. I was. Teresa, after a scary moment, said, "I think I'm all here." I pushed open the door on my side and rolled out into the snow. Teresa followed me. We stood, helping each other, and took a few steps in the snow. We were fine. But the sight before our eyes was not.

The Opel had come to a stop in the soft mass of an enormous deer that lay in the middle of the road. His eyes were still moving and they found us. A look of immense pain was in them. A second after, the animal died, taking with him his last image of life: us, huddled in terror in the snow, looking at him. The fractured glow from one of the Opel's still-working headlights framed the animal's hulking mass. A bit of moon came down now and then through the curtain of snow.

I am quite certain that at that moment something changed. I felt most affectionate toward my travel companion. I would not call this feeling love, but it was close. I still wanted to protect her. But I also desired her. A fierce will to live rose in me. I was sure now that we had taken a wrong turn somewhere. Unless the directions we had received at The Hand had been deliberately wrong, we should have arrived in the next village at least two hours before.

I dug through the contents of the glove compartment, which had spilled on the floor, for the Michelin guide. It was useless. Even if I had been able to make out the spidery map in the snow, it did not seem to correspond to what I knew about the area. But I was loath to wait helplessly. Our sheepskin jackets were already soaked through and through. We had no blankets or sleeping bags—having fled Hungary only with two personal files. We had to walk.

Teresa was of the opinion that we should continue to walk in the direction we had been driving in. I thought that we should walk back, in case we had taken a wrong turn.

While we sat debating this, a miraculous light began to cut slowly through the snow and the darkness. We heard the distinctive hum of an engine. Standing before the dead deer and the crippled Opel, we waved our arms frantically at the oncoming light.

An overpowering smell followed the lights. It was a suffocating stench.

"Someone opened the gates of hell," said Teresa.

It was an apt simile. The smell came in waves—a mix of burning hair and vomit—weaving through the snow and overtaking the fresh, pine-scented air of the mountain. When at long last the light-and-smell-emitting object came to a halt, we saw it was a truck filled with a squealing mass of pigs. They were crowded in the back, dark round shapes with burning red eyes.

Two drunken men emerged from the cabin. Kurt and Lajos, unshaven, full of cheap brandy, and no less smelly than their charges, helped us pull the dead deer from the road. They debated whether they should take the carcass ("Much good meat," quoth Lajos), but they decided that the pigs wouldn't stand for it. They would likely eat through it by the time they reached their destination. Kurt said that he would drop off the pigs, then come pick up the deer.

"How about us?" said Teresa.

The question stumped them. What were *we* good for? There wasn't much meat on either one of us. Though Teresa might be good for something. Before this thought had made its way completely from their groin to their voice organ, I proposed that we get a ride with them to the next town, in exchange for cash and whatever they could scavenge out of the Opel.

Lajos, who had a big scar running from his left ear to a corner of his mouth, nodded his head in agreement. I took the files from the backseat and we pushed the Opel to the side of the road, just behind the dead deer so that it was barely visible. It looked, in fact, like another dead deer just behind the other. Kurt and Lajos then uprooted a couple of pines by pulling them from the roots as easily as if they were house plants, and covered the two hulking masses.

"We'll drop the pigs, then get these," Kurt explained, as if it hadn't been perfectly obvious what they had in mind.

I couldn't have invented a better combination of idiocy, gruesomness, and odor if I had been the casting director for a new *Frankenstein*. Such village idiots in pristine condition aren't easy to find anymore.

Squeezed between Lajos and Kurt, overwhelmed by the depths of pig stink and unwashed men, Teresa and I felt very close to each other. I held her hand. The two drivers explained that the load of pigs was headed for a slaughterhouse at Alpsaug, a slaughterhouse town one hundred kilometers from where we were. Alpsaug was the sausage capital of Austria. Its sausages were known all over the world. They won sausage contests even in Germany, where sausage making was a high art.

Lajos reached behind him and pulled out a meter-long black sausage. He handed it to Kurt, who took out a gleaming knife and began to slice thick wheels out of it. Part of the black sausage was under my chin, while the part being sliced was next to Teresa's cheek. I watched the gleaming knife with growing apprehension, thinking that it could slip at any moment and slice my fair child. I was prepared to knock the blade from the pig driver's hand, but he was skilled. The slices were off before I could move. With his free hand, Kurt offered us slices of Alpsaug's pride. We could hardly refuse, particularly since the sausage was practically in our mouths already.

I closed my eyes and felt on my tongue the thick blanket of garlicky pig grease. It suffused the cavity of my mouth; it filled my nostrils with greasy smoke; and it made my eyes water. I held it there on my tongue like the devil's wafer, unable to swallow it. Fearing that I might vomit, I quickly rolled down the window and spit the pig chunk into the night.

"What?" said Kurt in his thick accent. "You don't like the glory of Alpsaug?"

"He's a vegetarian," said Teresa.

It was the right thing to say. The two men burst out laughing. They laughed so hard, the truck nearly rolled off the road hurling pigs into the darkness. We lurched back and forth with the spasms of the men's laughter. Alpsaug sausages came loose from behind Lajos's back and whipped about like fat black snakes. Belches of brandy and pig filled the air. If I don't vomit right now, I promised myself, I'll send a thousand dollars to the Vegetarian Association of America.

When their laughter subsided, Kurt said seriously: "We laugh because we never met a vegetarian before. We grow pigs, we kill pigs, we eat pigs, we talk pigs. We don't know what to do when we hear about vegetarians. We kill them maybe, like the Jews." They laughed some more.

"What did you do during the war?" asked Teresa. "I mean, when there wasn't much meat?"

"We ate the Jews," Lajos said.

"We always had pigs," said Kurt.

"War means nothing to a pig," said Lajos. "A pig lives to be eaten. He'll be eaten in war or in peace. Pigs don't fight."

That was unassailable logic, so we didn't speak for a while.

Kurt glanced at the stack of paper on my lap. "What's that?"

I would have liked to say, "Secret police files," but I wasn't sure how he'd take it. "My book," I said.

"That's funny," said Lajos. "You're a book writer and I can't even read. But I can count."

"What's the book about?" said Kurt, picking up some of the stack and then letting it fall back.

"It's about an evil old countess who used to live in these parts and kill young girls. I suppose you heard about her."

"We have," said Lajos. "She killed my grandmother. And you're going to write about her?"

That set them laughing again.

"You wouldn't be here laughing if she killed your grandmother," I said, trying to get into the spirit.

"And this young girl here," said Lajos, pinching Teresa's thigh, "what's she got to do with it? She's helping you write?"

To my displeasure, Teresa became warm after the lout pinched her. I could feel her excitement right through my wet sheepskin. I could also feel him rubbing his stink into her. I put my hand in her lap and found there the pig driver's callused paw. He didn't remove it. I withdrew and considered my options.

"Is there anyplace between here and Alpsaug where we can spend the night?" I asked. Suddenly the idea of going to the sausage capital of the German-speaking world in the middle of the night did not appeal to me.

"Yes," said Kurt, picking his teeth with a small strand of barbed wire, "there is Lockenhaus."

"Lockenhaus?" Teresa and I said this at the same time, rather astonished.

"It's a tourist place," said Lajos, "expensive. Isn't that where you were going? Your evil countess and all, that's where she killed the girls and stuffed them down the well."

"Well, yes, of course. That *is* where we were going," said I, Count Bathory-Kereshtur, master by birthright of Lockenhaus Castle. Of course, I had had no idea. The callused paw of fate was doing the driving.

The towers, donjons, and battlements of Lockenhaus looked like a fairyland strewn with colored lights. They sprung out of the darkness between snowflakes as if they'd been colored by a drunk impressionist. The imposing fortress, which had stood its own for many sieges, including a major attack in 1532 by the troops of Süleyman the Magnificent, had been restored and was now run for profit and amusement. In the fifteenth century this small garrison, with the help of its patron saint, Saint Martin, rebuffed a large Turkish army. Saint Martin, mounted on a white horse in golden armor, scattered the Turks with a sword made out of light. One century later, in the year 1600, Elizabeth Bathory added a new great hall, horse stables, and a tower, and strengthened the outer walls.

The pig drivers left us just outside the main gate, before a bridge on the dark moat. The sounds of drunken singing came from within the walls. After we entered the gate, a neon sign and arrow pointed to a tavern. The singing came from there. We descended the steps to the underground establishment.

The stone cellars of the cavernous restaurant were full of steam. Austrian and German tourists were banging beer mugs on long wooden tables, singing along with a gaggle of medieval wenches in peasant blouses cut low to expose ample bosoms.

A medieval ballad welled up in the smoky air just as we walked in:

She was a bad sweeper, she made too much dust
but she was pretty like a forest night flower
her mistress ordered her hung by her hair from the tower
but a man came from the moon
he cut her down and he took her to his silver house.

This all-time medieval favorite had roused the burghers to a frenzy. Some of them were weeping into their large plates of sausages, sauerkraut, and fried potatoes. Their emptying mugs were being refilled by waiters in velvet tights and courtiers' berets.

If ever I needed a drink, this was the time. I squeezed in at the bar between two barrels of Germanic flesh. I demanded a bottle of whiskey. Just as I got my wish, a family rose unsteadily from a table and stumbled out into the medieval night. Teresa seized the table, and we found ourselves wedged against each other on a bench in the cellar of Lockenhaus, a basement that had not always been a tavern.

Plates of half-eaten sausage littered the table. An empty tankard of beer with dried mustard on its lip tottered on the edge of the bench. I cradled my whiskey bottle like a baby and took long sips. I was ravenously hungry, but the sight of partly ravaged sausages congealed in pork fat reminded me of what we had just gone through. We were at the heart of sausage country here, a land haunted by dark legends. During the war, my father told me, people disappeared regularly, to be turned into sausages by unscrupulous butchers. Knowing what I know now, I could have told my father that his entire generation of patriots had been no better than unscrupulous butchers. Turning people into sausages was the big business of Mittel Europa.

I got some sour pickled tomatoes and a hunk of black bread. But I was hungrier for answers. I put my lips to Teresa's ear and said, "We were lost but now we're found." I don't know if she recognized this line from the lovely American hymn "Amazing Grace," but it touched her nevertheless, because she sighed and said, "I'm afraid so."

Before I could ask her what she meant, the wenches surrounded us and began to serenade. The drunken burghers joined in:

> They came on their horses from the snow
> They brought their cold hearts to our castle

The ladies made the great fires glow
And took the heavy armor off their masters

The wenches were neither young nor old, just loud. I made a gesture of dismissal and touched, without intending to, the stuffed bodice of a minstreless. Instead of withdrawing, she pushed her great globes into my face, smothering me. Gales of laughter filled the cave.

Above the din, I heard a familiar voice shouting, *"Long live the king!"* I freed my face from the pendulous breasts and looked up. Standing there was Lilly Hangress wearing an undecipherable expression on her beautiful face. Imre stood behind her, his mouth set at angry angles. He shouted again, *"Long live the king,"* then said angrily, "Do you think that you can escape history, Count?"

No amount of whiskey could banish the eerie feeling that I had lost control of my situation.

Lilly and Imre squeezed in across the table and stared at us. I stared at my bottle. When I finally looked up, I met their unflinching gazes.

"I don't suppose that I should ask you how you found us?"

"Ask," said Imre. "I will tell you. Or even better, let me tell you before you ask. We came down the information superhighway."

"I thought that I'd bought exclusive rights."

"Sure," Imre said ironically. "As if we had to pay for such things?"

"We?"

Throughout this exchange, Lilly sat impassively, smoking a cigarette and looking at Teresa. Teresa was crying.

328 · *Andrei Codrescu*

"Suppose we end some of this charade. Are you in this with the Megyerys, Professor Hangress?"

Lilly looked up from Teresa, who was shaking like a little bird, and turned her cold gaze on me.

"Am *I* in what, Count? I am part of something, it is true, but it is bigger than the Megyerys' puny little political puzzle. I have nothing but contempt for this little Fascist . . ." She blew a smoke ring at Imre, who winced but did not seem particularly surprised by Professor Hangress's opinion of him.

"Yes," she continued, "and I have even more contempt for his father, Klaus the mouse, the thief and the flimflam artist . . ."

Imre protested meekly, but she paid him no heed.

"No, my dear Count, I have but little interest in these contemptible weasels' power-sucking games. As I have told you during our lovely conference, I am beholden to other forces."

I must confess that once more the professor was intimidating me. But I knew that she had once been a high-ranking member of the Communist establishment.

"What forces?" I said. "Dialectical materialism?"

She laughed, but not contemptuously. "We must move our discussion to a higher plane, Count, if we are to understand each other."

At this point a din arose from the bar, where a fight had broken out. Two skinheads in leather jackets were swinging at a fat burgher in *spielhosen* who wheeled about inefficiently with a beer bottle in his hand.

"Still your dogs, Imre," said Lilly.

Imre shouted something that sounded like *dogwater,* and the skinheads spit on the burgher and turned their backs. Unfortunately, the emboldened burgher, who must have thought that it was his own prowess that had won the day, threw himself at the leather backs. Even Imre's *dogwater* couldn't stop them after that. One of them grabbed the man by the triple folds of his neck and banged his head on the wooden bar. It rattled there like a ripe gourd. The other one donned some brass knuckles and buried them with his fist in the small of the burgher's back. The fat man's family, eight fat offspring and a fat frau, surrounded the carcass and began wailing. The skinheads were done. They vanished up the stairs and into the great snowy outdoors.

"Why do you always create such vile scenes wherever you crawl?" Lilly asked, highly displeased. "When you were my student, Imre, you were bad enough all by yourself, but now that you have this little regiment of worms, you've become positively unpalatable." Her eyes flashed fire, and I could see that Imre was terrified.

"I can't always control them," he mumbled. "They are waiting for their moment to be heroes . . . Meanwhile . . ."

"Meanwhile, they are interrupting *me!*"

"I'm all ears."

"As I've said then, the political game is narrow. What is at stake here is the confluence of Retentio and Eros. To put this more plainly, the formation is here to allow for the fulfillment of Andrei de Kereshtur's game plan. Elizabeth Bathory will be reborn now, eternally beautiful and immortal. Her resurrection will signal the beginning of a new history, one in which immortality and beauty will reign. The domination of liberal ideas, democracies, ugly masses, Malthusian problem solving is at an end. We are all pieces of this puzzle that we must bring to a successful conclusion. There is no fleeing from this . . . What are you bawling about, you little goose?"

Lilly had addressed this last remark to Teresa, who had let loose a flood of tears.

I became very angry.

"OK," I shouted, "here is the thing. I do not wish to

accommodate any of your insane fantasies, whether the Megyerys' monarchist delusions or your even grander ones, Professor! I am not going back to Hungary to be a puppet on your father's monkey show, Imre, and I won't play your key-in-the-lock routine, Ms. Hangress!"

I looked at Teresa. Damp strands of hair were all over her tear-soaked face. She did not look at me.

"What's more," I growled, "I wish to protect Teresa from whatever she fears from you! If she wants to, she can come to New York with me!"

"Spoken like a true monarch," Lilly said admiringly.

I glared at Imre. "You and I have something to settle! You beat Teresa. Her whole body is covered with bruises!"

There was surprise all around. Even Teresa looked up sharply, forgetting to cry for a moment. Imre appeared baffled. But Lilly laughed. Then they all looked at me.

"I would never . . . never," mumbled Imre.

I became confused. Imre stared at me like a wounded rabbit. He may have been a strutting theoretical bully but was probably incapable of beating Teresa. Could I have been wrong?

I had been. Professor Hangress laughed. She reached across the table and took hold of a strand of Teresa's hair.

"I can pull it or I can caress it. Which shall it be?"

Teresa sat passive and still, as if the decision did not concern her one way or another. It was almost as if the Teresa I knew had vanished. In her stead was a submissive, vacant creature who was putty in the hands of her mistress.

I understood. Imre had not beaten Teresa. Lilly had. And it was consensual. I was embarrassed.

"Pull," I said.

Lilly caressed it and let go.

Creeping respect and—I admit—a bit more fear now attended my view of Lilly Hangress. As for Teresa, whatever the nature of her relationship with Lilly, she was momentarily beyond my ken. I understood also that all of them, including Teresa, were part of the game that involved my unwilling self. Still, I did not believe either Imre or Lilly. One wanted me to be king, the other wanted me to be the instrument of Elizabeth Bathory's resurrection. What did Teresa want?

After Lilly's assertion of power over Teresa, Imre found his voice. "Look, I expect that everyone's personal problems will be here long after tonight. I expect also that immortality can wait a little longer. But at the moment, at the moment, there is a grave crisis unfolding in our country. Our future is in peril. We need to think seriously. If Count Bathory does not wish to undertake the responsibility thrust on him by fate and history, so be it. But I have my orders. My orders are to bring him back to Budapest tonight. Professor Hangress kindly agreed to accompany me in order to persuade him. But if rational persuasion does not work, Saint Stephen's army is ready to carry out my orders."

"Rational?" I said. It was astonishing.

"Everyone has their own reasons," Lilly said. "Yours are sentimental, Imre's historical, mine are mystical. And Teresa, my dear Teresa, she has no reason at all, she only has her body . . . sufficient reason, I dare say."

"Frankly," said Imre, "if anyone wishes to be philosophical—and God knows, we have plenty of time for it, because it's snowing and we can't get out—I couldn't care less about this sixteenth century that you are all enamored of . . . I don't even care about royalty. I'm only trying to please my father on this score. I'm a nineteenth-century man! I see little point in history before that . . . historic forces nearly at a standstill for hundreds of years! Nothing but manners, codes, customs, theology! No *action* until the nineteenth! I simply want the restoration of hierarchy and authority. I want to create a climate that is once more conducive to the birth of heroes!"

Lilly shoved away the plate of half-eaten sausages, and it crashed on the floor. "What history do you disdain? The Reformation? The Counter-Reformation? The existence of Elizabeth Bathory? The person of our king? The virgin birth? The Hungarian national aspiration? Or sausage making? Your nineteenth century, Imre Megyery, is nothing but a coffeehouse full of shouting ideologues."

"History looks like a snail until 1848!" howled Imre.

And in their warm breasts beat faithful hearts
And men emerged from armor with swollen male parts!

wailed the wenches.

It was amusing all right, but it was all becoming stranger by the moment. I couldn't reconcile Imre's apparent conviction with his mission, which was to return me to my throne after making me remember my origins. That was a complex task, one that I had honestly believed him incapable of. And now he had just as much as admitted that he didn't care at all. Either beer was now releasing him from the constraints of his surliness or he had his own power game piggybacking on his father's. This was more than likely, and I had to admit that he was more personable this way, angry, with his bogus mission weighing him down.

In the smoky light of the tavern, with the whiskey finally warming me up, I considered my situation. I was the only one, it seemed, who did not know either who he was or what he was doing. The rest of them appeared quite certain of their purpose, even the wenches, who

seemed determined now to run through their whole repertoire of bawdy songs. Their bosoms rose majestically
over the besotted sausage eaters of Austria, unaware of
the prisoner-king and his jailers. Once more, there was
little I could do. Imre's goons were doubtlessly all
around. Snow had shut down the road. Ahead was Alpsaug, the sausage capital of all Deutschland. Behind was
Kereshtur, The Hand, and the hunchback innkeeper.
Beyond that was Hungary, where the government had
fallen. New York seemed very far indeed. And to top it
all off, I was falling in love with Teresa, who was
stranger than all of them. But she was the daughter of
my first love. I didn't want to leave her in the hands of
these people who had convinced her that she was a victim. Well, as the poet said, *"Enivrez-vous!"* Get drunk. It
was the only thing to do for the moment. I would eventually think of something. I got another bottle of whiskey.

The weather worsened. The winds were fairly howling
now, whipping the snow up the windows of towers. The
road was impassable. We had to spend the night at
Lockenhaus. It had been a huge day, a lifetime, and I
was exhausted. My sheepskin was filling with smoke and
sleep.

Imre was distressed. His orders had been to take me
back to Budapest to ready me for the takeover of the
television station by Saint Stephen's Knights next day.
Now the revolution had to be postponed.

Lilly Hangress, however, welcomed the storm. She
smiled widely and stretched like a cat. She patted my
hand and Teresa's cheek. "A night of delight before the
truth of light," she quoted from Sandor, the debauched
poet.

When I inquired after a room, the bartender said

that every room at the small inn was spoken for. I peeled a hundred-dollar bill from my wallet. Well, there might be something, the man remembered, but it was part of the museum, and strictly under the table. There was a big room in the tower with a bed, an historical exhibit. There was a fireplace up there, but it hadn't been used in a while, so it was probably freezing cold. He would consider allowing us to stay up there if we left everything undisturbed and got out long before 8 A.M., when the museum opened. He could be in big trouble if anyone found out that we had slept in the exhibit. For an extra fifty dollars he would bring us enough wood to make a good fire. That, in addition to the three-hundred-dollar fee for the room. And two hundred for a case of local champagne.

I was too tired to argue, but Imre also needed quarters for his goons. The interminable discussion finally led to the housing of the goons in the horse stables for some exorbitant sum. The only trouble was, Imre didn't have any money. Loath to have this drag on much longer, I paid for the storage of the goons. Paid, in other words, for the upkeep of my jailers. How much easier it would have been to let them freeze to death. I had been infected by liberal American ideas.

The square back of the man leading the way up the spiral staircase to the tower was familiar, like a dream. He had the kind of stooped back that could have been among those described in my gymnasium history book as "the long-suffering backs of the people on which palaces were built." There was something brutal about it, as if the back that built those palaces was also the back that strained under the effort of lowering an executioner's ax.

He opened the creaking door and went about in the dark, lighting candles. After the candelabra were lit, he bowed low and bade us to come in.

It was a round chamber with a vaulted ceiling. Tapestries covered the veined gray marble walls. There were five narrow slits in the thick wall. One could look out through these four-foot windows at the snow. They were just wide enough to insert a musket or an arquebus. The oval-shaped fireplace, where the shy fire was beginning to lick the frozen logs, had black marble edges. It was as big as a door, and I had the feeling that it was indeed a door. The barkeep had nearly disappeared within it while he labored to start the fire.

A four-poster baldachin bed with gold-threaded canopy stood at the center of the room, commanding the surroundings. At the foot of it rose a shiny column of black polished walnut. On one side was a tall brass cage that looked big enough to hold a man. On the other was a brass trunk that must have held nightclothes. Swaying slightly, though there seemed to be no breeze, was a round brass basket suspended from the ceiling by a thick iron chain.

"Home, sweet home," said Lilly after taking in the room with a sweeping glance. She then pointed to the cage. "Night Snow slept there." And to the brass basket. "That's where bad girls went nighty-night."

The basket looked small enough for a baby. I thought I saw the spectral shape of a leopard moving between the folds of light. A gilt mirror in a heavy frame hanging over a shell-shaped sink reflected the flames from the fireplace. A blackened crucifix sagged above a small devotional filled with ashes.

Lilly delicately scooped some of the ashes with the tip of her index finger. She pressed it to Teresa's lips. Obediently, the girl licked Lilly's finger, and then the ashes from her lips.

"For whosoever follows the trail of my ashes shall find her way out of the woods," Lilly said, collapsing traditions.

A waist-high panel painted with a fading hunting scene hid a tiny commode.

"Under this commode, if memory serves, is a tunnel leading to the river below. Should we need to dispose of a body, we will simply push it through here and the river will carry it to the sea." Lilly knew the room as if it had been hers.

"It is frozen this time of the year," said Imre, ever the punctilious technician. "A body dropped from this height might crack the ice, or it might not."

"There is but one way to find out!" Professor Hangress said. Her voice, half mocking, half didactic, chilled me. If I had been Imre, I would have slept with my hand on my dagger. I certainly wished that I had one.

Lilly was eerily amused by our surroundings. I didn't share her high spirits. Instead I felt a heavy psychic airlessness in the room. I took deep breaths, which came out as sighs. I couldn't get enough air. And I kept seeing things: the leopard shape in the stripes of light, a quick movement reflected in the mirror, a face laughing in the chandeliers. I was in for a long night.

A black glass vase filled with peacock feathers sat on a round marble table. Lilly plucked two of them and crossed them before her face as she teased Imre, "Come find the pearl behind the feathers, commoner!"

Imre made a vague gesture and sat on a small brocaded chair with the sign "MUSEUM EXHIBIT: PLEASE DO NOT SIT" clearly posted. I plopped down on a thick Turkish rug with rhomboid shapes and flowering vines, facing the fireplace. It was the only comfortable spot in the room, with the exception of the forbidding baldachin bed. Teresa sat next to me facing the flames, which had gotten quite high. Lilly, after moving happily among the objects that she seemed to know so well, reclined by Teresa after a time.

The pop of the champagne cork punctuated the silence. We passed the bottle around. Elizabeth Bathory's bedroom was singularly devoid of goblets.

"Ever since the king surprised her naked, she would bear no wine goblets about her chambers," Lilly explained.

I thought about the distribution of our bodies when time came to sleep, but in truth it was not something I was unduly concerned with, since at that moment I could have fallen anywhere and slept for one hundred years.

As the flames began biting into the wood and giving off more heat, warmth seeped in, and a dreamy laziness took hold of me. It was through the gauze of my drowsiness that Lilly's voice made its way:

"Will she, won't she, will she, won't she make an appearance?" she asked, plucking long fibers from around the eye of a peacock feather. In the light of the flames her face grew long and beatific like a Madonna's.

"I stand in my lady's sight . . . in deep devotion . . . approach her with folded hands . . . in sweet emotion . . . dumbly adoring her . . . humbly imploring her . . ."

Lilly knelt before Teresa with her palms together as if praying. "Bernard de Ventadour, one of the twelfth century's noblest troubadours, wrote that for you, Teresa . . ."

She handed her one of the feathers.

Closing her eyes, the peacock feather in her hand, Teresa responded in a whisper: "Thus, lady, I commend to thee . . . my fate and life, the faithful squire . . . I'd rather die in misery . . . than have thee stoop to my desire . . . That's Sordello, answering you in Provençal, *lengua d'amore* . . ."

While the women indulged their champagne-lit quotational reverie, I looked into the flames and saw Elizabeth Bathory, standing awkwardly, her dress draped about her. She was surrounded by a field of gold fleur-de-lys flamelets. She wavered in the fire about to speak, but she was painfully bound in the thousands of fiery threads imprisoning her. I studied her carefully, noting the thin lines of her lips, pursed in consideration of our arrival into the chamber where she had taken her pleasures and had suffered.

Elizabeth Bathory had indeed put in an appearance, but I was the only one to see her. She wavered like ripples in water before my sleepy eyes. Earlier that day, I had called on her at Kereshtur Castle, but she had not come. She had sent her hunchback alchemist instead. But now she was here. The drama of her reappearance was about to unfold.

I tried to point her out to the others, but by the time I had found the energy to speak, she had vanished back into the flames whence she came.

E LIZABETH'S RAGE WOULD PER-
haps have abated if her planned trip to Lockenhaus Castle in 1584 had gone according to plans. She had received a letter from Franz asking her to move the administration from Sarvar to Lockenhaus.

Franz wrote that, God willing, he might join her there at the end of the year. But during the long journey, her train of two hundred heavily laden coaches was met by devastation. The Black Death made its appearance.

Elizabeth noticed first the crosses painted on the door of village houses. Then they encountered a procession of penitents crawling in the dirt with heavy wooden crosses on their backs. The penitents blocked the road in front of her carriage, beseeching God in piteous tones to spare them from punishment. Many of them were already sick. Pustules had broken on their faces, legs, and arms. Some of them died before they finished crossing the road.

Since no servants dared descend to remove the bodies, Elizabeth's coachmen whipped the horses and rode over them. The penitents shook their fists after the aristocratic carriages. The aristocrats, they knew, were at least partly the cause of the Black Death. They used and taxed the people so sinfully, God had sent the Black Death as a warning.

But the dreaded disease made no distinction between serf and noble. It was as egalitarian as nakedness.

The bridges were drawn after the party entered Lockenhaus.

Elizabeth forbade anyone visiting or doing business to return home. The importation of wool and linen was forbidden. Villages were ordered to bury the dead at least six feet deep, as far as possible from any dwelling. The priests were ordered to consecrate ground in the forests for new cemeteries.

Ponikenuz, who had followed Elizabeth to Lockenhaus, found himself in his element. Flitting about like a black bird of prey, he excelled at his favorite occupation of delivering souls. He was assisted in this activity by Pastor Megyery, an equally stern Lutheran, who held the Lockenhaus staff and small garrison in the grip of fear.

He gave instructions to wall up together the occupants of the first village where the plague had been observed. The dead, the sick, and some who were still healthy were buried together in a common tomb. He also preached against the Jews, whom he held responsible for the plague.

But at the urging of Andrei de Kereshtur, Elizabeth issued orders for the protection of Jews. A messenger had arrived from Kereshtur just before Elizabeth had sealed the area, delivering news of a slaughter of Jews in which many had perished, including the learned Jew ben Lebus, whose books were burned along with himself. It was said that his heart had leapt out of the pyre intact and had vanished into the air.

The news saddened both Elizabeth and Andrei, who met to pray for the soul of their childhood acquaintance. Elizabeth's order to spare the Jews enraged both Megyery and Ponikenuz. They argued in vain that it was a well-established custom in Hungary to kill Jews whenever the Black Death made its appearance. The people believed that the Jews had poisoned the wells. She did not relent.

At Lockenhaus, floors were sprinkled and the inhabitants began washing their hands, mouths, and nostrils with vinegar and rose water. The doctors prepared expensive compounds made from powdered pearls and emeralds. Poultices of goat dung mixed with rosemary and honey were stored in jars, along with sulfur, peony root, powdered stag's horn, myrrh, saffron, potable gold, and oils of various sorts.

The first week of the plague passed gaily at Lockenhaus, despite the pastor's exhortations to prayer and fasting. The seven days of that week were a perfect time to practice Girolamo Cardano's *Book of Games and Chances,* as if they were living the *Decameron.*

Between games and titillating conversations, the shut-ins frolicked loudly in their chambers. Melotus, though nearly senile, found his amusing tongue again for a brief time and poured forth ribaldry and wit instead of gloom and *tristesse.*

The enforced intimacy of the castle affected others less happily than it did the nobles. Elizabeth's maid Teresa came to see her mistress. She was greatly agitated and very pale. Her romps with a new cook, who had insisted on making love the traditional way, had a predictable effect. Teresa was pregnant. This would have been no cause for alarm if not for the fact that her brutish husband had also been forced by the plague to take refuge at Lockenhaus. He kept a very close watch on her now and would be beside himself with rage if he found out. He had raped Teresa several times, but always in the Turkish style, which would not cause her to be pregnant. Teresa was sure that if the brute discovered her lover, he would kill both of them.

Telling her mistress was a mistake. Teresa had already talked to Darvulia, who had the matter well in hand. When Elizabeth heard that her maid was pregnant, she became unaccountably jealous.

That afternoon, Pastor Ponikenuz came to see Elizabeth again (for the third time!) about the need to fast and pray more. The good pastor asked her to advise the young people at the castle not to overexcite themselves with games. He recommended bland food, if any food at all, and continual prayer. Since no one was listening to him, he had taken to repeating his message as often as possible.

To get rid of him, Elizabeth told him that this was a bad time to discuss the matter, because one of her maids had marital problems. Pastor Ponikenuz told Elizabeth to send the girl to him for counseling.

When the preacher left, Elizabeth wondered if she had done the right thing. After all, it was none of the cleric's business. Nonetheless, she sent for Teresa, who came in shaking and crying.

Teresa had just aborted the two-month-old fetus with help from Darvulia. She cried uncontrollably about her baby and was in no condition to see anyone, let alone Pastor Ponikenuz, whose hardened features scared even hunting dogs.

Elizabeth ordered her to her feet, handed her a kerchief, and told her to go see the Lutheran. In her befuddled condition, Teresa went to the minister. In the presence of the Holy Mother holding the infant Jesus in a stained-glass window that allowed in just enough light to fill the maid with guilt, she broke down and told the pastor everything. She told him about her lover and her husband and about the bitter draught she had taken to abort the life in her. She had been deathly ill for two days, but it was nothing compared to the torments that she was now feeling. She told the preacher that she wanted to die and be with her baby in heaven.

Ponikenuz, who had been looking for just such an opportunity to prove that the plague was punishment for the sins of the devil worshipers in the castle, went to Elizabeth and demanded that the girl be imprisoned for infanticide and witchcraft.

Elizabeth promised to investigate the accusation informally, but Ponikenuz had already spoken to Megyery, who convened a commission headed by the captain of the guards. Teresa was accused of witchcraft for having aborted the baby.

Seething with rage, Elizabeth allowed the delegation to do its work, hoping that everything would be quickly forgotten. She did not want to antagonize the garrison.

Teresa was imprisoned as preparations for her trial began. There was little that Elizabeth or Darvulia could do except hope that Teresa would not implicate them all under torture. There had been a number of witchcraft trials in Hungary already, and church pressure was mounting for more. Despite the isolation, letters from the castle had found their way to churchmen all over the country.

The unexpected imprisonment of her maid made

Elizabeth ill. In such matters the church had jurisdiction. Teresa was being held in the Lockenhaus dungeon, which was guarded by Megyery's soldiers.

One midnight, using a secret passage, Elizabeth and Darvulia went to see Teresa.

Crumpled against the wall, her face streaked with tears, Teresa closed her eyes against the lights of the candles, but when she saw who her visitors were, she jumped happily up, rattling the chains fastened to her arms and legs.

The two women hugged the girl, but they didn't stay long. After consoling her for a few moments, Darvulia made a swift gesture and Teresa fell to the ground and lost consciousness.

Elizabeth returned to her rooms.

Darvulia, who was holding something tightly in her hand, went toward the kitchens. What Darvulia was holding in her hand was Teresa's tongue. She would now be unable to betray any of them.

Teresa was tortured pro forma because there was nothing to be found out. She couldn't speak, now that Darvulia had cut out her tongue. She had never learned how to write. She was found guilty of adultery and infanticide. The charge of witchcraft was not pursued. The despondent prisoner, her face grotesquely swollen, nodded assent to all the charges. She was condemned to burning at the stake.

Elizabeth urged herself to be strong. She told herself never to feel such worthless affection for anyone again. Teresa's sentence created a chill so severe among Elizabeth's women that many of them withdrew into stubborn silence, while others became so ill they could not rise from their pallets.

Only Darvulia spoke plainly to her mistress.

Darvulia said that women must depend on one another because they lived in a world hostile to them. Giving Teresa away to the preacher had been a betrayal of her kind, a betrayal sure to have consequences. Darvulia made some vague gestures toward the ceiling, and Elizabeth understood the reference to the moon and the night Darvulia worshiped.

"Are you threatening me, Darvulia?" Elizabeth asked.

"I love you more than my own life," Darvulia replied, "but the spirits that watch over us women are angry. Prepare to repent, my lady, and all will be well."

All was not well. The execution took place as swiftly as the trial. There was a sense throughout the castle that making a sacrifice of a young woman would help propitiate the anger of God, who had sent the Black Death to Hungary. People remembered the old days when sacrificing virgins to the gods of the forest had always had beneficial results for the community.

Teresa died well. Her swelling had receded, and though her face was pale, she looked almost beautiful.

On her way to the stake, Elizabeth offered her some words of comfort and came very close to apologizing, something she had never done before.

Teresa listened quietly. Elizabeth remembered all their games and frolics and felt her heart tighten. She remembered all the cruel pranks she had played on the silly goose, as she and Klara had called her. Teresa *was* a silly goose, no doubt about it, but she was good-hearted and without guile. This much Elizabeth knew, and she felt a tear fall from her eye. When Teresa saw her mistress crying, tears came to her eyes too. Elizabeth stroked her maid's hair. She remembered how many times she had pulled this hair now lying so pliantly and softly under her hand. She had certainly caused Teresa more suffering than Teresa had ever caused her. She had pinched her flesh, beaten her, abused her tender parts . . . and Teresa had always submitted calmly, almost joyously, never defiant.

Oddly enough, Elizabeth felt even now, through her sadness, a kind of excitement about all the bad things she had done to Teresa. As she rested her hand on top of Teresa's head, she had the strong urge to slap the stupid peasant in the face. Why did the silly goose have to confess? Why did she have to spill her secrets like a punctured wineskin? Teresa's docility was angering Elizabeth. The caress she had bestowed on the condemned girl tightened, and she grabbed a handful of hair and jerked Teresa's head up.

Elizabeth's original intention to comfort turned to rage. She slapped Teresa's face as hard as she could with her beringed hand. The surprised girl lifted her hurt eyes to Elizabeth, whose blazing eyes were so familiar to her. Blood streamed down her cheek and flowed over her lady's hand.

The people assembled to watch the execution gasped with horror. They had watched Elizabeth's tenderness and approved. But something had happened. Not one of them could explain it.

Elizabeth let go of Teresa, who collapsed in a shapeless mound on the ground. The countess lifted her bloody hand to a ray of light and looked intently. The blood dried slowly there, making her skin look more alive. The soldiers lifted Teresa from the ground and dragged her to the stake.

Is it possible, Elizabeth thought to herself, that blood causes the skin to become younger? Could it be that the living water that keeps one forever young and the mare's milk that rejuvenates the body are not water or milk at all, but blood? A warm feeling coursed through the countess, quickening her breath.

She rubbed more blood from Teresa's face onto another part of her hand. She watched it dry. Once more the countess saw that her skin became more elastic and youthful. She had to remind herself that her skin *was* elastic and youthful. Even so, Elizabeth had seen enough of the skin of older women to know that it was a fragile parchment subject to blemishes, wrinkles, and fading.

The stake had been erected at the center of the main court. A large bundle of sticks was stacked neatly beneath.

Pastor Ponikenuz walked before Teresa, who stepped lightly, as if she were floating on air. While Elizabeth had been slapping Teresa, Darvulia had managed to squeeze a powdered root into Teresa's hand. Now, as she was being lifted to the stake, Teresa swallowed the powder.

When she arrived at the foot of the stake, Teresa felt more alive than she had ever been. Everything looked brilliantly beautiful to her, even the stiff, straight, black-robed back of Pastor Ponikenuz. The sky was a brilliant blue, and she could see God's playful angels, including her baby, waiting there for her. Everything was filled with harmony.

She let herself be lifted onto the stake—she was light as air—and felt only momentarily the sharp pang when the executioner drove a nail through her right hand to fasten it to the stake. She was grateful to everyone. They had all loved her. Darvulia. Selena. The cook's assistant. Klara. Her mistress, Elizabeth. Even her brutal husband, whom she forgave. She watched the flames rise from below her, filled with tumbling gnomes and sprites. She saw that some of them had the faces of people she knew, and she said hello to them. As the flames rose higher, they licked the bottom of her cotton dress, which caught on fire. The fire was gentle, its tongues licked her slowly.

Instead of feeling warm, Teresa felt cold, but it was

not an unpleasant, freezing cold. She surrendered happily, and her soul shot up on the back of a spark and went to play with her baby.

After Teresa was delivered by the flames, Elizabeth's strength ran out of her like milk from a pitcher. She felt small and weak, like a bundled infant. She was helped to her bed by Darvulia, who held her in her arms as she had when Elizabeth was a baby.

"Tell me the story of the girl who bathed in mare's milk," Elizabeth whispered, curling up in her wet nurse's arms.

"Once upon a time," Darvulia began in the familiar tones of a faraway time, "there was a king who had a beautiful daughter. And so proud was he of her, and so jealous of her beauty, that he feared lest some man besmirch it.

"When the girl reached the age when the lads started casting long looks at her, the king was so afraid of losing her that he imprisoned her in a room in a tower.

"One day two strange wanderers happened to pass by. One of them saw who was inside the tower. It roused his anger, and he turned to his companion. 'Go and pull that dry stalk yonder and hold it up against that hole in the tower.'

"His companion pulled out the dry stalk and held it up against the hole. And the smell of the stalk pervaded the girl and filled her with longing.

"There was nothing her father could do to make her smile from that day on. The princess spoke with no one except to her maid, who loved her mistress dearly and would have done anything for her. But there was nothing she could do, and day by day her mistress's beauty began to fade.

"The king consulted a witch, who told him that the only way for her to keep her beauty was to bathe in mare's milk.

"But those same strangers who had held up the stalk to her turned out to be dragons, not men. These dragons fed on mare's milk, and they were so hungry that there was no mare in Hungary that had any milk at all. As soon as a mare filled with milk, the dragons sucked her dry.

"The king let all the young men in the kingdom know that if one of them could milk enough mares for his daughter to bathe in, he could have her for his wife.

"All the brave lads in Hungary went looking for mares, but those two dragons struck them all dead.

"One day a humble lad came before the king dressed only in a peasant's garb and asked to try. Everyone at the court laughed at the pale, frail youth, who didn't even have a sword. But the king, at the end of his wits, let him try.

"The lad went to the pastures below the mountains where the mares liked to graze and turned himself into a bucket perched on the edge of a deep well.

"When the two dragons came to milk the mares, one of them spotted the bucket. 'Go get that bucket,' he told his companion. 'We can fill it with milk so we can drink our fill later.'

"The dragon went to get the bucket, but when he touched it, the bucket moved very close to the lip of the well. When the dragon bent over to get it, he fell in all the way to the bowels of the earth.

"The other dragon went to see what happened to his friend, and he too fell in.

"The peasant lad then milked the mares, turned himself again into a bucket, and emptied himself many times over in a marble bath. He then blew over it and made the milk warm like a summer day.

"Next day, he brought the princess there with everyone in attendance, and the girl stepped in and lowered herself slowly into the marble bath full of mare's milk. She became even more beautiful than she used to be, after floating in there free of worries, washed by milk until her skin glowed.

" 'Now you must give me your daughter for my wife,' the lad said.

"The king sadly nodded his head and gave her to him.

"The lad took her far away to a land full of wild golden mares. When they got there, the lad took off his coat and peeled away his mustaches and his beard.

"He stood before the princess, who cried out when she recognized him. He was none other than her faithful maid, who had always loved her and would have done anything for her.

"They lived happily ever after, bathing in mare's milk whenever they wanted, and stayed beautiful for thousands of years.

"No one knew any better, but when people came by, her husband, who was also her wife, put on her lad's clothes until the visitors left. And even today, the only way to preserve beauty is to bathe in mare's milk."

When Darvulia was finished, a strong desire for mother's milk suffused Elizabeth. She pulled in vain at her old nurse's fallow breasts.

"I know what you need," her faithful servant said.

She left Elizabeth curled up on the bed and returned shortly with a young mother whom she had found nursing her baby in a corner of the kitchen.

She bade the frightened girl to lie next to her mistress. Elizabeth took her full breast in her mouth without opening her eyes. She sucked the sweet milk greedily until she fell into a peaceful sleep.

From that day on, whenever Elizabeth was tired and

weak, she demanded the milk of a young mother, which was the only way she could sleep.

Elizabeth had now spent one whole unhappy year at Lockenhaus, and Franz still had not come. That had been the whole reason for her moving to this accursed castle. Instead of Franz—who had been nicknamed the Black Knight by his enemies—she had been met by the Black Death. Elizabeth now thought of the plague as her husband's evil twin.

No sooner did the Black Death mount its horse and leave the Pannonian plain than Elizabeth was summoned to her mother's side at Kereshtur. Anna Bathory was on her deathbed. Franz had never joined her at Lockenhaus, but he wrote that, God willing, he would see her at Kereshtur before her mother left this world.

Upon arrival at Kereshtur after the two-day journey, Elizabeth was taken immediately to Lady Anna's chamber. The once beautiful Anna lay propped on a great many pillows, surrounded by preachers, doctors, and women dressed in black who moved softly through the room carrying basins of aromatic water.

The windows were covered, and the only light came from a few dim tapers floating in oil at the foot of the bed. It was hot, and it smelled of camphor and herbs and a sickeningly sweet scent of decaying flesh and infection.

Preacher Hebler, the monk Silvestri, and several churchmen whom Elizabeth did not recognize prayed quietly at Anna's bedside. They parted to make room for Elizabeth, who gasped when she saw her mother's face. Her once handsome features had been bloated by illness. She looked yellow and round like a gourd rotting in an autumn field. When Elizabeth approached, she opened her eyes, which were rheumy and nearly blind.

A whisper came through her thin, sore-covered lips. It was Elizabeth's name. Elizabeth sat on the edge of the bed and bent close to her mother's face.

In a voice racked by sickness, Anna Bathory told her daughter that upon her death, Elizabeth was going to become the undisputed mistress of the Bathory estates. Pausing to find the words of her well-rehearsed last speech, Anna entrusted to her young daughter the names of all her holdings, a litany that sounded mournful and cold like the grave. Becko, Becs, Kloster-Marienberg, Varanno, Ecsed . . . the names of castles and estates came dripping steadily out of her mouth. Elizabeth only half listened. This was not what she wanted to hear in her mother's dying hour.

She would have liked to know why her mother had tended so little to her when she was small and Anna was young and beautiful. She wanted to know why her mother had never held her, kissed her, or told her a story. She wanted to know why the withered bosom that lay dying in the great canopy bed had not held her close when it was firm and full of life. Battling back tears, Elizabeth whispered in her mother's ear, "Why didn't you nurse me, Mother?"

A shadow passed over Anna's tormented face. Sounding as if she were already speaking from the other side of the grave, Anna said that she had been with child nine times and she had lost seven of those children, five in childbirth and two to the bandit Dozsa. Only her Stephen, who was feeble-minded, and Elizabeth had survived. She had done her best to follow Luther's teaching to women to "bear themselves weary, or bear themselves out . . . This is the purpose for which they exist," but had been heartbroken when her babies died. She had been afraid that Elizabeth would meet the same fate and had not held her for fear of having her heart torn to pieces again.

Exhausted, Anna fell back into a half dream under her daughter's unforgiving eyes. But a little later she whispered again, asking Elizabeth's forgiveness. She then said, "I fear meeting your wet nurse's children in heaven." Not knowing what to make of this, Elizabeth bent closer to her mother's mouth. Anna said that her wet nurse Darvulia had killed one of her babies in order to nurse Elizabeth. Her other baby had died because it had been given to a sick woman to nurse. Darvulia had saved all her milk for Elizabeth.

This revelation made the airless, malodorous room spin about Elizabeth, who thought that she was going to vomit. She looked helplessly around and saw everyone frozen in the yellow light like a horrific tableau. Marching through the tapestries covering the windows were her mother's dead babies. They marched like little sheep, herded by the shadows of Darvulia's babies. "Luther be damned," thought Elizabeth, and then began to vomit. She blacked out.

Elizabeth woke up with a feral taste in her mouth. She had been taken to a small chapel next to the church and laid out on a small bed. Standing by her side was Hebler, looking as ill and spectral as her mother. The preacher asked her to pray with him for the imminent delivery of her mother's soul. Elizabeth turned her back to him. Speaking firmly but with what he thought was kindness, Hebler admonished her "to take a hold of the reins that were being handed" to her and to begin acting like the "great Lady Anna, who was passing" and who had never allowed herself to collapse in the face of inevitable sorrow. By means of well-chosen and fine-sounding words, Hebler exhorted and harangued Elizabeth, but to no avail. She stayed stubbornly turned toward the wall with her back to him. When he was finished, she asked to see the monk Silvestri.

Hebler hated the Catholic Silvestri with a great passion. The death of Anna Bathory was going to mark a turning point in the relations between the two of them. Hebler knew that Lady Elizabeth disliked him, but he had to do whatever was necessary to keep her within the Protestant faith. If Silvestri gained the upper hand, the great house of Bathory could revert to Catholicism. That was to be avoided at all cost, no matter how high. Silvestri could not be allowed to see Elizabeth. Hebler bowed deeply and promised to look for Silvestri himself and to bring him along.

Hebler trusted no one, but he had faith in the power of gold. Being an unsentimental and shrewd judge of character as well, he knew the weaknesses of just about everybody at Kereshtur, and that was nearly two thousand people, including the soldiers of the garrison. It didn't take him long to find Gabor and Vamos, two louts who spent most of their time sleeping in the cemetery by the village church when they were not busy digging graves.

The two sallow-faced gravediggers sprang to life when Hebler whacked them with his cane. They had been sleeping stretched out between two graves. Hebler explained his business succinctly and gave them each a taler. Another taler would be forthcoming when they finished the job.

Silvestri had spent every moment by Lady Anna's bed ever since she had become ill. He had been very happy to see young Elizabeth and was looking forward to a moment of respite from his prayers so that he could speak to her. After Elizabeth had fainted and been carried out of her mother's room, Silvestri had tried to leave several times, but each time he had been prevented by people falling to their knees and asking him for a prayer or a benediction. At long last, several hours later, after evening had already fallen, Silvestri was able to get away quietly. While Elizabeth was still resting, he was reunited with Andrei de Kereshtur, his beloved pupil, who had arrived with his mistress that day. He took Andrei to his laboratory in a remote part of the castle to show him some of his discoveries. He set the young notary at a long table filled with alembics and glass containers and gave him a big book of handwritten notes to read. He told him that he would try to see Lady Elizabeth, then return to continue their discussions.

It was a long walk from the old wing past dank walls and abandoned quarters from another century, but Silvestri knew the way by heart and did not need a candle. Now and then he glimpsed the starry sky through the ogive of a window. He nearly reached the last turn, where a spiral iron staircase was bolted to the stone wall, when he saw an immense shadow before him. A hooded figure holding an ax stood above him. Another hooded man appeared by his side, holding a length of rope in his hand. Silvestri commended his soul to God.

Andrei left the book open and picked up a container in which a mixture of sulphur was fusing with shavings of red sandalwood, bloodstone, and petroleum to form potent acid of spodium. At last the substance in the glass underwent a powerful change in color and texture. Andrei carefully lifted the glass from the low flame and held it admiringly under the lamp. At that moment he heard a thud outside, as of a body falling. Still holding the cooling acid, he opened the door of the laboratory and peered into the darkness toward the staircase where the sound came from. He advanced a couple of steps and looked into the well below the stairway. He saw shadows moving there, so he called in a loud voice, "Master Silvestri, is that you?"

When there was no answer, Andrei stepped down cautiously and descended, still holding the glass. As he stepped off the last stair, he bumped into the body of his teacher. Andrei nearly fell, but he steadied himself by grabbing the banister with his free hand. An unhooded face stood in front of him, with a bloody ax raised, ready to strike again. Andrei threw the contents of the glass vial at it. The murderer gave an unearthly howl, dropped the ax, and vanished into the darkness. Andrei began to scream.

Elizabeth had been sleeping when Silvestri was murdered. She did not hear the great commotion that rose from Kereshtur when the news spread. Everywhere, servants, soldiers, nobles, and children ran through their quarters shouting the news. Many of them were sure that the end of the world had come. Their great lady lay dying and her confessor had been murdered in cold blood by someone in their midst.

Hebler strode into the chapel with his hands together in prayer. Following him, people streamed into the chapel to pray. Silvestri's body was brought in and set on an improvised catafalque atop a velvet tablecloth. He had been strangled, and his wise old head with the big ears had been split nearly to the neck by a sharp ax. An old woman tied a kerchief about the tonsure. The wailing that had been held back for the day when Anna Bathory died now burst its dams and flooded the castle.

It was this sound that woke Elizabeth. She listened for a few seconds as she was coming out of sleep, and then knew what it was. They were wailing for her mother. Anna Bathory had died.

"Silvestri!" she called. "Where are you? I need you! My mother died!"

Darvulia, who had been fretting by her side afraid to

wake her up, embraced her. A whole flock of women rushed to her side weeping. "Where is Silvestri?" she shouted, while the women cried even louder.

Elizabeth jumped out of bed and saw, standing at the back of the distraught entourage, the pale face of her friend Andrei de Kereshtur. She ran to him and hugged him. Andrei felt the joy of her embrace under the terror and sorrow of what he had just experienced. His face was white as wax, and while his eyes tried to tell Elizabeth how happy he was to be her support, tears started streaming down his face. Taking his hand, Elizabeth walked past the bewildered throng that was milling all about them and began walking toward her mother's chamber.

"I know that she died," she whispered into Andrei's ear, "but I do not want to grieve too much." In fact, Elizabeth was not grieving at all. She was disturbed by Andrei's grief and his listlessness but attributed it to the shock of her mother's death and to deference to her own feelings, which, he must have thought, were devastating her. Elizabeth resolved to do whatever was expected of her as quickly as possible, and then, under the cover of mourning, cloister herself with Silvestri and Andrei.

"I marked his face for life! We will find him!" said Andrei.

"Find whom? Whom have you marked?" Elizabeth thought that Andrei was perhaps losing his mind.

"Silvestri's killer," Andrei said.

Presented with the dire events of the past hour, Elizabeth experienced an extraordinary feeling. She was overcome by a sharp lucidity. She saw, as if she were watching from somewhere outside herself, the whole pitiful panorama of people around her. She looked without pity on her mother's disease-ravaged body; she saw the antlike but aimless agitation of the grief-stricken subjects about her mother's bed. She even saw with blinding clarity in her mind's eye the Nadazdy household at Sarvar anxiously awaiting word from Kereshtur. It was as if she were floating above both places at once. Only a few people stood apart from the sorry throng of hypocritical and helpless humanity: Andrei, Klara, Darvulia, and Silvestri. But Silvestri was dead. Nonetheless she saw him as alive as he had ever been, looking kindly and concerned at her. "Good-bye, Silvestri," she whispered. The monk nodded his head and touched her cheek. She was flooded with a feeling of well-being and strength.

When Andrei and Elizabeth reached the chapel, the dense mass of humanity kneeling and standing there praying parted to let them through. At the altar, bent over Silvestri's body, was Hebler, looking like a buzzard about to devour the corpse. Still under the influence of her preternatural lucidity, Elizabeth saw Hebler in all his hideousness. He stood open before her like the pages of a book. She read his crime writ in large, red letters on his countenance. Letting go of Andrei's hand, she walked straight to the preacher and stood between him and the corpse. She did not look at the body of her teacher. She looked directly at Hebler, who did not lift his eyes.

Seeing their young mistress stand so defiantly before the cleric, the crowd became utterly silent. Elizabeth said loudly, "Damn your soul, murderer!"

Hebler straightened suddenly as if he had been struck by lightning. Eyes blazing with hatred, he said, "God is listening to your blasphemy, little spawn of Satan!" He raised his hand to strike her, but at that moment there was a shout from the door.

"Lady Anna is dead!" a voice cried out.

Anna Bathory was dead, and no one but her women had been with her when she died. And although she had received last rites from both Silvestri and Hebler, she had not had the solace of her ministers at the moment of her death. Her soul had left unguided.

The throng now renewed its wailing and began pouring back toward their lady's death chamber. The bells of the church and the castle bells all began ringing at once. Caught in the press, Elizabeth was swept away from her confrontation with Hebler, back to her mother's room. When she arrived, the funeral preparations had already begun. Women were strewing basil, balm, camomile, costmary, cowslip, daisies, sweet fennel, germander, hyssop, lavender, marjoram, pennyroyal, roses, mints, tansy, violets, and winter savory all over the floors of the death chamber.

Elizabeth allowed herself to be carried along for the next two days by nearly invisible hands, who washed her, combed her, and dressed her in fresh mourning clothes. She made sure that her friend Andrei was by her side at all times, and although they spoke little, they silently helped each other. Elizabeth's mind, though not still as lucid as it had been at first, was yet working calmly and deliberately. Her entire life had now changed. She had become the true mistress of her lands, the hand at the helm of the great ship that was the Bathory fortune.

This change was already evident in the way the staff at Kereshtur bowed and moved about her. Above all, however, Elizabeth wanted to finish her business with Hebler, who had not been seen since word of Lady Bathory's death had come. It was rumored that he had left on horseback in the direction of Prague. If that's the case, Elizabeth thought, our good relation Rudolf will have no choice but to hand this carrion eater back to me. Elizabeth recalled with some satisfaction that the

Bathory armies had defeated Rudolf's father, Maximilian, in battle no more than ten years before.

Silvestri's murderers were caught even before Lady Anna's funeral. A soldier watching the men digging the grave for the monk Silvestri noticed that one of the gravediggers was covered with a black hood. The soldier asked him to remove it. Meekly, the man did, revealing his hideously disfigured, still raw face. He fell to his knees before the soldier and confessed the whole episode. He threw the taler Hebler had given him into the open grave, and his companion did likewise. They were taken to the prison tower. They would go on trial after Lady Anna's interment.

With the funeral arrangements in progress, Elizabeth and Andrei found that they could spend a lot of time in each other's company. Pastor Ponikenuz arrived from Sarvar, and two Franciscans who had been Silvestri's boyhood friends were on their way from Florence. Dignitaries from Hungary and Transylvania as well as nobles from Vienna, Prague, and Italy arrived every day. But Franz, who was the one she was truly waiting for, did not arrive. Word came that a Turkish army had engaged him near Varna.

After greeting everyone politely, which is all that was required of her during this period of mourning, Elizabeth retired with Andrei to their favorite childhood salon, a small room overhung with tapestries near Silvestri's old quarters.

The young people spoke frankly. It was curious that, though both were living at Sarvar, they could unburden themselves only here at Kereshtur, where they had grown up. It was as if they had become children again. Elizabeth confessed her anguish at being the wife of a man she did not know. She confided her weariness of always being in charge. She also told him that sometimes she feared her own rage. She confessed that

Darvulia had begun to secretly teach her the arts of herbs and witchcraft.

For his part, Andrei told her about the alchemical teachings that he had begun to acquire, and his hope for Silvestri's tutelage. "Only now," he said sadly, "I fear that I am on my own, with only hard-to-understand books on my side." He had few friends among men of his age because they preferred the hunt and weapons of war to the study of books. He and Elizabeth discussed other matters as well. Affairs of state. Affairs of the heart. They commented on the great furor caused by Elizabeth's cousin the beautiful Susanna Forgach, who was living openly with her lover in defiance of her husband. They discussed beauty and the sorrows of beauty. The light flowed like honey through the stained-glass windows, framing them as they talked with great seriousness about perfection and mortality. The two pale young people stood under the waning light of an afternoon in the sixteenth century, trying to fathom the mysteries of youth, old age, time, decay, and eternity all at once, hungry for knowledge and fearful already of time's passing.

"Am I beautiful?" she asked her friend.

"Yes, my lady. More beautiful than the words of the sages." This was the highest compliment Andrei de Kereshtur could think of, and he meant it.

Elizabeth believed him. She loved the image of herself that every looking glass, everyone's eyes, and every bit of polished surface returned to her. She explained to Andrei her belief that the soul brought the skin to beauty wherever it touched it. Perfect beauty was achieved when the soul touched every inch of the skin from within.

The scribe reminded her of the story of Narcissus and admonished her gently not to become trapped by surfaces. Elizabeth drew herself up, stung by his didacticism, and said that beauty was the only antidote to the ugliness about them: the faces of the dying, the broken bodies of the punished, the misshapen gravediggers, the forests full of monsters, the fat merchants, the sallow peasant girls. Beauty, insofar as it was the work of the soul touching the skin, did not necessarily mean handsome features. There was beauty in apparently crooked bodies, and there were means to cause beauty to manifest by teasing or whipping it to the surface. There was an art to raising flowers from the ordure of commonness, an art that she was learning under Darvulia's tutelage.

"I am using all my strength to will my soul to illuminate my body," Elizabeth said passionately, holding her scribe transfixed in the glow of her immense black eyes. She compared the human body to a dark cave that needs to be conquered by the light of the soul's torch, an activity that required intense attention to everything one experienced.

"And should I fail," exclaimed Elizabeth, "your alchemical work will bear fruit. You will find the philosopher's stone, which confers immortal beauty!"

Andrei did not have the heart just then to repeat what Silvestri had told him long ago: immortality is but a metaphor for the Work. Only the Work is immortal: those who succeed along the way bask only in the reflection of the Work's importance. De Kereshtur himself only half believed this. Later, he wrote in his *Chronicles:* "At that time, being still unformed in Mind, I still believed in a magic Stone. And there was nothing I would have not done for my Lady. I wished with all my heart to find the Stone for her."

Palatine Thurzo arrived the morning of the funeral. He had ridden hard and looked cross. After the young countess bade him welcome, he extended his formal condolences in exquisite but cold form. Thurzo cloistered himself up to the time that the funeral procession began wending its way to the church. He walked stiffly behind the hearse pulled by the twelve black horses with silver bows on their manes, looking as if he belonged next to his cousin, who lay resplendent and peaceful in her jeweled casket.

Anna Bathory had become quite beautiful again, thanks to the art of her morticians. Elizabeth considered her lifeless beauty for a moment, a beauty like that of marble statues. Clearly the soul had fled her body, leaving only a shell behind. Elizabeth looked without pity or sorrow on her mother's form, thinking how similar she had looked during the few times that she had turned her eyes toward Elizabeth. On those rare occasions she had looked as dead as she did now, because she had withdrawn her soul. In her daughter's company only her dead form had been present.

As the priests sang and prayed and shook incense into the oppressive air, Elizabeth took leave of the childish love she had once felt for her mother. It had been mostly admiration anyway, the awe of a child for the royal bearing of a beautifully dressed great lady. Elizabeth suppressed a smile, thinking that one day she would have a number of mechanical statues built. They would be very beautiful in all aspects and would move graciously. She would present these statues to orphans who had lost their mothers and tell them to admire their grace. Yes, Elizabeth vowed to create a number of mechanical mothers for orphaned humanity. She looked up to the sorrowful Mother of God crumpled at the foot of the cross and thought blasphemously to herself that her statues would do for orphans what the Holy Mother did for everyone: give comfort. But her statues would give them something else as well: form. Heavenly comfort with splendid form. How clever!

Pastor Ponikenuz delivered a eulogy that made a strong impression. "Her Grace," he said, "fought the good fight against the devil, the world, the flesh, and sin. She carried out the word of God with forethought and love; happy is she gone to the Lord's table, and she did not spend her leisure time in idleness, but was dedicated to the reading of the Bible. She was as good as a mother to her subjects. She passed out food and clothing to the poor and supported the youth in their studies. She ate and drank sparingly and never overburdened her heart with excesses. Saturday and all days before holidays, she ate only once and then only sparingly. The more recognized and great she rose in the eyes of her husband and of her king and country, the more humbly she conducted herself, because any pretensions were far removed from her inner character."

No one who had actually known Anna Bathory recognized that lady in this eulogy. But then, Ponikenuz had not known her. Perhaps the preacher was hungry, because he referred so often to food. Elizabeth was amused by his conceits, but something about the conventional words troubled her. She did not know it yet, but these words were almost identical to the ones that the Lutheran pastor would speak at the burial of her husband, Franz Nadazdy, long hence.

Above the door of Anna Bathory's final resting place was written GRACE, WISDOM, AND STRENGTH. The coming ages, thought Elizabeth, will praise the one buried here for those qualities. No one will know how wrong they are.

During the five days of high mourning that followed, Lord Thurzo did not speak to Elizabeth, but on the sixth day, he requested her company. The palatine congratulated her on her dignity during the great ordeal that she had suffered. He then launched abruptly into his subject. The Bathorys, he said, are beholden by family tradition and wealth to support the king in all his endeavors. The wars with the Turks were going to require even more money than she had so far offered on behalf of the Nadazdys. The defense of Hungary was going to take place mostly in the border areas where the Bathory and Nadazdy estates were located. Naturally, he expected the two families to tend without delay to further strengthening their forts and preparing their armies for battle. In addition to these necessary works, the king needed more money from them for the defense of the crown. The Bathory family had been allotted the privilege of paying the crown an additional fifty thousand ducats in the coming year. It would probably be necessary to increase the taxes on merchants, on chartered cities, and on landholders. This would cause great hardship, which might result in peasant revolts. Thus, law and order had to be vigilantly maintained, and infractions severely punished. Any sign of weakness or lenience from the new mistress could cause a conflagration.

Lord Thurzo admitted that he did not know the young countess well, and he begged her forgiveness. He was being as frank as he could be, because in times such as these truth must take precedence over courtliness. He hoped that Elizabeth was made from the same stern fiber that other Bathorys were made of and that she did not subscribe to the sort of sentimental foolery that her cousin Susanna Forgach represented and that would ruin Hungary in the end if allowed to flourish unchecked.

There was another matter—and here the palatine's voice dropped confidentially—having to do with her cousin in Transylvania. The interests of Hungary and those of Transylvania were not the same. Should a conflict arise, God forbid, she had to stand firmly behind the Hungarian crown. To do otherwise was nothing short of treason. Lord Thurzo was emphatic on this point.

Elizabeth assured him that the Bathory family would do its monetary duty for the crown. She herself knew too little as yet about the great business of war, but she would endeavor to learn. As for the tomfoolery of sentiment to which Lord Thurzo had referred when he mentioned Susanna Forgach, she firmly believed that there were matters known to women that men did not understand. In these cases it was best, in her opinion, to judge the facts without discrimination. There are times when facts are on the side of the heart. Elizabeth did not comment on her Transylvanian relatives.

Lord Thurzo was shocked by Elizabeth's firm reproach. He had not credited her with an opinion on any of the matters he was discussing. He found that the young woman before him had a mind of her own, and one that, furthermore, dared to express itself clearly. The lord palatine gave grudging respect to the young Bathory. He resolved also that he must watch her. She was dangerous.

The trial of Silvestri's murderers took place one week after Lady Bathory's funeral. It was conducted in the main room of the garrison before Elizabeth, Pastors Ponikenuz and Megyery, and a number of select citizens. Captain Moholy was the presiding judge. The murderers, Gabor and Vamos, sat quietly through the proceedings, uncomfortably aware only of Elizabeth's burning eyes trained on them.

A moment of some uncertainty occurred when Andrei de Kereshtur was called to testify. Andrei told the assemblage how he had heard the falling of the monk's body, how he had gone to investigate, holding the vial of acid in his hand, and then he related throwing the acid in the face of one of the men, Gabor. Gabor's face was a raw red wound. Everyone turned to look at him.

"What kind of acid was it?" asked Ponikenuz quietly. He had not been expected to say anything, so his question was a surprise.

"A substance I had been conducting an experiment with," said Andrei.

"What kind of an experiment?"

"If it please the court," said Andrei, "I don't see what this has to do with anything."

Captain Moholy said that he agreed, but that in the interests of his own curiosity, he too would like to know what kind of experiment it was.

Andrei replied that the monk Silvestri had been teaching him the science of chemistry, which involved the mixing of various substances in order to study them.

Ponikenuz said that chemistry—he paused significantly after the word—was a legitimate field of study as long as it did not involve the invocation of demons known to reside in various compounds. There were too many people nowadays, even men of the cloth like the blessed Silvestri, who engaged in occult practices.

Elizabeth decided that she hated the preacher even more than she knew. Quaking with suppressed rage, she addressed the pastor: "I would like to be allowed to defend the memory of my teacher, who is not here to defend himself and who, furthermore, is not on trial. What the blessed Silvestri did can be observed in the great love of learning he imparted to us, his students. How dare a man who comes from elsewhere, who did not know him, insinuate that our teacher was invoking demons? I demand an apology from the pastor."

The pastor apologized ironically, in a manner that made it clear to Elizabeth that he did not feel apologetic in the slightest. Andrei de Kereshtur begged to be excused because, in addition to testifying, he was also the recorder of the trial. This was his first official trial recording, an exam toward his certification as notary. His father had allowed him to record this, his first trial, because he had been part of the events. The judge excused him, and de Kereshtur took the quill out of the ink pot where it had been resting during his testimony and began to write down, in a neat hand, all that had been said. Elizabeth watched his bent head intent upon its task and felt both affection and a slight tightening of her heart. She did not know that she would see him bent like this over his labors many years from now. He would be recording testimonies of witnesses against her own self.

Gabor and Vamos were allowed to tell their story, which implicated Hebler. Ponikenuz sat very quiet during this part, because he was painfully aware that the Lutheran Hebler's action against the Catholic monk had implicated all his fellow clerics.

The sentence of death was pronounced without any objections. Turning to Elizabeth, Captain Moholy said that among all those present, it was evident that Elizabeth had had the greatest affection for her teacher, and thus it was only fitting that she should decide upon the manner of the murderers' execution.

Elizabeth had thought about it. In a voice as calm and firm as she could make it, she pronounced that, first, Gabor and Vamos were to be tortured on the rack; second, they were to have the bones of their arms, legs, and ribs broken while still alive; third, they were to be impaled on stakes in full view of the village until dead; fourth, their heads were to be placed above the cemetery gates until crows had eaten their eyes; and fifth, their skins were to be removed and tanned and exhibited in some manner at Kereshtur.

The audience gasped as the young girl enumerated the many facets of the murderers' punishment. They were also filled with admiration, because many of them believed that nothing less would atone for such a heinous crime.

Elizabeth watched every stage of the punishment. She sat unflinching through the torture on the rack, paying no more attention to the men's screams than she would to the caws of crows in the field. She listened to the snap of their bones as they broke under the steel of the rack. She watched them being pierced by the iron-tipped stakes that penetrated them in the groin and came out of their necks. She listened to the death rattle that seized their throats as if it were the wind passing over a tin cup. She steeled herself to watch the flaying of their skins and peered carefully at the red meat and foaming viscera that spilled out when the envelope was removed. She was present when their heads were placed on the gates of the cemetery, two grinning gourds with swollen eyes.

She gave instructions to have Pastor Ponikenuz lodged in the small house by the church. This way, the murderers' heads were constantly in his view, whether he looked out the window or came out his door.

The gravediggers' tanned skins were given to Elizabeth in two rolls that looked for all intents and purposes like parchment. She handed these to her friend Andrei de Kereshtur and asked him to copy the records of his first trial upon them. This was Elizabeth's birthday present to herself.

A year had passed, and Franz had still not returned. The Hungarian army led by Franz Nadazdy, Erdody,

Zriny, and Bathany captured the Bacja fortress from the Turks and opened the way to Sziget. The campaign to take the well-defended fortress at Bacja, and Nadazdy's ruthless treatment of the Turks, made him famous throughout Christendom. Franz Nadazdy was nick-named the Black Knight, a title that he fully had earned.

Franz wrote to Elizabeth that he would return as soon as he recovered from a poison he had been given at Urmisz. The village of Urmisz near Bacja had met the Hungarians with complete submission, so there was little reason to suspect any difficulty. The priest had led the village elders, followed by women and children, to the edge of the road, where they kneeled before Count Nadazdy. The priest begged the count's forgiveness for the absence of the young men, who had been taken against their will into Turkish bondage to defend the fortress at Bacja. As was the custom in such cases, Franz let his men have their way with the village. The soldiers decapitated the old men and sliced the children with swift strokes of their long swords. They pulled the women up by their hair into the fields and raped them. The village was torched. The flames were a reminder to the Turks at the Bacja fortress that the same fate awaited them.

"My dear wife," he wrote, "after the torching of the village I spent the night in my tent, drinking with captains Erdody and Zriny. The wailing of the dying village and the screams of the women are a kind of familiar music, God forgive me. I sometimes think that I know nothing but the sounds of battle, that I have forgotten the pleasures of your lovely company." Franz recalled, in this letter to his wife, "the cherished memories" of their honeymoon. He dwelt sensually on their lovemaking. They had made love on a window ledge, where they were seen by soldiers of the garrison. They had frolicked on a bed made of young servant girls. With Elizabeth's kind permission, he had deflowered a twelve-year-old girl, who was then whipped by her. The few times when Elizabeth had received his seed directly in the simple way recommended by the church, Elizabeth had wept dreadfully. Each one of those times, she had had Ibis lick her clean until she fell asleep in the midst of sobbing.

Franz listed these episodes in the number of those that had given him pleasure. But he knew that they had not been of the same order as their other enjoyments. After each of their "simple" acts of lovemaking, Elizabeth became unaccountably cruel to her maids, particularly the ones who had submitted to Franz at her bidding. She punished them severely for the smallest infractions: for singing to themselves, for dropping a pin. At the end of their honeymoon, they had given up the sexual act as it was performed by men and women everywhere. Franz did not write this, but the unaccountable perversity of his wife had begun to bore him. He did not know what she was looking for.

Elizabeth achieved sexual satisfaction quite easily, it seemed to him, but she was incapable of resting even for a moment. She used her body as if it were a probing instrument, a surgery knife. Franz felt certain that Elizabeth was hoping to find something either in the extreme reactions of the flesh or just below the skin. She looked for something in the body to answer some question in her heart.

As he wrote his letter, the flames of the burning village threw eerie shadows on the tent walls. Franz's letter (which he was able to reprise only two weeks later) was interrupted by one of his captains, who came stumbling in followed by three wenches. They were the daughters of the village cobbler. He had found them hiding in a haystack. The wenches looked no older than fifteen, and one of them appeared to be even younger.

If they were more wholesome than the rest of the village girls, it was but an imperceptible difference. They reminded Franz of all the young girls Elizabeth hired. There was something infinitely dull and uniform about this class of girls, as if they'd all come out of the same mold. Their prettiness lasted but a year or two, and even their rosy glow of youth was depressingly similar. The same reddish or brown hair gathered in a braid on the back or piled up German-style on top of the head. The plump arms and the strong thighs used to field work. The brown shoulders beaten by the sun. The round faces with the eyes of uncomprehending beasts. The small foreheads. The round breasts better suited for nursing than for love. The lips, always full, were the only part Franz liked. That, and sometimes the surprising sparseness of down between their legs.

There was nothing more repulsive to him than an abundance of pubic hair between a young girl's legs. It was coarse. When they had been camping near Minger, Franz had had two girls brought to him and had ordered his men to shave them clean, including their heads. The girls allowed themselves to be shorn of their pubic down but raised a mighty howl of protest when Franz's men shaved their heads. Nonetheless, once they were smooth like eggs, Franz enjoyed sliding between them and was particularly fond of the slapping of their breasts over his body. He also made them mount each other while he sat on top of them, urging them on like a two-headed horse. But that had been his only indulgence so far during this campaign, and he had felt dull ever since.

Franz was annoyed by the interruption. He was about to send them off when one of the maidens spoke.

"If it please your lords," she said, "I would like to be spared."

That was so unexpectedly amusing that all the warriors broke into laughter. Even the other girls, who had been weeping and trembling, started smiling. When the gale of laughter subsided, Franz asked the girl, "If you give me three good reasons, I will not only spare you but give you three talers."

The girl said, "I am already engaged to one mightier than all the king's soldiers. I can make salves that can heal all your wounds. I know a secret way into the castle."

"Fine," said Franz, "let's start with the first one. Who can you be engaged to that is mightier than Hungary's greatest warriors?"

"If it please Your Highnesses, I would rather begin with the last. It will be better for everyone."

Astonished at the girl's persistence and at the calm in her voice, Franz gave her leave to speak in whatever order she chose. The girl said that there was a dry well, but a few yards into the forest, that led to the heart of Bacja Castle, right below the stables. She had often used this when she was a child to go into the castle at night.

"What were you doing in the castle at night?" asked Erdody.

"I met the one I am engaged to," she said.

"He's a noble then," said Franz.

"Most noble."

"You will show us in the morning. Go on to your second reason," said Franz impatiently.

"I have learned to milk snakes to make healing medicine. I can close any wound. If it please Your Highnesses, I have a small glass vial here." The girl reached between her breasts and took a small glass vial from a hidden pocket. "It must be applied with care in small drops mixed with honey."

"Bring it here," said Franz. "I have a scratch on my behind."

Everyone laughed again.

"Careful, my lord," said the girl when she handed him the vial. "Used unwisely it's a poison."

Franz, who had drunk several skins of wine, paid no heed. He clumsily took the little vial from the girl's hands. He undid the wide belt of his trousers and dropped them. On his bottom there was a huge rash in the shape of a crab. "You," he ordered one of the girls roughly, "come here and put a drop of this healing salve on my arse."

Despite the protestations of the vial's original holder, the girl Franz had called took the vial, uncorked it, and let a drop fall on the warrior's irritation. The liquid drop fell on the wound and made a foamy hiss that became a little cloud. Franz had started to laugh when he felt its sting, but his laughter turned into a rictus. His features became rigid, his whole body stiffened, and he fell to the ground like a corpse. As everyone cried out, the girl who had given him the vial rushed forward and wrenched it out of her sister's clumsy hand. She quickly fell to her knees before the fallen commander, put her lips directly onto the wounded buttock, and sucked as hard as she could. When she was out of breath, she spit a vile purple substance of mixed blood and poison onto the ground. She was pale and breathless.

"He will be fine now," she said. "He will sleep but a day and then he will rise. He will be like dead until then."

In truth, Franz slept for ten days and nights and was so groggy upon waking he barely remembered what happened to him. During the time he had been sleeping his men had taken the fortress. The girl who had given him the poison confessed that her lover was none other than the devil. She was put to death. When Franz was able to finally return to his letter, two full weeks had passed. He dispatched a messenger with it to Kereshtur, but as soon as he had departed, Franz made up his mind to return himself. He would convalesce at home.

Elizabeth received his letter at the same time that her notorious cousin Susanna Forgach arrived to visit. She set her husband's letter aside in order to entertain Susanna. She was most displeased. The letter, instead of announcing Franz's return, as she had hoped, further removed that longed-for day.

Susanna Forgach's visit had thrown everyone into a frenzy. Countess Forgach was just then the subject of every conversation in the realm. Her beauty had already given rise to songs and poems. Her love for her husband's best friend had made her into a figure of mystery and scandal. She was already living in her lover's castle, though not yet divorced from Count Forgach. The emperor and the king, at the urging of both the Catholic and the Lutheran churches, had become involved. If she was declared an adulteress, her rich domains would fall to the king or, worse, to the emperor! The Palatine Thurzo was representing the wronged husband, whose cause he had adopted for the sake of propriety, though he personally despised Count Forgach, whose weak chin and watery eyes he had once described in a letter to his wife as having "the consistency and effect of a puddle of dog pee." But the palatine relished his prosecutorial role without losing from sight his own interests or the interests of the family.

Elizabeth feared him. She hadn't forgotten their encounter after Anna Bathory's funeral. Thurzo, the chief justice of Hungary, was a formidable man with coppery mustaches that dipped down to sharp points like needles. His black eyes looked as if they were damning everyone they settled on. More powerful than the king, he dispensed justice in legal or semilegal forums as if he had invented the law. Before undertaking the prosecution of Countess Forgach, he had shocked Hungarian nobility by delivering to the emperor one of the greatest Hungarian warriors, Illeshazy, who had been accused of heresy by the emperor and the pope. So great was this betrayal that Thurzo became even more feared and respected. It was known, however, that despite his cruelty and treachery, he was extremely fond of his wife, to whom he wrote lengthy letters about the kingdom, baring his soul with such tenderness it was difficult to believe that the same man wrote them.

Elizabeth had followed anxiously the decisions of her uncle the palatine. She knew that she would incur his wrath by inviting Susanna to Kereshtur. But she also knew that other great ladies of Hungary, especially the widows, continued to welcome the beautiful adulteress, despite Lord Thurzo's anger and threats. The ladies' quiet defiance had received a public boost with the disclosure of an extraordinary document signed by Susanna's brutal husband, Count Forgach, in the presence of her lover Peter Bakics. In this document, Revay Forgach admitted beating his wife about the face and blackening her eyes, nearly strangling her to death, and locking her up for days without food or water. This confession aroused much sympathy for Susanna prior to her upcoming divorce trial.

Countess Forgach arrived at Sarvar accompanied by only six servants, a faithful retinue that had been with her through the entire drama of her flight from her husband and her subsequent residence at Peter Bakics's castle, where she had allegedly taken shelter solely for her protection. Elizabeth could barely hide her excitement when she sighted the approach of Susanna's carriage. In homage to Susanna's celebrated escape in disguise, she donned her favorite boyish tights and a red satin tunic trimmed with gold. Susanna Forgach had fled from her husband in the middle of the night dressed as a man, a detail that gave Elizabeth great pleasure. Elizabeth felt that she shared this very intimate preference with Susanna and that Susanna would somehow know, without speaking of it.

Susanna was even more beautiful than Elizabeth had imagined. Her hair was black, her eyes blue, her skin milky white, but most of all, her face was animated by her long suffering and by something that Elizabeth chose to think of as ecstatic joy. In addition to looking ravishing, Susanna smelled divine, like a mixture of crushed roses and attar. Elizabeth did not particularly condone Susanna's "great love," nor did she put much store by the chivalric romances originating in the French and Italian "courts of love," where such behavior was praised in the name of *Amor vincit omnia*. The principle for which Elizabeth stood ready to do battle was a woman's right to her physical dignity and her property. Count Forgach's brutality sickened her. Her own husband, Franz, had never struck her (he had never had the time) and had not even spoken harshly to her. Only peasants and serfs beat their wives. The property question was even more troublesome. If Susanna Forgach was found guilty, all that she had brought to her marriage would pass into the hands of her husband. It was a bad precedent.

But the discussion turned, even before dinner, to questions of love. One of the local ladies inquired, in a trembling voice that betrayed her impatience, whether Susanna had anything to fear from the king's court. After all, the lady sighed, "What does the law know about love?"

Susanna was graciously forthcoming. She quoted from Andreas Capellanus's *De Amore:* "Love teaches that no one can be in love with two men." Given that, the opinion of the court did not matter. She had given her heart to only one man, and that man was not her husband. Her husband had never, not even in the beginning, fulfilled his marital obligations to her. He did not, or could not, give her children. Therefore, all there was between them was a worthless paper writ.

Elizabeth also quoted from *De Amore*, but her purpose was less in finding out anything exciting about illicit love than in ascertaining certain material questions: "A woman who loves may freely accept from her lover the following: a handkerchief, a fillet for the hair, a wreath of gold or silver, a breast pin, a mirror, a girdle, a purse, a tassel, a comb, sleeves, gloves, a ring, a compact, a picture, a washbasin, little dishes, trays, a flag as a souvenir . . . any little gift that may be useful for the care of the person or pleasing to look at or that may call the lover to her mind, if it is clear that in accepting the gift she is free from avarice."

Given this innocent simplicity, could Susanna affirm without hesitation that her taking refuge in her lover's house, her accepting the use of his good horses and carriage, of the protection of his men-at-arms, and of the gold dishes at his table constituted blameless love?

It was a harsh question.

"Those things of which you speak, my lady," answered Susanna, "are not for my innocent pleasure. The madness of my husband makes it necessary for me to accept the protection of Peter Bakics. What would I not give to sleep between my own silk sheets, take my falcons hunting in my own woods, bathe in my own gold tub? I own far more substantial things and property than my husband, who is unlawfully holding them because I am a woman and don't have my own soldiers."

"Do you then believe," asked Elizabeth, "that your husband is persecuting you for love of your property?"

Susanna thought for a moment before answering. "Alas," she said, "that would make everything much simpler. It is not for love of property that he blackened my eyes and bruised me. He has in him a madness that he mistakes for love. God save us from such love, ladies!"

"And yet," one of the local ladies said softly, quoting *De Amore* again, "he who is not jealous cannot love."

"That may be so, my ladies," Susanna said patiently, as if she had answered such questions many times before, "but there is jealousy born out of the knowledge of one's beloved, and then there is the blind jealousy of a child over an object he possesses. An object he neither knows the uses of nor has any liking for."

The subject then turned, as it always did, to the love act proper, and whether anything was to be had from it by women, and who was more properly fit to give it, husband or lover. Our erudite Lady Elizabeth had little to say on the subject, but her entourage of ladies became greatly animated. Mainly to quiet them, and to interject some dignity into the proceedings, Elizabeth drew an opinion on the subject from a commentary on Aristotle by Albertus Magnus, hoping that such remote and illustrious scholarship would cool the ardent interest all about her.

Albertus asked whether the pleasure in intercourse was greater for men or for women. Since matter desires to take on form, a woman, an imperfect human being, desires to come together with a man, because the imperfect naturally desires to be perfected. Therefore the greater pleasure and appetite belonged to the woman. According to the great Albertus, the sexual climax was the indication of the emission of the female seed in intercourse. Double pleasure was better than single pleasure, and while in men pleasure came from the emission of seed, in women pleasure came from both emission and reception. Consequently, women conceived from having taken pleasure in intercourse. Judges, as it was well known, denied suit for rape if a woman became pregnant by assault. Aristotle said that the female seed, or the menstruum, gradually collected in the womb, increasing sexual desire as it accumulated. Menstruation, which was the equivalent of man's ejaculation, provided periodic relief. Therefore, though men's pleasure was more intensive, women's was more extensive. During pregnancy, when the menstruum was retained to form and nourish the fetus, a woman was at the peak of her sexual desire.

When Elizabeth had finished, she was met with an awkward silence, until one of the ladies asked, "If all women are weak and incomplete, how does one explain the complete greatness of someone like you, Lady Elizabeth, who has not taken a lover this whole year that our Franz Nadazdy has been at war?"

This was not exactly true, and the lady who had spoken knew it well. Elizabeth resolved to deal with the impertinent speaker later. There was no ready answer, she condeded, only that her desire for men had passed with Franz, who was the only man capable of weakening her. This was all to the better, because she could administer her estates now without being made speechless and unreasonable by a pair of mustaches.

Everyone then turned to Susanna, whose face had become very sad during Elizabeth's explanation. "I cannot proffer an opinion," Susanna said. "For me, pleasure has been so fraught with worry that I do not know the simple demands of my own body any longer. In the beginning, I did know a great deal. But now . . . I sometimes prefer to be alone with my best friend, Maria. Together we dress like boys and go swimming and mingling with people, without a thought for the sad facts of our womanhood . . ." Susanna admitted that she was weak and that she had been made so by love, and that she often wished she had never heard of it.

Elizabeth felt pity and disgust for the woman. Susanna's beauty, which she had until now taken as a mark of singularity and power, appeared to her in a diminished light. Susanna had allowed her beauty to make her the slave of two men, first her husband, then her lover. Elizabeth vowed that she would not let herself be made this weak by love.

The other women, however, had been aroused by their discussion and did not hear, or preferred not to hear, Susanna's remark. Like a pack of wolves they now gathered about the still-throbbing subject of their conversation and bit greedily into it. One of them referred again to *De Amore,* to the dialogue between two suitors of one lady. They "divided the solaces of love" and argued as to which half of their lady they would take, the upper or the lower. One of the knights contended that the upper was superior because its solaces were inexhaustible, whereas "the delight of the lower part quickly palls." But the lady disagreed: "Whatever lovers do has as its only object the obtaining of the solaces of the lower part, for there is fulfilled the whole effect of love, at which all lovers chiefly aim and without which they think they have nothing more than certain preludes to love."

Almost all those ladies present agreed wholeheartedly and felt the giddy heat of their lower parts. Elizabeth said nothing, because she was appalled at the frivolity of her circle. Susanna began to cry. Elizabeth was nauseated by the whole lot of them. She thought of the revolting blood that now dripped unfailingly between her legs every full moon. She had this in common with everyone at the table. The reality of her days was in the sanguine effluvium of her blood, not in the fanciful love invented by the poets. Her menstruum and her pleasure shared the same place, though they existed on different planes. Her blood was of the body, but pleasure was of the mind. She did admonish herself, however, that given the obvious excitement generated by such matters, she ought to investigate further, not dismiss out of hand.

When the few men worthy of the table joined them later for dinner, the discussion took on a somewhat different character, though more in its formality than in its content. Not all the men came. Pastor Ponikenuz sent word that he was ill disposed. Many of the husbands of the ladies who had been there earlier were at war like Franz. The men who came were, for the most part, at ease with ladies and good conversationalists. Benezzo, the harpist, came, of course, bringing with him a fresh poem that he had composed in honor of Lady Bathory. He begged the assembled company to listen to him before even the third course of viands came.

"Lady Bathory, flower of Hungary," he began pompously,

> All the world is ruled by unharmony,
> By the unchivalrous and graceless mob
> Not one dares to take up the flame of love,

and so on, extolling in one breath both her beauty and her courage, and offering himself at the end as some kind of "moss bank for you to rest your little foot on." And if this weren't embarrassing enough to the ladies present—after all, were they not also beautiful and courageous?—the poet Melotus stormed in, claiming that he too had a poem for Lady Bathory, "whose beauty had penetrated the darkness of his monkish cell like a sun swollen personally by God's breath." He then proceeded to recite his poem, which unlike the Italian's had no discernible rhyme scheme and was so unpleasantly laden with chilly metaphors from Hungarian folklore that all those present felt awkward.

Elizabeth thought that Susanna was going to cry again. She held herself stiffly like a glass flower, the folds of her white gown falling from her arms, the upper part of her breasts rounded and soft but unmoved by breath. Elizabeth held her breath too, resolving not to breathe until Susanna did, and she was nearly blue in the face before her guest's breasts rose suddenly, releasing her breath with a great sigh. Elizabeth had not either thanked the poets or, as was customary, addressed a witty rhyme back to them, so they all became gloomy. The Italian too looked as if he was going to cry anytime now, and Melotus, suddenly haughty, took a place at a lower table and sank his teeth into a roast.

Sensing her guests' distress, Elizabeth steered the conversation in the direction of state affairs and declared that she had heard that the palatine Thurzo had begun an inventory of the property of the great ladies of Hungary, including widows, unmarried children, and not yet betrothed young women. She wondered, mainly to herself, what his purpose could be. She hoped that he had not been swayed by the pope's agents at Maximilian's court to put the women's inherited rights under a new patrilineal law. She didn't say, but she fully suspected that the very public trial of Susanna Forgach was part of some plan to that effect. Elizabeth concluded that, given such dangerous circumstances, women must use their traditional weapons, namely, the poison of snakes, the deadly charm of sirens, the juice of poppies, the sicknesses of the moon, the long needles in their hair, and the cleverness of their speech.

"Brava!" cried Susanna, appearing animated for the first time.

Inwardly, Elizabeth was furious with herself for having expected so much from Susanna Forgach. Beauty is fine, she told herself. I am also beautiful. But my beauty will never be my weakness. My beauty will be cold and immortal, like the beauty of a marble Florentine angel. It will be everyone else's weakness.

It was at this juncture in the conversation that a servant burst in with the news that Franz Nadazdy's party had been sighted not far from Kereshtur.

The muddied company of soldiers fell on the food with gusto, and the festivities lasted all night. Husband and wife were not alone with each other until the early hours of dawn. Franz stretched his war-weary limbs next to Elizabeth and fell immediately into a soundless sleep. Looking at her husband's supine body, Elizabeth noticed how coarse the boy she married had become. He had grown hairy and sinewy, and there was an odor of steel and dust about him.

Now lying in bed next to her sleeping husband, Elizabeth felt weariness almost as great as his, as if the physical exertions of the recent past had also been a kind of war. This is the way one aged, she thought to herself. She rose in a panic from the bed and tiptoed across the room to her mirror. With trembling fingers she lit the candle and looked at her wavering shape. Her breasts were firm. Her skin was fresh and young, but Elizabeth read clearly the beginnings of fading, like the barely perceptible yellowing of a leaf at the end of summer. Anxiety welled within her. She threw herself on Franz, who groaned in his sleep and whimpered as his dreams changed but did not wake up. She fell asleep and woke only when her own dreams became too unbearable.

Franz Nadazdy stayed for one whole month. He did not assume command of the household. He did not question Elizabeth's administration of the estates. Together with his companions he spent the all too brief time in a state of drunken merriment, sprawled for most of the time before a blazing fire in the great hall. When he was sober enough to discuss matters of importance to their domains, he mainly approved his wife's decisions. Elizabeth did not object to his agreeable ignorance. She made sure that his soldiers were among the best armed and most finely clad in the kingdom of Hungary. She had Franz's black armor with the great gold cross in front mended and polished. The armors of his noble entourage were sent out for repair as well. The landholders, who wore black sheepskins with the red embroidery of the Bathory coat of arms on the back, took care of their own, as did the archers, the foot soldiers, the cannoneers, the grooms, and the cooks.

During her husband's stay, Elizabeth wrote letters to her peers, her vassals, and to her cousin Stephen Bathory, prince of Transylvania. Her handwriting covered the margins of carefully read accounting books. She kept logs noting interviews with her overseers. In a special ledger she noted gifts she had received, though she rarely gave any. She also bought more finery and jewels than at any other time in her life. Leather, silver, silk, and pearls topped her lists of purchases. On Sundays she went to church with Franz in town and allowed her subjects to see her splendid finery, to admire her horses and her coachmen.

When the month was over, she found to her surprise that she was relieved. She found also that she was pregnant.

Elizabeth gave birth to a girl, named Anna after her mother. Elizabeth granted neither Franz nor the groom Ficzko credit for the impregnation, preferring to think that the devil himself had taken the trouble to plant his seed in her during the full moon. In truth, Darvulia's ceremonies sometimes included masked men who arrived at the height of the frenzy and possessed the women in the middle of the circle. These men disappeared after the orgies. Darvulia paid them discreetly later, but the women believed that they had been loved by dark angels. It is possible that Elizabeth's spurned husband or her dutiful lover had in no way authored her spawn. The thought did not unduly distress Elizabeth. The birth had been such a harrowing experience, she did not wish to ever conceive again. Darvulia promised her that she wouldn't.

Announcing the arrival of the new Bathory, Elizabeth wrote to her husband from Sarvar Castle: "My much beloved Husband, I am writing to offer my services to you, my beloved Lord and Master. Your child, thanks to God, is all right. She has no flaws and I am feeling fine, even though I have headaches and eye pains. May God protect you and be with you."

It was the shortest letter she had ever written him. If she had written him what she felt, she would have wounded him deeper than a Turk's lance. She hated him for having disfigured her body. Despite Darvulia's ministrations, her headaches and eye pains grew worse. Motherhood, instead of soothing her, filled her with anxiety and pain. She charged Darvulia with the task of finding a wet nurse. Darvulia did, using as much care as had been used long ago when she herself had been hired. Elizabeth stayed as far as she could from the fruit of her womb, acknowledging her presence only at the christening.

For many months after Anna was born, Elizabeth's black moods rarely lifted. She tried to soothe the constant ache in her soul by traveling constantly between her castles and taking frequent trips to Vienna to hear music. She also became a great believer in bathing, because she had been told that mineral baths soothe and heal. She traveled to Piestany to bathe in the famous mineral waters there, where she also enjoyed being packed in mud and left to bake in the sun. She ordered special bathing areas built in all her castles. These rooms, constructed for steam and running hot and cold water, were filled with round copper vats. Her girls rubbed and kneaded her, hoping to chase the melancholy angel from her flesh. But nothing helped.

One day a merchant arrived from the German lands with a unique instrument. It was a cylindrical cage with sharp iron stakes inside. When suspended from the ceiling, it rotated very fast and contracted, driving the stakes into the flesh of whatever unfortunate creature happened to be imprisoned inside. This German, Philipp Imser of Augsburg, was the inventor of many refined and useful mechanisms. He had begun making instruments of torture because there had been a great demand for them in the wake of peasant rebellions. He had traveled to Hungary to make the acquaintance of the great Thurzo, whose hot iron throne for Dozsa he admired. He had constructed the cylindrical cage for Thurzo, but the palatine decided, for no discernible reason, to make a gift of it to his niece Elizabeth Bathory. Elizabeth wasn't sure what the gift signified, except a possible new demand for money, but she was glad to have it.

She had the object installed in her bathing hall at Kereshtur. It rotated there above her as she lay in her tub, a gleaming copper cage without a bird inside. Her contentment in contemplating the shiny mechanism was sharply curtailed by a scratch on her left breast. One of the girls who had been scrubbing her, a stupid Katarina from Slovakia, had scratched her with her fingernail. Elizabeth lashed out angrily, striking the servant. But when she found that her slap had been ineffective, she called on Darvulia to summon Ficzko. Still in her bath, she ordered her strong ex-lover and her women to tie up Katarina. The rotating cage was lowered, and Katarina was made to crouch inside. The cage was then raised.

As the motion threw the girl from side to side, the long nails pierced her body. Her gushing blood showered Elizabeth below. It was an extraordinary sensation. As the girl's blood rained on her, the gloomy angel left Elizabeth's soul, and a mad joy possessed her. Better than that, her skin, at the places where the blood touched it, became younger, glowing with new life.

For the next three years, the rotating cage became Elizabeth's favorite entertainment. When she looked in the mirror after one of her blood showers, she looked strong and pretty to herself.

The fate of the girls sacrificed to her well-being did not interest her in the least. The girls, their parents, and the villages they came from were her property. She was free to dispose of them as she saw fit. But her lack of worry was not shared by her servants, who, though helpful, feared being caught. Rumors about disappearing girls were creating great uneasiness among the people of the villages. Pastor Ponikenuz, who had never been allowed into the bathing area, tried to force his way in one day while women were washing away the blood and cutting the body of a victim into pieces for secret burial. He did not succeed, because Darvulia interposed herself and made him feel boorish for trying to invade a female area.

The rotating cage was only one of the strange contraptions that Elizabeth began collecting in the year following the birth of Anna. She also became fascinated by amusing but harmless mechanical novelties. She acquired many clockwork mechanisms that calculated not just time but the positions of the stars. She bought musical boxes and dolls that moved by means of hidden springs and gears. She met most of the clock-makers and mechanical craftsmen of her time. Many of them were invited to one or another of her castles, where they installed clever devices that opened hidden doors, gave warning of anyone's approach, or provided places to hide. From inside some of these objects Elizabeth's dwarf Ibis was able to manipulate levers that caused movements and sounds. Elizabeth used her toys to frighten her servants and to amuse her guests.

Her mania took a strange turn when she ordered the master clockmaker Imser to make her an iron maiden. Eventually, Imser made her six deadly mechanical dolls realistically resembling women. Elizabeth had them installed at all her castles and often traveled with one of them in her carriage, as if it were a creature of flesh and blood.

The big dolls reminded Elizabeth of her childhood. She became nostalgic for certain occurrences of that faraway time, particularly her magical flight into the forest after her sisters had been killed by Dozsa's men. She decided to visit the scarred people, but she found no trace of them. The place where the old woman Himlat had shown her how to gather roots was a small village now. The waterfall that seemed so big to her when she was a child had become but a trickle of water flowing into a dirty little stream where pigs were wallowing. The villagers fell to the ground when they saw the countess and didn't dare lift their eyes when she addressed them.

"Am I mistaken to think," Elizabeth mused loudly, "that people were less afraid in the old days?" No one answered. When she asked if they knew what happened to Himlat and to the scarred people, an old woman said that she had heard a story about such people, but that had been in the old days before the Turks came. Elizabeth laughed, even though she felt sad. "The Turks have always been coming," she said.

Yes, people were more afraid than they had been during her childhood. She felt more afraid herself but didn't know why. Perhaps, she thought, she was not wise enough. Certainly, for the people there was more to be afraid of. When the Turks passed their way, they left only ashes in their wake. Taxes on their miserable households had increased tenfold. The Black Death had raged through the area. And yet the people kept on surviving. "They are like grass," Andrei de Kereshtur wrote; "they grow stronger after they are trampled . . . they always come back."

Elizabeth turned her horse around and returned to the castle, vowing to forget whatever scenes of her childhood still beckoned to her. The herbs prescribed by Darvulia and prepared by her growing circle of wild-eyed girls made her nauseous. She had not made love to a man in a very long time. Her sole pleasure was the moment when drops of blood fell on her naked skin, a rain accompanied by the cries of dying girls. Her horse groom Ficzko had long ceased to interest her. She now relied on him only for his brute strength when she killed girls.

She considered briefly taking another lover, a dragoon who reminded her of her mother's lover, Captain Moholy. He was a strong and gregarious man. At the height of her infatuation with him, they had ridden into the countryside on a spring day. They stopped at a village on the way to drink cold water from the well. An old hag, bent under the weight of her years, was drawing water from the well. Her lover knocked the old woman to the ground in his haste to draw water for his thirsty mistress. The miserable wretch, sprawled in the puddle at their feet, hissed venomously at Elizabeth and said, "You laugh at me, young woman, but one day you'll be old and ugly just like me!" Elizabeth looked at the hag's wrinkled skin and felt keenly the terror of old age. At that moment, her love for the handsome soldier passed out of her like a vapor.

Elizabeth's witches, as well as the learned men who read her stars and spoke of transmuted metals, also began to bore her. She flirted briefly with the thought of becoming a nun, but her preachers repelled her more than anyone else. She tried praying but then had to admit to herself that she had quit believing in God a long time before, when no one could prove his existence through algebra and geometry. This realization caused her to try even harder to keep religious men away from herself. Unfortunately the preachers were multiplying, and they seemed to be having an increased effect on the people, who came to see them in greater and greater numbers the more miserable their lot in life became.

Intrigue was everywhere in the enclosed world of her castles, where hundreds of closely quartered souls pursued their aims and ambitions. Every woman in Elizabeth's service gave birth during those ten long years. Some of them had nine or ten children, while their mistress stayed eerily uninhabited. Only Darvulia, who was Elizabeth's closest confidant, made no new contributions to the race. Darvulia's full-moon ceremonies, which had so enchanted Elizabeth in her younger years, began to pall in significance when the devil stubbornly refused to show up. Elizabeth thought that the killing of black roosters was a childish offering. The devil did appear one time, but not to Elizabeth. Several of the girls he appeared to had black burnt stars on their backs after the dance.

Only travel seemed to help. She began journeying, often in the company of her aunt Klara, to visit nobles of her own rank. She was a frequent guest of King Matthias. She visited Emperor Rudolf in Prague and enjoyed his strange hospitality. Her town house in Vienna, across from the abbey of the Augustinian monks, was furnished in the best style of the late sixteenth century and was frequented by musicians, philosophers, and writers. Sarvar and Kereshtur also received distinguished visitors, though not as many as Vienna. Troupes of actors found Bathory's castles most enjoyable.

When Franz Nadazdy finally saw his daughter, Anna, she was five years old. Franz came home to stay a bit longer this time. He had never fully recovered from the poison at Bacja, though he lived on and fought in many more campaigns, until he came home one last time and died from wounds he had received at the battle of Bratislava. Anna was then sixteen years old, while Elizabeth was thirty-five. While Franz lay in a coma, a gust of wind struck the castle window. Fierce gusts of wind mixed with rain followed. A furious storm descended on them. Branches torn from trees struck the walls like war clubs. Sitting by his side, Elizabeth watched him die. She felt no compassion. She did not know this battle-hardened soldier for whom she had wasted her life, waiting.

After the pomp of the funeral, Elizabeth traveled to Vienna, where she planned to live what life remained to her. She was bitter over the loss of her youth. In her mind, everyone was guilty of stealing her best years. She forgave no one.

Your Honor, it has now been established that the storm that affected the Austrian sub-Alpine country on the night we were in Lockenhaus was the worst of the century. But of course I did not need a meteorologist to tell me what only I knew: it was the worst night of my life.

As the winds began to pick up, uprooting trees, loosening boulders, and snapping roofs off houses, the only buildings sturdy enough to withstand the fury of the elements were the towers of Lockenhaus. One might call this fortunate, but our physical safety was in fact our downfall.

Exhilarated by what she perceived to be nature's response to something that raged inside her, Lilly Hangress became positively wild. She began, mildly enough, with a proposition.

"Let's play the game," she said.

"*The* game?"

"At first it will be many games, then it will become *the* game."

"Perhaps we could sleep and dream the game instead," I said. "I am very tired."

"As if anyone could sleep," scoffed Imre. At that moment the terrible clatter of a mountain boulder slamming into the tower made his point. He did have one.

"We are already dreaming," said Lilly. "Now, here are the rules . . . I believe that you have this game in America; it is called Truth or Dare, like Madonna's movie . . ."

I protested. "I hardly know what the truth is anymore."

"Precisely," rejoined the beautiful tormentress, who was growing more vivid the wilder the storm. "Everyone has to tell an absolutely true story about one's intimate life, a story that was never told to anyone before. Count Bathory, we defer to you."

"My whole life is a secret I have never told anyone. But you forgot to tell us what is the object of this game. And what are the rewards and punishments? Who wins? At one time in my life I played enough games to know that such things are important."

Lilly waved her hand impatiently. "When you are finished with your story, you will surrender your identity to the group. We will take your clothes and your body and do with them as we please. The winner will be the best storyteller. She will be in control of all of you."

"She?"

"Naturally."

I had no doubt that Lilly had already assumed command.

Imre said, "I am not going to play." He had taken a leather-bound volume from a shelf and was reading, looking clerical and severe. He is both Megyery and Ponikenuz, I thought.

Your Honor, I had many doubts about Lilly's game. I knew that it was not harmless. I knew also that we were in the chamber of Elizabeth Bathory on a night of the sort often said to "bring the ghosts out of their cracks." I had even hallucinated my terrible ancestress in the flames of the fireplace. I had every reason to withdraw. I should have, perhaps, bolted out of the room and taken my chances with the elements. I did not. And the reason was Teresa, for whom I felt wrenching compassion. I had to protect her at all costs.

"Fine," I said, "I will tell you a story." I picked up the soggy stack of papers containing the secret police files of Klaus Megyery and yours truly. I separated my file from Megyery's and began to read, skipping now and then, adding and subtracting things at whim, following, it seemed, the cues of the wind, which grew and lessened at odd intervals.

I will not bore you with the details of this document, which I have entered in evidence, but I will highlight only the earliest story contained in it, which took the better part of an hour to read to my Lockenhaus companions.

It appears that when I was only a child, in Comrade Hebler's history class, I was asked to write a self-critique of my family. I had forgotten what it was that provoked Hebler, but Klaus Megyery, ever the accurate spy, noted it all down for his bosses. Comrade Hebler had asked the class to speculate on what it was that might have motivated the Hungarian tribes to be nomadic. Was it lack of resources, the search for food?

I appear to have answered, "The joy of plunder and rape."

The class burst out laughing, not because they found the answer wrong, but because it so obviously ignored the prevailing ideology, which found only the forces of production and class struggle relevant to any given situation, no matter how distant.

Hebler brought his ruler down on the desk with such force that it broke in two. "Feelings do not create history!" he shouted. "History is 99.9 percent sorrow! The only joy there is, is felt by people when they triumph over the rich!"

Comrade Hebler then reported me to the school authorities for my remark about the joy of plunder and rape. The Party committee charged with ideological vigilance at the gymnasium was well aware of my unhealthy social origins. My remark was viewed as a direct challenge to the new interpretation of history they were at such pains to provide.

I was called before the three members of the school's Party secretariat to explain myself. One of the judges, my physics teacher, was the mother of my girlfriend Mari. I was terrified that this incident might cause her to forbid Mari to stroll and study with me. The others were the Russian teacher, Comrade Angelou, and the school principal, Janosz Silvay, a former coal stoker on a ship who had come up through the Party ranks and had been put in charge of the school. Silvay secretly felt that he was unworthy to hold this position, which made him overzealous and overvigilant.

"Is this what your aristocratic parents have told you at home about the Hungarian people?" he shouted.

I mumbled in the negative. My parents never said anything at home. They hardly spoke to me, in fact. Or to each other.

"What did they tell you at home?" he insisted.

"Nomadism never came up at home, Comrade," I managed.

Silvay was at a loss. He turned to Comrade Angelou.

Comrade Angelou was a petite Greek woman, a young Communist who had been raised in the Soviet Union and sent to teach Russian in the satellites. She wore her skirts shorter than anyone in town. My gaze and imagination often traveled up her well-turned legs during the declensions of Russian nouns and stopped just short of the place I couldn't imagine but that made me break into a sweat anyway.

I know it's irrelevant, but at this point, Your Honor, everything is a clue. For the two years I'd been sitting in her class, I had not learned a single word of Russian.

"Not nomadism, perhaps," she said, "but there must have been other subjects. What, for instance, did you learn at home about the holdings of your ancestors?"

My family's holdings were news to me. I must have looked helpless, because she softened visibly. "Well," she said, "perhaps it was just a thoughtless remark after all."

Mari's mother was uncomfortable, but she did not want to seem lenient before Principal Silvay, who could have known about her daughter's friendship with the accused.

"There are ways of thinking," she said sternly, "that grow like weeds if left unchecked. History is full of such poisonous weeds. You must write a forty-page self-criticism of your family's history, demonstrating the correct point of view, using citations from Karl Marx, Friedrich Engels, and Comrades Lenin and Stalin."

The rest of the committee agreed.

I told my parents nothing of what had transpired, knowing how much it would worry them. I researched the matter on my own.

In a book published before Comrade Stalin made things clear once and for all time, I found that my ancestors, Arpad's successors, did not have much time to consolidate their kingdom. They were constantly involved in defending their borders against the Turks, who were advancing their plans for the conquest of Europe under the motto "God gave the seas to the infidel and the land to Islam." The Serb fortresses along the Danube fell in a series of battles. The end for the Hungarians came in 1526, when Süleyman the Magnificent destroyed their armies at the battle of Mohacs. Louis II, the Hungarian king, drowned in a stream while fleeing from the battlefield. As a result of the loss, Hungary was divided between the Ottomans and the Hapsburgs. Only the principality of Transylvania maintained relative independence. For hundreds of years after the defeat at Mohacs, Hungarian nobles walked a tightrope between Turkish interests in the east and Hapsburg interests in the west. A Hungarian noble might switch sides as many times as he changed horses during a journey from the Carpathians to the Danube.

To find out what Comrades Marx, Engels, Lenin, and Stalin thought about this wasn't so easy. Luckily, my friend Klaus Megyery's father was a Communist official. An entire wall of their apartment was covered by red-bound volumes containing the writings of Comrades Marx, Engels, Lenin, and Stalin. I told Klaus that I would like to avail myself for a short time of some of these volumes in order to extract citations for the history self-criticism I'd been required to write. Klaus, according to his own sanitized account, was afraid to let me touch these books, which were carefully dusted each week by his mother and were in pristine condition, having never been opened. I needed to persuade him somehow, perhaps by giving him some valuable object, but since the police raid on our house there weren't any valuable objects left.

Klaus's account skipped a bit after this, but I now remembered. After giving the matter some thought, I asked Klaus if he would like to watch me kiss Mari in exchange for looking at the books. I had not yet kissed Mari, but I figured that this was a good time, given the emergency partly caused by her mother.

Klaus said that just watching us kiss was not enough for the privilege of peeking into the sacred books. What Klaus wanted was to see Mari's "thing." For that, he would be willing to let me look into Marx and maybe Stalin. That was more difficult to arrange, but I worked out a complicated plan which involved pushing Mari's dress up while I kissed her so that Klaus, hidden in the park bushes, would get a glimpse, though I could not guarantee Mari's actual "thing," but only a glimpse between her legs.

Next day after school, I persuaded Mari to go to the park with me, despite her mother's injunction against seeing me until the self-criticism of my history was written. We sat on a bench in a shady area of trees near the gazebo where musicians performed in the summer. It was fall, and the park was nearly deserted. It was already getting dark when, after two hours of conversation with my arm thrown casually on the back of the bench behind Mari, I finally dared to lean close enough to kiss her. By this time, Klaus was no doubt suffering terribly because of his uncomfortable squatting position in the bush directly opposite, holding an old pair of opera glasses. When, at long last, my lips brushed Mari's lips, it was already dark. I tried lifting her school dress while we kissed, but I found her skirt pinned tightly between her knees. I used my hand to signal some kind of disappointment to Klaus in the bush, but Klaus had found the waiting too unbearable and had already left.

That evening we met in the alley between our houses. "Thank you," Klaus said uncertainly. I shrugged. "That was great," he said, sounding more convinced. "I saw her whole 'thing.'" He leaned confidentially into my ear. "The crack and . . . hair," he said, satisfied.

"A deal's a deal," I said. "Now for Marx and Stalin . . ."

Klaus tried feebly to wiggle out of some of it. "I said maybe Stalin . . ."

"No," I said firmly, "Marx *and* Stalin!"

Having obtained a copy of volume one of Marx's *Das Kapital* and *The Speeches of Comrade I. V. Stalin Before the IXth and Xth Congresses of the Communist Party of the U.S.S.R.*, before Klaus Megyery's parents came home from work I spent forty-five feverish minutes leafing through them in search of the correct interpretation of Hungarian history. I copied at random weighty-sounding passages that made little sense to me, and proceeded to apply them to my history.

I wrote that my great-great-great-great-uncle George Thurzo, a representative of the oppressive class, quelled the revolt of the peasant George Dozsa, which was unfortunate because Dosza was a member of the revolutionary class. I then dwelled at length on the career of the rebel, because I knew that the Communist Party approved of him more than they did of my ancestor. Streets in Hungary and Romania had been renamed in his honor, and a bronze monument of the rebel's head had been erected in the Square of the Republic in Budapest. Lord Thurzo "crowned" Dozsa by roasting him alive in a red-hot iron throne with a burning iron crown on his head. His captured followers were then forced to eat his cooked flesh before they were broken on the wheel and hanged. The crowning of Dozsa and the eating of his flesh were depicted in countless illustrations, including a woodcut in my history book. Dozsa's grizzled face looked past the flames into the future with a scary look. If I looked too long into those eyes—which, like an icon's, followed you no matter which way you turned—I found myself falling into their burning fire. My father had once said to me, "You were born during the end of the world," and I thought that in the depths of Dozsa's eyes I could see "the end of the world." But my father, of course, had been referring to World War II, a time of horrors still fresh in our minds.

Andrei de Kereshtur wrote: "Dozsa was punished in a fashion that warned rebels for all time. The dead are dead to the world; they are God's to remember and to judge. For us to recall their names, they must be of noble blood, possess valor or beauty, or die in a way that will not let us forget. There are those who are only by the manner of their death remembered. We do not remember those who die by the blow of the usual sword, or those of whom disease has made her meal. We do recall those whose hearts leapt out of the pyre to be eaten by their accomplices. We do remember the nobles impaled by Dracula on stakes as high as the Carpathian pines. We will remember Dozsa's throne of iron longer than the gold thrones of some past kings."

By dwelling so long on Dozsa, I believed that I had discharged most of my duty toward self-criticism, since Dozsa was such an obvious criticism of nobility and everything it stood for. It is true, I had taken great pleasure in describing Dozsa's roasting, but then so did my history book.

After that, I wrote only that Elizabeth Bathory was

my great-great-great-great-grandmother and that the unfortunate accusations against her showed that women had no equality in that epoch and they couldn't choose who they wanted to marry. Under socialism, Elizabeth Bathory could have chosen to marry anyone, even a peasant. I hesitated a bit before writing this, because I knew that countesses never married peasants, not even in 1953. Nonetheless, the remark seemed appropriate at this point. Happily, I never finished my family's self-criticism because Stalin died and we had three weeks off from school. When we came back, his portrait had been removed from our classroom.

The effect of my story, as reported by my childhood snitch, Klaus Megyery, had an interesting effect on his son. Imre, who had tried to ignore my reading of the file so diligently composed by his father, became interested despite himself.

When I finished, he furiously thrust the book he had been reading into my face and said, "Those lies about my father . . . you made them up! But . . ." A look of evil glee came into his eyes. "I will read to you what *your* forefather did and said!"

The book he had been reading was the first edition of the *Chronicles of Andrei de Kereshtur.*

And so, Your Honor, Imre Megyery was drawn against his will into Lilly's clever game. The storm picked up at this point. We could barely hear Imre read from the book, though he was shouting. I am quite sure that he had chosen the passage quite at random, but somehow it was appropriate. It was a letter from Andrei de Kereshtur to Elizabeth Bathory, at a time when her crimes were becoming common knowledge throughout the kingdom.

"I have been dreaming," wrote the notary, "that our

teacher the monk Silvestri has been teaching us again, and that we were both children. He was gloomy in my dream, and a lot more severe with us, his poor pupils, than was his nature when he was alive. He said that a teacher's mind is like an octopus full of ink; if it does not find enough suitable surface to write its teachings on, it becomes bloated and preoccupied with itself.

"I fear that he was speaking of my confusion regarding the researches I have undertaken. I was left wondering if you too are confused and feeling lost. By ourselves, we are not sufficient surface for his mind to spend its ink on.

"I must tell you how my researches began. Six months before he was killed, Silvestri wrote to me that he had dreamt a terrible dream. He said that he was summoned by you, my dear Lady, to the dining hall at Sarvar. He found the long table set with candles. Lying naked on the table was your mother, Anna, may heaven hold her dear. You, my Lady, were sitting in the shadows in the chair usually reserved for your mother, and you asked him to take a close look at her body because she had died 'from being bound to an invisible ship of fools.'

"Silvestri examined the body with a view to reading the last rites when the body exploded like an overripe fruit and blue maggots began streaming out of it. Silvestri was convinced that the devil had taken hold of our Lady, and he reached for his crucifix and psalter. He found neither as the body on the table expanded its boundaries, became formless, and started floating through the air animated by a terrible life. The windows opened and a great wind came through, pushing the body to and fro. Silvestri took hold of one of Lady Anna's hands, but the corpse floated above his head, showering him with worms. The hand came off and the body was sucked through a window. Silvestri tried to rise in flight after the body in order to follow it out the window to give it the last rites, but he could not rise. He heard you, my Lady, say, 'Let her go!'

"The dream was so vivid that when the Master came awake he began to pray fervently in a manner he had never employed before, hitting his head against the floor of the chapel. He interpreted his dream to mean that he was being called once more to delve deeply into the mysteries he had abandoned for several years.

"Many years before, when he had first come to Kereshtur, he had experimented enthusiastically after the manner prescribed by Trismegistus, Paracelsus, and Dorn. He had understood the problem of the *Mysterium Tremendum* to be entirely without description, consisting of the very fact that it could not be captured by any form of human devising. He had persisted nonetheless because he had loved his alembics, the variously shaped vases and containers, and the chemical reactions he elicited from his mixtures. He loved the transformations of matter, the stages of purification from putrid matter to blue flame. His dearest possession was a copper alembic of Arabic origin, which had been used by three generations of Seekers. The last owner, an Italian named Gregorius, had inscribed the bottom of the pot with the gold inscription *aurum*. When Silvestri achieved clarity in one of his reactions, he could see the glint of the gold letters through the top, and it was almost like having made *aurum*. He knew that it was an illusion, but it gave him pleasure.

"However, around the time that you, my Lady, were born, he abandoned his laboratory, allowing his alembic and his materials to gather dust. Asked by his friends how his researches were proceeding, Silvestri told them that he had abandoned his alembic 'in favor of human nature.' He did not, at first, know exactly what he meant, but as time went by he began to understand what he had casually said. The Great Work was but a symbolic representation of the purpose of human beings on earth. Fermentations, purifications, dissolutions, precipitations were but images for processes that took place in men's souls. The Purpose of the Work was also a False Purpose. As a young monk, he had often laughed at the stupidity of greedy patrons of alchemists, who fed and clothed them for years in the hope that they would produce gold. Even the stupidest alchemists knew that this wasn't the purpose of their activity, but they encouraged the belief because it kept them fed.

"What most of them believed, and this too was false, was that the Work involved the transformation of matter to such a degree that it would *perpetually renew itself.* The goal was Immortality, allowing the body to survive its decay. The *Mysterium Tremendum* was an abomination, the suspension of time in order to preserve eternally the body's youth.

"Silvestri had no illusions about whom this discovery would benefit. The same greedy princes who spent fortunes in search of gold also wanted to live forever. They cared not how many had to die for them to live. Many experiments used corpses, or parts of the corpses of servants, or even of other nobles. The more elevated the stature of the corpse, the more 'active' the *prima materia* was said to be. Until Guillaume du Dugaulville put an end to the practice in the fifteenth century, nobles even of the same family were quite willing to sacrifice one another in search of private immortality.

"Silvestri had lost patience with the physical aspects of the Work, dedicating his life instead to understanding the stubborn complexity of the human soul, without its depictions and icons. He hoped also to impart forbearance, resignation, and even kindness to the pupils in his charge so that when the time came, we would go joyfully to our deaths and to everlasting life.

"And yet, the dream of Anna Bathory's corpse disturbed him more than anything else had since he had abandoned his laboratory. He knew, of course, that despite the falsity of its Purpose, the Work could boast of evident successes, and that some of the powers uncovered by its process were formidable. His dream had been an alchemist's textbook in its clarity. He told me that you, my Lady, have reached the age when you became saddened by your mortality. For reasons Silvestri could not yet understand, he thought that you were going to make it your life's Work to reject the course of Nature, and that you had begun your Work, quite logically, with the destruction of your mother Anna's body. What surprised and terrified him was the ferocity of your purpose, at least in the dream, and your determination not to let the goodness of Christ stand in her way. This is why you shouted 'Let her go!' when Silvestri had attempted to offer Christian solace.

"And there was something else, my Lady. You were not alone in his dream. You were being guided, whether you knew it or not, by others involved in the Work. Silvestri thought that certain experiments were taking place at Sarvar, but unlike his experiments of the past, which had been naïve at best, the new Work was powerful. It was possible that you had engaged Workers to transform your mother's body, and that you had been made to believe that your participation would result in a new, immortal body for yourself. You were made to see this new body as beautiful, younger, better than your own. Silvestri thought that you were being deceived by evil beings. The very strength of your belief in their lies hastened the decay of your body, and you were being led by this deception to an unlit grave in the depths of hell.

"I must beg your forgiveness for the bluntness of my recollections, my beloved Lady Elizabeth. You are strong and intelligent. I do not wish to spare you the truth. The monk Silvestri, who knew you as well as I, was not surprised at your ability to lead this mysterious process. He knew, as I do, about your exceptional gifts. Silvestri admired most of all your curiosity and your ability to see through dogma. He said that, in time, your intellect would surpass that of most wise men of our time, if you developed enough feelings of kindness, affection, pity, and sympathy. You seemed to him lacking precisely in those qualities that we call feminine.

"Silvestri would have told no one about his dream, or about his understanding of it, if I had not startled him by writing about a dream of my own. I had been reading a book published in the year of our birth, 1560, called *Philosophia Naturalis,* by Albertus Magnus. I was very much disturbed by an illustration representing *animus mundi* containing the four elements and characterized by the number ten, which represents perfection. The man in the middle of the circle, opening his hands to display four cups floating on a mercurial substance, looked exactly like my father, the notary of Kereshtur. After noting the coincidence, and not thinking much of it, I had a dream in which I saw you, my dearest Lady Elizabeth, sitting before a mirror. Your hair was so long it reached the floor and it swirled over the entire room. The mirror was made of Venetian glass with a carved oval frame of black walnut. As you looked, I realized that the mirror was myself, and that you were looking at your reflection in me.

"At first, I felt great joy at being able to return the image of your beautiful face and body to you. But then I grew weak, as if someone else was directing my actions, and I began returning other reflections to you. I held up the image of an old woman whose hair was gray and patchy, whose once beautiful face had shrunk around two bony orbs filled with cold, bloodshot, dead eyes.

The skin on her arms and shoulders was wrinkled and loose and lifeless. When I held this image to you, my Lady, you screamed and began to tear your flesh, pulling off your skin and covering me with gushing blood. I made an effort to change back to the beautiful—as I know you to be—true image of you, but instead found myself holding an even more hideous figure before me. You were too weak to scream, so you gave but a low, insistent moan like a weary phantom. With a great deal of effort, I pulled myself out of the sway of whatever forces were directing these images, and was able, for a brief second, briefer than the spark of a sun ray on a pebble, to show you to yourself as you had been in the beginning. Exhausted, I fell into a deathlike slumber, but not before I heard you lamenting, 'Why have you done this to me, Andrei, my mirror?'

"To that question I had no answer, but when I woke the first thing I saw was the picture of my father in the book by Albertus Magnus. I felt in some obscure but powerful way that my father was responsible for my dream.

"I sought Silvestri's advice. The monk read my letter with unease and dread. He said that he was fond of me but that he could not spare me from a difficult destiny. Whether he liked it or not, he now had to advise me how to best embark upon the Work. He had hoped, while he had been reading my terrible dream, that there would be something that would indicate the possibility of another life, a monastic one perhaps. But our dreams, taken together, left neither one of us a choice. Silvestri wrote to me about his own dream, and then drew a new course of study for me, one that included only books on the subject of the Work."

Andrei de Kereshtur went on to reassure Countess Elizabeth of his devotion and wrote that his alchemical work had been "undertaken solely for your sake, so that you may not be threatened by the demons of dream and mortality."

Imre Megyery, who had begun reading sarcastically, became increasingly involved with the story, forgetting that the reason he had begun reading it in the first place was to respond to the unflattering portrait I had drawn of his father. As the old alchemist's words penetrated the air of the room, the flames in the fire began pulsing rhythmically like a heart. Twice during his reading I saw Elizabeth Bathory's ghostly form in the fire. And this time Lilly and Teresa saw her too.

The young man, who still held the leather-bound book in his hands, said sullenly, "My life is unimportant. Only you nobles have a history."

"That may be," Lilly said cruelly, "but something intimate about your life must be important enough to tell."

"So there is nothing you don't already know. You know more than I do. You have my father's file. And you know him from before I was born. I come to find, from *you*, that my father is a secret policeman, not a monarchist at all, a despicable liar, a snitch, a man without scruples or morals. He wants a king because he has a stupid plan to control Hungary. But you know what? I still love and respect his authority!"

Imre spoke so plaintively, it was almost a song, an old graveside lament. I almost felt sorry for him.

"And what exactly is Klaus Megyery planning to do with me after I play king?"

"Kill you. They always kill the king. It's an old story."

* * *

A gust of wind blew out the candles, leaving only the light of the fireplace. Lilly's face underwent a sudden change: her eyes widened, a pallor replaced the red in her high cheeks. When she spoke, her voice was husky and unfamiliar.

"I grew up listening to stories about the miraculous restorative powers of blood. Hungarian folklore is awash in blood. Blood and beauty are wedded in fairy tales, folk sayings, and conventional wisdom. Maidens prick themselves with sewing needles and sleep for a hundred years. They dance through forests of wild demons in blood-colored shoes and dresses.

"The war against the ravages of time takes the heroines of our legends through seas of liquid, most of it bright red. Religious, philosophical, courtly, and alchemical literature overflow with blood, which is both the supreme symbolic substance and the guarantor of life. The chief cure for any disease is the letting of blood.

"My pastors, Hebler, Megyery, and Ponikenuz, never tired of quoting Deuteronomy 12:23 from the Bible: 'The blood is the life! The blood is the life!'

" 'Little you know wherefrom you speak, Preacher!' I often rejoined inwardly. Outside of literature, in the real world, flowed relentless rivers of blood. The moats around my castles filled with the blood of soldiers time after time, year after year, as regular and periodical as my monthlies.

"Mass slaughters of peasants, the cyclical devastations of the Black Death, the unending battles, made my world an unsteady island on a sea of blood. There was literally and metaphorically no place for me to step without stepping in blood.

"Given this red liquid medium in which I spent my life, it would have been surprising if I *didn't* bathe in blood. To bathe in blood was simply to acknowledge the literal reality. Such acknowledgment was an act of sanity and thus, contrary to conventional wisdom, I was an eminently sane woman, a survivor."

"Elizabeth," said Teresa, "tell us about the village women."

"When I grew older, I started to imprint and to burn into the flesh of girls the symbols of the real world. I branded them with the dreadful realism of the world that had not yet happened to them. I said to them, 'I have lived and learned that life is sorrow, beauty a passing fancy, pleasure fleeting, skin only dry parchment . . . Let this be a lesson to you.' I was a moralist; I wanted to teach young flesh a lesson. I was doing my young girls a great favor, saving them from the slow, dreadful lessons of the world with my own swift, brutal teaching. And I did . . . for all ages. Even your flesh, my listeners, remarkably tingles from my brutal approach."

It was true. My skin felt oddly aroused, despite the cold, as if wings had passed over me again, close enough to startle my skin. Wings made of Lilly's—or Elizabeth Bathory's—cold, cold words. It did not seem strange to me then—though it does now—that Lilly Hangress had assumed the voice and persona of Elizabeth Bathory, the woman she had spent her life studying. In the ancient countess's bedroom, the only incongruity was my own story. Perhaps, I thought to myself, this is a variant of the Truth or Dare game, with rules unknown to me.

Still, I hadn't forgotten the bruises on Teresa's body.

"Four hundred years later you are as brutal as ever," I said.

"Not by a far shot, dear Count. Each year that has passed has limited my liberty. Teresa, did you resent my whipping?"

"No, my lady," answered the child of my first love.

"Elizabeth, had you no compassion for the poor girls?"

"Think. Where did these girls come from?"

I had read my *Chronicles*. I knew where they came from. Her Ladyship's maid Helena Jo said this about how the countess came by the girls she allegedly tortured and murdered: "These girls were brought first by Janosz Salvay's wife, then by a Jewess, and then by a Slovak woman . . . the wife of Janos Borsany also brought many. The wife of Janos Liptay had also procured two or three girls, and although she knew they would be murdered, she still brought girls, because Her Ladyship had threatened her. The wife of Janos Borsany had herself brought an aristocratic girl from Polany. The wife of Istvan Szabo, who lives in Vep, had already brought sufficiently many girls. Her Ladyship had given one of them a garment and another a fur piece as gifts. The wife of Balthazar Horvath, who lives near a monastery in a tiny town, also procured many girls."

"Think," said Lilly. "Why so many girls? And why were they all brought by wives? Why this unending stream of girls, of maidens, virgins, brought to me by an unending stream of wives? These girls were the daughters of other poor women just like themselves, or perhaps even their own daughters."

"Perhaps," I mused, "the wicked stepmothers in fairy tales were still alive in those days."

"They are still alive today," Lilly—or Elizabeth—said curtly, "but now their wickedness is more hidden."

"My mistress Elizabeth," Teresa said, "received the wives in the little hall at Kereshtur. When her husband, Franz, had been alive, the little hall had been the scene of many laughing, drinking parties. The poet Melotus sang his verses there. Harpists wrenched the sounds of heaven from the strings of their golden instruments, on which cherubs perched. The tapestries in the little hall did not depict heroic scenes of past wars like those in the Great Hall. They depicted scenes of love in the long-past Arcadia of the ancients and scenes from the *Decameron* and *Tristan and Yseult*. It was a warm room with stone fireplaces and long, narrow windows made of colored glass.

"But after the death of Count Nadazdy, my mistress received only wives here, wives who brought her shy and pretty girls from her lands in Slovenia, Hungary, and Transylvania. Seated on a carved throne, the velvet folds of her great dress spread about her like an astrologer's globe, her neck held tight by her ruffed collar, her pearls severely aligned, she studied the girls coldly, with the eye of one who had seen the blossoming of the flesh on a thousand bodies.

"The wives sat quietly while the countess appraised the shy blooms, and they calculated in their minds how much money they were going to get. My lady always paid cash, gold or silver, and there was often a little gift. A pair of lace gloves or a gold ring, a piece of fur or a precious stone.

"Later, after the wives left, she ordered the girls to work. She gave them tasks that I supervised. The girls took to these tasks joyously, enthusiastically, full of the vigor of their youth. They had no way of knowing that tasks such as polishing an immense Venetian mirror could not be accomplished by novices. And when they failed, my mistress burned the symbols of wifery, keys and money, into flesh that dreamt only of love and song."

"Why did the wives hate the virgins so much?" I asked. "Was it simply because they were young? Because they were still virtual, potential, possible? Were they killing them for the sin of *not being wives?* Was being a wife so inconceivably dreadful? Who appointed her slayer of youth, queen of crones, death angel of disappointment . . . ?"

I was most anxious to know. Suddenly, Lilly and Teresa seemed to me to know everything. I looked at Teresa, who had grown younger and prettier somehow. Something was released in the room, something bitter like a drop of wormwood.

I knew that Elizabeth Bathory didn't just burn keys and coins into the palms of virgins. In equally symbolic fashion, she pierced, penetrated, and ripped them. Over the centuries, the poison of her anger has dripped slowly down the line. I felt an immense loneliness.

Groping for words, I confessed how difficult I found it to imagine Elizabeth Bathory as a particular woman, an individual. The difficulty was manifold, I explained. She had lived in a time radically different from ours. I could find little in my own reality that corresponded to hers. I did not tell my companions that I found the darkness familiar. What was there *living* that would help me?

"In my profession, what separates the drudge from the great is only the occasional ability to experience the past," Lilly Hangress said, turning from the countess into the historian. "Your difficulty may not lie in imagining her life but in the fact that she was a woman."

I protested this, Your Honor. I had no difficulty imagining a contemporary woman, even a monstrous woman. True, my relationships with women had not been great. I had loved them in a complicated and anxious way that led inevitably to the dissolution of their affections. Yet I did not blame them. I understood why they had to leave me, to get away from my recurring melancholy, from my psychic heaviness. I have known many women. I did not have any difficulty imagining how they thought and what motivated them. Called upon to imagine a contemporary woman, a New Yorker, for instance, I would have no trouble extrapolating from what I know of our common space, the city. I could guess how she moves in it, where she goes, how the city affects her feelings. There is a choreography of contemporary beings that is accessible to me. What I found hard to imagine was how a great lady in the sixteenth century navigated the interiors of her castle and the corresponding labyrinths of her psyche.

"In what way were the people of Elizabeth Bathory's time like us?" I asked, increasingly desperate to know. I cannot explain this, but I felt suddenly as if I was on trial, a trial more severe and demanding than will take place in your court of law, Your Honor.

"I don't think that we were like you at all," said Lilly, resorting to the voice of Elizabeth again. "We were not like you in how we lived, how we loved, how we ate, what we ate, how we tasted what we ate, and especially how we *moved*. We moved within the constraints of our dress in a manner imposed on us by our home, by the architecture of the castle. God was more real, or closer, if you prefer. Love was a refinement that we invented to pass the time while men warred."

Lilly stared right into the fire, where her visions and her words seemed to be coming from. The image of Elizabeth Bathory had now become firmly visible. I could even count her pearls.

Teresa lay down on her back and put her hands under her head.

"All of this is mine," I said, bewildered.

"And so it is, Count Bathory," whispered Lilly. "And now comes the reward of the game."

"I am not prepared for any more game," I said. "This has shaken me quite enough, thank you. I beg your indulgence. I think I will stretch out here and doze off."

414 · Andrei Codrescu

I stretched out next to Teresa. I could smell her girlish scent and feel the warmth of her young skin.

"You may stretch," said Lilly, "and play the game like that, from a kingly position. But play you must. You may even call the rewards of the game. It does not matter what the rewards are, as long as the game continues."

"In that case," I said, weary beyond measure, "I propose that each one of us will imagine a scenario involving the others. Then we will draw numbers from one to four. The highest number will get the right to enact his or her scenario of rewards and punishments without protests from the others."

In proposing this, I had hoped to exhaust everyone. Eventually, we did have to sleep. Also, I must admit to a certain opportunism. I was not afraid to deliver myself into their hands. I was royalty, after all. They needed me. My own plans called only for sleep and then for escape with Teresa early in the morning. We would then fly to New York.

After a time, during which the flames in the fireplace rose to a great height, making the chamber almost unbearably hot, Lilly asked if everyone was ready. She took the copy of the *Chronicles of Andrei de Kereshtur* from the table.

"I will now open the notary's book. If the page number has a one in it, we will enact Count Bathory's scenario. If a two, Teresa's. If a three, Imre's. If a four, mine. I will close my eyes and put my finger on the page where it falls open."

Lilly closed her eyes, opened the book, and set her finger down on one of the pages. It was page forty-four of the *Chronicles.* At the top of the page were the following words: "For all that is preordained will be tested again."

"The number forty-four twice enforces my claim."

This was so.

"I will reveal my scenario in stages," said Lilly. "First," she said, "all four of us must sit in a circle."

Imre climbed reluctantly down from his museum chair and sat on the rug with us.

"Now, remove your clothes."

With expert familiarity, Teresa pulled her sweater over her head and wriggled out of her jeans. It was the second time that day, but at least it was warm.

Lilly Hangress's womanly body was voluptuous, with wide dark aureolas around her nipples, firm hips, and a luxuriant delta of Venus. Imre was pale like a sheet, but he was bony and solidly made, a soldier's body, taut and alert.

"Now, Teresa, you sit in the middle of the circle, while the three of us join hands."

The girl sat in the middle, glowing pink in the light of the flames. Her bruises took on vivid rainbow colors. Her girlish nipples perked to attention when our three pairs of eyes seemed to fasten on them at once.

"Now let us close our eyes and call our mistress!"

"She doesn't need to put in an appearance," Imre grumbled. "She's been here all along."

So he had seen her too. At that moment, I had the sense that everything had, indeed, been preordained. Even if I hadn't seen Elizabeth Bathory stand there, I knew that she lived in my blood and had been inert there, an inactive, centuries-old virus. Now she was about to come back to life. There was still time to resist, do something. But what? I felt tired, helpless, weak, and . . . yes, aroused. What Lilly had in mind was something quite delightful. I closed my eyes.

Lilly recited softly these verses by Dante Alighieri: "And there I saw a loveliness that when . . . it smiled at the angelic songs and games . . . made glad the eyes of all the saints."

"All strength lies in vulnerability," Teresa said, as if reciting a lesson. "A naked body is strong."

Indeed. After we had sat there for a few moments feeling surges of electricity pass from hand to hand, Lilly said: "And now to the core!"

Lilly leaned toward Teresa and bit her swiftly and hard on the lips. A trickle of blood showed where Lilly broke the skin. Teresa bit her right back. Both women were bleeding now and fed on each other's blood. Then they disengaged quickly and, to my surprise, started laughing.

My hands had grown sweaty. The surges grew stronger. My blood was trying to overflow its banks.

"Elizabeth's here," I announced.

"I hope so," said Lilly defiantly. "We are bringing her in on the tide of your blood and the passion of our bodies."

I leaned forward too, and licked blood from Teresa's lips. Lilly then pulled me to her and bit my lips hard. She licked my blood, and then the three of us brought our lips together and fed on the rusty iron of it.

The world must have felt like this in Elizabeth's grasp. I found it difficult to imagine the absolute power that my ancestress had over the lives of others. Common people were mere dirt to her. Their lives could be snuffed out at the twitch of her aristocratic nostril. Her carriage never stopped for peasants or for their children. Sex, like other appetites, was there to be satisfied by whatever means necessary. The place of morality was taken by an elaborate code of manners. Protocol was infinitely more important than kindness or the Ten Commandments. Elizabeth measured her power by the ruthlessness with which she took what she needed.

Lilly's lips, while firm and authoritative, still did not possess the deadly grasp of someone as powerful as

Elizabeth Bathory. I smiled at the comparison, but surrendered nonetheless to Lilly's vampiric pressure.

But what was Imre's role in all this? His strength was held in check. His hand had not lost its firm grip on mine, but he made no move to partake in the fierce kiss we were sharing.

Suddenly, Lilly disengaged.

Imre let go too.

"Count Bathory, you must now prove yourself worthy of kingship. The sacrifice is about to begin."

At this point, a gust of wind blew out the flames in the fireplace, leaving only the glow of the embers. It was dark. I could barely see the outlines of my companions. I wasn't sure what Lilly meant by "sacrifice," but I took this to be a metaphor for the continuation of our love game.

Imre took Lilly's hands and pulled her down. I took hold of her feet. She was now stretched between us. I felt Teresa's hot breath next to my ear and felt her hand grasp my erection.

"Take her," she whispered.

I obeyed, though a small voice within me protested. I closed my eyes. I covered Lilly with my body and entered her. Lilly was as hot as the burning wood in the fireplace. She drew me into her with hungry greed. I would have spent myself in a moment if a stern voice did not command me, "Hold your seed for Elizabeth's arrival."

I heard a hum in my ears like the Gregorian chant of monks. Voices I did not recognize crowded in my head, chanting the spell Teresa had once translated for me:

> AKAELOS KALENDRIA FUISOR
> RAMZET HALBUR KOLEMZI KRAH
> RAMEZAH HOLRAB ARK AMARGO
> PALER KMOSTREH HALBERUT

"Your shaman ancestors want their sacrifice now," said a female voice that was neither Lilly nor Teresa.

I pressed down deep inside my lover. I wrapped my hands around her neck. Felt the throbbing jugular through which flowed the river of her life. My thumbs closed in on it. I squeezed, feeling her blood slow and her breath fight for air. She surrendered to me gently like a child who trusted her mother to lead her to sleep. And I pressed harder. Then her soul, a comma-shaped spark, flew out of her body. She tightened brusquely around me and I released my seed at the same moment that the spark of her soul was sucked into the fire.

I was empty after that, Your Honor.

I had done the bidding of Elizabeth Bathory, who returned to this world then. The promise of Andrei de Kereshtur was fulfilled.

Only, right then, the flames grew tall again, and I saw that the body beneath me within which I had spent myself and whose life I had ended, was not the body of Lilly Hangress but that of Teresa, my sweet child. I had murdered the girl I had sworn to protect, the daughter of my first and only love.

Driven by horror at myself, I bounded out of the room. The frigid night shocked me as soon as I opened the door. The winter cold was multiplied in the frigid stones, and it slapped me with sudden sobriety.

I descended the freezing spiral iron staircase on the tips of my toes, passing the doors of other guest rooms behind which beer-sodden burghers snored away, moaning only now and then when the ice-cold hand of a ghost touched their wallets.

It was a long way down.

I found myself standing on the rough-hewn cobblestones of a small courtyard between the tower and a square building that had at one time been the stables. I heard Imre's goons snoring in there, between the moans of the wind. The main area of the castle with its circular courts and towers looked far away. One particular tower loomed both distant and forbidding, encased in moonlight and ice like a knight in silver armor.

It was difficult to say what attracted me to this tower rather than to any others. The only way to reach the place was to move by hugging the icy walls. The snow was deep enough in places that I sunk in it to my waist. But the snow felt almost warm compared to the outcroppings of cold stone and the gusts of fierce wind.

I felt very vulnerable indeed. I am sure that I wanted to die. The strength of vulnerability was a notion possible only in a heated room, lying on a rug before a fire. Outside, the only defense was a suit of armor, a weapon . . . I saw Teresa's lovely body still before the dying fireplace, and I was seized by a cold fiercer than anything my body was experiencing. I felt profound self-disgust. I was lost, lost!

As I crawled through the gate and then up the stone steps of the tower, I cursed the day I had returned to Hungary. Why did I return? It was punishment, I thought, for my masculine nomadic urge to escape, always escape from women. I was now being condemned to the icy interiors of an insane woman's life, a woman tortured by the mirror images of other women, living in a castle that was itself an interior of mirrors. This medieval castle was the ultimate interior: it twisted upon itself; it looped about its halls; it collapsed into its own histories; it was layered, intricate, absurd.

As I was freezing to death, I saw that Elizabeth Bathory's mind was only an image of these infernal interiors where she had spent her life. While her husband hunted Turks in the valleys of the Carpathians, burned villages, raped strange women, and covered vast distances, Elizabeth sat inside the tortured reflections of her endless interior, killing her likenesses in the mirror of time. Lockenhaus was itself a torture instrument. And here I was, foolish, drunk, a murderer. I had become her unwitting agent, following her through the maze of her mind, a cold stone maze.

A numbness that felt almost warm overtook me. The snow lit a sad-faced heraldic lion now and then or fell on a scene of mysterious pathos depicting ladies and knights frozen in faded gold thread on hanging tapestries. At the top of the tower was a round room that was empty and colder than the rest. Through an opening in the ceiling the lightning revealed a well. A round marble ring surrounded a pool of black water. I was certain that at the bottom of this well lay the bones of young girls murdered by the countess. Nearly paralyzed by cold and dread, I crouched on the edge of this pit, hoping to freeze to death there and fall in.

All that happened next belongs to another realm. I went through it like a spectator of my own life.

When I returned to the room, Teresa's body had disappeared. So it had been a dream after all.

That attempt at self-delusion did not last long. Lilly explained, matter-of-factly, that they had lowered the body into the tunnel under the commode. The river below would hopefully carry it off to sea.

Neither of my companions exhibited either remorse or any other sort of emotion. They were only concerned with the weather and returning to Hungary in time for the events unfolding there.

The storm abated in the morning. I allowed myself to be steered to Imre's station wagon. The events of the fatal night were mysterious and impossible, belonging to a different order. I watched the benign, sunny snow-

scape of Burgenland go by. The little village of Maunes-
burg, a clean place dominated by the church spire, was
riddled by neat signs at regular intervals that sported
the faces of what were obviously political candidates,
with the single word *Danke* written in black letters under them.

"The winners?" I asked.

"No," said Lilly, "the losers."

It was true. Austria was a polite little country. The
losers of the recent election had put up signs that said
"thank you" to the people who voted them out of office.

"They should say 'Fuck You!' instead," I said, suddenly remembering that I was an American.

We rode in silence to the Hungarian border.

The attempted Fascist takeover had taken place the day
before. It had been unsuccessful. Klaus Megyery had
gone into hiding. The skinheads who had taken part in
the attack on the television station were under arrest. At
the hotel there was a message from a magistrate requesting my presence for "an interview." It was ironic. I
was going to be questioned for my part in Megyery's
organization. My real crime was still a secret.

The national elections, scheduled for the end of the
month, were another matter. It was widely predicted
that the Fascist parties, including Saint Stephen's
Knights, would garner a majority of the vote. Taken together with similar electoral results in Russia and
Romania, the undeniable resurgence of the long-buried
beast terrified the world. In Budapest the atmosphere
was turbulent.

I watched from the window of my hotel as groups of
demonstrators bearing placards with the unmistakable
face of the dictator Horthy gathered to listen to
speeches. A gang of skinheads with black armbands loi-

tered about the lobby of the Gellart. They followed me when I went to answer the questions of the magistrate.

Predictably, these were about Saint Stephen's Knights and my eventual position, should monarchism become an issue. The magistrate was overly polite. Hedging his bets. If I turned out to be of consequence, he could always point to his behavior. I answered curtly and absentmindedly. No, I was not interested in politics. I wanted to leave Hungary as soon as possible.

But there was something I had to do. I had to tell Eva that her daughter was dead.

I called Horoarspital and asked for an appointment. I was put onto the chief resident.

"Have you not heard?" he said. "She has recovered. She left the hospital yesterday."

"I didn't think it was possible to recover from her condition."

"It is a puzzle," he admitted. "We have heard of cases in the United States of people waking from a long coma with the aid of a new drug. But we did not administer this to Eva. It was completely spontaneous. Sometime during the night of the terrible snowstorm, something happened. Next morning, she came to my office and said, 'I would like to go home.' Of course, I was not willing to allow her to go without further tests, but she was extremely persuasive. She said that she had been sleeping and was now awake. She was going to go home."

"Where is home?"

The doctor hesitated. "Well, there is a problem. We had only an old address and, foolishly, I admit, we allowed her to return there. But when I went to visit there today, I found that the building had been demolished. We don't know where she is. Perhaps, you can help us . . ."

"How did she look?" I asked.

"Well, that is another puzzle. She looked younger and more beautiful than when she came in . . . I had the impression, when I spoke with her, that she was growing young before my eyes . . . absurd, I admit."

"Has anything of this sort happened in your experience before?"

"It is like a fairy tale. Unknown in medicine. Unless you want to compare Eva's condition with that of Hungary, who has also awakened from a long sleep . . ."

The doctor was a philosopher. It wasn't a bad analogy. Hungary, and all of Eastern Europe for that matter, had woken after a long sleep, and her demons were coming out of their graves.

I promised to let him know if I heard from her.

I had to find her. Eva had recovered at the precise time my hands had put an end to her daughter's life. *At that very same moment.* I had the chilling insight that Elizabeth Bathory had not returned to take residence in the body of Lilly Hangress but in that of my first love, Eva!

I tried to reach Lilly after I had spoken to the doctor, but she was unavailable. "She has gone to a funeral," her secretary said, predictably. I went to her house and banged long and loud on the door. No one answered.

With Klaus Megyery in prison, Imre too became suddenly unavailable. The only company I had was an occasional visit from a police lieutenant who strongly suggested that I return to America. My presence was an embarrassment to the government. I had been abandoned by everyone. I was alone with the memory of Teresa.

I spent the next two weeks calling Lilly, Imre, and the chief resident at Horoarspital in Budapest. Lilly and Imre did not answer. The doctor told me that there was no news of Eva but that he had heard that a woman who was growing younger and younger was traveling throughout Hungary, followed by an entourage of beautiful young women. They were a traveling bordello of some sort. Of course, he wasn't sure whether this was Eva or not.

"All of Hungary," he added, "is a traveling bordello these days."

A FTER THE DISAPPEARANCE OF the singer Ilona Harszy at the end of the year 1599, rumors of Elizabeth Bathory's evil deeds grew alarmingly. Lutheran preachers Ponikenuz and Megyery preached against her in the churches, calling her a witch and demanding that she be burned at the stake. Ponikenuz wrote to both King Matthias and Emperor Rudolf demanding an investigation. King Matthias, who still loved Elizabeth, summoned his prime minister, the palatine Thurzo, and ordered him to look into it. Thurzo became extremely concerned. He was not so much worried about Elizabeth as about the reputation of the Bathory name and the disposition of her great fortune, which was in danger of falling into the king's hands if she was tried and convicted.

Emperor Rudolf in Prague was secretly gathering evidence as well. His spies in Pest reported every rumor to him. His own interest, like Matthias's, was motivated by greed, but in addition, he was fascinated by the allegations of witchcraft. Rudolf let no rumor of supernatural intervention go unchecked, no psychic talent untested. He searched high among the studious monks with their books full of symbols, but also low among healers, herbalists, and witches. He instructed his spies to "gather anything pertaining to lotions, magic roots, incantations." One spy, a certain German silversmith named Heuss, reported back that "Hungary water" was frequently used at Countess Bathory's court for occult purposes, and he enclosed the recipe for his emperor. It was "based upon oil of rosemary but was later reinforced and sweetened by the addition of oil of lavender. The hermit who presented the fragrance to the countess assured her that it would preserve her great beauty unimpaired until her death." This news was of interest to the emperor, who knew that rosemary was an ingredient used in making witch's brew, which made witches fly. The Spanish called it *romero* and revered it because it had been the bush that gave shelter to the Virgin Mary. He instructed Heuss to obtain a sample of Hungary water, which Heuss did and sent to Prague, sealed inside a silver flask bearing his seal. He also elaborated further on the precise nature of the process: "One and a half pounds of fresh rosemary tops in a gallon of white wine that must stand for four days . . ."

Following this communication, Rudolf requested formally from King Matthias II that "the heretical woman Bathory must be seen by the Imperial Court and by representatives of the Holy Roman Church to ascertain her faith."

The king answered Rudolf with more than his usually minute sense of humor: "His Majesty is welcome to divert a Hapsburg regiment on its way to vanquishing the Turks in Wallachia to the Kereshtur fort to offer the countess His Majesty's hospitality . . . provided that she is in good spirits." No Hapsburg regiment was anywhere advancing on the Turks. Kereshtur was on Turkish lands and was unassailable. Elizabeth Bathory's regiments could have seized Hradschin in Prague before Rudolf's regiment arrived halfway to Kereshtur. As for her being "in good spirits," that was a double joke, alluding both to her temper and to her alleged dealings in the occult.

The question of proper jurisdiction in investigating Elizabeth Bathory was the subject of letters between Hungary's Palatine Thurzo and King Matthias II. The palatine Thurzo, her uncle, maintained that the proper forum for the investigation was the family court. "Insofar as Countess Bathory is said to have offended the laws in her own courts, the matter of extent and gravity is for the family court to put in proper form for Your Majesty. There is also the question of the debts the crown owes to Countess Bathory, which have to be paid before any jurisdiction that may cause the dissipation of her fortune. We must also protect the memory of Count Nadazdy, our Christian knight whose valor is praised throughout Christian lands."

The palatine was nothing if not blunt. If she was to be found guilty by the king's court, her considerable fortune would have been confiscated. He wasn't going to allow it. Another letter, from the palatine Thurzo to King Matthias II, was dated April 8, 1609, before any allegations were officially recorded. Once more Thurzo explained to the king the necessity of investigating Elizabeth under the aegis of the family court. "It is far better that the woman Bathory's child be allowed to fairly consider such mother's infractions, so that she may cleanse the family name and not cast shadows on the reputation of her father, the valiant Count Nadazdy, hero of the wars for Hungary." It was tortured prose, but the palatine's meaning was clear. The family name could not be allowed to go down with the criminal countess.

The king, understandably, argued for a trial by the crown. "The gravity of the accusations . . . has gone beyond domestic jurisdiction. Countess Bathory's name is spoken outside of our borders. She has been mentioned in correspondence between ambassadors and their courts." The king did not say how the privileged correspondence between ambassadors and their courts came to be known. He did not mention the 600,000 gold florins he owed the countess. He also did not mention his own secret desire to have Elizabeth imprisoned in his own dungeon, where he could see her whenever he wanted. His violent passion for the Protestant countess continued unabated.

In the end, the palatine secretly convened a commission of inquiry on behalf of the family. The chief commissioner was the palatine Thurzo, but the high commission included also Elizabeth's daughter, Anna, and Anna's husband, Sandor. Neither the king nor the emperor was in a position to force the issue.

The killing of Ilona in the snow was the first recorded act of foul play concerning a daughter of the nobility. Others followed: the twin daughters of a Russian princess; the only daughter of an Austrian widow connected to the Hapsburg court. After getting a taste for well-educated, well-dressed, sweetly smelling aristocratic girls, Elizabeth lost interest in peasant girls. But there were not enough noble girls who presented themselves to her castles to satisfy her appetite. Darvulia and Ficzko conspired to dress up peasant girls in noblewomen's finery after bathing and scenting them. These girls were brought to Elizabeth's table, where they sat as they had been instructed but rarely opened their mouths for fear of betraying their coarseness. After dinner, the countess ordered them enclosed in iron maidens or tortured them herself. Often, during torture, the illusion of the girls' aristocratic upbringing was destroyed by their rude screams. The countess then became "fierce like a wolf with red eyes and white foam about her mouth," according to Jo-Anna, who was also a participant in these orgies.

In late November of the year 1610, Elizabeth traveled to Cahtice with her entourage of women. Cahtice was one of her smaller holdings, an impressive but ill-defended castle in Slovakian country. The day after she arrived, a cold wintry day, she ordered a feast for the Christmas holiday, and also in honor of her aunt Klara's fiftieth birthday. Snow was falling gently from a leaden sky, but despite the weather, Cahtice teemed with life. Butchers killed and skinned lambs, pigs, and deer for the winter larders. The sparks from the anvils of horse-shoers mixed with the smoke coming from the tanning shops. In the stables, horses were brushed, fed, and groomed. Soldiers polished their weapons and wiped clean the barrels of the cannons atop the walls. Some of them sat chatting with the servant girls, who ran back and forth with pots full of steaming water for the kitchens. The smell of roasts cooked with dried rosemary and dill filled the air. Merchants from town, who had been promised an interview with the countess better than five hours before, sat on cold benches in the connecting halls, impatiently tapping their fingers on bundles filled with gloves, looking glasses, laces, beads, ribbons, thimbles, needles, girdles, buttons, fringes, soaps, sweet-scented oils, Cyprus powder, wigs, and a hundred other different items the countess was known to fancy. Whenever Elizabeth arrived at one of her castles, the merchants flocked like starlings to her rooms.

But by the afternoon, not much of it mattered to Elizabeth. The growing feeling that old age was ravishing her as Dozsa's soldiers had ravished her sisters was in her heart. She could hardly believe how ancient Klara was. In her thickly insulated tower, Elizabeth lay on embroidered Turkish pillows, pearls from a strand she had just broken strewn around her. She stared fixedly at a black walnut pole, polished to a dull sheen, that rose from the floor halfway to the vaulted stone ceiling. Elizabeth had commissioned an Italian painter to cover the vault with a scene from the Last Judgment, but she had become enraged when the man painted the face of her new maid Dorika on one of the angels. She had ordered the man flogged and driven out into the snow. The outlines of demons and half-finished angels of darkness above her were only enigmatic patches of black, purple, and gold that she would have painted over as soon as a new artist could be summoned. Staring impertinently from the unfinished heavens was the beatific face of Dorika.

The countess ordered the glazed lead windows covered with black lace. Very little winter light filtered through the lace, making intricate patterns together with the flames in the fireplace and the light of a few gold candles. She ordered Dorika brought to her.

The young girl was barefoot, dressed only in a white muslin shift, smelling cleanly of soap and rose water. Her hair had been vigorously combed, but it was curly and looked unruly as it cascaded past her freckled shoulders. She trembled with fear and asked her mistress what she had done to displease her.

"What has she done to displease me?" the countess asked her trusted Darvulia.

"She was given the job of polishing the mirror in the great hall, my lady. She made it dirty."

This mirror at Cahtice had been allowed to stand in deference to her guests, but Elizabeth required that it be covered in black muslin whenever she entered the hall.

"There," said the countess. "Now do you understand?"

Dorika knew that she had failed. It was a tricky job:

no sooner did she achieve perfection in one section in the middle of the glass than the rest of it began to cloud. She did not know that cleaning a Venetian looking glass was a difficult art. She'd sweated and cried until Darvulia had come for her and taken her to the baths. There she had been soaped and scrubbed on every part of her body with swift, harsh, but competent strokes that only reminded her of her woeful inadequacy with the mirror. "I will do better! I swear!" she promised the quiet old woman who now dried her with a rough linen towel and sprinkled her with rose water from a blue bottle. The girl felt grateful for the bath, but she could not understand why she was being treated so nicely when she felt that, in truth, she should have been punished for her inadequacy. She felt relieved when Darvulia made her lean over the rim of the copper tub and lashed her with birch saplings that stung fiercely. This she could understand. She had been birched for smaller infractions since she had been a little girl. Her whole body glowed with the pink infusion of her healthy young blood. When Darvulia stopped birching her, she said, "Now, let's see what the countess thinks of your work, you little devil!"

Dorika fell to the floor and kissed the embroidered slippers of her mistress.

"Ficzko," the countess called out, "this is the worst girl I have ever seen!"

Ficzko, broad shouldered, nearly square, stepped from the shadows behind the fireplace where he always sat waiting. He was holding thin leather strips that looked like bootlaces. He pulled the girl roughly by her hair away from Elizabeth's feet and tied her to the walnut pole. While the girl cried and promised to do better by her ladyship's mirror, Ficzko fastened her legs and wrists tightly.

Elizabeth rose laboriously from her pillows and

walked up to the girl. She slapped her face. "I wanted to give you a key to my rooms, you little whore! Now what did you do? You spit on the key to my rooms, you filthy shit!"

The girl sobbed loudly and swore that she would never again dirty her lady's mirror and that she would do anything to carry the key to her ladyship's rooms.

"Well then, my lovely, so you will!" cried Elizabeth. She tore the muslin shift from her body. The naked girl started to shiver, while her breasts became hard from the cold.

The countess took a ring of keys from a hook on the wall and tossed them to Darvulia. "Give her the keys to my room!" she shouted.

Darvulia caught the keys in midair. She pinched them between the smoke-blackened arms of a pair of tongs resting against the fireplace. While she heated the keys in the fire, the countess alternately slapped and stroked the helpless Dorika, who cried and shouted so much she lost her voice. When the keys were red-hot, Ficzko untied the girl's wrists and held her small hands in his large ones. The countess walked behind the girl, grabbed her hair, and made her look at the ceiling where her angelic countenance floated in the unfinished paradise. At that moment, Darvulia let the hot keys drop on the girl's upturned palms. The sizzling metal burned the flesh, but the girl was no longer conscious. She did not see the burning lines of fate written on her palms. She did not see the faces of the countess and her helpers as they watched her flesh melt away. And she certainly did not feel Elizabeth's sharp, pearly teeth sink deeply into one of her small breasts and tear away a piece of flesh. The smell of burnt flesh that still sickened Darvulia and Ficzko (still! after all this time!) thrilled the countess to her core. She inhaled deeply as if drinking in the scent of a rare flower.

It was her last killing.

Count Thurzo led a surprise raid on Elizabeth at Cahtice Castle on December 29, 1610, during the Christmas holiday. Upon recognizing her uncle's colors, Elizabeth allowed the lowering of the bridge over the moat, not suspecting anything. As soon as the armed party crossed into the courtyard, Thurzo's soldiers disarmed Elizabeth's guard, which was surprised inside the barracks having a holiday dinner. They then surged up the staircases and fanned out into the interior.

One of Thurzo's lieutenants, a knight named Palosz, wrote in his memoir many years later that

> the dead bodies of young girls lay everywhere, some of them half eaten, some without arms or eyes. Many soldiers became sick, even ones that had seen the wars of the Turks. A body with round burns was inside a fireplace, blackened by the flames that had gone out before consuming her. The accomplices of the heinous countess tried to hide the bodies, but we found them easily, because the hard ground prevented them from digging deep. Our dogs clawed down through shallow graves and brought us hands and limbs from maidens no older than my daughters were at the time. We watched with horror as the dogs ran about with parts of the girls in their mouths.

Such gory scenes would have certainly received some corroboration from other witnesses, but Palosz was alone in his description. When Count Thurzo wrote to his wife, Aloyssa, to whom he always wrote frankly, he told her only that "as we directly came then upon certain men and female servants in the manor house, we found a girl at the house, dead due to many wounds and torture. I took the woman [Bathory] into custody; she was immediately taken to her fortress . . ." There was no mention of the dogs, the shallow graves, the moat choked with cadavers. The Thurzos had known Elizabeth since her childhood. Was he trying to spare his wife the terrible details? There was no such reticence in any of his other letters. He wrote to her unsparingly about beheadings, burnings, sexual license. Men and women of that time did not shy away from the physical truth.

Count Thurzo did not stay at Cahtice long after the raid. He spent less than an hour speaking privately to Elizabeth. He then commanded the captains of her guards to swear allegiance to him, and put them under the watch of his men. Would the thoroughgoing palatine leave such carnage as Palosz described without investigating further?

Witnesses later identified the dead girl Thurzo mentioned in the letter to his wife. Her name was Dorika, and she was said to have been punished for "stealing a pear before Christmas." She had had her hands burned and her breasts bitten by Elizabeth Bathory with the help of her maid Darvulia and master of horses Ficzko. Thurzo later reiterated that he found no evidence of outlandish sexuality, blood-drenched moonlight orgies, or any of the other fantastic activities later attributed to his niece.

The official inquest of the palatine, who presided over the family court, began in 1611. Over a period of four years, 350 witnesses testified about the crimes of Countess Elizabeth Bathory, mistress at Kereshtur, Sarvar, Lockenhaus, and a score of other castles in the kingdom of Hungary. The judges rendered this opinion about the necessity to investigate:

His Highness Count George Thurzo was elected Lord Palatine of Hungary in order to protect all good persons and punish the evil without fear or favor. His Highness, not wishing to close his eyes and turn a deaf ear to the satanic terror against Christian blood and the horrifying cruelties unheard of among the female sex since the world began, that Elizabeth Bathory, widow of the much esteemed and highly considered Franz Nadazdy, perpetrated upon her serving maids, other women, and innocent souls, whom she extirpated from this world in almost unbelievable numbers, had ordered a complete investigation of the accusations leveled against Countess Nadazdy-Bathory.

On two days alone—January 7 and January 11, 1611—thirty-five witnesses were called to testify. They had all been tortured and made to sign oaths to tell the truth. Among them were the countess's close associates Darvulia, Jo Anna Tohka, Dorothea Tohka, Helena Jo, Selena, and Ficzko. All but Darvulia confessed that they had helped torture and murder the many girls who had crossed the threshold of her castles and never returned. Jacob Silvazy, the overseer at Castle Cahtice, produced in evidence a register in the countess's own handwriting where she had recorded the names of 650 girls she had killed.

Six hundred and fifty girls! The shock of the judges, the greater for their being intimates of the woman, reverberated throughout the proceedings. Elizabeth's daughter, Anna, present at the inquests, took great care never to speak to her mother again. She did not mention her in letters, and she forbade her children to mention their grandmother. As she listened to the litany of charges, the excruciating variety of tortures, the tales of cruelty, she thought back to her mother's coldness. She had never nursed her; she had never even smiled at her. The killings had taken place over the years she had been unknowingly playing her childish games and missing terribly her beautiful and distant mother.

Jo Anna Tohka testified that "she had the girls undress stark naked, thrown to the ground, and she began to beat them so hard you could scoop up the blood by their beds by the handful . . . She bit individual pieces from the girls with her teeth."

Dorothea Tohka, her daughter, said, "The countess also froze naked girls to death in the snow by pouring water over them. She watched while they had their breasts cut off." By far the most voluble witness, she went on: "She liked to bite pieces of a girl's flesh or shoulder. She stuck needles into the girls' fingers, and said, 'If it hurts, you old whores, pull them out!' But if the girls did, the countess cut off their fingers."

She recalled that: "Once, when my mistress bit into flesh, all color fled from her face. She was deathly pale, and her eyes were full of fire. The devil had her and us in his grip. I held down a girl while my mistress bit her. I had to use all my strength, because the girl, Anika, was kicking hard. I sank my teeth into her too, but my mistress slapped me hard across the cheek."

Dorothea's riveting testimony impressed the judges with its wealth of detail and its vividness. Murmurs of disbelief rose from their ranks when Dorothea described the eating of living girls' flesh. When she confessed to having partaken of it herself, the high commission felt as if they were themselves participating in the delirium of the cannibalistic orgy. The black-robed men seated on the high dais felt the hot flame of the devil's tongue lick them. Dorothea's testimony did not lose either credibility or vividness when she claimed to have seen the devil himself sit in Elizabeth's lap, "clawing his red, knotty sex organ that looks like a birch root."

Andrei de Kereshtur's blood boiled with indignation as he listened to Dorothea, whom he knew to have been deflowered by Franz and whipped by Elizabeth and who, therefore, had more than enough reasons for lying. But he was not empowered to shout or to ask questions. His job was to record and be silent.

Asked by the palatine if she had ever had intercourse with the devil, Dorothea batted her lashes flirtatiously and answered, "Yes, Your Highnesses, many times. When he touches you, there is nothing you can do, because his birch root is so strong there is no woman can resist the advance and fullness of it." And just to make sure that the men understood her, she said, "Compared to a man's corresponding organ, his is much hotter and fatter." The men understood and ordered her to the torture chamber.

The other witnesses were not as forceful, but they all recalled having either been present at or hearing about tortures and murder. Of all those questioned, only Darvulia steadfastly refused to betray her mistress, saying only that "at times she may have punished girls for not obeying her, but I have seen no killings." She said also that, quite contrary to what was being rumored, her mistress often called her maids by endearing nicknames. Pressed by the court to admit that she had been enslaved by the devil in Elizabeth, she said that she had been "fascinated by her eyes," but that was only natural since "I was her wet nurse and have gazed into her eyes since she first opened them."

The groom Ficzko readily admitted that he had been

her lover and described diverse torture machines made for Elizabeth by craftsmen "from the German cities." She had used torture racks, revolving cages, procrustean beds with mechanical saws, crushing balls, and iron maidens. The maidens were realistic "sculptures of women with deadly interiors made out of sharp iron spikes." These devices were as esthetically pleasing as they were deadly. "Often," said Ficzko, "she appeared more interested in the workings of her mechanisms than in the sufferings they inflicted."

Pastor Ponikenuz, reporting hearsay, said that "we have heard from the very mouths of the girls who survived the torture process that some of the boys were forced to eat the girls' flesh roasted on a fire. The flesh of the other girls was chopped up fine like mushrooms, cooked and spiced, and given to young lads who did not know what they were eating."

Barbely Ambus, a folk doctor, told the high commission:

No one was allowed into the mistress's bedroom but her three or four trusted maids, who brought her girls. One time being called to minister to a sick girl, I went to her room and saw four bodies wrapped in shrouds. Only their mouths could be seen, but not their bodies or their faces. I put drops between their lips and knew that they were alive because the bitters made them swallow hard. I think that they were tied in their shrouds because their limbs did not move. I didn't know these people or whether they were men or women, and I don't know if they ever left Her Ladyship's room. But if they were dying anyway, why was I called to administer tinctures? This I do not know.

After their testimonies, the witnesses were sentenced to die. For her refusal to talk, Darvulia was condemned to having her breasts cut off and her eyes put out, after which she was burned at the stake. Jo Anna and Dorothea Tohka were sentenced to having all their fingers, which they had used in their crimes, torn out by the public executioner with red-hot pincers. After that, they were burned alive at the stake. Ficzko was decapitated and his body was drained of blood. He was then thrown into the fire. Darvulia, Jo Anna and Dorothea, Selena, and the others were burned alive and scattered to the winds.

Lady Klara Bathory, who was warned about the inquests, fled to Transylvania, where she took refuge at Stephen Bathory's court. Later she traveled to Italy and then to Spain. In 1615, already an old woman, she sailed to the New World and settled on the island of Cuba.

The testimonies of the witnesses against Elizabeth Bathory were written down in a neat and firm hand by Andrei de Kereshtur, who kept his head bent low over the parchment for fear that his eyes might betray his anguish. He tried to copy the words that indicted his friend as if they were in a foreign language. But little by little they became understandable to him again. Elizabeth, his confidant, his patron, and his idol, who had seen to it that he received the best education available —his dearest friend—was being slandered and turned into a monster by his own handwriting. All of her life, Elizabeth had kept him informed of her doings, just as he had kept her abreast of his. At no time did she confide in him such things as these witnesses contended.

While his heart raged and his head split, his pen flowed obediently across the parchment for all posterity to see. This was the only time in his life that Andrei de

Kereshtur hated his calling to the scribe's profession. It was the hardest thing he had ever done. He swore to himself that after her death, which now appeared inevitable, he would chronicle all the important memories of their common lives and redeem her. Elizabeth had written more letters to him than to anyone else in the world. But even as he resolved to do so, he began to doubt. As witness after witness wept and betrayed their mistress, he could not deny the sincerity of these voices speaking haltingly and painfully for hours and hours about crimes so unspeakable he could barely keep his quill to the parchment.

Andrei was not an innocent child. He was a man of his century. He had seen executions and had watched rows of the dead. He had taken depositions after witnesses had been tortured and left with only swollen tongues in bleeding mouths to whisper the few things expected of them. But the testimonies of these women were of an entirely different nature. They were grotesque, unseemly accounts of acts that he could not associate with his beloved Elizabeth. They described nearly identical crimes that had taken place over many years in castles distant from one another. Witnesses from different castles did not know one another.

As the testimonies of the first inquest were drawing to a close toward midnight on January 11, 1611, Andrei's whole being hurt. He felt betrayed by his friend. But there was also something else, flowing directly in the wake of the intense pain in his heart. The scribe realized that Elizabeth had meant more to him than he had ever thought. He realized with a start that she had been the love of his life. He had dedicated his life to ascetic study in order to remain wholly devoted to her.

Andrei would have liked to attribute to his friend the saving grace of a philosophical passion. Failing that, he would have liked her to be the victim of a passion that transcended mere human feelings. But such thinking could hardly be sustained as he listened to witness after witness. According to Ficzko, her onetime lover and the only male servant involved in the tortures and killings,

> if the folds in the countess's dress were not smoothed out, or if the fire had not been yet lit, or if one of her garments had not been properly ironed, the girls responsible were tortured to death. The noses and the lips of the girls were burned with a flatiron by Her Ladyship herself or by the old women. The countess also stuck her own fingers in the mouths of the girls and ripped their mouths.

What could redeem such cruelty? Andrei remembered the agitation of his mistress on several occasions when an important visitor was expected. He tried to imagine the extremes of such understandable agitation. Suppose that moments before the great Kepler was due to arrive at Sarvar, Elizabeth found that her garments had not been properly ironed. The enraged countess may have taken hold of the hot iron herself. "I will iron you!" she may have shouted to the slovenly girls, and then done so. One of them decided to talk back. Talk back! At a time such as this! The countess inserted her fingers in the girl's mouth and ripped it open. That will show her to talk back!

Andrei was aware of the ridiculousness of the scene he was imagining, but felt himself becoming agitated too, because he could imagine it so well. He could see and feel Elizabeth as she ironed the girls and ripped out their mouths. Worst of all, he could see her laugh. He saw her laugh cruelly and uncontrollably as a wave of pleasure washed through her body. The unexpected sensation delighted her. Andrei knew that Elizabeth discovered pleasure at the peak of her anger, because she had told him. A pleasure that could moreover be repeated at will and often. Pressing her bloodied fingers to her lips, she must have willed herself to stop laughing. The expectation of an evening of sublime intellectual stimulation gave her other kinds of pleasure. "Her Ladyship singed the private parts of a girl with a burning candle," Dorothea had confessed.

Andrei de Kereshtur feared to delve too deeply into the matter, because he was beginning to experience pleasure himself. He did not trust the potency of such false imaginings, because they distracted him from his true purpose, which was to understand and perhaps exonerate his friend.

Thinking of the needles under the girls' fingernails, Andrei later wrote, "We live in a pierced world, from the broken arrows sticking out of Saint Sebastian's body to the sharp stakes on which the Wallachians impale their enemies."

His friend's world, as well as his own, was a sieve in the making, a continual fabric of piercing pain that let in the evil energies of a malignant cosmos. She may have taken it upon herself to ensure that her Lord's crown of thorns and the piercing of martyrs continued unabated. She may have tried to avoid pain by causing it, attempting to be a piercer, not a piercee, that is, a woman. Andrei could only imagine how deeply Elizabeth had suffered. Pain and its icons were the constant companions of their lives, despite the good moments. There was pain within, in his teeth, eyes, and ears. And pain surrounded them, in the visible deaths of others redeemed only by the image of Christ bleeding on the cross, surrounded by his equally wounded saints. Andrei knew that Elizabeth did not want to be a woman in the obedient mold prescribed by Luther, and her suffering was doubled by not knowing what other kind of woman she could be. Did she want to be a woman at all? The terrible punishments meted out to her young servants may have been in retribution for their being women. The girls were also punished because they were *young* women. The affront of their youth was to contain within itself the sweet antidote of desire that occasionally blotted out the pain. Elizabeth may have lost that antidote, and she may have believed that it could be found in the virgins' sweet blood. Andrei de Kereshtur wasn't certain where his thoughts might lead him, so he stopped himself again, fearful of the hellish depths she had opened in him.

The testimonies of the witnesses interviewed by the palatine's commission were carefully edited when the results were relayed to the king. With a view to the church, all references to witchcraft were excised. Since most of the witnesses were sentenced to death and executed immediately, their testimonies could not be duplicated. Elizabeth herself was never called to testify, and she was never formally charged. The palatine's court decided against filing formal charges.

When sufficient evidence was first obtained in the year 1611, Thurzo ordered that Elizabeth's imprisonment at Cahtice be made permanent. The countess, who had first been placed under house arrest at Cahtice, was then walled inside her own chamber. An opening was left in the wall for food to be passed through once a day. Because no formal charges were lodged against Elizabeth Bathory, the great fortune stayed in the family.

The most damning conclusion of the family court report had to do with the great number of sophisticated torture instruments found in her residences. Reluctantly, the commission concluded that "these carefully designed devices are proof that she was not simply the victim of uncontrollable anger." In other words, she may have begun by cruelly lashing out in an accepted manner at her insubordinate servants, but in her maturity she had prepared refined, sophisticated means of gradually and skillfully arousing pain and, very likely, pleasure. She orchestrated her pleasure like music. "Hers were the harmonies of hell," the report concluded. The report was sealed in Palatine Thurzo's archive and did not emerge again for four centuries—until Prof. Lilly Hangress found it and used selected parts of it for her book.

In the grip of uncertainty, in the shadow of war, and under the protection of the great Lady Elizabeth Bathory, my friend and my mainstay, I have been conducting certain Researches into the Nature of the Physical World in the hope of illuminating the Dark Paths of the Spiritual. The *mysterium magnum* was mother to all the elements, a grandmother to all stars, trees, and creatures of the flesh; for all sentient and insentient creatures are born of the *mysterium magnum.* I have achieved the Milkiness of certain compounds of which Paracelsus speaks as being Indicative of the Light of *mysterium magnum.* Being alone, without my beloved teacher Silvestri, and unable to interpret the Reactions, I found myself in a sort of Reverie and saw a Creature with rays that came out of its head like the Sun. It had the breasts of Woman and around its stomach was a Sphere with stars blinking in it. The Creature sat between two steep Cliffs. On each cliff stood an Animal, half Bird and half Lizard, pointing fiery tongues at the Creature. I asked the Creature about the Meaning of Milkiness, but when he was about to Speak, a black Cloud passed and obscured the Scene. I prayed then to the soul of Monk Silvestri to guide my Research, and to bring back the Creature so that it will Speak.

This is how Andrei de Kereshtur begins to explain the difficult work of saving Elizabeth's soul.

During Elizabeth's imprisonment at Cahtice, other trials were held throughout Hungary, involving witchcraft, marital infidelities, or both. As Ursula Nadazdy had once suspected, the great lords had begun moving against the properties of wealthy widows.

Until the hour of her death, Elizabeth claimed her innocence of the deeds that she claimed were the invention of priests. On the matter of witchcraft, Andrei de Kereshtur left no doubt that Elizabeth was taught magical and folk arts from a very early age. The world of the women at Kereshtur, Sarvar, and Cahtice was steeped in it. Witchcraft was the women's craft, just as alchemy and astrology were its manly equivalents. Andrei de Kereshtur, who was himself an alchemist, found it amusing that all the preachers and priests who were constantly around these activities were rarely able to obtain positive proof. He speculated that one of the better tricks of witches was to make men of the cloth forget what they'd just seen and heard. "The truth of daylight is a veil over their eyes."

After Elizabeth was imprisoned at Cahtice, Pastor Ponikenuz wrote a long letter to King Matthias describing a visit with the distinguished prisoner. Elizabeth, who made no secret of her hatred for the Lutheran minister, repeatedly accused him and his fellow preachers of having led her into a trap. Pastor Ponikenuz defended himself by describing to her acts of witchcraft he had himself observed the countess practicing. She disregarded his tales with a derisive laugh. This was not her subject. Ponikenuz himself seemed to forget the subject (until he recalled it in the letter) and followed the countess's train of thought instead. He became most indignant when the countess said, "For this you must die first, then Megyery. For the pair of you are the cause of my bitter captivity." Ponikenuz argued that he never denounced her by name when he made his sermons. Elizabeth said that there was nothing to denounce.

She said that she had never done anything wrong. Peasant girls, she said, sometimes died of blood poisoning, of consumption, of overwork. Some of them, heavy with child, threw themselves from the castle parapets. Hundreds of girls had presented themselves to her castles over the years, looking to enter her service. She had been most generous to them. After five years of service, they earned a dowry that enabled them to marry. This dowry was their hope, and the hope of their parents, peasants who scratched the land all year and barely fed their bellies. As for the girls who never returned, they were undoubtedly better off dead. Elizabeth had seen the filth in which the peasants wallowed in their hovels. They were brutish, cruel, and covered in sores. When the girls' humble parents came to the castle to ask what happened to their daughters, Elizabeth ordered them flogged. She was enraged when preachers and priests sometimes inquired after servant girls on behalf of their parents. To their inquiries she replied that the girls had died after being ill. Ponikenuz, writing to King Matthias, claimed that "the lives of her servant girls were of no account to Countess Bathory. She looked on them as so many stalks of summer squash. Her hounds and her falcons were more precious . . ."

Elizabeth had been imprisoned within a walled-in chamber for five years without the solace of a single ray of sunshine. Outside, the life of the household went on as if she didn't exist. News of the world was withheld from her. She was treated as if she were dead and entombed.

As the world receded from her, she told and retold herself the story of her life, as if it were a weaving that she wove and unwove. Each time she told herself the story of her life, it became clearer to her that she had been the victim of her evil preachers.

She had been allowed to bring to her living tomb only a small writing table, her box of pearls, two plain gowns, and her gold candleholders. Her hair grew long and unruly and became first gray, then dirty white. Her body odors filled the room like a protective cocoon no one dared approach or regard. The woman who had spent her life forcing her subjects and her equals to look at her spent long years without as much as a glance from anyone. Finally on August 7, 1613, on her fifty-third birthday, she dipped her quill in the nearly dried ink that she moistened with her saliva, and wrote to her dearest friend Andrei. When she was finished, she set about the business of dying with the same determination she had exhibited in living and killing. Seven days later the Hungarian chronicler Istvan Krapinski reported: "Elizabeth Bathory, widow of Count Nadazdy, His Majesty's chief master of horse, who was notorious for her murders, died imprisoned at Castle Cahtice on August 14, 1613, suddenly and without crucifix and without light."

The August 7 letter reached Andrei de Kereshtur at Kereshtur Castle on the very same day that the countess's soul, in which she no longer believed, left her nearly transparent body.

My Dear Friend,

My curious life is coming to an end. I have seen the figure of my death and I welcome it. You and I have been friends since we were both children at Kereshtur, when we dressed alike and no one could say which of us was the girl or the boy. During my confinement I have thought often about those days, and I have come to believe that they were the best of my life. Those things that happened to us later did not diminish my affection for you, Notary. I forgive you for writing down the dreadful lies of those women bewitched by the preachers. You have served me faithfully and are alone among those I have known to have stood unswervingly by my side. You have been my mirror, Notary. I release you from this painful duty now and command you to ensure that my name will be forgotten. This is the last demand from your capricious and often neglectful countess. I want you to ensure that no writings about me will leave the malicious pens of men who have not known me. You will destroy our letters and will beg of my child that she do the same. I crave oblivion more than I crave death. I have craved death for all the hours of my life these past five years. I have heard nothing but the lying voices of the preachers on the other side of this wall. The squealing of rats under the stones at night has been more comforting to me. All this time I have not seen the body of a living man or woman, only their hands shoving my bowl of gruel through the slit they made to pass things through. I should have died a long time ago from shame alone if not from the lack of light. I blame the preachers. They will all be tormented eternally, Hebler, Ponikenuz, Megyery. To think that Hebler is free to spread his poison while I languish in this chamber!

I don't know what has kept me living, Notary. The strength of the life in me has always been a mystery to me. My desire to live has been stronger at the darkest times, even when my beloved Teresa was consumed by flames. They say that I have killed

innocent girls. Did I? I have punished them for
their inattentiveness, for their stupidity, for their always lowering their eyes before everyone and everything. I did not kill them. Their resignation and
stubbornness took away whatever was left living in
them. Death has always increased my appetite for
life. I have thought of nothing but death these dark
years, but instead of weakening me, these thoughts
made me stronger. Our beloved teacher Silvestri
once said that one's own death is the only one that
matters, with the single exception of the death of
our Lord Jesus Christ. I must have taken his advice
to heart, at least as far as I am concerned.

Do you remember the visit of the great Kepler
to Sarvar Castle? He was renowned the world over
for his horoscopes. I believe that he had seen something in my stars that he did not tell me. I did not
know what he saw until I was put in here, alone
until the end. I now know that the stars foretold my
loneliness and he did not find it in his heart to tell
me. He must have looked at my horoscope and
seen the absence of stars, a dark night sky without
light. I have only been happy when I was exhilarated by beauty or genius. Johannes's faith in the
beauty of what is written moved me, as you moved
me with your passion for your chemical researches.
I was moved when I was a young girl and burned
with impatience to hear our teacher Silvestri . . .

Andrei remembered well. He recalled the visit of Johannes von Kepler, because it had been his first meeting
with the great astrologer. He remembered also his mistress when she was a young girl and they were both
consumed by the vastness of what there was to know
and saddened by the brevity of their lives, which would

never allow them to know all of it. Their discussions about the hidden design of God's plan had given him a direction for his life. He had dedicated himself to studying and revealing God's plan. There was joy in this endeavor, yet it was not the kind of madness that made one want to "singe the private parts of a girl with a burning candle."

Andrei de Kereshtur looked desperately for a reason that would explain his friend's action. "Perhaps there was a passion in her I could not understand," he wrote, delicately alluding to his own ascetic calling. He was a monk who had resolved to forgo the flesh, though he often wrote that he understood the flesh. He did not resort to a convenient demon to explain Elizabeth. He did not believe that she was possessed. He insisted on finding a reasonable explanation for her actions, perhaps because he knew her so well. He asked:

Was she driven by the beauty of God's celebratory celestial candles to pluck one of them from the sky in order to set fire to the very source of human life? This source, belonging as it did to a young girl, a virgin, had not yet participated in the creation; it was an unused passage for souls from the other world into ours. The girl's virginity was, in its potential state, the source of all possibility. Why did my Lady want to close it?

During the long nights that followed his transcription of the witnesses' words, de Kereshtur tried every reasonable approach. He attributed the loftiest reasons to his friend, whom he knew to be intelligent, logical, and well read. He speculated that she had perhaps been aroused by Kepler's celestial harmonies to deplore the fallen, unharmonious state of a humanity that could participate in God's creation only through an intellect such as Kepler's.

She may have wanted to stop the passage of the girl's soul from a state of musical bliss into the sorrowful world of flesh. Like an anti-Lucifer, she may have wanted to extinguish the flame of unworthy life that Lucifer, contrary to God's wishes, had given humanity to keep and to fan. She may have thought that she was serving God.

Andrei wept as he read Elizabeth's last letter, but he did not honor her request for oblivion. He wrote down what he remembered, for the sake of his soul if not hers.

An unusual number of storms were recorded in the last decade of the sixteenth century as Andrei de Kereshtur trusted his thoughts to parchment. There were more than the usual number of travelers stranded at Kereshtur Castle during those winters, but he paid them no mind. These storms were said by astrologers to correspond to spiritual upheavals in people's souls. They coincided also with the political events that marked the beginning of the modern age: the beginning of the waning of Ottoman power and the rise of the Hapsburgs, the spreading of the Protestant faith into all the German countries, the end of the Inquisition, the beginning of nationalism, and the fabulous wealth of the New World. Each storm was different from the one that came before, but each one was more intense than the last, with high winds that leveled villages and so much snow that only the church spires could be seen in certain towns. According to the astrologers, these storms caused disturbances of which Countess Bathory's alleged acts of madness were but an example. Andrei de Kereshtur listened to none of it, writing without respite, listening to the winds but never believing for a moment that the heavens had been responsible for the life of his beloved Elizabeth. Using his quill, he called other orders to the fore.

*W*hat follows is Count Bathory-Kereshtur's last testimony. The judge then retired to her chambers to consider all that she had heard.

My liberty was bitter, Your Honor. I was a free man. A marvelous bird of our century whisked me back to America, the land of my beloved anonymity. Elizabeth would have loved the airplane. It would have matched her inner velocity. Her gradual fascination with small and large mechanisms, astrological clocks, iron maidens, trapdoor springs, revolving cages, had slowly turned her castles into infernal machines from which there was no escape. She became a prisoner of her mechanical web, a web that has grown to monstrous proportions in our time. Our mechanisms have grown, but our murderous sentiments differ little from Elizabeth's. We have killed more and better since learning to fly.

Looking down on the verdant mountain valleys of Austria, I saw the iron rods and springs of Europe's infernal machine, not trees, farms, and rivers. Trapped at the heart of it was my monstrous ancestress, calling for blood through the centuries, condemning her posterity to a terrifying, heartless interior.

I had escaped from the land of my birth. But even America was not safe from Elizabeth Bathory. While she stroked her wildcat and played with the feathers of birds from the New World, the diseases brought by Columbus devastated the natives of America. Only 10 percent survived their "discovery."

I accuse myself of Teresa's death, judge. Of all of us, she had been the only one without blame. It is always the blameless who are sacrificed. I feel guilty and want to be punished, unlike Elizabeth, who had been guilty but felt no remorse, only outrage at her fate. Guilt is the only new thing in the intervening centuries between me and her, the acrid flower of the blood of generations.

In Hungary, trapped among representatives of every temporal authority, I felt only the smooth walls of everyone's guilty prison. Imre inside his hatred of his father. Klaus inside his hatred of foreigners. Lilly inside hatred against her own fate. Guilt was the key to these prisons. I felt as if I held it in my hands. A big, awkward key intended for dank medieval gates.

Only Eva remains a mystery. If she has indeed become Elizabeth Bathory, an immortal, I will doubtlessly hear from her. She has all the time in the world.

The burden of my murderous ancestress will never lift from my soul. She was a powerful woman from whose ashes has risen the modern world with all its horrors. To escape from Countess Elizabeth Bathory, to escape from the evil heart of the old empire, is a work of generations, Your Honor. I am only a man, and a timid, unloved one at that.

I once listened to Imre in a restaurant berate, in order, Jews, Gypsies, Romanians, and Americans. I was filled by rage. Later that day, I startled myself at the Budapest City Museum when I looked at a woodcut of Transylvanian burghers impaled by Dracula. I imagined on the highest stake the body and head of Klaus's son. Imre stared back at me from the woodcut, blood dripping to the sides of his neck where the sharp stake was sticking out. That is where my feeling had placed him. Every time I banished the image, it returned with irrational strength.

One may escape Europe but not her images, Your Honor.

I presented myself to this court to confess to a murder I believe I have committed. I want you to find me guilty. I have delivered to you every detail in my memory, but I will find more if this is not sufficient. I know other sorry sins of our sad corner of Europe.

Provided the court cares, of course.

My native country may never overcome its cursed inertia, inherited from centuries of cruelty and sloth. But I accuse myself of all her sins.

I realize that, personally, I have overcome nothing.

I am no one. I am the king of Hungary.

monstrum creavit
July 25, 1994

AKNOWLEDGMENTS

The author is grateful to the Hungarian State Archive, the Museum of the City of Budapest, and American Airlines. He wishes also to thank the following people for their gracious help: Noah Adams, who was intrigued by the story of the countess one snowy afternoon in Budapest; Jonathan Lazear, for insisting that he look for her; George Csicsery, for his enthusiasm and research; Janos Angy, for unknowingly providing a character; Katalin Peter, for discussing the countess at length in Budapest restaurants and also modeling for a fiction; the author's mother, who carried out translations from old Hungarian, despite the nightmares the material gave her; and all his dear ones, who suffered with him through the madness of the countess's emergence.